To Cheyenne —
Enjoy the Tale!

Irene Baron

Mindreacher

Irene Baron

The author/publisher assumes no responsibility as this is a work of fiction, the author's imagination, creative writing efforts, and is purely coincidental to real world events or are used fictitiously. The writing style or genre may be classified as "faction," a contraction of fact and fiction. It is also in the "speculative fiction" genre as an adventure novel. All rights reserved

First Printing: 2019
Amazon Press

ISBN: 978-1096303923
Library of Congress Control Number: 2019903478

Irene Baron
P.O. Box 1203
Zanesville, OH 43702

www.irenebaron.com
www.mindreacher.com

Cover design by Greg Hetherington
Cover Image: Mindgarden by Leon Alegria

*An asterisk will show the first time a glossary word is used.

v

INDEX OF ABBREVIATIONS

ACCM	Alternative or Compensatory Control Measures (USN Black Budget)
AISC	Army Intelligence Security Command
BRN	Barisan Revolusi National, SE Thailand
CIA	Central Intelligence Agency
COMINT	COMunications INTerception
CONUS	Continental United States
CRI	Cascades Research Institute
DARPA	Defense Advanced Research Project Agency
DCI	Director Central Intelligence
DIA	Defense Intelligence Agency
DNA	DeoxyriboNucleic Acid
DOD	Department of Defense
DSS	Diplomatic Security Service
ESP	Extra Sensory Perception
FAA	Federal Aviation Administration
FAST	Fleet Anti-terrorism Security Team
GMT	Greenwich Mean Time
GS	General pay Schedule
HALO	High Altitude High Opening
ICT	IndoChina Time
JPEG	Joint Photographic Group
JSOC	Joint Special Operations Command
LPS	Laboratory for Physical Science
LTTE	Liberation Tigers of Tami Eloam
MARSOC	MARine Corps Special Operation Command
MEG	Magneto encephalography
MFF	Military Free Fall
MSOR	Marine Special Operations Regiment
NAVSOP	NAVigation via Signals of OPportunity
NCTC	National CounterTerrorism Center

NRI	National Research Institute
NRO	National Reconnaissance Office
NSA	National Security Agency
NSC	National Security Council
NT	NonTelepath
OBE	Out of Body Experience (Remote Viewer)
OSD	Office of Secretary of Defense
OUB	Out of Body
PDF	Portable Document Format
PhotinT	PHOTographic INTelligence
PIV	Personal Identity Verification
SAP	Special Access Programs
SAST	South Africa Standard Time
SATCOM	SATellite COMmunication radios
SCI	Sensitive Compartmentalized Information
SDI	Strategic Defense Initiative
SEAL	SEa-Air-Land Navy SpecWarrior
SIGINT	SIGnals INTelligence
SLC	Satellite Link Card
SOF	Special Operation Forces
PC	Satellite Phone Card
TSCC	Top Secret Crypto Clearance
TS-SCI	Top Secret-Sensitive Compartmented Information
USAP	Unacknowledged Special Access Program
USID	United States Identity Card
UW	Unconventional Warfare
VESPER	Virtual ExtraSensory Perception Experimental Research
Wfirst	Wide-Field Infrared Survey Telescope

CHAPTER 1

JFK International Airport
Jamaica, Queens, New York
1 August 8:45 AM DST

The President of the United States spent anxious moments with advisors planning how government agencies would respond if terrorists acted on their recent threat to use weapons of mass destruction within the United States. He insisted these terrorists be identified by any means possible. When sarcastically told only mind readers could identify a terrorist, he envisioned telepaths working for the government who could locate and identify terrorists. To that end, he initiated his highly classified Virtual ExtraSensory Perception Experimental Research, or VESPER project, to seek superior telepaths.

Realizing legislative changes were inevitable, he assigned a legal team to analyze existing laws and future legitimacy for VESPER procedures. The nation had to be prepared for issues arising from psychic terrorist identification methods. The public was not alerted to the existence of his VESPER project. It was hidden in abandoned corridors beneath the John F. Kennedy International Airport (JFK) runways.

Previous administrations had enlarged the corridors to house a secret, subterranean, disaster emergency facility for government administrators in case of attack. The JFK facility can accommodate over five-thousand persons for six-weeks. It is a facility for the president to conduct civil and military affairs. The newly appointed VESPER staff was placed in one section of the massive subterranean facility to work on the president's visionary telepathy project to identify and locate terrorists.

* * *

Standing in the JFK airport terminal before a maintenance elevator door, Colonel Andrew Jackson Anderson, USMC, surveyed the area. Psychiatrist and Medical Director of the president's newly formed VESPER project, he was assigned to lead the psychic testing program once telepaths were found.

Telepaths were rare. He had never met one. Although the VESPER project appeared feasible, it wouldn't work until they began to find superior telepaths.

Al Qaeda terrorists were intent on planning history-changing attacks on the United States. The latest threat of destroying American civilian and military airports with plutonium bombs loomed over his head. An established and reliable source had advised that detonations were planned for Thanksgiving weekend in three months. The informant was found murdered the following day. No government agency could find the terrorists.

Anderson appeared confident, intelligent and robust. From all outward appearances, no one would know he was a left leg amputee from the knee down due to a combat injury. Men not as severely wounded often relinquished their military rank for civilian life. Not Anderson. He was assigned to solve difficult problems using his superior intelligence, willpower and dedication. The more complex the problem, the more he relished solving it. His brilliance was exactly what the president demanded.

Formerly assigned to a desk within the Special Operations Command, Marine Special Operations Intelligence Battalion at Fort Bragg, Anderson had been enjoying the ease of his current orders. The president had declared VESPER highly classified. If the project were made public, the media would ridicule him out of office. Not wanting to be identified by telepaths, terrorists would try to destroy the VESPER facility and personnel connected with it. VESPER had to remain hidden.

Within the hour Anderson would present information to the new VESPER Directors. Implementation of his proposal could ensure success in finding superior telepaths. He tried to guess which Directors would balk at his disclosures.

His graying-black hair, dark skin and intense light-hazel colored eyes made him appear younger than his fifty-three years. Thankful psychic ability was not required to work within this unusual government project, he looked forward to the day terrorists would be positively identified by VESPER telepaths and subsequently dealt with by the government. Although this assignment would be easier than his previous work with the most elite and secretive special ops at Fort Bragg, Anderson knew he would miss the excitement of his former position. He reminisced about prior black op assignments as he leisurely entered the elevator when it arrived.

Hearing a shout, he turned to see a man slide to a stop at the entrance, grasp the closing elevator doors and violently push them open. A tall, thin, dark-skinned man stepped inside the elevator. He brought with him a stench of urine. The intruder stared at Anderson with fury. Anderson's outward appearance of a graying, uniformed officer in a relaxed position belied the fact that a lethal martial arts expert resided within a well-honed body.

The intruder's oversized suit gave Anderson the impression of someone not used to the fit of American clothing. Then his eyes locked on what appeared to be multicolored wires and the corner of a bomb pack hidden beneath the huge jacket. He now knew why the suit jacket was oversized.

"Thanks for not waiting," the newcomer said with a sneer. "Didn't you hear me call?" Sunglasses partially concealed the intruder's angry eyebrows.

"No, I didn't hear you." Anderson was reminded of a feral dog by the man's discolored teeth and sharp incisors. He recognized the Pakistan accent from having been formerly assigned in Karachi.

The new passenger demanded, "Punch in the VESPER level old man."

With a querulous expression, Anderson offered, "You go ahead. You're closer to the controls." The colonel wanted to know how this man knew of the hidden facility housed deep beneath the airport runways. Except for employees with high *security clearances, only a handful of the nation's defense personnel were aware of VESPER's existence. Persons in the know were positioned at the top of their department or agency didn't talk about the president's new project. Anderson worried how the president would react if he learned VESPER information had been leaked.

Curious, Anderson let himself be subdued when the Pakistani lurched forward, raised a sturdy forearm against his neck and rammed him against the back wall. The action gave the Colonel a closer look at the bomb vest. The elevator's polished metal wall reflected a stiletto being drawn from the intruders back waistband.

"Make this elevator go to VESPER," the intruder commanded, the stiletto point at Anderson's neck.

Trying to appear subservient, Anderson responded, "I'm so sorry. Who's Vesper?"

"Listen man, don't mess with me. This elevator won't let me go anywhere but up. I know it goes down." Pushing hard, the man rubbed his arm back and forth across Anderson's neck. In a threatening manner he barked, "Punch in the code, infidel."

Anderson recoiled from the stranger's sewer breath and feigned fright. "How can I? I'm pinned against the wall." The attacker gave him a questioning look. Using the break in attentiveness, Anderson rapidly struck the assailant twice in the groin with alternate knees while disarming him. He tossed the stiletto into the corner. To keep him from arming the bomb, Anderson grabbed the man's wrists and pulled them toward the floor. The assailant collapsed forward. Anderson kneed him in the side with his metal knee, grabbed both ears and smashed the intruder's face against the wall with a thud. Blood splattered from the would-be-bomber's crushed nose, lips and teeth. One broken, bloody tooth remained impaled in the aluminum wall.

"Jackal," Anderson said. "Don't ever threaten a Marine."

As the unconscious man dropped to the floor, Anderson stifled a kicking urge. He flicked a few drops of blood off his uniform and tapped a gold earsphere in his right ear to activate the transceiver. Hearing a soft tick of acknowledgement, he instructed his secretary, "Jen, I just subdued an elevator intruder with a bomb vest. Tag my position." He requested security and a bomb squad. "Alert Herman Wald." Wald, the VESPER CEO, could be counted on to be focused, analytic, and calculating.

When asked if anyone was injured, Anderson replied, "Only the perp. I want to know who he is and what he knows, ASAP!" At that, he turned off his earsphere. "Damn," he said, "that felt good. I've been out of action too long."

CHAPTER 2

VESPER Conference Room
1 August 9:45 AM DST

In the well-lit and windowless VESPER conference room located two stories under the runways, seats around a conference table were being filled.

Colonel Anderson, standing impatiently behind a folding metal chair, hoped cushioned chairs had been requisitioned for the fledging organization. Gleaming white walls lightened the room. Wall-to-wall government issued, light-brown carpet absorbed sounds.

Scrutinizing expressions of VESPER Directors present, Anderson wondered if the security leak could have come from one of them.

Until telepaths could be located, VESPER had hired seven out-of-body (OUB) remote viewers (RV) with no mindreading skills. Their subconscious mind could enter targets such as locked and sealed facilities in any country. The RV's physical body back in the lab was guarded by an OUB coach sitting beside him. At Anderson's request minutes ago, an RV was mentally present in the conference room to look for evidence of a potential traitor. The *remote viewer had been instructed to read individual notes taken during the meeting and look for negative body language. A debriefing would occur later.

Anderson had had little opportunity to know the staff intimately. Glancing around the room, he questioned if the OUB watcher was floating around at ceiling or eye level. He looked in vain for a visual clue as to the watcher's location. He questioned if remote viewers created a temperature change in the air when they moved and made a mental note to ask.

All seats were filled, including one near the door he'd left for Major Jonathon Coulter, USMC. The Major had been assigned as liaison officer between VESPER and OSD, the Office of the Secretary of Defense, at Anderson's request. The moment Anderson learned of Coulter being severely injured during a black operation in the Middle East, he began filling out paperwork to have the Major temporarily transferred to VESPER upon recovery before returning to active duty. Anderson believed a rear job would allow Coulter productive recovery time. Within VESPER, only Anderson and CEO Herman Wald were aware of Coulters' heroic exploits. A natural leader with courage, intelligence, and integrity, Coulter personified the ideal soldier. His six-foot tall outward appearance hadn't changed except for recent facial scars. Calm, intelligent, hazel eyes continually scanned his surroundings. Dressed in civilian clothes, except for his haircut, confident attitude and posture, he blended in and looked like all the other attendees.

* * *

Coulter didn't appreciate his new assignment. He didn't believe in psychics or telepathy and didn't want to be near personnel associated with what he called "stupid mental gyrations." After attending to business with the foreman of his four-hundred acre Montana ranch, he had reported to VESPER as ordered. Despite having respect for Colonel Anderson, Coulter had applied for leave time to escape from VESPER in the near future.

Coulter flexed his back and shoulders. He wasn't healing as fast as expected. Anyone not knowing of his recent combat injuries would erroneously assume he was in top condition. He and Colonel Anderson worked at keeping his compromised fitness level quiet. Coulter leaned back and crossed his arms, impatient for the meeting to begin.

Herman Wald sat farthest from the entrance door. A heavy set and large-boned man, rosacea gave him rosy cheeks set in a ruddy complexion. He sat straight and smiled between sagging jowls. His rumpled beige shirt, brown suit and nondescript tie belied the fact that he was an unnoticed power in private and political sectors. His past successes at creative thinking and problem solving were why the president appointed him as VESPER's CEO.

Wald shot a glance at Anderson and snapped his pen loudly against the table top. Conversation ceased. Eyes turned toward Wald. With a serious expression and calm voice, he began, "As you know, the first official government psychic organization, the *Star Gate Project, closed in the 90s. I expect the VESPER Project to be more successful. Without a strong telepath, we've had no success using Star Gate type psychics to identify stateside or international terrorists. Although we may not understand exactly how OUB viewers work, we're familiar with their techniques. Their minds somehow travel out of their bodies to different locations around Earth.

Exclamations were heard.

It's been proven they can observe areas unavailable to us and watch others. They can't read minds. In the past 48 hours, terrorist threats and incidents within the United States have escalated to a critical point. We believe these threats are from *al-Qaeda, ISIS, the Islamic State or one of their amoebic offspring. To that end, I requested Colonel Anderson to present a viable option for us to consider." All heads turned to face the still standing Anderson, who straightened, clasped his hands behind his back and slowly walked around the room.

"The Stars and Stripes," Colonel Anderson began in his reverberating voice, "is a weekly newspaper available to United States military personnel stationed around the world. A 1980's publication had an article about a group of superior children born in Johannesburg, South Africa."

Security Director, Shelly White, interrupted. "Colonel Anderson, what do you mean by superior? Physical or mental?

"Above genius level. Over one-sixty IQ. I was assigned to Ramstein Air Force Base hospital in Germany. Reading the story aroused my curiosity. Taking leave, I grabbed a military hop to South Africa and found the story was true." Anderson crossed his arms. "An incredible story," he reminisced. "I guarantee its authenticity. A gynecologist in Johannesburg tried to make his pregnant patients more comfortable without medication. Remember thalidomide babies?"

Most every head nodded.

"They were born to European women who allegedly took thalidomide pills for pain. Over forty-thousand babies were missing hands, feet, arms, or legs and sometimes all four limbs."

Anderson scrutinized his audience. "Knowing the vulnerability of developing embryos and fetuses, Doctor Reginald Beckman didn't want to prescribe medications. Instead, he devised a portable vacuum chamber to enclose their torso. He theorized that if atmospheric pressure outside the body was reduced during gestation, mothers would find relief from pain and internal uterine pressure."

Communications Director, Philip Arnold, appeared to be an enigmatic man. He sat across from Anderson quietly absorbing information. He remarked, "Creative idea," and touched a small American flag lapel pin while looking over half-glasses. "Did it work?"

Arnold was usually ensconced in his office or his Satellite Communication Pit with satellite links. His hard eyes bored into Anderson.

Anderson had never seen Arnold without his flag pin and wondered if it was planned to promote a patriotic ambiance. He believed the man was intelligent, for he'd been at the top of the lists as a intelligence officer in cybersecurity. Since Arnold kept pretty much to his computers, no one at VESPER seemed to know him. Smiles he offered were on his lips, not in his eyes. Average looking with dark hair and eyes, he usually faded into the woodwork. Anderson was pleased the man had spoken.

Wald slapped his hand against the table top with a loud bang. "Don't keep them in suspense, Andy. Tell 'em what happened." Then he leaned back to listen.

"It worked," Anderson continued with a smile. "Pregnancy pain receded. With oxygen and nutrition through umbilical cords unimpeded, perfect fetal brains developed as Mother Nature intended."

Wald added, "Their minds were Adam and Eve perfect."

Anderson raised his eyebrows and looked for questioning expressions. Seeing none, he continued. "It's been rumored that the Joburg children treated by Beckman used telepathy to communicate with one another." Startled glances were exchanged. Exclamations were heard around the table.

Wald affirmed with enthusiasm, "In addition, it was communal telepathy. When one child learned something, instantaneously so did all the others. Can you imagine the implications?" He paused to let the concept sink in.

Feeling excitement growing in the room, Anderson commented, "There's no other instance of communal telepathy in written history. These now middle-aged telepaths could ferret out terrorists. They'd instantly identify a terrorist and learn their plans just by listening to thoughts. To stop telepaths from being targeted by our enemies and to protect them, we must keep their existence secret. If we could find these mindreachers and convince them to join VESPER, global terrorism could be eliminated. Dismantling terrorist threats could lead to world peace. War-mongers may be neutralized." He waited for comments during stunned silence.

Elbows on the table, Security Officer Shelly White adjusted her glasses before raising a hand. At fifty-years old, she was an efficient, short haired, platinum-blonde with a medium build. She wore a doldrum suit to hide a slightly over-weight figure and brown oxfords for comfort. A retired administrator from the Department of Defense, White had joined the VESPER team with anticipation of someday learning how to become a telepath. Her neck wattle moved as she asked, "How many children are we talking about?"

"Approximately twenty," Wald answered, making a quick survey of facial expressions at his response.

Wide eyed, White sat back in her chair with an expression of incredulity. "Whoa," she choked out. "I was thinking three or four. It'd be difficult to monitor so many and keep them safe."

"Agreed. Those we hire must be protected. We don't know how many we may need. That depends upon their capabilities." There were concurring nods of agreement.

Wald added, "Tell them about the break in the communal telepathy link."

"According to one report," Anderson shared with excitement in his voice, "the mental link to one child was broken when his family went on a holiday over 500-miles away. Distance evidently presented a barrier. I interpreted the interruption to mean each child's reach was a maximum of two-hundred-fifty miles. Continent to continent their communal telepathy wouldn't work. Realizing their predicament, parents craving a normal family life prepared to leave Johannesburg to distance their child from the others."

Herman Wald leaned forward and tapped his pen sharply on the table. Again the room grew quiet. "Imagine if you will," he began, "parents welcoming a beautiful baby into their lives to nurture and love while they grew into a perfect family. Didn't happen." He shrugged, extending open palms. "The first year wasn't bad. By age two…" he held up two fingers, "the children began speaking in complex sentences. By three, they were devouring books and asking questions. Eliminating the slow, oral communication of normal humans, the telepathic children found it more efficient to instantly communicate by reading each other's' minds. They plucked desired information from adult minds. It's rumored that some of the children used mind control on antagonistic siblings."

With a concerned expression, White interrupted. "Would you clarify the word 'communal' again?"

Anderson responded, "When one of these children used telepathy, others with the same telepathic ability instantaneously received the mental conversation. When one learned a new word or fact, they all learned at the same time. They remembered what they learned. Their knowledge must have grown exponentially on a daily basis."

"Or hourly," Wald corrected.

"Thank you, gentlemen," White replied. "Having thoughts of others entering my mind would drive me crazy. They must have been able to block each other's thoughts. How else could they survive the mental onslaught?" Answering her own question, she continued, "Guess they got used to it. What a frightening thing to have babies reading your mind. Yet the concept…" she hesitated, grasping for the right word, "is exhilarating."

"They must have frightened others," Anderson said. "That became a good reason for parents to hide their remarkably talented child. Who knows what frightened people would do to the children?"

White inquired, "What would you call a person with such superior psychic talent?"

"I created the word 'mindreacher' to define those with ability to mentally communicate with someone over a hundred miles away."

Wald affirmed, "The moniker fits."

slammed his fist onto the table. Exclamations and loud conversations continued until Wald raised his hand signaling for quiet.

In the sudden silence a new voice was heard. VESPER Finance Director, Scott Galbraith, began, "How do terrorists get nuclear devices into the United States past border guards? Wouldn't they be detected?"

White responded, "Simple. Parts are small even for city busters. Small bombs can destroy a city. Picture a tube twice as long as a can of hair spray. That amount or less is how much plutonium is needed to create a dirty bomb." She paused to see if there were confused expressions. Seeing none, she continued, "Smugglers move illegal materials across our borders all the time."

Galbraith replied, "If they destroy airports, our country will come to a standstill."

Straightening her suit jacket, White added with a determined expression, "By destroying public and military airports, these November bombers may think they'll stop air travel in the United States." Shaking her head at their ignorance, she explained, "These jihadists don't know American history."

He commented, "I don't understand what you're referring to."

White replied, "President Eisenhower prepared for future wars fought on our soil. He requested and ensured two miles of unencumbered straight stretches of highway were constructed about every fourteen-to-twenty miles throughout our nation's interstate highway systems. Be assured, no matter how many airports terrorists destroy, we have landing strips throughout the nation on all major highways."

Andy commented, "On the Alaskan highways, airplanes already have right of way. If terrorists destroy our airports, our highways will become runways."

Leaning forward, Galbraith exclaimed, "Eisenhower was a wise man."

White continued, "General Eisenhower was a five-star general in the United States Army and served as Supreme Commander of the Allied Expeditionary Forces in Europe before becoming president. During World War II he witnessed the effectiveness of moving people and equipment on German autobahns. He wanted such fast transportation throughout the United States."

Galbraith said, "I can't imagine life without interstate highways."

White said, "Our military has to consider strategies to deal with ground-based bomb attacks. SDI, the Strategic Defense Initiative, has the technology to neutralize incoming nuclear warheads, not ground-based ones. One point to note. Knowing the history of terrorists and their proclivity to use advance planning, cell members may already be employed at targeted airports."

Anderson cut in, "Good news. Homeland Security restrictions have been removed from us. Whatever we need will be available. I've been checking out facilities and technology available from all armed forces, government agencies, and *DARPA, the Defense Advanced Research Projects Agency. We're now allowed to accomplish our mission using any technique and equipment they have available."

Arnold nervously cleared his throat. "How do you plan to find these mindreachers if only a telepath can identify another telepath? You only have a few remote viewers who couldn't identify a mindreacher any more than I could." Crossing his arms, he leaned back into his chair.

"Not a valid statement," Anderson responded. "A psychic phenomenon can be recognized by a trained person observing human reactions. They do have to know what to look for. Once they recognize human reactions to a psychic event, they should be able to find the catalyst or person causing the reaction. The psychic."

Galbraith commented, "Please explain."

"Anyone can be trained how to recognize human reactions to a psychic event. A trained individual may hit the psychic jackpot and find a mindreacher. The odds are in our favor we'll find one stateside."

Arnold scoffed, "You want us to believe you could train anyone to find a psychic?" He glanced at what he considered a he-man jock seated nonchalantly near the entrance. "Even him?"

The man Arnold referred to was Major Jonathon Coulter, USMC, an experienced officer in the Intelligence Support Activity of the Joint Special Operations Command. It was true

Coulter believed remote viewing or telepathy impossible. When first assigned to VESPER as liaison officer with OSD, he'd tried in vain to embrace the psychic concept. It was due to his skepticism that the Secretary of Defense believed the Major would remain unbiased.

Coulter glanced at Philip Arnold as though looking at an insect. Ordered to wear civilian clothing, his gladiator-type body was camouflaged. Appearing innocuous, he had been ignored.

Anderson believed Major Coulter had more testosterone in his little finger than Philip Arnold had in his entire body. With gleaming eyes Anderson answered, "Yes, even him." He was proud to have Jon as a longtime friend and colleague. With a stern voice Anderson addressed Arnold. "Major Coulter is one of the finest officers I've known. A weapons expert and hand-to-hand combat instructor, he's served on many successful covert operations, some with Navy SEALs. Major Coulter has served this country with distinction. Once trained in techniques to identify a psychic, if he is in the vicinity of a psychic-caused phenomenon, he will recognize it as such and identify the telepath causing the incident."

With a raised and questioning eyebrow Coulter respectfully stated, "Colonel, I'm in possession of too much classified information to be exposed to mind readers. I've put in for a transfer."

Knowing Coulter's transfer request had been tucked safely away in his desk, Anderson gave him a sympathetic look. That request wouldn't see the light of day until Coulter was back in prime fighting condition.

Wald exclaimed, "This has to work. The United States needs VESPER to survive an ever growing terrorist threat."

In a soft voice, Arnold warned, "You may never find a mindreacher."

Anderson caught Arnold's sullen look. Hearing the "you" and not "we" when the man referred to VESPER, Anderson questioned the man's loyalty. "You may be right, Mr. Arnold. In the past, we've advertised discretely for psychics. Those we've found to date have had limited abilities. Right, Mr. Lopez?"

Sitting at the end of the table near the exit, Miguel Lopez straightened in his chair and looked at Colonel Anderson. "Except for remote viewers," Lopez replied, "as psychic evaluator, I've not tested anyone showing significant psychic ability. We know remote viewers can't read minds. They only observe the physical world. I believe a minor telepath could identify a mindreacher." He looked at Anderson. "I agree with Colonel Anderson. If we fly a mindreacher over cities of interest, they could definitely pinpoint terrorists."

Anderson advised, "Failure is not an option. There is something we can all help do to help break this log jam of progress. In the immediate future, all our highly classified employees will be trained to identify and assigned to be on the lookout for psychic phenomena. I suggest we include training of selected American military and government personnel around the globe." He looked at Lopez. "I've asked Mr. Lopez to conduct online classes using a double encrypted government network."

Lopez addressed the group. "Training classes are ready to begin. Those trained can be on the lookout for psychic phenomena within the week."

"Fantastic," Wald exclaimed. "Using computers, Lopez can electronically train hundreds at a time. That will allow for an increasing base of observers. Who knows how many trained men and women we'll have in place by next week?" Lopez gave Wald a thumb up.

Arnold raised his right hand and demanded, "Make sure I'm included."

Wald said, "We need to find the mindreachers and rid the United States of terrorists. It doesn't matter what they call themselves, al-Qaeda, ISIS, ISIL, Tahrir al-Sham, or whatever. If they're terrorists, we deal with them."

Seeing confused expressions around the table, Anderson glanced at Miguel Lopez. "Mr. Lopez, when can you begin?"

Lopez took a deep breath. One of the few Hispanics in the VESPER fold, he had olive-colored skin with graying dark hair on both sides of his short forehead. Scraggly gray hairs extended randomly from his heavy, dark eyebrows. Thick glasses enlarged his intelligent brown eyes. A yellow and grey plaid tie contrasted with his immaculate black shirt, the long sleeves rolled under at the cuff. His shoes and slacks showed little wear. Three identical pens were attached to a plastic holder in his shirt pocket. On the right middle finger he wore a gold ring with a movable, small gold sphere turned to the inside of his palm. Absently rotating the sphere with his thumb, he looked at the Colonel.

"By the time you have authorization to begin training," Lopez said, "I'll have training schedules"

Wald said, "Mr. Arnold, as Communications Director, you will coordinate video equipment and create a temporary studio for interactive transmissions and recordings. Once the sessions are recorded, you won't need Lopez to teach them. Just continue to run the session videos to selected audiences."

Lopez smiled at Andy and hooked his thumb toward Coulter. "Major Coulter and Mr. Arnold can be in the first class."

Jon Coulter slowly shook his head in frustration.

Wald added, "Imagine how far reaching this project will become in protecting the world from terrorists." Eyes intensified on him. Fingers flew on electronic pads. "A reminder. Standard Operating Procedure is for all employees to use only VESPER provided electronic equipment. No personal electronic devices are to be brought into this facility. We had an potential lethal attack this morning proving knowledge of VESPER is on the street. I see some of you are using electronic pads. Ms. White, please ensure they have email and messaging disabled before they leave this room. VESPER electronic devices are not to be removed from this facility. Right, Shelly?"

"Affirmative. Approved communication is only through our double encrypted lines. VESPER's electronic pads have been tagged to set off alarms at exits."

"Thank you, Mr. Lopez," Wald said. "I know you've been concentrating on a training program. We appreciate your hard work." Lopez leaned back in his chair.

Anderson looked at Coulter and chuckled. He knew Coulter found the thought of being near psychics repugnant. Now the skeptic would be trained to find one. Anderson tried to contemplate military chains of command decisions once mindreachers entered the picture. Military personnel followed written or verbal orders given by superior officers. The thought of a military officer having to decide whether to accept orders given by a non-combatant and non-verbal telepath, rather than a superior military officer, would create ripples throughout any command. He questioned whether mindreachers could, or would, be given command authority since they could theoretically read minds of combatants within two-hundred miles. They would probably remain information sources and let command make combat decisions. If VESPER reached the president's expectations, command decisions from telepathic officers might become the norm. Future ramifications of mindreacher telepathic intrusions into common and covert military operations may increase in complexity. To learn how to make combat decisions, mindreachers would have to study military strategy at the war college. Letting out a deep breath, he pondered the future of combat.

Wald offered. "The president's fighting an uphill funding battle for our existence. Success at finding these November terrorists is imperative. Time has become a four letter word. Even though we must tread lightly, let's crank our treadmill up to a run."

CHAPTER 3

Virtues Golf Club Restaurant
Nashport, Ohio
15 August 11:00 AM EST

Two weeks later, Major Jon Coulter was enjoying leave time while driving toward his Montana ranch. By remaining a bachelor, he had paid off his mortgage, had a good ranch foreman, a sturdy truck, horse trailer, tractor, round bailer and backhoe. Registered with both the American Quarter Horse Association and Foundation Quarter Horse Association, his stallions brought income. Montana grass allowed him to maintain a small herd of cattle. Through selective breeding his foreman kept the ranch profitable.

Coulter had decided to take a break from driving to enjoy a game of golf at the Virtues Golf Club in southeast Ohio. He sat at a small table in the back corner of the Overlook Bar listening to buzz about the parkland-style course. He had moved the table and his chair. His back was in the corner of the room, the paneled wall on his left. He appreciated the rich paneling and furnishings which created a comfortable ambiance. The bar offered an expansive view of the last five holes on what was considered the best public golf course in the state. Gentlemen seated nearby discussed the easiest holes on the course and the tricks for dealing with the tough ones. Looking forward to seeing who would be in his foursome after lunch, he couldn't stop reminiscing about his recent past.

When assigned with USN SEALs, Coulter learned operators were considered perishable military assets when wounded or killed while accomplishing their objective. Unexpected variables in the field multiplied risks. With intelligence supplied from the office of Joint Special Operations Command and occasional others, every scenario his team could possibly encounter was evaluated and rehearsed prior to deployment. Seemingly impossible and dangerous missions were most often completed successfully with no one left behind. During his last mission, he had to be carried out. Without his combat team, he wouldn't be alive.

He had no idea what field to enter if he was unable to return to the prime fighting condition of a Marine. His current assignment sucked. He hated being around psychics.

Nationwide panic had been avoided by not announcing the Thanksgiving terrorist threats. Keeping terrorist targets quiet was SOP with Homeland Security. Until the 2013 NSA surveillance security leaks, the public had no idea how many narrow escapes there had been since the Twin Towers were attacked. Terrorist ring leaders had been located and disasters averted. But this time was different. Government agencies attacking the problem had been stymied. The president knew the bomb threats were real. There was just not enough information to find the terrorists.

Vigilant and aware, Coulter contemplated his recent VESPER training to recognize psychic-caused activity. He questioned his ability to recognize such an event. His personal attitude toward working with what he termed "weirdo psychics" was of no consequence. He obeyed orders. *Semper Fi.* Those orders required VESPER personnel to find a strong telepath. "Be continually observant of surrounding activities no matter where you are, even while taking a leak," Lopez had taught. "Keep your eyes open for unusual events."

Military training taught Coulter to continually scan for concealed firearms, especially when entering a new situation. Hearing an increase in the volume of conversations, he scanned the sports bar. Determining it was clean except for law enforcement, he ordered another fire-brewed beer. His glance turned to an attractive blonde about to enter the room at the stairway entrance.

* * *

A few minutes earlier, across the room from Coulter, a woman named Ana Masterson and her friend, Josie Garcia, had paused at the top of the entry staircase relaxing in the congenial atmosphere of golf enthusiasts. Josie, a sheriff's deputy in full uniform, was taking a lunch break. She looked less like a deputy than anyone in the Licking County Sheriff's Department due to her short height. No observer would suspect that in the line of duty she had tangled with and defeated men twice her size.

A keen observer might realize blonde Ana Masterson is unusual. A rare, invisible energy surrounds her. Individuals in any room she enters have no idea why their lives are suddenly positive and exciting. They become more energetic and talk louder as their mental activities increase.

Ana Masterson looked around the room. She admired the comfortable way light filtered through north-facing panoramic windows. The stone patio was filled with patrons enjoying their meal or having a drink. One large flat screen television hung above a lengthy granite topped bar. Laughter and predominantly male voices brought a sense of camaraderie. Blended aromas of grilled steak and onions made her mouth water. She thought, maybe a steak sandwich instead of salad?

Josie cocked her head and asked, "Any bachelors here?" She was the only person outside of Ana's family who knew Ana was a telepath.

Psychic from conception, Ana Masterson had begun to telepathically learn about her world as a fetus. In addition to using her parents, she learned about life from nearby animals. Her brain's neural connections became more complex as she absorbed information. Her cerebral cortex was continually resculpted in a constant state of learning. Additional neural and *glial connections evolved in specialized regions of her brain allowing solidification of telepathic techniques. By birth, Ana's use of telepathy had become as natural to her as breathing. Because her innocent, childhood telepathy resulted in anger, assaults and death threats to her family from others, she had been forbidden to use it. From daily parental reprimands and guidance, she learned secrecy and fear.

Ana confided only in Josie. As teenagers, she'd told Josie that a person in love had a specific brain site with increased temperature. She called the hot spot a "love site." If a love site had normal temperature, the person might be available. Over the years of their friendship, using love sites to know whether couples were friends or lovers, Ana frequently located straight, single guys for Josie. The process was a secret joke between them.

"Those two guys in matching green polo shirts," Ana told her after surveying the crowd. "They're a couple."

"The rest of the guys are straight?"

"I can only tell if they're currently in love. There are a lot of guys here wearing wedding rings with no love site activity."

"Meaning?"

"They're not in love with their wives. They just use them as an asset."

Josie's eyebrows scrunched up and her lips puckered. She had a confused expression as she glanced up at her friend. "An asset? Like a pension?"

"Think about it. Couples are invited to more social events than singles. After sharing lives in marriage, passionate love may stop. Yet they still provide companionship and care when their spouses are ill. Some people are more afraid of being alone in old age than of staying in a loveless and unfulfilling marriage."

Josie chuckled. "Annie, you never cease to amaze me."

Although Ana professed ignorance about how telepathy worked, she had spent much time researching structures and functions of the human brain, especially glia. She believed she had more glial cells in her brain than normal. Through her studies, she knew glial cells could act like stem cells and change into neurons to facilitate internal brain repair if needed. She enjoyed tracing energy moving through glia and neurons in minds of others. Acts of neuron groups passing electrons created rhythmic acoustics. Each person's unique rhythmic pattern became their identifying signature. To Ana, such unique identification was more accurate than fingerprinting, iris scans, retinal scans, or voiceprints. She called such rhythmic neural patterns in the brain "mindsongs." They were mental identification signatures varying only in velocity. Neural scientists called such signatures "oscillations" or "rhythmic patterns" as groups of neurons fired electrical signals.

Over the years, she recognized that children with a calcium deficiency had slow mindsongs with an associated lower intelligence. Since glia required calcium to function, she thought her personal calcium craving directly related to a high glial count. She consumed several gallons of milk a week along with cheese, yogurt and ice cream. Especially butter pecan ice cream.

Ana theorized a complex mindsong indicated higher intelligence. What always surprised her had been finding similar mindsongs within a family. By comparing family mindsongs, she discovered that males appeared to inherit neural rhythms from their mother while females inherited neural rhythms from both parents. That was a sign mindsongs may be inherited through the *X-chromosome. Everyone's mindsong nuances evolved with time, yet their basic mindsong remained an easy identifier.

Sometimes there were so many individual mindsongs within her listening range, she likened hearing the chorus of them to mental mayhem. To cope and relax within the mayhem, Ana imagined her telepathic energies as living entities emanating from her mind. She pretended they existed in vivid colors of turquoise, rose, blue and green creating a swirling rainbow of energy. The colors, in three dimensional masses, moved out from her in all directions. She believed each telepathic type had a unique vitality and hue as though alive. She closed her eyes and conjured images of the vibrancy moving from her mind into space surrounding her body and beyond. This helped process energy flowing around her.

* * *

The two women were looking for empty seats at a table when Ana was jolted into psychic awareness. The bolt of awareness was caused by someone visually scanning for a firearm.

"What in the world?" She reacted too late to home in on the scanner. It had given her an impression of intelligence. She turned to Josie. "Who's law enforcement here?"

"Why? What'd you see?" Dark eyes sparkling, Josie's right hand automatically moved to rest on a holstered firearm. She looked around.

"Someone just scanned me for a gun."

Josie's sharp eyes reviewed the room. Her short, black hair bounced as she looked around. "No one here from my department." She lowered her voice. "Do your mental thing and find 'em." She grinned and rubbed her hands together in anticipation.

The times Ana had used her psychic power when the two were together, something unpredictable always happened. Her telepathy created excitement in an otherwise blah day. Except for unruly students in her high school classrooms, she rarely used telepathic power. Her family received death threats when she used it as a child. They wouldn't allow her to use her telepathy talents. When she did read a mind, she made sure it was undetected by the subject.

"Okay, Josie. You're still sworn to secrecy."

Josie chuckled and looked around the room in anticipation.

With apprehension, Ana used her pent-up psychic energy to telepathically scope the large room. As her psychic energy flowed through the room, heads turned toward her in a wave. Customers glancing at her were unaware of the psychic energy surge, but became more audible and animated.

Within seconds, Ana zeroed in on the weapon seeker. She thought, he's an alpha male. Recent scars across his left eyebrow and nose. Cleft chin. Military buzz. Muscled. Looks like a paper-thin watch. Must be a Rado. That means he's either wealthy or single. Intelligent eyes. Can't see finger gold. Sits strategically where no one can step behind him. Who is he?

She skimmed his mind to find a name. When she discovered he worked for a psychic organization called VESPER, she immediately pulled out of his mind. Who is he? If he's psychic, she thought, he'll feel me. Wonder what he does? Maybe they'd hire me. Any non-teaching job would be a win. If I could be hired as a telepath, I'd be in seventh heaven. Need to learn more about this VESPER. I'll Google it later. She whispered quietly to herself to remember the name, "VESPER, VESPER VESPER."

* * *

Major Jonathon Coulter, when noting the unusual motion of heads turning in a wave toward the stairs, executed a double take. He couldn't believe his eyes. People whose heads turned in the wave nonchalantly continued about their business apparently unaware anything unusual had happened. Due to his recent VESPER training, he realized what he'd just seen wasn't normal. Trainer Lopez had stressed recognizable unusual events may be effects of psychic energy. To Jon, the head wave proved an active psychic was in the room. Excited, he tried to find the catalyst who caused the head turns.

"Unbelievable. A psychic event," he said under his breath. Like his father, Coulter was a patriot with an inquiring mind and conservative political views. He had doubted psychics existed until witnessing the head wave. During the head wave, eyes were aimed at two women standing by the entry staircase. The shorter one in a deputy uniform looked Hispanic. The blonde was average height, clean cut, trim and perhaps in her thirties. She looked athletic in fluid white slacks and black T-shirt. He tried to guess which of the two women was a psychic or if they both might be. He settled in to focus on them.

The blonde surveyed the room. When their eyes met, without breaking eye contact, Jon saluted by lifting his beer mug in her direction. Seeing her teal-colored eyes, he assumed she was wearing tinted contacts and gave her a point for trying to push the appearance. Her friend's a deputy, he mused, so blondie must be living on the right side of the law. That's two points. If she's a powerful psychic, he predicted, she could become a walking terrorist target.

* * *

Ana froze when their eyes met. She felt panic. After Coulter saluted, she casually looked away. She told Josie about him as they walked to the only vacant seats which were at the bar.

Once seated, Josie whispered, "Never saw him before. Good looking."

Ana nodded and checked her appearance by telepathically entering the optical nerve center of a female bartender as she approached to take their orders. The smiling bartender had the name Kathy on her plastic name plate. She had no idea that Ana was checking her own hair using the waitress's eyes as though looking into a mirror. Ana smoothed an errant wisp of hair.

Josie whispered, "Is he carrying?"

Ana shrugged. Perspiration rolled down her back. She thought, thank goodness he doesn't know who I am or what I can do. She cautiously gathered Coulter's thoughts about VESPER and remarked to Josie, "He's with some psychic organization."

"Really?"

"We need to learn more about him."

Josie elbowed Ana's arm. "What do you mean we? I need to get back on duty." When served, Ana enjoyed a leisurely lunch while Josie ate quickly and left.

While eating, Ana observed Coulter through optical senses of others. He checked his watch before moving confidently between tables toward the bar, glass mug in hand. She wondered if his confidence was earned or innate. She knew he'd pinpointed her as the head wave cause. Eyes widening, she leaned against the tall, bar stool's wrought iron back rest with crossed arms. She refrained from waving away his Marlboro odor when he stopped beside her.

"Hi. I'm Jonathon Coulter. My friends call me Jon." He motioned at the empty seat beside her. "I wondered if we could talk."

CHAPTER 4

Virtues Golf Club Restaurant
Nashport, Ohio
11:32 AM DST

"Hi Jon." She nodded to the leather-upholstered bar stool Josie had used. "Have a seat. I'm Ana Masterson."

He asked, "May I buy you a drink?" In studying her, he saw irises flecked with shades of teal and blue. Rosy cheeks highlighted creamy smooth skin. Curly chin-length hair had various shades of light ash blonde. Small, laser cut, gold hoop earrings showed off a slender neck.

"Thanks. I'm having soda water with lemon and lime. No ice."

Jon placed his mug on the shiny granite bar with a thud, establishing claim to the seat. Ice on the outside of his mug slid to the bar as slush. After ordering refills from bartender Kathy, he asked Ana, "Do you golf here often?"

"No. Just here for lunch." She asked Kathy, the friendly bartender for her bill.

"I'm just passing through," he said noncommittally.

His presence brought her a sense of adventure.

He spoke cautiously, "I saw what happened when you entered the room. Neat trick." The bartender served their beverages.

"They always forget and add ice." She complained, stalling to think of a good rebuttal. She asked herself if she was excited or nervous. Her hands were shaking. She lifted the lime off the edge of her freshened drink, squeezing juice into the glass. As its pungent flavor was released into her club soda, citrus aroma filled the air. She stirred the drink. Ice clinked against the glass.

She slid the swizzle stick slowly across her tongue before taking a sip.

Ana asked, "What trick are you talking about?" She turned innocently away, eyeing Jon using optical senses of others.

In a lowered voice he replied, "The head-wave. When everyone looked at you. Don't deny it. I saw it with my own eyes."

She was amazed he'd observed reactions to her energy scan. Memories flooded into her mind of childhood incidents when others had suspected how different she was. Challenged and confronted many times in the past, she became wary of his scrutiny.

* * *

Jon observed the woman. Surprised to find a female telepath, he wondered if her skill was strong enough for VESPER. She needed to be tested. He figured he could probably get her into bed, but to New York? He couldn't use force. He'd have to proceed with diplomacy and caution.

* * *

Looking over the rim of her glass, she sipped at the contents. Suddenly apprehensive, she gave a nervous laugh. "I've heard many come-ons. Yours is definitely an original." She worried he would let everyone know she was a telepath. She mumbled, "I better leave," and picked up her bill.

Jon blocked as her toes touched the floor. "Where're you heading?"

"Out of here." She turned away from him.

"Did I hit too close to home?" At her hesitation, he immediately regretted his comment. "I'm sorry." He stepped back.

Her face reddened. "What are you driving at?"

He relaxed his stance and pleaded, "Five minutes of your time's all I ask. Look around. You're safe. We're in a public place."

Questioning if she were in her right mind, Ana looked around the room before grumbling a suggestion. "The head turns were guys just checking out the merchandise."

He wiped condensation off his mug. To ensure no one overheard, he leaned closer. "Would you laugh if I said your government needs you? I'm assigned to an agency searching for telepaths to jump-start a new project. The security of the United States is at stake and time is running out." He looked reluctantly out to the golf course and back to Ana who was tapping manicured fingernails on the bar. "What it boils down to, we need telepaths to identify terrorists. You may be exactly what ... uh... who we need."

"Or maybe not." It was a struggle for her to consider she might actually get paid for using telepathy. She felt her heart beat faster.

"You give off psychic energy without even thinking about it."

Downplaying her ability, she differed. "I don't think so." Ana knew telepathy was as automatic to her as eating or driving. When using telepathy, her frontal lobes were galvanized into action. They were a region of her brain where emotions were experienced and assimilated. Unconscious thought processes gave those emotions meaning and significance. Without actively thinking about Jon, his presence was causing her to experience heightened emotions in her frontal lobes. In the past, if she became highly emotional about anything, psychic energy surrounding her body could increase and affect others nearby. She craved anonymity and tried to prevent such occurrences. Jon Coulter was affecting her. She wanted to know more about him. Anything she scanned of his mind made him appear honorable.

"Who's in charge of your organization?"

Jon answered solemnly, "In charge? Hummm, let's see ...," he looked into her eyes. "Right now it's an alphabet soup. There's the OSD, the Office of the Secretary of Defense..., the DIA, Defense Intelligence Agency..., SOCOM, the Special Operations Command, the Army Intelligence Security Command, maybe a dozen others. Of course there's Homeland Security. It goes as high as the White House. The President receives updates each Wednesday morning during a Daily Brief." He smiled at her. "You may be the next topic."

"Is there a telepathy protocol used by your staff?"

"Protocol? Can't answer your question. I know someone who can." He told Ana about Colonel Andrew Anderson.

"Andy's been involved in government operations with Army, Air Force, Navy, and Marine Corps Special Op commands. Even the Coast Guard. Over the years, he's had a hand in all types of military tasks. If you want to get anything accomplished, going through him makes it easier. A genius with a handle on everything."

"Is he psychic?"

"Never asked."

"Are you?" He shook his head. Deciding he wouldn't know if she entered his mind, she skimmed his mind again. Bless him, she thought, he thinks I'm in my thirties. "Were you a Marine?"

"No such thing as a former marine. Once a Marine, always a Marine."

"What's *Semper Fi* mean?"

"*Semper Fidelis*. Latin for "always faithful. Would you go to New York to get tested? Can you get away from your job for a few days?"

"Right now I'm on leave. I'd enjoy being tested for psychic ability." She leaned against the cushioned, leather back of the bar stool in anticipation of learning more about VESPER. "In the past I've been criticized and threatened for my psychic abilities. Now your VESPER wants to hire psychics." She beamed. "How can I lose?"

"What do you do for a living?"

" I teach high school."

He grinned. "How are students now days?"

"More interested in cell phones than learning." Excited about VESPER and future employment opportunities, she rested her hands on her thighs to keep them still and thought, don't blow this opportunity.

"Any pets?"

"My dad and I share rights to Charlie, our Bernese mountain dog. He's with dad days and with me nights and weekends."

"Any obligations to stop you from flying to New York tomorrow for testing?" She shook her head. "If it's okay with you," he suggested, "in the morning I can drive us to Columbus or meet you there to catch an early flight. We can be at JFK by noon. Let me check with Andy."

He punched Colonel Anderson's number on his cell phone. "Andy," he began at the pick-up, "I'm at the Virtues Golf Course in Nashport, Ohio. Would you believe it? I think I found one." He sat back with a satisfied smile directed at Ana. "Name is Ana … Ana Masterson. Can I bring her in tomorrow?" Jon listened to Andy's affirmative reply. Andy told Jon someone from VESPER would immediately check her out. "Great, see you about noon. Before closing the connection he added, "She wants to know if VESPER has a protocol for telepaths." After receiving a negative answer he thanked his friend and punched off. "Andy probably began a background check on you the minute I closed the call."

Her eyes opened in surprise. "I hope this is a good move."

"It is." Jon phoned his favorite airline to check departure times from Columbus International Airport. "What time can you be ready in the morning?"

She replied immediately, "I'm an early riser."

"Good."

"I'm stunned. You're the first person I ever met who not only identified me as psychic, but wants the government to make me a job offer to work with other psychics." She leaned back and sighed, "There is a God!" While Jon checked flight times, hairs on Ana's arms stood on end. "I can't see you," she whispered. I can feel your presence. Definitely male. Are you from VESPER?" She knew an invisible someone was beside her, but there was no response.

Jon booked the first morning flight out of Columbus International Airport to JFK. He gave Ana the logistics of the drive to Columbus and flight to New York. Someone would retrieve his BMW from the airport and store it.

When they parted, Ana walked outside and put on her aviator sunglasses. Knowing a solo flight would boost her spirits even more, she headed for PARR airport.

* * *

At the highly classified VESPER facility hidden under JFK International Airport, information critical to national defense was never discussed on outside phone lines. However, someone with an intricate knowledge of the in-house communications system had prepared for such a random and significant conversation. Although there were no traceable wiretap devices on desk phones, all VESPER land line conversations to the outside world had been compromised. Because of such advance preparation, Coulter's information to Anderson concerning Ana Masterson had been clandestinely recorded. The call would be automatically forwarded to an outside radio receiver. By midnight, an operative within a New York city terrorist cell would also be running information background checks on Masterson.

CHAPTER 5

JFK International Airport
Jamaica, Queens, New York
16 August 10:00 AM DST

When Ana and Jon deplaned at JFK the next morning, he led her to a freight elevator in one of the passenger terminals. When the elevator car arrived and the door opened, Jon ushered her inside. He placed his Personal Identity Verification, or PIV card, near the elevator's right wall. A hidden panel slid open to reveal additional elevator controls. He placed a knuckle near a button which lit when it sensed body heat.

"If I'd made contact with the button," he informed her, "this panel and the elevator doors would've closed, locked, and security alerted. Someone would arrive to find out who set off the alert. This is the only VESPER entrance located inside an airport terminal and requires security measures." An unobtrusive metal detector in the elevator had determined they were not armed.

"How many people have accidentally touched the pad and gotten sealed in?"

"Not many."

Ana grabbed the handrail at a slight feeling of levitation. She had expected the elevator to go up. It moved swiftly down. "VESPER's underground?" She swallowed a gulp of air to disguise distress and the beginnings of panic.

"VESPER's highly classified. No one's supposed to know it exists. Everything's hidden underground." The elevator slowed and began a horizontal shift before accelerating.

"It goes sideways?"

He nodded. "These subterranean tunnels extend far beyond the runways."

Astounded, she tightened her grip on the railing. "It's so quiet. What makes it move?"

"Magnetism." He patted the wall. "Horizontal elevators make for easy transit. Install powerful suspension magnets and off you go."

"It's so smooth. How fast are we going?"

"Maximum speed could be eleven miles per hour. This facility isn't big enough to use those speeds yet."

"How many elevator cars are there?"

He answered, "Four. Only two are in use. In case of a national emergency, the others will automatically be deployed."

"Can they ever collide?"

"No." At her raised eyebrow, he added, "They're in shafts with technology to avoid collisions."

She rolled her eyes. "This is exciting and scary at the same time." Fear rolled through her body. To keep her mind off being trapped underground, she thought about etiquette rules when using telepathy at VESPER. She took a deep, trembling breath. "How many floors does this subterranean place have?"

"That's classified information."

Once they reached their destination, the door slid open and Jon walked out. Ana poked her head out to check the corridor in both directions. Regularly spaced imbedded wall sconces fanned light in all directions. The floor was a smooth gray concrete, the walls brushed aluminum.

Ana said, "There's no sunlight. No windows." Warm, damp air invaded the elevator. "How long will this meeting take?" She struggled to breathe.

Across the corridor from the elevator, a young security guard sat at a desk facing them from a small alcove. Three computer monitors faced him. Jon's PIV card had triggered an identification program as soon as the elevator door had opened. The guard checked a matching image on one of his monitors and motioned for Jon to approach. The two men talked briefly.

"I need your cell phone," Jon said to her. They surrendered their cell phones to the guard before a temporary visitor pass was issued for Ana. Surveillance cameras documented every action.

Turning to hand over the visitor pass, Jon was surprised to see her tortured expression. "Is there a problem?"

Her breath became shallow. Her glance darted back and forth. It was difficult for her to say the word. "Claustrophobia."

"Just don't think about it." He'd worked with such superbly trained men on his special operations teams, he'd never considered being saddled with imperfection. He took a deep breath.

"I'll try." She stepped away from the elevator. When the door closed, she felt trapped. Her escape route no longer existed. In her mind, the corridor walls appeared to close in as the ceiling lowered. "I can hardly breathe." She twisted her hands as a wave of heat hit. Her breath became more rapid and shallow.

Jon asked, "Is there anything I can do to help?"

"I don't think so." She frowned. Her mouth tasted of acid.

"We go this way." He led her into the corridor to the right.

Walking at a funeral pace, Ana tried to get her mind off the situation. Upon seeing the periodic protrusions of small squares from the ceiling she asked, "Video monitors?"

He answered, "Surprised you noticed since they only protrude a few millimeters."

She declared, "They contain more than video."

"You're right. They have monitors for chemicals, static electricity, and humidity. Actually, this is a smart building. Air filters and sensors are part of an underground, interconnected safety network."

"What kind of sensors?"

"Biological and chemical substances during attacks," he answered. "See those cylinders?" He motioned to a dark Plexiglas faced cabinet flush with the wall.

"Fire extinguishers? The walls are metal. They won't burn."

"Read what's written on the canisters."

She leaned forward to read the small print through her reflection on the grey Plexiglas door. "One contains foam developed by *Sandia Laboratories to neutralize nerve gas. The second one's for other biological agents. Neither one's for putting out a fire. I never knew there were biocanisters like these."

"Because you're not a warrior or a geek," he teased with a wink.

Although somewhat distracted, she didn't appreciate being trapped in a maze.

He explained. "Working together, all the systems automatically react to create a safe underground site in case of attack. One sensor can automatically seal the building from the outside world. "

"VESPER's that important?"

"Not yet. This area's been stocked as a disaster-preparedness facility. Materials needed for the survival of several thousand people for months are stored and replenished periodically."

"You mean food and water?"

"You bet," he answered. "Anything needed in an emergency. Cots, sheets, blankets, cribs, diapers. Add communications to the outside world. It's for government top dogs if a disaster hits the United States."

"Lots of computers here?"

"You wouldn't believe what they have here. It's updated whenever something new comes along. Right now it rivals Titan, a Cray XK7 system at the Oak Ridge National Laboratory. VESPER has unlimited access to it. New corridors are being built down here to house more computers."

"Are VESPER computers different?"

"Thumb and disk drives are disabled. Personal communication devices are not allowed. Staff are provided with needed electronics."

"Can anyone break into VESPER computers?"

"There's software encryption for sensitive data. A two-person authorization or sensitive encryption keys open them."

"You must have a lot of sensitive data." He didn't answer. She gestured to the space around her and commented, "To have all this underground preparedness for an emergency, VESPER must be tremendously secure."

"In case of disaster, if the president can get here, he'll have one of the safest living quarters and the most secure, high-tech, communication nerve center in the world. This is one of several underground safe sites in the United States. "

"Wouldn't terrorist bombs destroy the tunnels?"

"Most blasts go up, not down. This is considered the place to be during or after an attack. Ever hear of the deep underground cities built for millionaires?" At her nod, he said, "This one's made with tax dollars for government officials in case of war."

Perspiration beads dotted her face and chest. Feeling a trickle of moisture between her breasts, she unbuttoned her suit jacket.

"I need air. A window. A fan. I can't take this closeness." She stopped and put a hand against the wall for support. "Jon, I... uh, I don't do well in enclosed areas." She could hardly get the words out. "I don't know if I can work here. What if there's an emergency? I could barely see the elevator control and I stood right in front of the dumb thing. How can I get out?" She muttered, "Stupid phobia will keep me from working here." Near tears, she could barely walk or talk. She thought this was another dream heading for the gutter.

"Take a deep breath," he suggested. "Do you feel faint?"

"Wait a minute." Ana had the ability to release endorphins from her brain to feel better and did so. Her natural endorphins would begin to work within seconds to counteract pain and stress. With the growing sensation of inner calm came a floating sensation. "I want to get my mind off this tunnel. Talk to me. Tell me about this place while we walk."

Gently grasping her elbow to provide support, he began. "The first tunnel construction started in 1990 by the Port Authority of New York and New Jersey which operates the airport. The tunnels were constructed to move passengers and luggage between terminals."

"Who paid for it?"

"The airlines. There was supposed to be a central, underground terminal with eight tunnels connecting to above-ground airline hubs. Existing terminals were to be demolished for more runways."

"Then what happened?"

"The airlines stopped construction when costs exceeded estimates. For all the public knows, these tunnels were abandoned. Out of sight, out of mind. I doubt if many New Yorkers remember they exist."

"Why's VESPER underground?"

"The President put it here to keep it hidden. This project took over a section of a twenty-one million dollar tunnel system to nowhere.

She stopped. "I'm trying to be calm. I feel so closed in." On the verge of hysteria, she tried to act nonchalant and grasped his arm. The hallways didn't provide enough light to give her a sense of freedom. She wanted blinding, bright sunlight. She slid her right hand along the wall as they walked. "How many exits are there?"

"Several, but if I told you where they're located, I'd have to kill you," he teased.

The duo passed many opaque, glass doors to reach their destination. Jon said, "Doors here have cipher locks. You need to enter key pad codes to proceed or have someone let you in. He stopped an arm's length from one of them. The door became transparent as his PIV card triggered an electronic signal. A seated, brunette female receptionist inside glanced at them and back to a computer monitor *embedded in her desktop.

"She's matching my face and irises for identity verification," he explained. "Jen must've been too busy for a positive ID as we approached or she'd have unlocked the door by now."

"You referring to biometrics? Electronic recognition?"

He gave a curt nod, lips pressed together. "Bioscan data is held by the FBI and other agencies for face recognition. There're seven national databases in the United States each holding regional data. By the way, if you work here you can't wear specialized contacts."

"Specialized?"

"For example, the words 'Cleveland Browns' printed around the edge of your contacts would stop iris Bioscan identification."

She exclaimed with a grin, "That's my team!"

"Since they scan the outer ridges of the iris, words and designs on your contacts make them useless for identification."

"When would they scan someone like me?"

"Electronic earspheres automatically transmit iris data when they send tracking info. Can't use fingerprints taken down here. Construction dust clogs fingerprints and makes sweat pores on the ridges impossible to see."

"Could my data be stored on some computer system?"

"For sure."

"Aren't they primarily for criminals?"

"And politicians."

"Politicians and criminals. Why am I amused by such a grouping?"

His quick glance and crooked grin acknowledged her humor. "I could take a picture of a criminal or spy, enlarge it and copy the iris for scanners. Could probably do the same with fingerprints. Ever see a picture of a spy?"

"No."

"Exactly. They know how to avert having their picture taken or have their picture removed from all data bases."

As the receptionist aimed a smile toward Jon, the door slid quietly into the wall jamb. Cooler air flowed past them into the hallway. With it came the slight scent of Chanel No. 5, Ana's favorite cologne. The receptionist typed on a keyboard with her left hand while manipulating a small object in her right palm with her thumb.

"Hey, Jen." Jon's voice had a happy lilt to it. "You're more beautiful than ever!"

"Well ... hello, Jonnie," Jennifer replied before standing. Combining a low sensual voice with a mischievous grin to greet Jon with a hug, her playful gray-green eyes sparkled bright in contrast to a spray-on tan. "Long time no see!" She laughed and pulled back, holding onto his shoulders to look at him. "I thought you were on leave." Her face dimpled when she smiled. She was dressed in a pastel, blue suit with no blouse under the closed jacket. A white opal on a gold chain resting near her cleavage sent off pastel fires of green and pink with each breath.

Jon said, "Jennifer Clark, meet Ana Masterson." He put an arm around Ana's shoulder. "She's an exceptional original."

"Pleased to meet you, Jennifer." Ana extended her hand. As they formally greeted one another, the warm miniature gold sphere of Jennifer's ring rubbed Ana's palm. At the same time, the cursor on the computer screen moved. Ana realized the sphere was a thumb-operated wireless trackball.

A social smile on her lips, Jennifer replied, "My pleasure."

Hairs on Ana's arms moved. The alert told her someone was observing her. She followed the observation feel to a miniature video link embedded in a watercolor seascape behind the reception desk. The end of a fiber-optic cable had been hidden within a small flag atop a racing sloop in the picture. Had she been able to see the cable, she would know it was a strand finer than one of her blonde hairs. A laser beam turned it into a video link. The opening in the wall was smaller than a pinhole. When she sent the watchers a mental hello through the link, it closed within a second of her send. She figured anonymous viewing was the norm at VESPER and wondered when she'd get to meet any psychics.

"I'll see if the Colonel's on schedule," Jennifer said, and activated the intercom. "Colonel Anderson, Ms. Masterson and Major Coulter have arrived." Ana's eyebrows rose at the realization Jon was an officer. She tilted her head and reexamined him.

After a momentary pause, they heard Colonel Anderson respond in a deep, booming voice. "Send them in."

The colonel stood and stepped forward as they entered his office. He shook her hand. "Welcome to VESPER Ms. Masterson. I'm pleased you were able to join us today."

"Thank you Colonel. I'm pleased to be here."

"Call me Andy."

She acknowledged his request with a corresponding dip of her head. "Call me Ana."

"Thank you." He motioned to one of two folding metal chairs facing a massive and intricately carved, walnut desk. She was comforted to note Andy was a barrel-chested, robust man similar to her father. His khaki-colored, long-sleeved shirt was tailored to skim his torso. It created a handsome contrast with his mahogany-colored skin. Andy sat.

Jon sat on the remaining chair. He said, "Andy's the friend I called back in Ohio. I've been trying to get him to retire and play more golf."

"I will when I have room at home for this desk," Andy quipped. "Son moved back." His eyes crinkled with a friendly smile. "I retired once. Got bored. When the President initiated VESPER, I made sure I was on board. Love to solve problems." After an infectious laugh, he sobered. "Knowledge of VESPER's on the street. The President is not pleased."

While the men talked, Ana took even breaths and tried to relax. She reflected that two days earlier she would never have discussed her telepathy.

Andy removed papers from a folder on his desk and studied her, fingers gently tapping the desktop. "Has Jon told you what we're about?"

"A little." She fanned her face. "Did you send a remote viewer to me yesterday? There was a presence of someone I couldn't see after Jon called you."

With raised eyebrows, Jon turned his head to look at her.

Amused by her directness, Andy chuckled. "Affirmative. I wanted to see if you were as telepathic as Jon insisted."

"Your conclusion?"

"The remote viewer couldn't tell. They use only sight. Visuals. By acknowledging his presence you confirmed your psychic awareness." She opened her mouth to say something, but didn't.

"We discussed VESPER," Jon said. "Nothing classified."

Andy said, "Our security classification may be changed. Even though our presence may have been discovered, the President doesn't want public awareness. He believes if the classification is lowered, more people will find out about us. The National Reconnaissance group wants security lowered to TS-SCI, Top Secret-Sensitive Compartmented Information. The OSD, Office of the Secretary of Defense, wants us to stay classified as USAP, an Unacknowledged Special Access Program to keep us hidden. I think our psychic work embarrasses them." He studied the face of the woman before him. "For having been here less than an hour, you've certainly generated attention."

Lowering her eyes she offered, "Other than that video in your outer office, I wasn't aware of any attention."

Andy asked, "Before we begin, is there anything I need to know?"

Ana squirmed. "I think it's important for you to know I'm claustrophobic."

"And...?"

"Being underground like this is stressful. No matter where I go down here, I feel boxed in. Like I'm suffocating. I can't survive this. There's no windows. No sunshine."

"Thank you for letting me know. That's something we can positively address."

She visibly relaxed.

He looked at Jon. "Anything you need to tell me?"

"Not that you don't already know."

"Ana, you've been living topside in a non-psychic world. Here, you'll be immersed in a psychic-heavy atmosphere. I hope you'll consider what VESPER has to offer."

"Yes sir," she replied, "but not remote viewing. I like my body too much to leave it."

He laughed. With elbows on the darkened, padded, chair arms, Andy brought his hands together in a prayer fashion. Tapping his fingers against one another, he assured, "We're moving in another direction." He paused for a moment and cocked his head, as though listening to someone before speaking.

"Several of our psychic staff detected you as you descended from the airport terminal. Since this facility is shielded from above, they were amazed. You also caught them unawares with the amplitude of a message you just sent through an observational link in Jennifer's reception area. You'll note I said "observational." It wasn't designed for telepathic messaging such as you demonstrated. You opened a can of worms, my dear. We'll be exploring the link to see how your message was transmitted." He laughed. "They're thinking electronically while you're thinking telepathically." He picked up a silver pen and flipped it rapidly between thumb and fingers. Reflected light flashed as it moved. "From what I've been able to determine, you're widowed."

"My husband developed terminal cancer two years into a beautiful marriage."

"I'm sorry for your loss."

Tears welled up in her eyes before she looked away.

"I'm impressed with your teaching accomplishments and awards. You'll be missed."

Her face glowed at the insinuation she'd leave teaching.

"If I read you right, VESPER's going to suit you to a 'T'. If you'll oblige us, tomorrow we'll run tests to identify your specific talents. If all goes as planned, we'll have employment papers for you to sign and security clearance applications to fill out. Does this meet with your approval?"

"It does," she said with a growing smile. She longed to be recognized for the telepath she truly was and use her talents without criticism. She questioned how those in VESPER would react if they knew exactly what her talents encompassed. She decided to not expose them all. After being stifled in telepathy by her parents, she didn't know if she could freely open up to use all her psychic techniques practiced in secret.

Andy took a deep breath of satisfaction. "If you join VESPER, we'll do our best to accommodate your abilities. Tell me about yourself."

Ana told him about her parents forbidding her telepathic use. "My mom was a little psychic. No one else. My parents often wondered why I developed it. My mother thought a burst of energy moving through the universe hit my brain when it was an embryo of just a few cells. She also thought dad had been on drugs when I was conceived. He thought it was my mother's diet. She was a strict vegan, ate only organic food, and used all kinds of herbs and spices including marijuana. She didn't know marijuana causes chromosome damage. Could that have caused my telepathy?"

I can't answer that question," Andy said, "Once you record your history, we can try to figure out what may have caused your telepathy. We're desperate to find telepaths. We need them right now to identify the latest batch of terrorists threatening the United States infrastructure. Would you be interested in becoming involved in such an operation?"

"Working with VESPER would be an honor."

They conversed a few more minutes before Andy stood and gestured them to the door. As they walked through the outer office, Jennifer extended a sheaf of incoming message forms to the Colonel. Looking pointedly at Ana, she said, "Messages are nonstop."

Andy directed, "Arrange hotel accommodations for Ms. Masterson and Major Coulter. Then call for a driver." With an amused expression, he took the thick stack of telephone messages from Jennifer's hand with a flourish. Softly whistling and waving the papers, he demanded, "Jon, take excellent care of this talented woman. If we're lucky, tomorrow may prove to be a pivotal day for VESPER."

CHAPTER 6

Holiday Inn Hotel
Manhattan, New York
16 August. 6:20 PM DST

In her sixth floor hotel room, Ana thanked Jon for handling her luggage. She took a few moments to memorize the escape path posted on the back of the door. Peering out the window she watched curls of high, cirrus clouds brush across the sky's blue palette. Tall, soot-smudged buildings jutted up at irregular intervals while lower ones presented blackened roofs filled with air conditioners, water towers, pipes and cables. She pushed at the bottom of the window frame with no result. Fanning her face, the large room appeared to close in.

Seeing her distress, Jon asked, "Claustrophobia kicking in?"

She stopped fanning. "Can't help it. I'm an outdoor type." She stared out the window.

"Would you prefer another room?"

"I'll be fine." She continued fanning her face and neck thinking, am I having a hot flash?

Jon pulled a protein drink container from an inner jacket pocket. He unscrewed the cap and held it out to Ana. "Want a swig?" At her "no thanks" he downed the liquid, crushed the container, and tossed it into the waste basket. "What do you hear when listening to telepathy? Normal talking?" He settled into an upholstered chair next to the window.

"I hear soft vibrations of electricity moving through synapses during neural activity. I call them mindsongs. They are so addicting. When whales share songs, their songs change. When I listen to mindsongs, changes seem to occur. So I don't stay long."

She paced the room as she spoke. "We have a well-constructed brain contained in our multipurpose body. It holds our conscious and unconscious self, our soul, and for some fortunate ones, the Holy Spirit. The physical body is a support system. I believe the power of my being, of who I am in my conscious or unconscious existence, could be changed by listening to the neural mindsongs of others." During the following silence Ana worried she'd said too much.

He had a perplexed expression. "Explain."

"Without telepathy, people unconsciously react to body language such as eye reactions, facial expressions, posture and so on. I use it sometimes when scanning senses." Too much info, she thought.

"I thought you didn't scan people."

"I normally don't."

"Can you describe what it's like?"

She struggled to formulate an accurate description. "It can be different with each person. It's hard to pull out of brilliant minds. When I do pullout and become a singular person again, I feel like an essential part of me is missing. Experiencing the expansiveness of a vivid life is an ultimate experience. When I've had the enriched mind of a genius intermingling with mine, I feel I'm in heaven. It should be on every bucket list."

She didn't see him roll his eyes.

"I have a sense I didn't ask for and am trying to live with in a positive manner. It's a gift. Think of it this way … when you travel to a new place, you have open and fresh eyes for different views. It makes your adventure exciting. I experience adventures like that with each mind. If I found one exciting enough, I could stay there and withdraw from the world."

"What an invasion of privacy! For the record, don't enter my mind. Okay?" He looked into her eyes with a stern expression.

She nodded.

"Were you ever trapped in a mind?"

"Once. It was scary. I soon developed a nanosecond mind scan. Want me to tell you about your mind?"

"No! Don't let your mental fingers near me." He moved to the window, leaned against the frame and watched traffic below.

48

"Something you need to know," she confessed. "When I use telepathy I'm not aware of anything else." She looked out the same window, leaning on the sill with both hands.

"That could be dangerous."

"It is." She turned and tucked her hair behind her ears. A few strands escaped. Glancing in the wall mirror she thought, I need to lose a few pounds. Her image was silhouetted against the back light of the late afternoon sun. Translucent curls created a blonde halo. Turning, she pressed her forehead against the window overlooking the street below. Her hair crinkled between skin and glass. She smelled stale cigarette smoke clinging to draperies. A few pedestrians were on the sidewalks below. Yellow taxies darted in and out of traffic.

"If you can read student minds, aren't you better off than other teachers?"

"Absolutely. Administrators admire how difficult students behave in my classes. They attribute it to classroom management. Actually, I can be aware of student's nasty ideas as soon as they think them. I learn who to watch and can stop disruptions."

Jon looked skeptical with squinted eyes and a raised eyebrow.

"Other teachers do the same thing with eye contact, questions, standing beside the nasty kid. Nothing mental. My advantage? I know planned behavior instantly, not after the fact." She chuckled. "Actually, sometimes it's hard not to laugh at their antics. I have to admit, I admire a creative mind."

Jon broke into her reverie. "Do you remember when you realized others weren't like you? That no one else was telepathic?"

Her eyes flicked back to him. She asked herself, is he beginning to accept me? "It was a gradual realization. I learned to hide my talent or be ridiculed and attacked." She pensively put a thumb under her chin and rubbed her lips with an index finger. "I frightened some kids. Made me feel like I was from Mars or something."

"Women are from Venus," he commented with a chuckle. "I can understand why they were negative. The idea of telepathy is repulsive."

She closed her eyes and took a deep breath at his demeaning comment.

He continued, "Does your mind feel different when using telepathy at greater distances?" He stood beside her and gazed at the street scene. Uneasy silence stretched between them. The sky had grown grey and pink along the horizon with the lowering sun highlighting lavender smog.

"To answer your question," Ana began, " it does feel different when I project farther. Awareness pulses from my frontal lobes." She touched her forehead with fingertips of both hands. "I face the direction I want my awareness to go. If I put my hands against my forehead like I'm praying, the impulses going out seem stronger. I don't know what kind of energy it is." She slid her hands into her pockets. "Maybe someone at VESPER can tell me. Perhaps your friend, Andy. What's he like?"

"Wise beyond his years. Good man to have on your side."

For amusement, she telepathically used the touch sensation to create an itch on Jon's earlobe. He scratched it. "Why'd you just scratch your ear?"

"It itched."

"I wonder why," she asked in a teasing tone." She expected him to be amused.

Seething under his breath, he frowned and walked to the door. "Showing off your power? Who do you think you are, Ms. Masterson? I told you I don't want anything to do with your so-called psychic power. Quit creeping around in my mind. That's sick."

She held his heated stare. "I thought you'd be amused, Major Coulter." She walked toward him. "All I meant to do was…"

He raised an open palm toward her. In a clipped tone with cold eyes, he said, "Number one rule of engagement, don't mess with me. I never want to second-guess you. Mental maneuvering disgusts me. It's also a matter of security. I know too much." Resentment simmered within him.

She deflated. "Thanks for telling me."

"For telling you again," he added with a disgusted expression, stalked out of the room and slammed the door.

She thought she heard muttered cursing grow fainter as he left. Leaning against the door, she lamented, "At least VESPER appreciates my telepathy skills."

CHAPTER 7

Office of Medical Director
VESPER Facility
17 August. 9:05 AM DST

The next morning, Andy told Ana and Jon how psychic tests were given.

After the explanation, she said, "I hope claustrophobia doesn't affect test results."

Andy answered, "You'll be fine."

"I'd feel more comfortable if someone familiar was there. Maybe Jon?" As soon the words escaped her mouth, she froze. He may be starting to detest her.

"I'll help where I'm needed," Jon commented in a formal tone.

"He can sit in the observation room. You won't be able to see him."

"Thank you," she said.

Andy capped his pen and tapped it lightly on the desk. "Mr. Lopez is anxious to learn what you can do." Handing Ana a PIV card dangling from a red lanyard, he directed, "I'll trade you pass cards. You'll need to wear this one. VESPER's a hot facility."

As she handed him the PIV card she'd received earlier, she asked, "Hot?" She flipped the new card over. USID VESPER was imprinted on the other side with a number.

Jon tapped his card, "Hot means VESPER has more detectors and gadgets than any building in New York. Your smart card is different from those used in stores. It has six memory spots each holding mega data. Each memory dot carries enough data to fill more than a hundred DVD disks. It's a radio frequency card with oomph. Has an encrypted signal broadcasting a radio wave to track you. While wearing this, if you enter an unauthorized area within VESPER, it'll trip an alarm to lock doors in your vicinity. A security team has to release you. If you're authorized in the area, your card will unlock doors and elevators and activate wall lights as you approach."

She flexed the transparent card and tapped a fingernail against it. "I don't see any memory dots."

"What looks like print on the card is imbedded material holding nano-sized dots." He chuckled. "One minor segment of a memory dot can carry your digital signature, iris scan, facial-recognition biometric data, hand geometry, medical and dental data, X-rays, embedded security holograms, anything we want. Regular staffers have their photo etched into the card. This technology is similar to the wireless antenna in your biometric passport, only better. It can be coded for satellite pick up. Like any digital data capture, over time the information begins to disintegrate."

"Like CDs?"

He nodded.

"You mean I'll lose my music?"

"Earth's magnetic field causes disintegration of all digital data. When smart card data becomes corrupted, we replace the cards."

"What if I lose it?" She lightly rubbed her finger over the card's smooth surface.

"Don't worry. VESPER cards require a pin before the secure template can open. Stolen ones can't be used without the pin. One neat thing, no one outside the system can scan through its lock. It's off technological grids."

"What powers it?"

"The print contains a semiconductor. It draws energy in the form of radio waves from the objects scanning it."

"Where's yours?"

He tapped his right ear. "I don't need one. I have an ear transceiver. Most VESPER employees have one." He let her visually examine his metallic gold earsphere.

"A two-way radio?"

"Indeed. This will outperform any PIV card."

Ana frowned. "Talk about lack of privacy."

"It can be turned off. It's time for your test." Andy led them into the hallway. He and Jon discussed golf while they walked.

Ana was too exhilarated to plod docilely along and slipped behind them. Her claustrophobia was present, but she was coping. If she could have danced a jig or clicked her heels in the air without attracting attention, she would have. Instead, in the excitement of anticipating her future, she gracefully lifted her arms and whirled once while sending out an awareness of exhilaration. She had no idea her excited mental energy created havoc as it moved through VESPER.

* * *

Psychics performing remote sensing felt Ana Masterson's powerful energy wave hit them physically and mentally. It left them flailing, lost in the searching and exploration mode of their extended minds. The sense of a now fatal existence enveloped thoughts of out of body viewers. Neither they or their coaches knew how to reconnect mind to body. With great patience, experimenting and effort, remote viewers were finally linked back to their bodies, exhausting their coaches.

A few non-working psychics, surprised by the mental interruption, tried to zero in on the origin of the energy jolt. Using their transceiver earspheres, they communicated with one another to discuss what had just happened and the implications. Knowledge of the near-fatal disruption of the favored and brightest OUB workers at VESPER moved throughout the facility. Terrified remote viewers feared the event might happen again. They refused to continue their research.

CHAPTER 8

Testing Laboratory
VESPER Facility
17 August. 10:00 AM DST

Ana studied Miguel Lopez as he stepped into the testing room. She couldn't tell if it was claustrophobia or excitement causing her heart to beat faster. Her throat burned and her back was wet with perspiration. What happened in this room could legitimize her telepathy. It would be the biggest career move of her life.

Lopez smiled as he introduced himself. He motioned for her to sit in an oversized brown recliner.

Never having been tested for her psychic ability, she wondered how long it would take.

Lopez lifted his head from his papers, a questioning look on his face. "Do other members of your family have psychic ability?"

"No." Because Lopez used the present tense in his question, she didn't mention that her deceased mother had had some psychic ability.

"I understand you hear sounds in minds of others. Is it a humming or words?"

"It's music. I call them mindsongs."

"Good word. How would you describe a mindsong?"

Shifting in her chair to be more comfortable, she answered, "The closest comparison would be a harp being played by a skilled musician with a soft orchestral background."

"You make it sound ethereal."

"It is."

"Does everyone have the same mindsong?"

"No. Each person has a mindsong flavored with what they've experienced. It evolves with life experiences."

"Interesting," he commented wistfully.

"Mindsongs of children in my neighborhood are jumbled until birth. They become more organized at about two to three months of age. They begin to distinguish what they see, especially facial expressions." Ana wondered if he'd remember she could listen to minds in a womb or if that would make a difference. She realized VESPER may be the safest place in the United States to talk about telepathy, but past experience told her to be careful."

Lopez asked, "What do you think accounts for mindsong differences?"

"One child who was experiencing a terminal illness had a slowing and lethargic mindsong. Another, who traveled extensively with her parents, had a rich mindsong with intermingling melodies and resonance. Experiences definitely alter them." She tapped near the top of her head. "They appear to be generated from deep within the mind."

"Mind or brain?"

She stopped a moment to think before answering. "Maybe both. My guess is they're created by rhythmic sounds of electricity charging through neuron synapses and glia of the brain ... or both." She grinned.

"What's funny?"

"When people sleep, their mindsongs sometimes go backwards. I was just thinking of babies I've listened to as they fall asleep. It's funny to hear their mindsong lull and then change. It's like hearing an orchestra stop playing and start tuning their instruments. Truly, they actually play backwards."

Lopez lifted an eyebrow with a quizzical expression. "The cause?"

"Maybe it's just nerves cleaning themselves of memory? Getting ready for new memories? Reorganizing synapses? I don't know. I do use mindsongs to identify people."

"Like fingerprints?"

"Exactly. Once I hear your mindsong, I'll be able to identify you in the future and know what type of person you are. The catch? I have to be fairly close to hear it."

"How close?"

"It varies." She omitted a definite answer and smiled. Hoping the answer would be yes, she asked, "Do other psychics hear sounds caused by neural activity?"

Lopez said, "I don't know."

I'd love to know if we hear the same resonances. It might prove what I hear is measureable energy." She tilted her head. "When I concentrate, I hear an undertone … a hyper-thread. The brain executes two concurrent streams of music, the continuing undertone and the changing melody. The streams appear to originate from both sides of the inner brain. It's comparable to two multiprocessing organs."

"Have you found the exact area within the brain where the tones originate?"

She thought for a moment before answering. "No. I'd have to magnify sections of the brain and I haven't learned how. I do know the songs are electrically generated from pinpoint spots and travel outward in all directions simultaneously. Sometimes they're distorted. It's possible a section of the brain occasionally malfunctions. Maybe neurons misfire or glia chemicals change." Lopez remained quiet. "It could be," she reflected, "mutations in the brain are caused by what we eat or drink." She saw him raise an eyebrow. "There are dangerous chemicals in some drinking water. I drink only steam-distilled water." Rubbing moist hands together, she cleared her throat. "I know for a fact chemicals cause body changes. If your body doesn't know what to do with strange chemicals, they're deposited in the brain. That affects neurons and glia which affect everything else."

Lopez said, "You keep mentioning glial cells in the brain as if they're as important as neurons."

"They are. I evidently have an excessive amount of them compared to neurons." When he raised his eyebrows in question, she explained, "I crave and drink milk all the time. I used to worry about that until I learned water in milk is retained in the body longer than the identical amount consumed as pure water. I couldn't figure out why I was so addicted to milk for a long time. I finally learned glial cells were constructed primarily of calcium. My abundance of glial cells require mega amounts of calcium. If I hadn't been drinking milk every day, my glial cells would have begun to die. By age thirty-five, I'd begin to have dementia."

He laughed. "I need to read up on glia."

Laughing with him, she affirmed his comment with a brief nod. "Look at the dementia in our senior citizens. As young adults, they stopped drinking milk to drink coffee, tea, alcohol and soft drinks. Their glial cell system began to die probably by age thirty-five. Poof! There goes their memory. It didn't happen overnight. They brought it upon themselves over many years." Entering his optical senses, she viewed herself through his eyes and straightened her posture.

Lopez asked her, "Tell me your theories about memory."

"To remember a fact there has to be a connection with another memory in your personal history. Each memory has multiple connections to other memories. For example, when you see a Bernese mountain dog, your mind brings up relationships about that species. How big they are, colors, friendliness, gentleness and silky feel. One memory can bring forth hundreds of others waiting for your correct association. Everyone has automatic response memories for sight, sound, touch, motion and so on. To respond without thinking, including the act of creativity, requires connections with other memories. Unused brain cells are waiting for input. The younger the person, the more unused brain cells there are. It's been proven brains continually grow new cells. We can continually learn."

Lopez said, "I agree. Facts have to be included to make our memories. What, when, where, who was there, feelings experienced, what you saw and so on."

She said, "Memories are partially caused by repeated patterns in the neural pathways. The more often a memory is recalled, the easier it'll be recalled in the future. By recalling them often, such as during your job, hobby or daily activity, they get stronger. Using memories causes additional neural patterns to be formed in those sections of the mind. The person gets better and more creative at the task with more intense neural patterns."

"True." He nodded.

"What amazes me," she continued, "is the number of neurons and glia in our brain and how they continually form new synapses, or connections, in response to what happens in our lives. Each experience creates new chemical and electrical neural connections which in turn help to create memories."

Lopez inhaled and leaned toward her.

She said, "Electrical impulses can't cross the synapses, the spaces between neurons. Electrical impulses trigger chemical changes to enable impulse crossing of synaptic spaces. When these connections are repeated in an exact pattern from an old memory, the older memory is brought to the surface for us to recall. Why that happens I don't know. Recalling a memory many times strengthens that neural pathway to make it easier to retrieve. Mess up neural connections with medications or drugs and there goes your memory."

"Tell me about your family, Ms. Masterson."

"Dysfunctional. My parents demanded quiet. I wasn't allowed to have friends over to play or visit. Being the only kid in the neighborhood, I spent many hours in the top of an old maple tree in our back yard listening to infrasounds some of the birds could hear. They were below my audible hearing range, yet when I tapped their minds, I could feel vibrations or hear them in my mind."

He laughed. "Bird brains!" For the next fifty-five minutes, he conducted tests on her telepathy ability. After a lavatory break, he said, "I'm going to see how well you do as a human lie detector." He checked clipboard notes, snapping the clip loudly. "As you know, polygraph machines used by law enforcement primarily provide info on breathing, perspiration, blood pressure, nerve jumps, and pulse."

He unconsciously kept smoothing his papers. "Terrorists from undeveloped countries aren't familiar with the machine. They show no fear. The polygraph is useless on them. There are also what we call "cleanskins," persons with no previous criminal record. With them we have nothing on which to base our findings. Can't depend on body cues."

He crossed his left leg over his right knee and leaned back. "Some wounded terrorists can't be interrogated. Doctors may tell us they have amnesia. Could you tell if they are pretending?" He leaned forward to hear her answer.

"Instantaneously."

He did a double take and stared at her. "We don't know the mental differences between telepaths and other psychics. We've been brainstorming how to best interview them. Can you help our understanding?"

"Maybe." She sat up straighter. "A question. When lie detectors are used on sensationalized, television talk shows, do you agree the results may be incorrect?" She watched for his reaction.

"Absolutely! Polygraph results can be incorrect. An overly nervous, innocent person may cause the same results as a guilty person. The body reacts the same way in both situations. No expert could tell if they were innocent or guilty. Results for an innocent person could be interpreted as though they were telling a lie."

Ana had watched persons on television who appeared innocent and were accused of lying after a polygraph test. Their lives were changed forever by someone misreading their polygraph.

With a raised voice, she said, "Television producers and hosts should be told. Think of the innocent lives damaged by such actions! What injustices to innocent people caught in a TV web of lies."

"Knowing they could ruin innocent lives makes no difference to television producers, Ana. They're out to make money. Sensationalism sells. Totally innocent persons get accused of horrendous acts on national television due to faulty polygraph test results. Victims and their families can be destroyed just for the sake of TV ratings."

She grimaced. "Programs promoting the idea that polygraph tests are foolproof should be banned."

"You know people lie. Remember watching TV shows with the a good cop versus bad cop? During terrorist interrogations, if you're the good guy, you get more information. Unfortunately, if the guilty planned their story ahead of time, the technique doesn't work."

She raised her eyebrows in question. "Why is that?"

"If you ask them something totally different from what you were discussing, you can trip 'em up. It disrupts their thought processes. Gets them away from a rehearsed story. They hum and haw which can help prove they lied. If they're telling the truth, the story naturally changes over time as they remember more. Liars don't change their memorized story. Investigators asking about details in a reverse sequence can often find liars."

She asked, "Eye witnesses don't remember everything."

"True. Especially when it comes to colors. False memory can take place in the brain's hippocampus. For unknown reasons, neurons change to give a visual trace of a new memory. A true method of lie detection is using infrared cameras to determine eye temperature. There's an instantaneous, violet, lie-signature in the eyes. A slight thermal change in the eye's more accurate than a polygraph test."

She didn't stop him to confess she could determine eye temperature change without an infrared camera.

He continued. "The problem is, you have to have the equipment on hand to measure eye temperatures when the lie is told. The terrorist has to be facing the camera. A terrorist with training will keep changing the direction he faces. They know interrogation rooms have video cameras."

She glanced at the mirror knowing Jon Coulter was sitting behind it. "Don't eyes dilate involuntarily right before the thermal change when someone lies?"

Lopez's eyebrows rose and his eyes opened wider. He nodded.

She thought Jon would approve of thermal imaging for his special ops teams. "Recording of infrared signatures should be put into military night lenses. Soldiers should be able to record what they see through thermal lenses. A small memory chip should do it."

Lopez tilted his head to his right, listening to his earsphere. "Let's begin, shall we?" Moistening his lips, he opened the door to admit a man smelling of sweet tobacco. A heavy set, white-haired gentleman of her height wore a light blue lab coat with a pipe stem sticking out of the breast pocket. His face had many age spots. Hands in his coat pockets, he leaned against the door frame. She entered his mind.

Lopez said, "Thanks for volunteering, Patterson. You know the procedure. Use your discretion."

Patterson showed tobacco stained teeth and a missing upper tooth when he spoke each yes or no. She could sense excess energy created within his inner brain at each spontaneous lie. His frontal lobes and eyes increased in temperature as further evidence. Patterson held a poker face. To her satisfaction, she noted the human lie indication of enlarged electrical and neural activity within his stomach. Pitting her observational skills against findings within his brain, she conceded her human Pinocchio was an inveterate lie expert. To his credit, there was no instantaneous tensing of his forehead or light, telltale blush of heat around the eyes.

"Everything he said was a lie," she reported to Lopez.

"How do you know?"

Not sure whether to be truthful, she answered, "Intuition." Patterson agreed and left. When Lopez tested her with a second person, Ana purposely missed a few to create the impression she was fallible. After a lifetime of hate and horror aimed at her because of telepathy, she still wasn't feeling safe. She couldn't bring herself to trust Lopez.

"Terrorists don't care who they harm," he told her. "They're unsuitable for a normal polygraph test. The ones captured have been brainwashed to hate Americans. Such hatred invalidates tests by skewing them. We need a way to know whether they're telling the truth, ratting on terrorist cells, or spreading lies and propaganda. What it boils down to, can you use telepathy to tell truth from lies?" Lopez looked at the floor, shaking his head in frustration. "Most international terrorists don't speak English. Interrogators may not be using their language to ask questions or interpret answers correctly. Talk about screwing with results! There aren't enough interpreters to go around."

"What if you had them read their own questions? Record their answers? Have several different linguists interpret the results?" She was enjoying the conversation. It took her mind off the closeness of the tiny office in the subterranean facility.

"Most can't read. They're uneducated. That's why they can be easily swayed to become suicide bombers. They believe what they're told. They could tell us anything. Misinformation. Lies. How would we know? Investigations are ongoing with brain imaging machines, electroencephalographs, and even magnetic resonance imaging, the MRI. Finding the lie is becoming more complex. Are you familiar with MEG? Magneto encephalography?"

"That's a mouthful. Never heard of it."

"It's a scanner to track microscopic changes in the brain occurring as people think. It tracks how ideas move through the brain. Investigators can watch the progression of thought on a screen."

There was a light tap at the door. Lopez opened it to find Jon Coulter.

"Come in, Major, we're nearly finished." Jon stepped into the room. Lopez asked Ana, "Can you can locate a target in this facility who's repeatedly thinking your name?"

"I can try." She stood. From the zenith above her head to the nadir beneath her feet, she made awareness extend outward in a smooth, vertical, scanning plane. She next rotated her body with the awareness staying in front of her. The plane extended far beyond her usual reach. It was strong enough to penetrate shielded VESPER walls. For a reason Ana could never fathom, although right handed, her scan would only take place when she rotated to her left.

"He's about two-hundred feet to my right, two stories lower." Yowza, she thought, this place is a labyrinth! Letting my mind go in here would be the ultimate game. She repressed a smile.

Lopez broke her chain of thought. "Thank you. Now locate a person outside this facility thinking your name."

Slower in her rotation, with apprehension she blurted, "In my hotel room? You invaded my privacy!"

Astonished at the distance and gender identification, Lopez ignored her question. "That's miles away."

"Only because your own name is an easy locator. I couldn't do it otherwise." Furious with the intrusion of her personal space, she made fists with her hands to stop them from trembling.

"I've overtaxed you, haven't I?"

She was annoyed by his chauvinistic comment and stated satirically, "You consider females fragile and simplistic." Her comment sailed right over him.

Jon opened the door. "Can we call it a day?"

"Ana, you've presented me with new viewpoints."

She flexed her shoulders, barely mollified.

"I hope we didn't overwork your brain, Ms. Masterson."

Frustrated with his attitude, she glared at him. "Believe it or not, Mr. Lopez, you haven't even scratched the surface." She tossed her jacket across a shoulder and confidently walked out the door.

Eyes locked onto Ana's swaying backside, Jon followed her. His body shook in repressed laughter.

Lopez tapped his earsphere and called Herman Wald. "Miguel Lopez here, Mr. Wald. Do you have time to talk?"

CHAPTER 9

Conference Room
VESPER Facility
17 August, 4:35 PM DST

VESPER Directors assembled in the conference room with anticipation.

Hands clasped on the conference table, Anderson sat opposite the doorway quietly observing the last few persons entering the room. Nearest the door sat Herman Wald. When Wald stood and tapped his pen with a sharp snap against the table, conversation ceased.

"Ladies. Gentlemen." Wald began. "Sorry to call you away from your work. We have new developments." He glanced around the room. "Ana Masterson was interviewed. She's not a mindreacher. She's a telepath who can penetrate our wall shields." As he talked about Ana Masterson, with each word spoken, he pointed his pen to a different person. His voice resonated with authority. "She identifies people with what she calls mindsongs originating from their neural patterns. She has distance limitations. Let's hope we'll be allowed to keep this woman. Other agencies might requisition her talents as soon as they hear about her." Thinking of all the implications, his mouth grew dry.

Scott Galbraith stood in alarm. "Do you mean to tell us she could put suggestions into our minds?"

Wald referred the question to Miguel Lopez, who responded. "Compared to a Johannesburg mindreacher, she would be classified as a low-level telepath. If I had to guess, I would answer your question with a yes. Appended to the yes, I'll say she appears to be a highly moral and ethical woman."

"Do we need protection from her?"

Wald shook his head.

Galbraith addressed Miguel Lopez. "Colonel Anderson told us mindreachers extend their thoughts two-hundred-fifty miles. How far can Ms. Masterson extend her telepathy?"

Lopez cleared his throat before replying. "The human brain is so attuned, we can hear our name whispered across a noisy room. In telepathic terms, she heard her name spoken from several miles away. She'd know if a mindreacher were nearby." His visual sweep included everyone. "We have no telepath strong enough to verify her ability. However, there's current research ongoing in *biofusion. We could study her brain and see how she's different. Research is also producing machines with thought imaging techniques." He turned to Wald. "Do you think VESPER should be added to the list of agencies receiving information about such machines? Perhaps they could be used in the absence of a telepath when interrogating terrorists."

Wald turned to his young male secretary. "Try to obtain a 'need to know' priority with the thought imaging machines." The secretary nodded once and continued checking his electronic pad to ensure the machine was transcribing conversations correctly. Wald continued. "In the situation room this morning the President commented he wasn't satisfied with our progress in identifying terrorists. He's right. We haven't identified any yet. I'd hate to have VESPER eliminated just when we found Ms. Masterson. The woman is easygoing and optimistic. From the non-invasive blood chemistry monitor during testing, we found she released an endorphin, perhaps on command."

Anderson clarified, "Endorphins from the pituitary gland in the center of the brain are more potent than morphine to remove stress or pain. With her abilities, she may be able to relieve pain in others or teach them how to do it themselves. Pain treatment may be revolutionized."

Lopez looked at the ceiling. "Amen. The end of pain meds."

Communication Director, Philip Arnold, raised his hand for attention. "Can she physically move objects with her mind?" Blinking rapidly, his mouth worked noiselessly.

The room grew quiet.

Anderson spoke first. "Psychokinesis? Good question. Mr. Lopez?"

Miguel Lopez leaned back in his chair and shrugged. "I've no idea."

Arnold said with a pompous attitude, "Did you ask?"

Lopez looked at the floor and then to Anderson. "Colonel Anderson, I apologize. I didn't ask Ms. Masterson that question."

Anderson nodded.

"Regardless," Wald bragged, "we have a remarkable woman on our hands. She'll be invaluable in HUMINT, Human Intelligence. The U.S. security requirements continually increase as terrorist threats grow more frequent and sophisticated. Until we find a Joburg mindreacher, she'll be our human firewall for terrorist activity. The Office of the National Counterintelligence has been searching for someone of her caliber. In reality, if Coulter hadn't been trained to recognize psychic phenomenon, he'd never have spotted her. Right now VESPER is in a remarkable position."

Scott Galbraith asked, "Is she a security risk?"

Wald checked his watch. "She'll be fine. Security with reference to information concerning Ms. Masterson is USAP with other agencies. On second thought," he reflected, "why don't we let the SCI staff limit access for us? The Sensitive Compartmentalized Information office." Those present nodded confirmation.

Anderson leaned toward Galbraith and made eye contact. "Mr. Wald inquired earlier if we should test her further," he paused for emphasis, "and use her at the same time." With a spark of excitement in his eyes, he continued. "On site in South Africa, she may be able to verify the Johannesburg incident." He included each person in his gaze around the table. There were looks of astonishment at Anderson's expectations for Masterson. "It'd be clandestine. No one outside of VESPER connected agencies would have a need to know."

Wald gave an imperceptible nod, alert to the possibility of reaching a dream. He knew the President would be pleased. If they were successful, elimination of anti-American terrorists would be accomplished through the President's VESPER project during his first term in office.

"There's one major consideration to be addressed," Wald admitted. He looked at Lopez. "The President wants additional personnel immediately trained to find psychics." Seeing confused looks around the table, he offered, "In the past twenty-four hours, White House decisions have been made to have selective training in psychic phenomena recognition. The President wants action. He ordered training of additional selected National Guard, Coast Guard, Navy, Army, Air Force and Marine Corps troops. The Deputy Chief of Staff for Doctrine – Concepts and Strategy of the U.S. Army Training and Doctrine Command, the USN Commander of the Navy Warfare Development Command, and the Commander of the Headquarters Air Force Doctrine Center are all on board. They'll be looking to VESPER for guidance and training of their personnel."

Miguel Lopez opened his mouth in astonishment and closed it, realizing he would have to instruct and supervise trainers and direct more advanced training videos.

Seeing questioning looks, Anderson added, "Verifying the Johannesburg mindreachers will ensure success of our mission to identify terrorists in the United States. The first task is to stop the November airport bombings. Masterson will be the catalyst to find the first Joburg mindreacher. Then we'll kick some terrorist butt."

Shelly White, rubbing her hands together, broke into the conversation. "It'll be open season on terrorists,"

Wald studied her, straight faced. "No one's surfaced from the Johannesburg incident in over thirty years, but I'm optimistic."

Anderson added, "If Ana Masterson locates even one mindreacher to prove the rumor, I guarantee we'll find all stateside terrorists. For Masterson's protection, we can team her with a proven military winner. Perhaps we could use Major Coulter. The Secretary of Defense can find a liaison officer to replace him."

Phillip Arnold cleared his throat. "What kind of a winner is Coulter"

"He's with MARSOC."

"Which is?"

Anderson barked his endorsement. "The United States Marine Corps, Special Operations Command activated in '08. In MARSOC he served with Navy SEALs under Naval Special

Warfare. Most recently with the Foreign Internal Defense. He was involved in counter insurgency of covert operations against al-Qaeda, and Islamic states. Is he a winner? Absolutely. Next time he wears his dress uniform, check out the display."

Arnold reluctantly nodded. "Colonel Anderson, let me see if I understand this. You've discovered one maybe okay telepath and are assigning her to locate a Johannesburg mindreacher. Correct?" A sneer flicked across Arnold's expression.

"Affirmative," Andy replied. "Do we expect her to find a Johannesburg mindreacher? Yes, if we're lucky. Masterson's intelligent. She has superior on-the-spot reasoning ability. Add her telepathic ability and you'll realize our best chance in locating a mindreacher."

Wald tapped his pen lightly against the table top for attention. "Can we narrow the possibilities as to where mindreachers are located? No. Their parents may have headed to metropolitan areas in hopes of getting lost within the populous or into the countryside to be absorbed by peasants of whatever country in which they settled. Our target area? The world." He looked around the table. "Let's do it."

Arnold slammed his hand onto the table top, "Yes!" He rubbed his flag pin as though imparting a shine.

Galbraith's raised voice brought attention, "Speaking from experience, it's my opinion we use an untraceable black budget. Perhaps task this quest to ACCM, the Alternative Compensatory Control Measure. It'll fit there. Definitely assign Coulter to the team. He's trained and battle-tested."

"Don't consider Coulter a throwaway," Anderson demanded. "Being he's a personal friend, I want to make sure they both return. He'll be the sole, real time protective detail to cover and evacuate this woman twenty-four-seven. If word gets out about her talents and this project, she'll be targeted. Watch your enthusiasm. This is a highly classified and need to know project."

Wald added, "The President believes we're the solution to the November crisis. He wants action."

Sitting with a rigid posture, Arnold injected into the conversation, "I understand Coulter was recently wounded in Afghanistan. Is he ready for this assignment?"

Wald and Anderson exchanged glances. Both knew Coulter's medical information had not been made public.

"He is," Anderson replied and dissected Coulter's background to the quiet, concerned listeners.

Wald asked, "Any questions or comments?" He waited the standard five-seconds after asking a question. At continued silence, he loudly tapped his pen against the table, solemnly rose, and left the room.

Everyone exited the room with expressions of concentration and reflection except for Philip Arnold who looked grim.

CHAPTER 10

Satellite Communications Pit
VESPER Facility
17 August. 5:30 PM DST

By five o'clock, VESPER Communications Director, Phillip Arnold, had turned off his earsphere and walked toward the Satellite Communications Pit. His assignment of supervising computer servers, satellite photography and surveillance, was to also maintain radio relays for remote viewer coaches and future telepathic field personnel.

Doubt had been cast on his success as a future al-Qaeda cell leader in New York City. The doubt was caused by rapid, global, leadership changes in the growing number of networks and splinter groups affecting Islamic terrorist organizations. Arnold thought changes were due to funding loyalties. Whoever guaranteed the most funds generated the largest terrorist following. Money talked.

Hands in pockets, mumbling to himself, he was pleased with his listening devices in every VESPER office. He questioned whether any offices had been debugged recently by an outside agency without his knowledge. White's security team usually let him know when scheduling such procedures. Whenever one of his wire taps was discovered, he acted shocked. After wires were ripped out, he replaced them. He had also compromised the VESPER computer system linked to the massive server of the emergency preparedness facility. He compulsively checked his data drops of international al-Qaeda information hidden within the bowels of the server to ensure they were active and working. Every technologically literate terrorist leader had access to the system he'd created.

The love of his life was his blue Satellite Pit. The stillness within the spaciousness made it feel like a sanctuary. Surrounded with imagery, he leaned against the wall next to the door and watched the floor-to-ceiling interactive wall monitors displayed on the massive wall to his right. Most were on-line to keep them working. They had been installed for use in the communications grid in case of a national emergency.

The centered and largest Alpha Monitor showed a satellite view of a current remote sensing site on a four-by-eight foot screen. A red tag showed an active remote viewer's location. Other displays, one-third Alpha's size, showed additional scenes of Earth's surface with grids of activity and data pertinent to intelligence monitoring. Two technicians were engaged. One wall monitor exhibited a moving scene over several degrees of longitude within a North African vista. Arnold couldn't remember why a remote viewer had been assigned to a Tunisian site.

His local terrorist objective was to report progress made within the VESPER community. On his way to becoming a master handler of global information, Arnold wanted to burst into the ring of handlers to organize international terrorist events. The knowledge of mindreachers and their ability to alter the terrorist world would put his name on the map. The recent leap forward by the Masterson intrusion had created a new set of parameters. He questioned whether to report her abilities to his contacts or withhold information about her for a future bargaining tool.

As a youth volunteering in terrorist organizations, Arnold found leadership changes within the radical Islamic community rampant. Usurping power by an up and coming activist was common. If his current terrorist affiliations were exposed, his life would be over. By working in communications, he assumed he'd avoid seeing any telepath. Now he cringed at the thought of accidently meeting one in a corridor. He had to stop Masterson before she brought him, ISIS, al-Qaeda, and all the peripheral terrorist organizations around the world to a standstill. Masterson and any other telepath had to die. If he played it right, he could stymie the VESPER project.

Assaults against the United States with which Arnold had been involved stretched back to when he was a teenager. He'd flubbed lines leading the Pledge of Allegiance during a school assembly. His mistake resulted in unmerciful teasing with harassment following him through college. Underneath his gentle appearing exterior, he was conniving and vengeful. A personal vow to create private terror against families of those who were most atrocious to him was yet to come. Planning progressed.

Arnold aligned most of his views with radical Muslims. They believed in no material wants or needs, only selfless duty. He hated greedy, warmongering corporations and politicians speaking to the world as though everyone was an imbecile. He'd often quoted "the blind leading the blind" to his al-Qaeda associates. Every body bag returning to the United States brought him pleasure. Pleased to be a key part of terrorist activity and deception, he was proud to have helped bring terrorist horror stateside. He hated the farcical American flag pin on his lapel. He wore it to give the appearance he was a patriot. As far as he was concerned, ideals of life, liberty and the pursuit of happiness were crap.

Nervously twisting the lapel pin, he uttered softly, "No slut's going to stop me. I've worked too hard to get where I am. So, VESPER wants to begin a seedpod of mindreachers? Well, I'll show them." He crossed his arms. His eyes grew cold. "I'll follow Masterson electronically. Using her leads, I'll find Joburg mindreachers and start growing weeds of my own. They'll work for me or I'll have them eliminated."

The Satellite Communications Pit was the place to keep a ground situation in view. The floor of the large room was several feet lower than the corridor, hence the name "Pit." There were three four-foot wide steps to the main floor. The high wall to the right of the entrance contained the expansive bank of oversized displays of Earth from different satellite vantage points.

They were easy to observe in the subdued lighting. It created a calm ambiance in the pale blue room. Two technicians worked each shift controlling satellite cameras as needed. After completing observations for other government agencies, the two technicians would often be kept busy by the remote viewers in the field making observations for the Pentagon. This would be SOP until telepaths were in the field.

Arnold scanned the Pit muttering, "I'll know everything that goes on through the implants put into Coulter and Masterson. I'll know what they know in real time, where they're heading and where they are. That'll make it easy to alert in-country assassin teams."

The assassins he had in mind were members of cash-strapped terrorist groups who would jump at a chance for funding. It would be a simple task for them to put a woman into the ground. Since Bin Laden's death, such groups had proliferated around the globe, each vying for leadership within their growing number of al-Qaeda type splinter cells.

Cowboy Derek Riggle was the cyber technician in charge of the Satellite Pit. Riggle's neck lanyard had a mass of electronic equipment hooked onto it. Two silver festooned holsters at his waist held cell phones. Arnold watched as Riggle rolled his chair from one computer to another. He shoved his cuffs up before attacking the next keyboard. The innocent cowboy, using electronic bits and bytes, would unknowingly help eliminate Masterson. With satisfaction, Arnold left the Pit.

Walking the empty halls with a lowered head, he processed his recent concepts to hasten the telepath's downfall. "Masterson's like an earthquake epicenter. With a little push, she'll precipitate enough energy to destroy us all. I have to make her appear horrific. How? Misinformation? Yes! I'll create a false information base to generate interest in eliminating her. She won't last a week. I have to get word out about her bodyguard's combat injury. They'll take him out of action fast."

In his office, after putting his earsphere in a desk drawer, Phillip Arnold straightened his desktop. Knowing only security personnel and satellite Pit technicians worked after hours. He headed to a server room to admire his wire taps and get an ego boost before going home.

When introduced to the emergency preparedness computer banks, he had believed he was obligated to steal unused memory from the massive computer for international terrorists. In the short time since VESPER began, he'd clandestinely created illegal connections and memory drops in the main server. The computer ironically existed in the bowels of the organization whose mission it was to find terrorists. The government had no idea their emergency preparedness site provided computer access to terrorist groups. Arnold glowed with satisfaction whenever he thought of his accomplishment.

* * *

Arriving at the server room, he admired the stacks of shiny grey cabinets. Their glass doors showed inner-lit works. The first one in each row showed three glass side windows for additional observation. Computers in each row of twelve cabinets, within in his visual range, appeared to be working perfectly. Upon hearing a shuffling noise, he moved to the back of the nearest row of computer banks and found a hefty, black woman nosing around near the base. Her fingers were following one of his wiretap connections.

He shouted, "What do you think you're doing?"

Startled, the woman jumped backwards and fell against a cabinet. Losing her balance, she landed on the floor. Embarrassed, the young woman got to her feet. She stood smacking the top of her head.

"Just checking the system," she replied with a smile, continuing to hit her head.

"You have lice?"

"No sir. My weave's too tight. It hurts. Hitting it makes it feel better. After a few days of growing, it'll be fine."

"What are you doing here?"

"The regular tech's sick. I'm not familiar with this installation so I thought I'd stay late and check it out. Don't worry. I'm not on overtime." She leaned forward. Her three-inch diameter gold hoop earrings swung above a chambray shirt and denim overalls.

Arnold narrowed his eyes and said, "As Communications Director, I'll determine who checks what. What's your name?"

"Vienayetta Bodanski," she replied with a grin, a wide gap showing between two front teeth.

"What are you doing?"

"Just following a connection. If I didn't know any better, I'd say it's a wiretap. Look here at this twenty-four gauge wire." He watched her dark fingers follow the line.

"Wiretaps aren't made with wire anymore. They'd just electronically shunt a line for monitoring."

"Maybe this was a dumb wire tapper."

He frowned at the personal affront to his wiring. That was all it took to anger him tonight. His thoughts turned lethal. Wire taps were a priority. This woman had to die.

"Follow it to the two ends," he directed. Without taking his eyes off Bodanski, he reached to the top of the cabinet where he'd earlier placed leftover insulated wire and grabbed it. He slowly wrapped the ends around his hands several times and pulled to make the wire tight. He left several feet of wire between his hands. "Where's the hall guard?"

She didn't look up. Her fingers moved on the wiretap line. "He's not on duty in this area after hours. Why do you ask? You think it's dangerous here?"

"No," he said with a smirk. He repositioned himself behind Bodanski as though examining what she found. With a swift motion, he whipped the wire over her head, anchored it around the back of her neck and jerked.

The woman reacted by trying to get her fingers under the wire. Arching her back, she leaned toward him. Her legs buckled and shook.

Arnold kneed her in the back for leverage and pulled harder. She uttered gurgles. With each jerk, blood oozed from underneath the wire entrenched within her flesh. Weakening, she flailed, trying to break his hold. Her fingernails gored his arms and hands. Cursing, he jerked the wire again and winced at the pain it caused his hands. He felt it cut through her neck cartilage and trachea, an effective garrote.

"Die, slut," he whispered viciously, "or I'll rip your head off." His back hurt from supporting her heft. He uttered more curses. Her hands dropped from his bloody wrists. When she stopped jerking, he waited to see if she was dead.

After a few minutes, he dropped her to the floor and flicked the wire from her neck. Spatters of blood flew in all directions. He wiped the wire on her overalls. With a few twists for compaction, he placed the bundle into his jacket pocket. He'd burn the jacket later. He wasn't worried about forensic testing of blood or skin evidence. His DNA had never been recorded. It would never be matched to him.

VESPER's video surveillance control unit was in the same server room. He methodically erased evidence of the previous two-hours throughout VESPER and delayed further video-taping for another two-hours. He cleaned any touched surface. Checking to ensure the corridor was empty; he slipped into silence and took the elevator to his office hallway. Inside his office, he stuffed his bloodied suit jacket into a briefcase and slipped on a spare blazer kept in his closet. He combed his hair in a different direction and readjusted the length of his tie. He mopped his face. Sweat ran down his armpits and back.

He took the maintenance elevator to the terminal. Stepping out, he averted his head from a surveillance camera. Changing his posture, gait, and mannerisms, he adopted an altered appearance. Entering a restroom, he closed the cubicle door and sat shaking on the toilet. Amidst much profanity he whispered a vow. "I'll never kill again. Gotta' pay someone else to do it." His shaking diminished. "I have to calm myself." He took a ragged breath. "The wiretaps have to be changed so techs won't find them. With a new design, maybe I can get a patent on illegal wiretaps." He chuckled.

In his attempt to erase evidence, he rolled his shirt's bloody cuffs under his jacket sleeves. He mumbled, "Need an excuse for my arms. I'll trim roses when I get home and bring some to the secretary tomorrow." That's when he saw blood spatters on his shoes. He spit on toilet tissue and wiped them clean, flushing the evidence of his efforts.

Within thirty-minutes he walked out of the restroom maintaining a false posture and gait. Head averted from cameras, in an isolated area of the passenger terminal, he ensured there were no listeners and dialed an al-Qaeda associate from a throwaway phone.

"Jack? Phil Arnold," he whispered. "Problem. I need another government job. Fast." After listening for a few moments, he closed the conversation. Jack would help. Until Masterson was killed, he had to leave VESPER or risk being exposed through her telepathy. Dreading the call alerting him to a murder in the computer stacks, he rushed home knowing he'd be in his wife's' rose garden within the hour.

CHAPTER 11

Office of Medical Director
VESPER Facility
18 August. 9:30 AM dST

"You're looking mighty pretty this morning Ana," Jon commented as the two entered Andy's outer office.

Relieved he didn't appear angry, she grinned. "Aw, you're just saying that 'cause it's true!"

He laughed. "Still interested in working here?"

"If I get hired, you'll never see me in a classroom again."

"You're making a big decision."

"The right one."

Andy acknowledged the comment with a brief nod and leaned forward, hands clasped on his desk. "I hate to start off with bad news." He alerted them to the murder of the computer technician the previous evening. "No one knows if more than one person was involved. They knew enough to tamper with video feeds in the server stacks, hallways, and elevators. They had to have a working PIV card to navigate the hallways. One was lost a few weeks ago. The owner thought he misplaced it. That may be how the murderer entered VESPER. Unfortunately, our PIV card use isn't archived yet. White's team is handling the investigation. Because of national security implications, she called in Homeland Security."

Andy told them about the Joburg babies. Ana leaned forward listening for clues to her own telepathy origin.

"Think what was unleashed on the world," Andy exclaimed. "The implications of having strong telepaths are enormous. Hopefully they learned ethics and were nurtured in many different fields. Imagine them in politics. Ana, do you have any idea why they were born telepathic?"

She nodded. "I'm not sure, but I have a pretty good idea."

"Tell me."

She ran fingers across the curls at the top of her head. "I'm guessing. Our family doctor told me when babies are born they have twice the neural connections in their brains as adults, ready and waiting for input. Those connections decrease as the brain learns what's important for existence. He theorized my connections never sealed off and continued multiplying. It's possible the same thing happened to the Johannesburg mindreachers. I may have something in common with them. I never told Dr. Cruthers I used telepathy before I was born."

Andy exclaimed, "Before birth?"

"I tapped into senses of others and nearby animals."

"I want to hear details when I have recording equipment. Ana, you are going to be like the breeze before a storm, going in the opposite direction of others." He leaned forward and slowly shook his head, staring at his prodigy telepath. "Any questions about the Joburg babies?"

"Were they hypnotized to forget their telepathy?"

He leaned back, clasped his hands over his abdomen and answered solemnly, "No one knows. The fact that I reacted to the Stars & Stripes article made the difference. I had accumulated leave time and flew to Johannesburg. Learned a little. Like a politician, I'm glad everyone has short memories. Until you arrived, I figured the Joburg babies would never be found. You may not have the same depth of telepathic power as they, but you'll sense their presence. You sensed our remote viewer in Ohio at that golf course."

"When do you need a mindreacher?"

"Within a few weeks."

Ana blurted, "A few weeks? Do you think that's possible?" Her wide-eyed skepticism made an impression on Andy.

"On a scale of one to ten in difficulty," he said, "I'd put it at a ninety."

"What's the rush?"

Andy explained what he knew of the terrorist threats to nuke America's airports during Thanksgiving vacation.

She asked incredulously, "Can't the FBI find the terrorists?"

"No government agency has been able to do so."

She studied Andy's face. Her pulse and claustrophobia feelings increased. She desperately wanted sunshine. She tried to relax her face, jaw and forehead. She blinked her eyes to moisten them. She kept thinking, stay calm... stay calm....

Andy said, "I notice you're feeling your claustrophobia. It's a learned condition and can be unlearned."

"I know. I'm trying to control it. I've just never been in a place like this."

"Does the task of finding a mindreacher intimidate you?"

She shook her head. "If you were me, how would you begin to find a mindreacher?"

Andy gave her a big smile. Her comment let him know she would accept the assignment. "Start in Johannesburg, South Africa ASAP."

"What about using your remote viewers?"

"They can't reach into minds to see what's there," Andy replied. "Or turn pages of archives to research information. They have to have a site in mind before they go out of body and can't go from one unknown site to another. They have to know where they're going. You, on the other hand, could find terrorists by listening to mindsongs. We have no concept how telepathy works. If I had your ability, I'd probably go crazy."

"I know nothing about terrorists. Can you give me some background?"

Jon began, "NATO allies backed al-Qaeda cells in Iraq. Those cells became AQI which evolved into ISI, the Islamic State of Iraq. ISI then moved into Syria. The world was told ISI and 'Jabhat Al-Nusra,' joined to form ISIS."

"That sounds like a foreign language."

"It originally meant Islamic State of Iraq and Syria. ISIS is now short for Islamic State of Iraq and al-Sham." Andy added, "The names keep changing."

She asked, "Then what's ISIL? President Obama used that word."

The men exchanged glances. Jon answered, "Islamic State of Iraq and the Levant."

She raised her eyebrows. "Levant?"

"Land between Turkey and Egypt."

"What's the difference between the ISIL and ISIS?"

"People using the term ISIL believe that the land which Israel claims belongs to the Islamic state of ISIS."

"This is so confusing. What are we supposed to call terrorists?"

Jon straightened. His face looked haggard. "Five major terrorist groups joined to form Hay'at Tahrir al-Sham. Translated, it means 'liberation of the Levant organization. They're independent and distancing themselves from al-Qaeda. From what I know, they're getting in deep with the Syrian insurgency. They've been urging other factions to join them. When President Trump claimed they were defeated, they had been pushed back so far, he didn't think they would regroup. It's believed they continue to break up into many smaller groups."

Andy assured, "Don't worry about names. Your objective is to find a mindreacher. You're our only bet, Ana."

"These South African mindreachers were more powerful as kids than I am as an adult. Think how controlling they'd be. What do I say when I find one? Excuse me, sir, do you use telepathy?" She shook her head in frustration and lamented in a quivering voice, "I just don't know."

Andy took a slow, deep breath. "The circumstances of the moment will determine your approach. You'll be fine. Jon will be right beside you."

Incredulous, Jon exclaimed in a loud voice, "I don't want to be saddled with a telepath." He glanced at her. His eyes narrowed. His expression grew stern.

Surprised by his outburst, she looked dumbfounded. Her mouth dropped open and eyebrows rose.

Andy replied professionally, "You're an officer."

Jon added, "… and will follow orders."

"You're perfect for this mission, Jon. Brains. Brawn. A walking weapon. Plus, you think outside the box. And you know Ana. Of equal import during this assignment is that you'll be training for a new type of military presence. You'll be gaining intelligence for future troops interacting with telepaths." At Jon's responding glare, Andy tried to placate him. "I know. There'll be heavy resistance from the brass. Mark my words. Telepathy will be launched into military ranks."

Jon put his head back and rolled his eyes before glancing at Ana.

Andy continued, "Ana will be your buddy, your only asset in the field. There is one problem." He watched Jon cross his arms and tilt his head questioningly. "You project confidence and posture of an elite warrior. You'll have to become an actor and blend in with the masses. No attention can be brought to either of you. No photographs. No publicity. Nothing."

Jon gave him a disgusted look. "Hotel Sierra!"

Andy saw her questioning expression. "Ana, at all times you must follow Jon's lead. He'll know what to do in any situation."

Jon was unconvinced. Having her referred to as his buddy was monumental. Buddies were a team. They didn't separate and they kept an eye out for one another. They communicated easily and knew each other's' movements during combat. She wouldn't know anything. Every ounce of responsibility would fall on him. Calming, he demanded, "She'll have to change her thinking. Learn how to be safe."

Encouraged, Ana asked, "Can you teach me?"

Putting elbows on his knees and head between his hands, Jon groaned.

She straightened her shoulders and sat up straighter. "I've questioned all my life why I have the gift of telepathy. This may be the reason. Finding terrorists by reading their minds is so logical, it's a wonder I never thought of it."

"Umhum," Andy murmured in agreement. "Mindreachers may wonder the same thing. So far, VESPER's footing has been questionable. You're our first rock. You need to get to Joburg. Read every document you can find on these kids and their doctor. Follow clues. Locate a mindreacher and bring him here. We'll do the rest."

Andy never failed to see potential in others. He knew Jon was organized, trustworthy and observant. Sensitive to nuances of personal behaviors, he'd use visual clues to evaluate Ana's unseen thought processes. It was a fact Jon detested psychics. That made him critically analyze what he would experience with her. He'd ID enemies and react to protect her. Back at VESPER, Andy would cut through red tape put in front of the duo. He quietly informed them Ana's identity as a telepath would remain concealed with Jon assigned as her bodyguard.

"Don't worry," Andy reassured. "You'll be wired. You'll each have a subcutaneous transceiver with two-way radio capability. They're made of softened, miniature computer chips with neural connections. Inserted behind your right ears, they won't be noticeable when, uh … observed." He nearly said 'examined,' thinking of a coroner working on their bodies. "Using a *NAVsop system, we can locate you anywhere on Earth within half a centimeter."

Ana realized Jon wanted nothing to do with her. She was beginning to dislike him. He might be protection, she thought, but not a friend. She asked, "What's a NAVsop?"

"British system. Made GPS obsolete. NAVsop is alphabet for Navigation via Signals of Opportunity. Uses Wi-Fi, TV and mobile phone signals. GPS units use one easily jammed signal. NAVsop uses hundreds of signals. Resists jamming. Can be integrated into our satellite systems. It detects signals deep inside buildings with frequencies from Low Earth Orbit Satellites.

"Are you using transceivers because you don't trust me?" She enjoyed his deep and spontaneous laughter. "If I were in your shoes, I wouldn't trust me either."

He laughed again. "Most tracking implants are smaller than a rice grain. Your implant will be nano-thin and two millimeters square with a unique identification code. We'll know it's you."

"Like a transponder in an airplane."

"Exactly." He anticipated objections. "Transceivers are becoming standard in government operations. Don't connect them with a trust issue."

"Understood."

"We have the United States to defend. We must know your every move. If anything would happen to you, we could go back to the transcriptions for help. We'll need to know how, why, and where your search ended. We'll continue from there. You're correct with the trust issue. I want to trust you but have red lights going off in my logic. Your transceivers will be two-way transmission capable, have NAVsop and GPS capability, satellite links, auditory neural links, and so on."

Ana put a finger to her lips, took a deep breath and asked, "What if our body rejects them?" Since her brain was so different, she worried the transceiver might do irreversible damage. "How would anyone know if it affects my brain? My mind? My existence?" She rubbed the area behind her right ear. "Do you think, since I'm telepathic, an electronic device connected to my nervous system might be dangerous to me?"

Andy shook his head as he said reassuringly, "There should be no problems. There've been no rejections in test subjects." He disclosed, "Some companies are requiring all employees have simple implants in their hands between their thumb and index finger. One day it may be SOP. They're coated with a fuzzy monomer to shield them from your autoimmune system."

Jon asked, "What's a monomer?"

"When the molecules of a compound are linked end to end, they create a long molecule called a polymer. Poly- means many. Mono- means one. If there's just one molecule, it's called a monomer. If we have to communicate with you, the message will go to your auditory nerve to be translated by the brain into sound. It cannot be heard physically. No one else will be aware of it." He chuckled. "Except for Ana and mindreachers."

Ana reached to her ear. "What powers them?"

"Solar power. Skin is translucent. Sunlight will go through it."

She teased, "Do they have little blinking lights to show they're working?"

Both men grinned. Andy replied, "No."

Jon asked, "Are these implants turned on all the time?"

"They can be turned off when needed. By the way, they have a double encryption for safety. No hacker will be listening in. In case you need me, just say my name aloud twice. Any segment with my name will be tagged, transcribed, and immediately sent to me via earsphere transceiver or email. So, if you get into trouble, verbalize. Your transceivers will be constantly monitored."

Ana asked, "If I need help, I just say Andy?"

He nodded. "Twice. If I don't respond within a few minutes, repeat my name several times. I should be tagged quickly and get back with you. Crypto-level technicians will be monitoring your frequency twenty-four hours a day. They will make sure transmissions are checked thoroughly before they leave the Satellite Pit. We've become bio-literate in areas more than DNA. You'll be given a mesh bar code. Your genetic subtype will be checked. If anything happens to you, with your permission, organs will go to a genetically matched person." He noticed her confused look. "What's your question?"

"If I'm hired," Ana asked, "can I tell my father about my job?"

"In the field you can let him know where you are, not what you're doing. With our classification, you can't tell anyone."

"What about Star Gate? It was public knowledge and a government psychic project."

"Star Gate closed decades ago."

"Technicians will know our location at all times?" She clasped her hands and stretched her arms forward.

Andy said, "They will." He looked at Jon. "You current on shots?" Jon gave a nod. Turning to Ana, he said, "The local military clinic will know what sets you'll require for international travel. We'll begin malaria prevention. Ever had sets of shots for yellow-fever, cholera, typhoid, hepatitis, or tetanus?"

"Sets?" Her eyebrows rose. "Just how many shots are you talking about?"

The men laughed.

"Less than twenty," Jon replied.

Ana looked back and forth between them. Does this mean I'm hired?"

"Congratulations, Ana. You are now officially a VESPER employee. You'll be asked to fill out a mass of paperwork for your security clearance and obtain a *GS rating."

"GS?"

"It's a salary rating. Human Resources will go over with you what that entails when they give you the security clearance paperwork. "

CHAPTER 12

Technical Laboratory
Defense Advanced Research Projects Agency
District of Columbia
19 August. 10:00 AM DST

Major Jon Coulter and Colonel Andy Anderson arrived at the Washington D.C. Laboratory for Physical Science, LPS, at the University of Maryland where research for spy craft technology takes place. As far as the public was concerned, this laboratory pushed the limits of technology as the most extensive language study site in the world. In reality, there were also areas for testing of equipment developed by DARPA for use by the National Security Agency, a national-level intelligence agency of the United States Department of Defense.

Knowing Ana would become a terrorist magnet, VESPER CEO, Herman Wald, had insisted the mindreacher search team be issued the most efficient, defensive equipment available.

In the LPS facility, Jon and Andy met engineer Denise Baker. A slim woman in her thirties, Baker had shoulder-length, brunette hair hiding her hearing aids. Wearing a white shirt, black slacks and flat shoes, she looked ready to tackle any job. She told Andy, "When you called, you requested international technical support. Colonel Walton and I will give you a tour to see a few of the latest developments. I think you'll find what you need."

"Thank you," Andy replied. "A woman by the name of Ana Masterson is our best piece of equipment."

Baker tipped her head and gave him a thumb up. She then escorted the two officers to Colonel James Walton, USAF, the Director of Operations. After introductions, Andy and James Walton briefly renewed their friendship while touring the laboratory.

At one stop, Walton handed Jon a cotton-lined, plastic pill vial containing seven aspirin-sized pellets.

"Careful," he warned. "They're porous silicon and will explode if their outer coating is scratched. Each pellet will create a larger mini-explosion than mankind has ever seen from such a small amount of chemical." Jon examined the vial with curiosity.

"He's not exaggerating," Baker confirmed. "Handle with care."

Jon asked, "Why seven?"

Walton answered, "Returning operatives report seven is the quantity most convenient to have."

"Can you touch them?"

"As long as your fingernail isn't seven on the Mohs scale of hardness. As soon as the outer coating is scratched, the chemical is triggered. Original units had reactions only under cryonic conditions, way below zero. This version works at room temperatures."

"And my fingernail hardness is…?"

"One or two. Depends on your diet."

"Is there an upper temperature limit? We're heading to South Africa."

"No reaction above one-hundred degrees Fahrenheit. The colder the better." Walton turned and directed, "This way gentleman." He led them to a laser demolition area, handed them goggles, and waited as they positioned themselves behind a transparent protective barrier. Holding his hand out for the vial, he opened it and dropped a pill-sized pellet in his hand. "Observe." He threw the pellet against a concrete practice wall. The resulting explosion breached the wall.

Jon let out a low whistle. "Good diversionary tactic. Nice and small. Can you use these with a sling shot?

"If the sling is a soft material."

What's the physics on these?"

Walton returned the vial to Jon. "It's chemistry, not physics. The silicon pellets are extremely porous with a hydrogen outer coating. Create a crack in the hydrogen allowing oxygen in, then KABOOM!"

"Are these exclusive to the States?"

"Developed in Germany. Refined in this lab. Other countries haven't evolved past super-cold applications."

Jon tightened the lid and slipped the vial into his pocket. "Think I'll need them?"

Andy answered, "You'll be traveling with Ana. Terrorists will want to use her abilities or eliminate her."

Baker asked, "Do you smoke?" At Jon's nod she said, "I can have them inserted into cigarette filters to conceal and protect them. Can be easily popped out."

Walton instructed, "We'll reconfigure them to look like an unopened pack of cigarettes."

Jon suggested, "Can you put them in a cigarette box instead of paper for protection?"

With a nod, she accepted the vial from Jon and moved off in another direction. He accompanied her.

With a concerned expression, Walton addressed Andy. "I've heard rumors about VESPER."

Andy glanced around to check their privacy. "VESPER information is on the street." He shifted his weight. "We had a murder in house. Don't know who did it or why."

"The why? Simple. You expose terrorists."

"Not yet."

Walton handed Andy a card-sized white box. "You requested these. Your telepath will find them handy in the outback of any country."

Anderson hefted the parcel. "How many?"

"Two-dozen." Handing over a second small container he added, "Here's your implants. They exceed your specifications. Have your surgeon call me if he needs info."

"Will do." Andy pocketed the boxes as Jon rejoined them. "A mindreacher might turn our telepath against us. I want to know everything that's being said."

Jon warned, "With telepathy you won't hear anything."

"I'll hear conversations. Plus you'll be with her."

Jon reminded, "I have no weapon against mind control."

"Ana's your weapon."

Walton remarked, "Your international travel will be a good test for the implants."

Jon asked, "How do I turn the implants off once they're installed?"

Andy said, "I'll show you later."

Walton remarked, "If the implants are turned off, they can still be hacked by anyone knowing your satellite signal codes. Like a cell phone, your geolocation would be exposed. There shouldn't be any problems. VESPER techs will know where you are and can use other technology to zoom in and capture images."

Jon looked skeptical. "Even during storms?"

"There's a real time digital KH-11 simulator on a Hubble-type telescope used to compensate for atmospheric disturbances."

"Wasn't the Hubble discontinued?"

"Equipment on the Hubble used by DOD was transferred to new telescopes. Son of Hubble, the James Webb scope, won't be used by the defense department because it's partially owned by other nations. However, back in 2012, the National Reconnaissance Office, the NRO, donated two Hubble-twins, formerly top secret KH-11 Spysats. They were called *Stubby Hubbles. Highly complex, the two telescopes were gathering dust in upstate New York. Built around 2000 as spy telescopes, they're better quality than the Hubble with bigger mirrors and advanced technology. It's hard to believe the NRO considered them obsolete."

Jon said, "Makes me wonder what type of reconnaissance satellites the NRO has now if Hubble equipment's considered primitive."

Baker added, "If we can have access to such phenomenal spin-offs, I say more power to them. NASA orbited both scopes. They're working just fine. NRO-1 is aimed outward in the Wfirst project, or Wide-Field Infrared Survey Telescope, to find dark matter and exoplanets. The NRO-2 is aimed toward Earth. It has enough resolution to find something smaller than a grapefruit."

"Like my head?" He ran a hand across his buzz cut.

Walton joined Baker's laughter and said, "For sure, but not your face."

Andy quipped, "Thanks for that," and laughed.

Walton pointed toward the back of the building. "The envision office back there can turn such data into 3-D images. We can zoom in on streets, alleys, and doorways, giving you directions through your implants from looking at the satellite data while you move around. We're one of twelve envisioning offices in the United States and there's more overseas. Even Kuwait has one." Walton turned from them to answer an employee's question. Jon lit a cigarette, inhaled and blew smoke out his nostrils in a steady stream.

Andy commented, "Smoking causes wrinkles and premature aging. I look so young because I don't smoke." He guffawed, knowing he looked his age. "Jon, VESPER's been a perfect assignment for you. Giving you time to heal. The security level on this mission should keep your activities quiet. Since Ana's capabilities are on a need-to-know basis, you shouldn't have any problems keeping her safe."

Denise Baker approached. "Major Coulter, this is a non-smoking facility. We have a sealed ventilation system."

"My apologies." He pinched the ember with two fingers before slipping it into his pocket.

She continued, "We're having our tailor prepare two pairs of multi-pocketed, long-sleeved shirts and cargo pants for you and Ms. Masterson. They're made of a new material combined with *spidersilk. Fibers have toughness of steel. Spider DNA was transferred into female goats. During lactation, their milk produces spidersilk. When woven, the silk reacts like micro-thin body armor. It's so strong, a strand as thin as a pencil could stop a 747 in flight."

Jon quipped, "You're joking, right?"

"Clothing designers for the rich and famous are beginning to use carbon nanotube fibers as bulletproof material. They're stronger and harden on impact. It costs about fifteen-thousand dollars per ounce. Our LPS contractor inserted liquid-acting, magnetic nanofibers which react to impact by solidifying even tighter. They'll stop a bullet. Impact force may still cause damage." She looked around and added, "Front and back shirt yokes will be padded with multiple layers to resemble safari wear."

"Is Kevlar body armor outdated?"

"There's micron-diameter sized Kevlar fibers woven around the spidersilk strands, Don't discuss it. This stuff is patented and donated to us for experimental use and testing."

"Is it waterproof?"

"Better than *Gore-Tex."

"Sweet."

Baker continued, "Between layers of spider silk we're inserting a flexible, thin, transparent material resembling kitchen plastic wrap. It's a superconductor. A product called *Graphene. It's considered one of the thinnest materials on the planet. What's remarkable is the claim it'd take an elephant balanced on a pencil to break through it.

"You sure have strong pencils around here," Jon teased. A smile danced around his lips.

"Can't recall hearing about Graphene," Andy commented with a thoughtful expression.

"Not a common material," Baker replied. "It's made of layered carbon one-atom thick. In a pure state it'll stretch and conduct electricity. Many layers are put together to the thickness of plastic kitchen wrap. Picture chicken-wire within the layer, made of *fullerenes and rolled into *nano-tubes. What they're doing with it is so classified, I don't even know how they cut it. Most seams are glued."

Jon asked, "Any glitches with it?"

"Humidity might affect layer bonding. Don't worry about it."

"What's a fullerene?"

Baker replied, "It's a carbon molecule in the form of a caged sphere." She cocked her head. "Your bullet proof clothing will be our first application incorporating Graphene. If it works out, this material may become standard for military uniforms. Our troops will live through events that would have killed them earlier. It's flexible and impermeable. Rain won't penetrate. It also insulated. That might be a problem in tropical climates."

* * *

Leaving the building, Andy told Jon, "Ana is the most important part of your team. Sometimes she'll lead. With her telepathy she'll know where to go and who to meet."

Jon gave him a sour look. "She can't be team leader. She knows nothing about combat."

"She'll have to make crucial decisions when interacting with mindreachers. You're the muscle. With the *Shaolin Temple's Kempo and martial arts training you had in China and your advanced Marine training, you're a lethal weapon. Don't let your guard down for a second. Be polite and respectful to everyone you meet, but have a plan to kill them."

"Where have I heard that before? I understand the rules, but I don't intend to injure innocent children or noncombatants if possible."

"She can't be replaced."

"And I can." Twisting his neck and tilting his chin toward Andy, he said, "CCW."

"Concealed carry? Whatever you need."

His lips curved up. "My *SIG."

"P227?"

"P226. Nine-millimeter."

"You've come a long way since growing up on your farm with an air rifle."

"I still have that rifle." They both grinned.

"You'll be traveling as a civilian. Let me have your SIG before you leave. Within twenty-four hours, I'll have it and your ammunition delivered to you incountry by diplomatic courier wherever you are. You already know not to piss off local police. They hate civilians with weapons better than theirs and will take 'em if given the chance. The presidential directive is to protect Ana no matter the cost, human or otherwise. Do you realize what an asset she'd be during field operations? Imagine having someone in combat able to verify enemy troop locations and tell command what the enemy is planning. Special op teams could have mindreachers assigned to them. You won't regret this pivotal assignment. It's a first in the history of our country. Expect an extensive debriefing when it's over."

"*Semper Fi.*"

CHAPTER 13

Johannesburg International Airport
Johannesburg, South Africa
22 August, 12:00 PM SAST (South Africa Standard Time)

The duo of Ana Masterson and Major Jon Coulter reached the city of Johannesburg, South Africa at noon. The metropolitan city, located over a mile above sea level and receiving less than ten-inches of rain a year, was experiencing South Africa's dry season. They headed for a recommended hotel.

Ana said, "Hope it doesn't have bed bugs."

Jon chuckled. "When you go in your room, put your luggage in the bath tub or shower. Then examine the mattress and sheets. If you find any bed bugs, we'll ask for other rooms."

After settling in, the two agreed to look at records of children born between 1979 and 1981 for their mindreacher search. In a city of over ten million people, the task of finding such information seemed impossible.

Using the occupation of journalists as a cover, for three days Ana and Jon spent hours in various public Joburg archives to find records of nurses who worked for Doctor Reginald Beckman. Ana looked for the Beckman name as attending physician during births. Birth statistics of interest were photocopied while Jon cross-referenced newspaper articles mentioning the doctor. Available parent names would be used for international searches.

* * *

On 26 August, their fourth day in Johannesburg, they hired a local private investigator. Chihambuane Mohr was requested to locate any woman who had been a patient of Dr. Reginald Beckman during the years of interest. Sitting at Mohr's desk, they requested he check government archival records from which civilians are forbidden access. Documents over twenty-five years old were accessible only to South African business associates. Mohr and his staff could legally access the Central Archives of the Cape Archives Depot in the city of Pretoria. The detective asked the Americans no invasive questions.

The detective flashed them a toothy smile. "My staff will appreciate this assignment. Weapons will be holstered for a change." He slicked back a few strands of nappy hair on his perspiring, shiny scalp. He was a heavy set man with a continual smile. Exposed ebony skin on his neck had numerous skin tags of all sizes, the biggest with a red and yellow tattoo border. A matching tattoo encircled a large mole on the back of his right hand. A diamond stud graced his left ear.

Ana ran a hand through her curly hair. "What types of jobs do you usually contract?"

Mohr unconsciously tapped his fingers on the wooden chair arm. "In this City of Gold, we keep busy investigating murders, rapes and retail thefts. There's quite an impressive number daily. You'll find armed guards at most commercial establishments." As he talked, Ana listened to languages spoken in the small office. Seeing her interest, Mohr boasted with a wave to his staff, "Lord bless Africa, my staff speaks the official languages of English, Afrikaans, and Zulu."

"What's with the clicking noises?"

"You're hearing *Xhosa language, Ms. Masterson. Makes you think of champagne bottles opening, doesn't it?"

She grinned. "I don't think I could talk like that."

"You have to have the right mouth anatomy to speak a click language." At Ana's quizzical expression, he added, "The roof of the mouth is higher. With your tongue, feel the bump between your upper teeth and the roof of the mouth. They have no such bump."

She tongued the roof of her mouth. "I never noticed that before."

Turning to Jon, Mohr admonished, "You're in the carjacking and rape capital of the world. A rape occurs every thirty-or-so seconds." Ana and Jon exchanged glances. "Indeed. Crime keeps me in business." Pressing his full lips together and inhaling noisily through wide nostrils, he leaned back into his chair. "The crime rate here is triple the rate of your Chicago or Detroit. We have over twenty thousand residential burglaries a year in Joburg. Thugs show no fear. They even robbed a TV announcer while his staff taped him for a newscast."

Ana leaned closer to Jon as she addressed the detective. "Does South Africa have terrorists?"

Mohr folded his arms, resting them on his protruding stomach. Silent a few moments, as though deciding how to respond, he began in a quiet voice, "Many African nations are in a position of economic instability and social unrest. Our breached borders allowed one of the biggest terrorist groups to infiltrate our country. The Al-Shabaab. It's a Somali group that branched out to make their civil war international. They created havoc throughout our country. With corruption and bribery of officials and citizens, terrorism grows. We have the presence of the Shabaab organization established. South Africa has also been a haven for other terrorists. Our government supported the Renamo terrorists in Mozambique to help get rid of in-country terrorist groups. As far as you're concerned, I never mentioned it. I don't want to be red-flagged."

"Understood," Jon supplied. "Do you know if the American Embassy in Pretoria is still under a high state of alert?"

"Today it's okay. Tomorrow I can't guess. For your own safety don't use public transportation of any kind, here or in Pretoria. I can lease you a nondescript car in any city you visit … at a good price." He produced an infectious chuckle. Ana laughed with him. At Jon's nod, Mohr looked over his shoulder and called, "Katerina, did you hear?" A traditional, large boned, black woman with a beautiful smile and cascading braids sat across the room at a desk filled with papers. Katerina looked at him and thumbed agreement. "Ms. Masterson, Mr. Coulter, would you like a cup of coffee or tea?" When they declined his offer, Mohr looked to Katerina, brought his thumb and index finger together and with raised fingers, tipped them toward his mouth inferring, 'coffee please.'

Katerina walked toward a coffee pot as Mohr continued.

"Westerners are targets. Wear dark, inconspicuous clothing. No flashy anything. Don't carry or flash cash in the form of greenback dollars or our South African rand. Don't let credit cards out of your sight. Water is a precious commodity. Carry what you need. You may not easily find potable water south of here. With only ten inches of rain a year, this is desert country."

Lengthening the strap of her black rip stock *Ameribag,Ana repositioned it to fit diagonally across her body. "What about restaurants?"

"Portable credit machines are available city wide. Request one at your table when the bill is presented or pay cash. Terrorists are indiscriminate when bombing restaurants, hotels, or places catering to western tourists. Remain vigilant. Exercise caution. Continually look for escape routes." As he talked, his stained, bottom teeth became more noticeable.

"Thanks for the reminder," Jon said, making an effort to not appear controlled and lethal by relaxing into his chair.

Ana removed a pen and writing pad from her Ameribag. "Do we call 911 in an emergency?"

Mohr chuckled and spread his arms wide. "Now that you ask," he began with exaggerated modesty, "I rent in-country cell phones for a small fee." A large-toothed smile remained on his face while he removed a cell phone from a desk drawer and passed it to Ana. "We keep them registered to a phantom existence. Emergency numbers are in the contacts section."

Katerina delivered his coffee with small jar of ground cinnamon. Mohr spooned cinnamon into his coffee, stirred it and put the stirrer and cinnamon back on Katerina's wooden tray. After taking a sip he sighed.

* * *

The next morning, after an email check from their hotel rooms, Ana and Jon flew to the city of Durban at the southern tip of the African continent bordering the Indian Ocean. Durban boasted two major industries, scuba diving and deep sea fishing. Because they were trying to find someone who may have sold wetsuit material to Dr. Beckman for his vacuum device, Durban seemed a good place to begin searching for names associated with mindreachers.

After visiting most of the dive shops, they were finally referred to an old barrel maker who remembered making Beckman's vacuum device because it was so unusual. From the barrel maker they obtained the names of two others associated with the doctor. There were no leads to patient names. They regretfully returned to Johannesburg and dropped off information for Mohr to investigate. With an impending sense of urgency, the two Americans examined accessible, public archival records.

* * *

On 28 August, detective Chihambuane Mohr's assistant couriered the first positive result to Jon at the hotel. Jon skimmed the results and rushed across the hall to Ana's room.

"We have a hit," he exclaimed. "A Verwoerd family. Parents are Hans and Stella Verwoerd. They live in Soweto, a town south of Johannesburg."

She quickly stood. "Great! How far is Soweto?"

"About twenty miles." He had a somber expression.

"Wow. We'll get to meet our first one? A true mindreacher. I'm so excited!"

"I hate to tell you this, but we'll only meet her parents, not the mindreacher."

"Is she out of town?"

"No. The daughter died in a car accident as a teen." Jon chewed on the inside of his cheek, unsure how Ana would accept the information.

She sat and lowered her head.

He didn't break her silence. Instead, he lit a cigarette and sat with his back to the window.

After several minutes she asked, "What else do you know?"

"Detective Mohr's report said it was a hit and run."

"I'm sorry to hear that. I hope her parents know of another mindreacher in the area."

He shrugged. "With their abilities, these kids probably had all kinds of problems."

"Their parents too. I can sure empathize with them. Life was hard for me and I didn't have a fraction of the ability those kids had. Did Mohr provide any other names?"

"He'll let us know if he finds any while we're here in Joburg. Once we leave, he'll email info to Andy. I put him on a retainer."

"Do you think the girl's parents will talk to us?"

"Let's find out."

* * *

Nearing Soweto in Mohr's nondescript rental car, the duo drove by a community of dilapidated huts constructed of metal sheets leaning one upon another. If one in the row were to tilt sideways, hundreds of huts would topple. Disheartened by the sight, Ana was further discouraged to see skimpily clad children playing with trash in the narrow, dusty lanes. In one lane children played around a water pipe sticking up out of the ground. They were splashing mud and giggling. It was a sharp contrast within a nearby cosmopolitan city full of wealth and beautiful architecture.

Jon studied Ana at every traffic stop. "Are you aware that people stare at you?"

"I have a large aura."

"A large what?"

"An energy field. I give off energy. I don't know how to stop it." She clasped her hands together in front of her chin and looked at him with innocent eyes. To lighten the atmosphere, she said, "With all the electric lines along the streets, I wouldn't think my energy could be felt."

He gave her an incredulous look. "People of all ages whip their heads around to see you. It makes no difference if they're walking, on motor bikes, in buses or cars. They all gawk."

"My parents used to freak out when that happened. I'm so used to it, I forget about it." She leaned her head back and closed her eyes. "Relax," she muttered to herself. Her fisted hands opened.

"Does Miguel Lopez or Andy know about how you unconsciously attract attention?"

"I never thought to tell them." She skewed her mouth into several positions while looking out the window.

"Andy said not to attract attention." He examined her face.

"I don't know how to stop it." She looked at Jon's worried expression. "Quit staring. I'm not an alien." Concerned, she slowed her heart rate and breathing.

"Do you think mindreachers will attract attention too?

She took time to think before answering, "I have no idea." Using the GPS unit provided with the car, they soon arrived at the Verwoerd cottage. Grey paint peeling from the neglected siding showed a green paint underneath.

Jon knocked at the door. A small boned Caucasian woman opened it a few inches. Dressed in a faded grey house dress the color of her unkempt short hair, she appeared tired.

"Good morning, Mrs. Verwoerd." He introduced Ana. "Would you consent to be interviewed for a magazine article?" Hesitating, she glanced backwards.

"No interviews," a man commanded from across the room. He walked to the door. "Why do you want to interview my wife?" When he elbowed her from the door, Mrs. Verwoerd crossed the room and sat on a worn, wicker sofa. Both Verwoerds and their room looked disheveled.

Jon maneuvered himself through the doorway and continued in a calm, smooth voice. "We're researching how parents cope after losing their teenager in an automobile accident. We're sorry for your loss."

With pain of grief etched in his face, the father said, "There's no drama here. No sex. No drugs. Leave us alone."

"Anika is gone," the mother commented as a shadow passed her face. "Let her rest in peace." She twisted her hands together.

"We just want to ask a few questions," Ana broke in with a soft, persuasive tone. "Any information you give us could be a tremendous help to other parents in the same circumstance. By telling them how you coped may make other lives easier. Anything you say can be anonymous." She projected a sense of calm into their minds.

Mr. Verwoerd looked back and forth at them. "What magazine do you work for?"

His wife interrupted, "Hans, if it'll help others, perhaps we should answer a few questions?" She looked to her husband for approval.

Mr. Verwoerd huffed in exasperation and glared at Ana before relenting. He turned to Jon. "Don't judge us. Our hearts are still broken. We loved her so much."

Jon sat and gave an introduction to their bogus research while Ana listened to the couple's active thoughts. The wife was thinking of an Asian couple not part of the white enclave. Searching deeper, Ana sensed the name, Meay Jayachettha. Meay had been employed evenings to clean Dr. Beckman's office. Pregnant Meay's husband had helped his wife secretly use the doctor's pain relieving, vacuum machine. When the doctor found out, Meay was fired. Ana gathered a few more facts before interrupting Jon's conversation.

"Do you remember a woman named Meay?" The Verwoerds glanced at one another before Mrs. Verwoerd looked to her red hands. Gleaning thoughts, Ana learned of Meay's past travel plans and obtained the words 'nong' and 'khai.' Mrs. Verwoerd's mind exhibited fright. She thought Jon and Ana were sent by a local drug lord.

With a motion to be silent, her husband barked, "We don't know any Meay, do we Stella?" Agony in her expression, his wife gave a miniscule shake of her head.

Ana saw both of them exhibit the classic traits of deception. Mr. Verwoerd looked haggard.

"Enough questions," Verwoerd stated. "Leave us."

Jon and Ana moved toward the door. "We thank you for your kind cooperation," Ana said, disappointed at not having time to delve into the father's thoughts.

Jon reiterated thanks and offered his hand. He had to whip it back as the door was slammed in their faces.

* * *

In the car, Jon made a U-turn on the Verwoerd's narrow street and observed a car nearby parallel his action. "We're being followed."

Ana looked back to see the tailing car. "That green car?" At his nod, she said, "Can you lose them?"

"Sometimes it's better to know your enemy. If I lost them I might pick up another tail I didn't know about. I wonder what they want?"

"Money? The car?"

"Not this heap."

She responded by scooting lower in her seat. "While you drive, I'll tell you what I learned. You already know the daughter's name was Anika. Her mother believed Anika's mindreaching caused the murder. The daughter must have accidently uncovered a drug dealer and passed information to the authorities without telling her parents. Like most parents, they didn't always connect with her. Because of that, they feel her death was their fault."

"Lack of communication isn't unusual with teenagers," Jon replied.

"They believe someone in the police department leaked the name of the informant to seal Anika's fate. She was murdered by a hit and run driver on the way home from school the next day. Had she not confided her involvement that morning to her parents, they would've accepted her fate as an isolated accident. As proof of their suspicions, they've had many threats from drug lords since her murder. Evidently the drug machine thinks the parents were involved. Shunned by their neighbors out of fear, they finally moved to that small house and kept to themselves. I'm afraid our arrival put them into a state of shock. Their daughter must have been very special."

"What a loss." Traffic hindered Jon from distinguishing the make of the car pacing them. Traffic circles were bumper-to-bumper moving chaos. Cars in front of them couldn't easily enter the circles. Once in the circle, a slow car in the outer lane made it difficult to get out.

"Dumb tourist! Get a brain." He swore at a driver and narrowly dodged a car darting in and out of traffic.

"You realize we're dumb tourists too?" Her giggles infectious, Jon laughed.

Finally seeing a mangled right front fender made the trailing car easy to distinguish. He decided to verify the tail with a left turn signal. When the tail duplicated the signal, he made a rapid right turn into a narrow side street. The suspect car continued straight on.

"Must not be a tail," Ana suggested.

"This could get tricky," Jon mused, analyzing their surroundings. The street was lined with cars. There was barely room for their car to move forward. As he proceeded slowly, the green car that had been tailing them angled across the intersection ahead of them, skidding to a stop. It effectively created a chokepoint. Two firearms were aimed toward them.

Ana blurted, "We didn't lose 'em."

The street was too narrow to make a fast 180-degree sliding turn. He couldn't escape back the way he came .

He said, "Get in the back seat. Behind me. On the floor. NOW!" He muttered obscenities. The rail frame supporting their car was about a foot inside the wheels. He lined the car up so that front passenger edge of that rail frame was aimed at the point behind the blocking car's rear door, its C-pillar. Then he began to slow down to make them think he was coming to a stop. When he was about twenty feet from the green car, he punched the gas and stayed on it. The car responded, accelerating rapidly.

Ana yelled, "What are you doing?"

"STAY DOWN!" Sitting lower, he continued accelerating as the tires squealed and spun. Bullets ripping through the windshield and rear window shattered the laminated glass into spider-like webs making it hard for him to see.

Ana quipped, "Guess this rules out the carjacking theory."

He chuckled. The continuing barrage peppered the finish and added more holes in the front and back window glass. "Hold on," he called, knowing a wrong move would make them fodder. "We're going to spin them out of the way."

With a loud crash, the right front of their car met the back right fender of the blocking green car. Metal hitting metal jarred both vehicles. Momentum of their car spun the green car ninety degrees to face the lane they just left. It was partially in the intersection. The space created by the ramming allowed Jon to barge past. Shouts of innocent bystanders mixed with sounds of handguns. Amidst the outrage of other drivers, Jon decelerated to blend in with traffic and swerved into the slow-moving traffic.

He shouted, "Move, idiots, MOVE!

A glance in the rearview mirror showed the rear tires of the rammed car smoking from burned rubber. Its driver slid the car's back end in a tight circle to turn around.

Jon cursed. He didn't know the city. He couldn't plan an escape path. Judging an approaching traffic light in their lane was about to change to red, he kept their car moving at a fast pace. When the light changed, he accelerated around cars that were stopped ahead of him. To the chagrin of drivers who had started into the intersection from left and right, he barreled through amidst horn blowing and tire squealing, narrowly escaping three collisions. Had he not been trained in evasive driving, he would have lost control. Oncoming vehicles and resulting traffic tie ups stopped the green car from entering the intersection.

Making several quick turns into side streets, Jon skidded their car into the shadowed parking alcove behind a church. He turned off the motor and took a deep breath.

Ana had been banged around, but not hurt. Anxious, she waited a few moments before asking, "Is it safe to get up?" Hanging on to the back of Jon's car seat she said, "My heart's beating a mile a minute!"

"Stay down woman," he commanded sternly.

Irate, she replied, "My name is Ana."

"I need to hear." Under his breath he murmured, "They could've killed you."

"Us," she corrected.

At the sound of tires squealing in the distance and heading away from them, Jon relaxed somewhat.

She asked, "Who were they?"

"Someone who wants you d...." Catching himself, he said, "... stopped." He looked out the side windows. "The mindreachers you'll identify will change intelligence modes of operation all over the world with mind-boggling implications. No matter where they hide, terrorists will know they'll be identified through telepathy. They're running scared. You're right in that someone masterminded that attack. I wonder who?"

"How did they find us?"

Jon fingered the implant as he helped Ana out of the car. She leaned against the church while he grabbed the tire iron out of the trunk. In a rage, he knocked out what glass was left of the front and back windshields. When the car was safe enough to drive, he brushed glass off the seats. Being windshield glass the pieces were small and thick.

During the drive back to the hotel they rehashed the Verwoerd visit.

When they arrived back at the hotel, Jon parked the car between trash dumpsters in the back. He next called Detective

Mohr, gave him necessary details about damage to his vehicle and information as to the car's location. Placing the keys on the top of the back left tire, he escorted Ana to the front of the hotel. He asked, "Why don't you use your telepathy more often?"

"Habit. I was forbidden to use it when growing up."

"You won't find a mindreacher if you don't open your mind. You have to use your telepathy to find a telepath."

"I'll do better." She covered a yawn. "What's a nong and a khai?"

"Nong Khai is a town in southeast Asia. We'll travel to the Pearl of the Orient and from there to Nong Khai. At least we have the mother's name to go on."

"Pearl of the Orient?"

"Bangkok. It's the capital of Thailand."

CHAPTER 14

Don Mueang International Airport
Bangkok, Thailand
30 August, 10:20 AM ICT (IndoChina Time)

When Ana Masterson and Jon Coulter arrived in Thai airspace, their flight was diverted to the older Don Mueang International Airport, the busiest airport in Thailand. An aircraft sequencing foul-up left no open slot for their airplane at the terminal. It had to be parked on the far side of the tarmac where transport buses to the terminal awaited passengers.

"Wow," Ana exclaimed when she stepped out of the air-conditioned airplane. Heat and humidity hit her as a physical weight. She wrinkled her nose at an unpleasant odor. She peeled off her suit jacket and looked around. Recent rain steamed off a glistening tarmac. Shielding her eyes, she barely glanced at the hazy blue sky before donning sunglasses.

Jon said, "Welcome to Southeast Asia."

She asked, "What time is it?"

"Ten-thirty. Ten thirty at night in Ohio."

"No wonder I'm tired."

In the terminal, passengers reveled in air conditioning. Retrieving their luggage, The duo moved through customs in the faster green lane for persons having nothing to declare.

Visitors to Bangkok often arrived with empty suitcases to fill with Thai merchandise. The ancient city was filled with canals, Buddhist temples, statues and sky reaching hotels. A woman's shopping paradise, tourists bargained for hand crafted wood carvings, silks, bronzeware, precious gems, jewelry and antiques in numerous shopping centers at prices less than stateside wholesale rates.

Ana tried to follow direction signs to areas designated for arriving passengers while Jon tried to lead her toward the Departure Hall for travelers leaving the country.

She asked, "Why the Departure Hall?"

"See those people getting out of taxies at the Departure Hall entrance? We'll grab one of their cabs and be out of here without having to wait. Everyone else going into the city will wait for a cab from the legal line farther down the lane."

She looked in the direction of unusual music coming from the entrance hall. Eyes open wide, she exclaimed, "Look!" She pointed to tourists surrounding female Thai dancers wearing long-sleeved, black fitted silk jackets. Their crimson, satin knickers were filled with metallic embroidery. The tips of their fingers were adorned with curved, three-inch, gold cylindrical extensions tapering to a point. During elaborate motions, miniature bells at their ankles jingled and glittered amidst the jeweled toe rings. Each dancer kept their bare feet at right angles to their legs as they danced. Sparkling gilded tiaras rested on each head. Theatrical makeup on frozen expressions accentuated the presentation. Long necked stringed *sitars were being played by three seated musicians dressed in traditional Thai costumes.

Ana inhaled a pleasant sweet aroma before she noticed jasmine leas about the dancer's necks. The ringing of brass finger cymbals sounded to the music beat. She thought the whole scene exotic. When she began to walk with the rest of the arriving tourists in the direction of the entertainment, Jon grabbed her elbow to hurry them outside.

She removed her arm from his grip with a tug. Hands on hips and eyes glittering in challenge, she turned to face him. Exaggerating each word, she asked, "What is your rush? I'd like to watch this." Bystanders began to look at them.

In a low voice, Jon answered, "Look around. We're in a crowd of unknowns. It only takes one person to target you." Scanning for unknown threats, he added under his breath, "Let's keep moving and not draw attention."

They headed outside to the line of recently vacated taxies. Not seeing anyone keeping them under surveillance, Jon hailed a driver who had just dropped off two young backpackers. By not heading for the popular Sky Train and avoiding the legal queue of taxies lined up for city-bound tourists, he kept Ana from possible dangerous exposure.

The taxi driver addressed them in a lilting, singsong voice. "Sawadee, krup." Bowing, he placed his hands in front of his chest in a prayer attitude. His palms were together and fingers pointed up. "Guten Tag. Bonjour. Hello." When he saw her response to "hello," he knew she spoke English. "Want taxi? Have good price." The driver furtively searched the area looking for police. Taking fares away from legal outbound queues further down the lane was frowned upon.

Before Jon loaded their luggage, Ana took a small red bag out of her suitcase. Once seated in the taxi, she lamented, "Just our luck. No air-conditioning."

He handed her a bottle of water before memorizing the driver's registration name in English.

She drank half of it before asking, "Is milk safe to drink here"

"If it's imported."

"What difference does that make?"

"Electricity's an expensive commodity here. No electricity equals no refrigeration. If you can't store it, you don't buy it. So, there's little market for dairy products. Most weaned kids in this part of the world don't have milk except for occasional treats of sweetened canned milk.

She fanned her face. "I'm burning up."

"No matter what the temperature is, the TAT and the local radio announces it as less than one-hundred degrees Fahrenheit. Keeps the tourists coming. If the temperature's one-hundred and ten degrees and I tell you it's eighty-nine, you'll put up with it and attribute the discomfort to humidity." He smiled at her enlightened expression.

"TAT?"

Tourist Authority of Thailand."

The driver agreed, "Vury hot."

Jon examined cars passing them on the divided Don Mueang Toll way. The road had been built above the older Vibhavadi Rangsit Road to Bangkok. He could see the elevated Sky Train tracks in the distance. He told Ana, "I checked hotels on the Internet in Johannesburg and reserved two adjoining rooms in an older hotel off the tourist tract. We don't want to be on anyone's radar."

As they approached the city, they could see the faint lavender-gray smog enveloping the skyline.

She mused softly, "Mindreachers must have successful lives if they're so intelligent. Why would any want to work at finding terrorists?"

"Just find one. Leave incentives to VESPER."

"Incentives such as?" She wrinkled her nose and looked around to find the source of a sewer smell along the road.

"Green. American dollars can be spent anywhere."

"What if he's nasty?"

"Don't worry. We'll tread carefully."

She looked at her clasped hands in her lap. "I'd lose in a mental battle." She wrinkled her nose again. "What's that smell?"

"Smell is from klong, madam," the driver announced respectfully. "Klong is canal. City have many klong." He motioned to the canal paralleling the highway.

She rubbed a finger under her nose as though to dispel the smell, marveling at the views. Thailand was more unique than she could ever have imagined. She thought, here I am in a strange land with a handsome escort from the United States government and working with anti-terrorists in psychic espionage. What's next? Leaning back into the seat with a contented smile, she said, "I think I was born for this."

The driver said, "Bangkok neung ... ahhh ... one meter above sea. If you dig hole one meter, find water." The driver turned to grin at her.

Jon said, "Early Bangkok canals were for transportation. With the influx of tourists and cars, the main thoroughfare canals were filled in to make streets. Existing canals are used for bathing, fishing, washing clothes or dishes, cleaning hair and teeth, sewage and so on." He watched the narrow, shallow klong they were paralleling.

"Being so close to sea level, they must have good water purification plants."

He asked, "Did Andy give you a pack of Australian *Graphair water filters?"

She patted her pocket. "He said to always keep them on me."

"Good. You never know when you might need one. They'll remove almost one-hundred percent of all contaminants in one pour through."

"That's what Andy said." She glanced at the driver and whispered, "Is the Thai government friendly to the United States?"

He whispered back, "Yes, ever since we helped them during World War II. We give them dollars for counter-terrorism, peacekeeping training, counter-insurgency, and military equipment to buy from us."

"We give them money to buy stuff from us?" He nodded. In a search for lipstick, she opened her Ameribag and pushed aside a small, red, zippered nylon bag.

He turned his head to peer into her purse. What's the red bag?"

"My emergency stash." She unzipped it. A white box the size of card deck and tied with a rubber band rested at the top. She put it aside.

Jon followed the box with his eyes. It resembled a container Colonel Walters passed to Andy back in Maryland.

"Okay, here's what I have. A mini flashlight..."

"Good, it's xenon."

"It'll blind an attacker at night."

"Not for long."

"Long enough for me to wop them over the head with it and knock 'em out."

He grinned. "You'd have to know where to wop."

"It's pretty heavy." She lifted it for his inspection. "I have to be careful when I hold it. One end has sharp edges." She gently fingered the sharp end.

"You'd really hit someone with it?"

"No. I'd run away," she admitted, stifling a chuckle.

"We use similar flashlights in the field." He pointed to the sharp end opposite the lamp. "This is razor sharp. Swing your flashlight across an attacker's skin and you'll leave deep slashes." He held the flashlight wrapped in his palm and gently grabbed her earlobe. He secured the lobe between his thumb and the sharp edge at the end of the flashlight. With a gentle tug, he illustrated how her head would follow his hand. "See how ---"

Ana slammed her elbow into his side and hissed, "Stop it. That hurts."

"Where'd you learn that move?"

"I'm not stupid." She glared at him.

"Here, try it on me." He flinched as she grabbed his ear lobe with more force than necessary before letting go.

"If you think I could grab someone's earlobe during a fight, you're crazy. I doubt if I could grab one if they were standing still." She turned her attention back to the kit. "Here's my Johannesburg map."

"Toss it."

"My Swiss army knife." The worn, red knife was less than three-inches long.

"Kinda' small."

"It's not the size that counts." He smiled while she unscrewed the top of a small, red plastic canister to show him wooden matches and three small safety pins. A compass was imbedded in the lid. The other end was a whistle. She pulled out a metal tin formerly used for mint candy. It contained an antibiotic ointment tube, a small super glue tube and three Band-Aids. In separate sealed plastic bags were Imodium tabs and additional Graphair water filters.

"I have two black trash bags, a high energy bar, a parachute cord bracelet, ten dollars in singles, photocopies of my passport and birth certificate, a small concave signal mirror and another small packet of personal Graphair water purification filters." She held up the filters. "I also brought a small magnesium spark rod to start a fire, and earplugs." She held out a shiny metallic pack small enough to fit in her palm. "Emergency blanket."

He added, "You can use it to signal someone and as a tarp or poncho."

She took a satisfying breath. "What have I forgotten?"

"Fish hooks? Duct tape?"

She whispered, "I couldn't clean a fish."

"You could if you were hungry. Why a concave mirror?"

"To start a fire with sunlight."

"I assume the energy bar contains chocolate?"

She laughed. "I'm a chocoholic. If you ever buy me chocolate, buy the best. Most brands have paraffin to keep them from melting. They're like eating a brown candle. I think paraffin is what clogs arteries. Your body doesn't know what to do with it." She held the energy bar at one end and watched it slowly bend in the heat.

"Toss it. Why garbage bags?"

"Shelter? Camouflage?"

Jon chuckled. "Bet you were Girl Scout."

"A very good one!" They both laughed as she repacked her kit. "What emergency gear do you have?"

"Leatherman, paracord, tactical pen, duct tape and such. Not much."

"You know," she whispered, aware of the listening driver, "we might go for months and never find our man. We could be tripping around the world for years at the expense of Uncle Sam."

"I always dreamed of having a rich relative." A confirmed bachelor, Jon didn't think any female would appreciate his treacherous occupation and attitude on life. However, if he could get used to Ana's mental abilities, she might become someone special. She'd be a good friend if nothing else. He appreciated her patriotism and dedication to finding a mindreacher even though it put her life in danger. Looking forward to teaching her self-defense, he pointed to the driver and to his own forehead.

She grinned and whispered, "He's anticipating something good."

"Probably a big tip. I've got American green and Thai baht. Since the city of Nong Khai is near Laos, I'll get Laotian kip there."

"Green is good, sir," the driver commented. He spoke better English than he let on.

Jon motioned out the window at scaffolding and construction cranes as they neared Bangkok. Pile drivers, pounding what looked like twenty-foot long telephone poles into the ground at two locations, shook the earth. "This is like Rotterdam. Water-soaked clay won't support buildings. Poles are pounded in the ground one atop another for over twenty meters."

"How do you know so much?"

"I read a lot."

"What traffic!" Her attention was absorbed by sights and smells as they entered the city. Petrol exhaust and smog hung heavy in the air. Vendors and shoppers crowded sidewalks. Cars, trucks and buses jammed streets. Motorbikes and scooters, guided by drivers wearing breathing masks, scooted in and out of traffic with finesse. Motorized three-wheeled taxies called *tuktuks* or *samlors*, driven in the side streets, had one to three passengers on the back seat. Part rickshaw and part motorbike, the driver told them the open-air vehicles were outlawed on main thoroughfares.

Eventually, their taxi was traveling east on Sukhumvit Road. Ana noticed paved, one-lane *sois* or small streets alternated off the four-lane road. No two *sois* were opposite one another. Even-numbered *sois* were to her right, odd-numbered ones left. She peered into *sois* busy with pedestrians and small businesses. In some of them she could see houses were protected behind tall concrete block walls. Jagged shards of glass topped the walls. She caught sight of two German shepherd dogs jumping over one ten-foot high gate. She didn't realize dogs could jump that high.

Their conversation and Bangkok scenes distracted them from noticing a following, small black car.

CHAPTER 15

Satellite Communication Pit
VESPER Facility
29 August 6:00 PM DST

VESPER Communications Director, Phillip Arnold, had skillfully misdirected attempts to find the computer room killer. Employees were on edge not knowing who committed the on-site murder. Personal safety was an ongoing issue.

Expressionless in the Satellite Pit while staring at large wall monitor projections, Arnold sighed. His technicians continually accessed the massive emergency preparedness computer system to keep it functioning. Government technicians, expecting VESPER to keep computers in working order, rarely tackled the multiple server banks. He glanced at the giant monitors of two geo-stationary satellites above the equator and noted who was on duty in the Pit. Expecting one of the current two-man crew to leave for a break in a few minutes, he leaned against the wall to watch.

Technician Derek Riggle, a redneck cowboy, was assigned the Joburg team satellite frequencies. Riggle was engrossed in interpolating figures in a Computer Aided Design, or CAD program, on two adjacent machines. A wizard in electronics, the engineer could complete electronic tasks with rapidity and minute attention to detail before moving to his next assignment.

Arnold thought Riggle looked ridiculous in his everyday black cowboy shirt and bolo tie with a massive turquoise slide. He knew a gigantic, silver belt buckle was hidden under Riggle's fat roll. He chuckled at the thought Riggle was probably sterile in such tight jeans. A black Stetson hat hung precariously on the corner of an unused desk monitor. Engrossed, the cowboy didn't notice his supervisor. Riggle was enjoying a relaxed night duty.

It was daytime for Masterson half way around the world. Arnold knew if anything was going to happen to Masterson, it should be during this shift.

Riggle noticed Arnold and hustled to obtain current latitude and longitudinal coordinates of the Masterson telepath.

Arnold asked, "How's it going, Riggle? Much movement today?" He kept his distance from Riggle's cologne overdose.

Riggle stood and spoke in a slow Texas drawl. "Evenin', Mr. Arnold. Nice to see ya'." He unconsciously rubbed a cuff against a silver phone holster attached to his belt.

Arnold touched two fingers to his eyebrow in an unofficial salute. "What's happening?"

Riggle began, "Cane't tell if they're movin' 'rot now." He gestured toward one of the wall monitors. "Satellite's just goin' outta' range." He handed Arnold a lined yellow paper marking Masterson's latitude and longitude with large numbers in ballpoint pen. "Another satellite'll pick 'em up in 'bout twenty seconds. When it connects with their transceivers, GPS data'll be on thet screen." He pointed to the larger of two screens on the monitor wall.

Arnold read the data Riggle gave him. "Enlighten me. What hotel?"

"Don't know the name yet. It's on 'Sue-Come-Vit Avenue. 'Jist a second. I'll bring it up." Shifting uncomfortably, Riggle aimed the narrow beam of a red neon-laser penlight to a monitor showing a hybrid satellite view of Bangkok. With one deft motion he changed the view to show street names and buildings. He used the laser to pinpoint a larger building. "Thet's it. Bin' listenin' to 'em. Not much import'nt jawin'."

"Whether you think it's important or not, have every uttered word automatically transcribed. I want to know what's said no matter who says it or how inconsequential you think it is." He paused before adding as an afterthought, "By the way, Colonel Anderson said he's too busy. Email me the transcriptions. I'll see he gets his copy."

Anderson would receive altered versions. By the time the Colonel figured out what was going on, if he ever did, Ana Masterson would be dead and Arnold would be gone.

"Yes suh, be glad to do thet for ya'." Checking the wall display, the cowboy rolled his shirt sleeves and exposed a wide silver and turquoise watch band.

Arnold headed topside for the nearest public Internet café without video monitors. His Al-Qaeda contacts had to be made from anonymous computers to keep him safe from suspicion.

* * *

At the Internet café, Arnold contracted a *sniper associated with a Sri Lanka group. Since the death of the primary Sri Lankan terrorist leader and defeat of the Liberation Tigers of Tamil Eelam in 2009, off shoot terrorist cells had been in dire need of funding. They were easy to locate through al-Qaeda Internet links. Working with the Sri Lanka Internet site, he learned a large portion of the Muslim empire now stretched from Indonesia through Thailand. Radical Islamists heavily infiltrated terrorist cells in those regions. Arnold recorded Southeast Asia cell leader names, electronic contact numbers and addresses to his home computer.

He questioned which terrorist cell in Thailand to contact. Which could do the job best? He decided to send several different photos of Masterson along with her recent coordinates. Her death would be soon. Within an hour on the computer, Arnold had reached several Southeast Asia terrorist groups. He was elated to contact a member of the infamous Jemaah Isamliya team with links to al-Qaeda. With a wide grin, he recalled the Jemaah group wanted to make all of Southeast Asia an Islamic state.

"With all of their international ties, they travel unimpeded. No matter where Masterson and Coulter go, these guys could follow." He wondered if he could afford them. They were one of the better militant organizations which had executed successful attacks throughout Southeast Asia. At their acceptance of the soft target assignment, Arnold advised them how to obtain data from illegal Internet sites he had previously constructed.

"Have your men use hollow point bullets," he directed. "They're hard to trace and deform on impact. Fill 'em with poison and seal 'em with a dribble of wax." When he received objections, he offered more cash. "I want a close kill through an eye socket. If she doesn't die from the bullet, poison will complete the task."

Arnold had known of victims who were shot in the head and lived to tell about it. He next requested the teams run a wire cleaning brush through the bore of their rifle to alter the ballistic marks after the kill was made and to get rid of ejected shells. He wanted no possible match to the weapon in any forensics lab during ballistic tests. Although he didn't expect much in the way of forensic labs in Southeast Asia, he wanted no lead back to him. He sent his directions through an email site which bounced through several countries.

* * *

At home later in the day, Arnold logged on to his desktop computer and linked into a server operated by a large company in Minnesota. He'd been illegally using their server for over ten years to drop data into the bowels of its memory. He transferred all his data from the Minnesota computer to the inner depths of the massive Emergency Preparedness and VESPER computer system. He smiled knowing the techs in Minnesota will be perplexed wondering where all that released computer memory came from.

An admin entrance link was created so he could access the data no matter where he lived. No one would ever suspect one of the most highly classified government electronic systems in the United States held and serviced numerous data drops and message boards for Islamic terrorists. To maintain the clandestine and illegal system under the nation's nose brought Arnold extreme pleasure. He could easily imagine himself as an old man managing his illegal site with money pouring in from terrorists needing information.

Within VESPER's system, he clicked on a public Internet site he'd designed, enlarged pixels in a prearranged position and inserted information for his contractors. It was much easier than using code. Using space allotted for data, he inserted Masterson's location, a grainy photo of the woman, information about Coulter's right shoulder wound, and orders to kill the woman on sight. Arnold chuckled as he worked the site. To be a kingpin was a power fix and fed his ego. He loved making others do his bidding, especially murder. What a rush!

CHAPTER 16

A Hotel
Sukhumvit Road
Bangkok, Thailand
30 August, 12:24 PM ICT

Once registered at their hotel, Ana Masterson and Major Jon Coulter were escorted to their adjoining second floor rooms. Ana's room smelled of cleaning chemicals and stale cigarettes. Jon put her luggage in the bathtub. She threw back the bed comforter and sheets to expose the mattress. No bedbugs. The night stand held a digital clock radio, low wattage lamp, telephone and hotel directory. Two small upholstered chairs rested beside a small round teak table by a small window. A flat television screen hung on the wall facing the foot of the bed.

After turning on and muting the television, Jon located an English language station on the FM radio.

"What are you doing?"

"Checking for bugs."

"I already checked the sheets."

"Electronic bugs. The listening variety."

"Why? No one knew we'd be here."

"Just sweeping the room to be safe." He glanced at the television. "The TV broadcasts are in Thai." He grabbed a laminated television guide and handed it to her. "You'll find English translations by using FM radio. Each language has a separate FM frequency so foreigners can watch TV in their own language."

Out of habit, he began to dry clean the room for electronic bugs by turning the analog radio dial to the lowest frequency, below eighty-eight megahertz. Since no FM station is assigned below such a low frequency, anything heard there is suspicious.

Increasing the volume, he moved the dial to the right until he came to the first commercial FM station. He whistled as he scanned the dial's low and high ends. The whistling was not heard from the radio.

"How does whistling work?"

"I tuned the radio to a silent frequency and carried it around the room while whistling softly. If there is a bug, the radio will begin picking up its transmissions and make a squeal. By moving the radio around, I can zoom in where it is loudest and find the bug.

She watched him work.

"Your room's clean. Being so close, it cleared my room too." He turned off the TV and readjusted the FM to an easy listening music station before turning it off. "What are your immediate plans?"

"Sleep."

"What about going with me to check out the hotel? I don't like leaving you here." He locked the door joining their rooms.

"No thanks."

He cleared his throat. "Andy said you're my buddy on this mission. Buddies stay together. You shouldn't be alone."

"What can happen with the door locked?"

"Give me your word you'll stay here." At her nod, he said, "Lock the door behind me. Use the bolt. No matter who knocks, don't open either door. Understand?"

"Got it."

"Put your satphone on the window sill to charge. Call if you need me. "

"Will do." She heard him stop when he walked out the door until he heard the bolt slide into place. Ana kicked off her shoes and undressed. Garbed in camouflage-colored lace panties and bra, she glanced at her image in the mirror and jumped into a defensive position. Satisfied she looked dangerous, she found her digital reader, put on her reading glasses and reclined on the bed. She opened her reader to a bookmarked point before resting it on her chest and began talking to herself. "How in the world am I going to search for a mindreacher? Man! VESPER needs an alternative plan. Lots of alternative plans."

Catching motion out of the corner of her eye, she turned to see a four-inch long, light-brown lizard scampering across the pillow a few inches from her face.

"AAAIIIIEEEEEE!" she squealed and rolled off the bed in the opposite direction. Her heart beating fast, she dashed across the room and jumped onto an upholstered chair. Tottering with one foot on the arm and one on the seat, she leaned precariously to reach a hotel bathrobe from inside the closet. She put it on and leaped toward the door. Releasing the bolt with a loud, slamming motion, she jerked the door open and ran into the hall. A hotel porter was nearby.

"Help!" She waved him over.

The uniformed, young man approached with a bow. "May I help madam?" He pronounced madam as 'ma-dom.'

"There's a chameleon in my room! A lizard!"

While the porter entered her room, a dark-suited and sullen looking Asian man was walking down the hallway. Seeing Ana's blonde hair, the man stopped to observe the fracas. Reaching into his shirt pocket, he pulled out a small paper. Comparing an image on the paper to the woman standing in the hallway, with an imperceptible nod and lurking smile, he slipped the paper into his pocket and stepped behind her open door.

The young porter reassured in a singsong voice, "Oh, madam, is *chinchuck*. Not to worry." Smiling, he soothed, "*Chinchuck* not hurt you." The lizard was climbing her hotel room wall.

"I don't care what it is, get rid of it!" She stomped her bare foot and cinched her loosening bathrobe.

An amused cleaning woman walking by handed the porter a broom. She covered a smile with small hands and leaned against the banister to watch the spectacle. Beyond the banister was a wide, spiral staircase of white marble covered with a burgundy carpet. The stairway opening, near the elevator, was about twenty feet from Ana's room.

"Not to worry, madam," the porter repeated and started to leave.

Get rid of it, Ana demanded telepathically.

The young man froze in his tracks. "Yes, madam." He gently swept the lizard from the wall toward the door.

"*Keep going,*" she admonished, Grasping the front of her robe. She was poised to run if the lizard darted toward her.

The cleaning woman hurried away as the porter guided the frightened *chinchuck* along the hall carpet toward the banister. The animal skittered on its four short legs under the banister and disappeared over the floor edge. With its suction grip feet, Ana thought it might walk down the wall to the lower floor. She opened her awareness to track the reptile.

In the confusion, no one noticed the furtive, middle-aged, dark-haired man standing behind Ana's door. His lips curved into a wicked smile. If Ana had known he was there and listened to his thoughts, she would have known the man's bad knee began to ache. He also had the worse case of heartburn he'd ever experienced. Money that his al-Qaeda cell would earn depended upon his next decision. Escape routes went through his mind. With a killers' predatory stare, he pictured how the American woman would die. Flattening himself against the hinges behind Ana's door, he waited.

The porter walked past Ana, down the hall and around a corner. Holding the bannister rail for support, she craned her body outward. Concentrating psychic energy to find the creature and make sure it wouldn't return, she spotted it scurrying across the curved wall toward the lower floor.

The Asian man stepped out from behind her room door. Checking to ensure the hall was void of witnesses, he lowered his right shoulder and ran toward Ana in a battering ram position.

At that moment, the porter walked back around the corner and saw what was happening. He ran toward Ana calling, "Madam. MADAM!"

While using telepathy, she heard nothing. Satisfied the lizard was gone; she straightened and brought her mind to the present. Turning, she saw a man running toward her. She knew his intent. Raising her left forearm as a block, she turned away from him and leaned against the banister. Her right hand gripped the underside of the railing for an anchor. She didn't want to be catapulted over it.

"Lord, help me," she cried out.

"Die, infidel slut," the man uttered in a gravelly voice as his shoulder hit her back left side below the waist. The blow bent her toward her right. Her breath blew out with a whoosh. Their legs tangled. Toppling, her feet lifted off the floor. Knowing his body might stop her twisted fall over the banister, she kept her legs entangled between his. As she was shoved by his momentum, her rising legs slammed into his groin.

"AAGGhhhhh," the man groaned as he was knocked off balance.

She grabbed a fistful of his shirt to pull herself back. With the momentum of his run, her upward kick into his body and pull against his shirt, he was propelled over her. When he flew past her head, she smelled his rancid odor. He grasped at her hair which was too fine for a good grip. Both of them were thrust over the banister.

While being shoved aloft, Ana slid the hand holding the railing further through the opening. Because of her bent arm, her elbow caught when it hit the railing. She pulled her body close to that elbow anchor, tightly grasping her hold on life. The action didn't stop her from flipping over the banister. Her elbow had become an awkward but effective fulcrum. Suspended in space, the weight of her body rested on the elbow of her right arm.

"Allah...," her attacker yelled as he flew across empty space. When his head slammed against the side of the marble staircase, he was knocked unconscious. Gravity accelerated his limp body toward the lobby.

Ana's reading glasses fell off as she screamed.

* * *

Walking across the lobby, Jon was startled by a scream. Then a limp body smashed head first onto the white terrazzo floor about ten feet from him. Breaking bones echoed as blood and brain splattered in all directions. In the frozen instant of silence, Ana's titanium-framed glasses hit the terrazzo and shattered. Jon whipped his head around and looked up. His heart plummeted upon seeing Ana dangling from a banister by one arm. Her long white terrycloth bathrobe was tangled around flailing legs. Pandemonium erupted in the lobby.

Galvanized into action, Jon ran for the stairs, leaped over the first five steps and took the rest three and four at a time. Using obscenities every other word, with clenched teeth he snarled, "Why'd she leave her damn room?"

"Oh nooooo," she yelled.

She would have fallen to the lobby had she not wrapped her right arm around the banister railing. Sharp shoulder pain made her slip a few inches. A furrow of pain arced across her face. Sudden perspiration made her arm slippery. Breathing hard, she kicked at the bathrobe impeding her legs. She tried to grab the banister with her free hand.

Leaning over the railing, the porter grabbed her free arm and pulled. She placed a knee on the floor edge. He helped her over the banister, grunting with the effort. Knees wobbling, she grasped the railing with both hands to steady herself before taking a deep breath. Gathering the robe, she rubbed her elbow and shoulder. Her heart pounded and teeth chattered. "D-d-did you see that?"

"Yes." The frowning porter leaned over the rail to see the bloody scene below and jerked back in shock. "Why did he do that?"

Ana didn't know what to say. How could she tell this young man a terrorist wanted her dead because she could read minds? She slowly shook her head back and forth once.

"Is madam hurt?" His frightened face conveyed alarm.

She cinched the loose robe again, sighing in exasperation. Her knees trembled and teeth chattered. Her shoulder pain was excruciating. She didn't know how normal people not able to release pain killers from their mind could survive life.

"Thank you. God bless you. You s-saved my life. W-what's your name?"

"My name is Samri." He bowed and stepped away. Exhausted from her ordeal, she supported her wrenched elbow and shoulder while padding barefoot back to her room. The porter stayed near the banister and watched her.

In the hotel lobby below, shouting employees and shocked guests appeared frozen in place.

Jon's anger increased with each step. Barely winded, he reached Ana's hotel door just as she was entering the room..

His lips drawn back and teeth clenched, he said, "Fancy meeting you here. I thought you were going to stay in your room."

Eyes opened wide, she stared at him. "I...I..."

"You okay?" He grabbed her shoulders, letting go at her wince. He scanned for another assailant. "Are there more?"

She shrugged. "I don't know." The adrenaline rush made her hands shake.

Jon gently manipulated her arms and shoulders to determine if they were dislocated or broken. "I was in the lobby," he explained. "Ran up here when I saw you." He took a deep breath and expelled it slowly, his anger not subsiding. "What happened?"

"He bulldozed me over the banister."

"I thought you were going to stay in your room."

She related what happened and asked, "He's dead?"

"He is."

"I want to see him."

"Not a good idea."

She defiantly lifted her chin. "I have a r-r-right to see who t-tried to kill me." Tears welled up in her eyes.

"Didn't you hear his mindsong?"

"I was deaf and dumb because I was following that stupid lizard. I killed that man."

"Ana, you defended yourself against a murderer and survived." His piercing eyes narrowed. "You should have stayed in your room."

She opened her mind and listened to him thinking about their compatibility. He was thinking she was a danger magnet, never listened to him, didn't follow directions, and did whatever came into her mind. Humbled, she had to admit he was right.

He continued. "This situation is serious. I need your total cooperation. Any instruction I give you is for your safety."

With a haunted look, she again started to explain what happened. "It was a lizard. I panicked." She appeared to deflate. "I'm so sorry." She wiped moisture from her eyes. Her lips trembled.

"How big was this monster lizard?"

Ashamed, she held her index fingers four-inches apart.

"It's okay. You're safe." Wrapping an arm around her good shoulder, he applied a comforting squeeze. "It's my fault, I shouldn't have left you alone." When he stroked her delicate strands of hair she leaned her head into his hand.

After a few moments, she demanded, "I want to see the body." In anguish over the man's death, she felt guilty being alive.

His stance one of defiance, Jon snorted before he inclined his head. "Get dressed. The police'll want a statement anyway."

A short time later in the descending elevator, he said, "I have to keep you alive to find a mindreacher. We don't know our enemies. In the future, for your own sake, follow my directions."

"I wasn't aware of him until it was too late." She rubbed her burning elbow. Her lower lip disappeared between her teeth. "I hope it never happens again."

Jon quipped, "Being tossed over a banister?"

She answered in a trembling voice, "Being so close to dying." She knew she'd lost his trust and would have to earn it back.

In the hotel lobby, guests were circuitously avoiding the bloody landing site. Uniformed cleaning crews were scrubbing the area with mops and pails of water. Hotel workers hurriedly carried buckets of clean water to the site and buckets of red water out.

"Where is he?" She cradled her right elbow.

Jon spoke with the hotel concierge who led them into a corridor off the lobby. Two Royal Thai policemen stopped them. After explanations and collaboration from the porter, Ana was allowed to see the sheet-covered body on a gurney in the center of a small room.

Jon lifted a corner of the sheet for her to see the lifeless and unknown man.

Blood drained from her face. She whispered, "It's hard to believe he wanted to kill me. He didn't even know me."

Back in her room, Jon helped ice her shoulder and elbow. The hotel's medical doctor arrived and confirmed Jon's diagnosis by proclaiming nothing was broken or dislocated, just strained. She was ordered to rest and apply ice to sore areas as long as it was helpful. Before leaving, the doctor requested she stop by his hotel office in the morning.

Jon paced in her room. "I want to find out if your attacker acted alone. I need to check out several things here in the hotel. After what just happened to you, I don't want to leave you alone. Do you feel up to walking?"

She looked away from him and said, "I think I'd better stay here. I'm exhausted."

He gave her a stern look. "Not alone."

"After what's happened, I won't budge from this room. I swear. On my word."

They heatedly discussed what to do. When Jon finally accepted that she would honor her word to stay in her locked room, he walked out and stopped.

She softly closed the door before angrily slamming the deadbolt into the lock position. Leaning her head against the door, she lamented, "Why was I afraid of such a small animal?" She picked up and shook her suit jacket to rid it of any lurking animals or insects and put it on a hanger in the closet. Next, she jiggled the draperies back and forth, looked under furniture, and examined inside her closeted shoes. Ready to jump at the first hint of another lizard, she called out, "Any more of you here?"

Slowly opening her awareness, she located cockroaches behind the baseboard. Wishing for bug spray and keeping her mind open for a lizard, she grabbed the satphone and punched in Jon's number to apologize again.

With no warning a fluent and powerful male voice entered her mind.

Sawadee khrup.!!!!!!!!! Khum cheu! Arai!
Ahhh...Americane! Woman?

The man pulled out of her mind as fast as he had entered.

Too surprised to be shocked, she shivered, struggling to recall what words were sent to her. She had just started to hear his mindsong, before it was cut off. Never having experienced such raw mental power, cold sweat formed on her back. Remembering the taxi driver at the airport, she knew the first two words he'd spoken were "hello." She murmured, "He attached an emotion through his send. I wonder if I do that? He knew instantly I'm American and female." She took a deep breath and expelled it. "Now what?"

She was deep in reflection when Jon's voice startled her.

He asked, "What's up?"

She'd forgotten she was holding the phone to her ear. Shaking her head to get back to the present, she reported, "I just had a mind send. From a man."

"You locked in your room?"

"Yes. You won't believe how it felt. He sent feelings! Words with feelings! I'm so excited." She closed her eyes to remember the pleasurable sensation of the send.

"Are you locked in?"

"I am."

"I'll be right there."

Within a few minutes he arrived. By the time she finished describing her experience and her impressions of the contact, she'd calmed somewhat.

"Tell me again what happened," he demanded. "Don't leave anything out." He listened to her story a second time. She theorized her mental search for a chinchuck was detected by an aware mindreacher. Her voice quivering, she repeated his telepathic message.

"You're scared."

With a shocked expression, she said, "If he wanted, he could have controlled me like a puppet. He was that powerful." She was sitting with crossed legs in one of the upholstered chairs. Her feet were nervously jiggling up and down. Her hands tightly gripped the chair arms. She kept looking up, her glance moving back and forth.

"I leave you alone for a few minutes and look what happens," he teased.

"It was so exciting. No one ever used telepathy to contact me before."

"We should celebrate. Why not order the best they have from room service for dinner?"

"Oh, no you don't. I want to experience what I can in the short time I'll be here. Let's eat out and enjoy Thai cuisine."

"Let's lay low. Our best option for now is the hotel restaurant."

"You think I'll be contacted again?"

"Count on it."

"It had to be a Joburg mindreacher." She bit her lower lip. "His touch was so strong! It invaded my mind as though it was the most natural thing in the world."

"We should've been expecting a contact," he reminded. "Telepathy isn't a one way street. You'll no longer be the telepathic initiator."

Her face was pale. Her expression solemn. She looked at him with apprehension.

Jon asked, "Can you re-establish the link?"

"I don't know how." She crossed and uncrossed her arms. Her gaze flicked about the room. She was in constant motion.

Gently, Jon put his hands on her shoulders. In a low, calm tone he said, "It's okay. Relax. Just be open to another contact."

"I'll work on that after dinner."

Trying to calm herself, she took a deep breath. Now that the experience of a mindreacher had been thrust upon her, her heart beat fast and furious. She wanted to meet the mindreacher, but dreaded contact.

She said, "My talent is nothing compared to his." Fear began to enter her realization of what had happened.

"I'll be with you."

"What if he takes control of me? Or you? You wouldn't even know."

"Would you?"

She stopped moving, sat down and stared at him.

"I don't know." In frustration, she thrust her head back, clenched her hands into tight fists and thrust them skyward. Opening her hands wide, she closed them again while bringing them to her chest. Crossing her arms onto her chest, she brought her hands under her chin and put her head down. Her shoulders expanded upward with a big breath. "There was a friendly feel to him." Seeing Jon's look of skepticism, she continued regretfully, "There might not be another contact for days."

"Can you take notes during telepathy?"

"I never have…"

"I'm trying to work with you." Lowering his head he looked into her eyes. "How can I protect you if I don't know what's happening? My clues are only visuals and sound. I need your telepathic information. Lots of information."

"I'll try to tell you everything."

Jon thrust his open hands toward her and shouted, "Try? You'll try?" He shut his mouth to keep from swearing and clenched his teeth. His face reddened. His hands clenched into fists. He wanted to give her a dirty lecture.

"You have to work with me."

Feeling frustrated and ashamed, she stood, lowered her head and stepped back. "I know. I know."

He didn't believe her. "Keep your suitcase packed. We may have to leave quickly."

CHAPTER 17

Hotel Restaurant
Sukhumvit Road
Bangkok, Thailand
30 August, 7:30 PM ICT

Upon entry into the restaurant, Jon scanned for firearms and noted customer positions. Enticing aromas filled the darkened room. Glasses clinked. Background chatter was light. When seated at a four-chair, linen-covered table, Ana requested recommendations for local dishes from the waiter.

The young man responded with, "*Khao! Phat. Muu?*"

Surprised, Ana asked, "Did you just say "cowpot moo? Doesn't sound very appetizing."

The waiter smiled. "Taste vury good. Not spicy hot. Many farang enjoy with pork."

"I don't usually eat meat." She leaned toward Jon and whispered with raised eyebrows. "Can you picture something called cowpot?"

"Madam, our chef can cook with no meat. Is fried rice."

"Okay. I'll try your cowpot with no meat."

Jon said. "I want a thick Kobe steak. Rare. Baked potato and salad."

She asked, 'What's Kobe?"

"The best steak I've ever had," he replied and tossed the menu to the table.

"I'm not much of a meat eater."

"Would you like some milk?"

"I'm too thirsty. Water first."

""---no ice with lemon and lime," they recited at the same time and laughed.

The waiter asked Jon, "What will madam have to drink?"

"One cold and capped Dasani for the lady. Do you have pasteurized milk?"

"Yes sir."

"Bring a glass of milk for the lady and a long neck beer for me." The server acknowledged their order and bowed as he backed away. "I'd rather have Scotch, but better stay alert."

She asked, "Is Kobe a breed of cattle?"

"There's more to it than that." He scanned the room as he talked. "They were bred in Japan over 2,000 years ago. The cattle are fed beer to increase their appetite in the summer and given corn and other foods to fatten them up. They're massaged to work layers of fat into the muscle. The meat's pink, not red. So tender, you can cut it with a fork. I'll let you try it."

Their waiter served Ana's milk and a sealed bottle of water with a small upside down glass over it. Jon was given a bottle of Singha beer with a small glass.

Placing a container of sweeteners on the table, their waiter suggested, "Milk is better with this."

Jon popped the lid off his beer and quickly drank half the contents.

An elderly, Caucasian gentleman with white hair, a sparse goatee and floppy gut at the next table leaned toward them. Speaking with an impeccable English accent, the man commented, "Enjoy our local beer, my friend." He smoothed his sparse goatee. "One preservative they've used in local brews has been formaldehyde." His grin showed a deep jowl line in each cheek. He introduced himself. "Warrington. Arthur Warrington."

Ana's eyes widened. "Formaldehyde's poison."

Warrington nodded.

"Is Singha the brewery name?" She examined the label of Jon's beer.

"Yes and no." He twitched his beard. "It's a mythical creature similar to a lion. You're new here, eh?"

"We arrived today," she answered, a sparkle in her eyes.

Jon glowered and whispered, "Don't talk to him."

She whispered back, "He's trying to be nice."

"What about following my directions?"

Showing no remorse, she glowered back. "He looks innocent."

Warrington asked her, "How do you find the Thais?"

"I love the respectful bowing," she answered.

"It's called a sawadee," he explained in a soft voice while leaning toward their table. "These people make time for courtesy. Sawadees show everyone who has higher status. The lower someone bows their head, the more honored the person they are sawadeeing. However, no one's head may be higher than the king's."

"I hope he's tall," she said with a chuckle.

"Legend has it a Thai king once reclined on the floor of the palace throne room to make an approaching adversary keep his head lower by slithering like a snake. What a sense of humor!" He chuckled. "These are a wonderful people, but life is expensive for them. Tariffs are over two-hundred percent on about everything but books. We transplants buy local products when possible." Warrington lifted his wine glass in salute, "We *farangs*, or round eye foreigners, have to stick together and share information."

Ana leaned toward the Englishman. "Why do they say hello differently? One will say *sawadee kha* and another *sawadee khrup*.

"It's sex." Warrington chuckled. "Everything revolves around sex. *Sawadee kha* is 'hello' spoken by a woman. *Sawadee khrup* is the male version. By the way, you'll love the food! A multitude of spices to burn out your nasal passages. To prove we foreigners can't stomach local foods, an unscrupulous cook might add extra hot sauce as a joke. Destroys taste buds for weeks." He laughed. "Here …," he gestured about the room, "it's well prepared, safe, and delicious."

"Keep your guard up," Jon whispered, stood and walked away toward the entrance. Keeping Ana in his eyesight, he called Andy on his satphone. When Andy answered and greetings were exchanged, Jon asked in a low voice, "When will my friends arrive in Bangkok?"

"Should have arrived today."

"Timely."

Andy asked, "What's the problem?"

"Check the transcription."

"On it."

"Expect to be surprised. Ana may have found you a mindreacher. Let me know what's happening at your end."

"Will do. Charlie Mike." Andy's comment of "Charlie Mike" meant to continue the mission.

Terminating the connection, Jon pocketed the phone and looked forward to hefting his SIG.

A oval plate of fried rice arrived with a large spoon. The mound of rice in the center was decorated around the edges with thin slices of cucumber, tomato, hard boiled and quartered egg, parsley, lime wedges and miniature ears of corn. Sprinkling the concoction liberally with lime juice, Ana sampled the dish, savored the taste and ate with gusto. Jon wolfed down his meal.

"Umm, this is good," she exclaimed between mouthfuls. She kept looking at Jon.

He said, "Is something on your mind?"

"My contact. Do you think he could have manipulated my mind?" She paled.

"I admit my ignorance of your mental rigmarole. I don't know a thing about it except to observe reactions of others." He caught the waiter's attention and held up the empty beer bottle. The waiter acknowledged the request and left. "Next question?"

"What's the primary religion here?"

"Buddhism. Indians are primarily Hindu."

She cracked a smile and met his gaze. "I'd like to have the translation of *Khum cheu! Arai.*"

"I'll get it for you after dinner."

When Jon later escorted Ana to her room, he admonished, "Lock yourself in. Don't leave the room."

"I'll be here." She disliked being bossed around. Within five minutes, when he knocked on their adjoining room door and identified himself, she opened the door.

"When he said, *Khum cheu! Arai,*' he was asking for your name."

"Next time he contacts me I'll tell him."

"If he's a mindreacher, he already knows."

She made a slight groaning sound. "I wonder what else he knows?" She made a questioning gesture with uplifted palms.

"Whatever he wants, I would guess. How fast can he scan your mind?"

"Good question."

"Can you initiate contact with the guy? Home in on his beam or something?"

She laughed. "It doesn't work that way."

"How does it work?"

"Beats me. Sometimes I feel I'm just a passenger when my mind goes out to play."

"Can you turn it off?"

"Not easily."

He gave her an appreciative once over. "You want me to stick around?" He leaned against the door frame, hands in his pockets.

"No," she answered with a grin. Slow to continue, she added, "I'll be fine."

I can sleep on the floor, your chair … or your bed." He stifled a grin.

She tilted her head. "No need. I learned my lesson. I'll stay here."

Before Jon left her room, he called the American Embassy. When an after-hour Marine guard answered, he introduced himself and asked, "Do you have a package waiting for me?" Hearing an affirmative answer, he said, "I'll pick it up early tomorrow morning." He paused and added, "How much advance notice do you need to arrange a flight to northern Thailand?"

Ana sat quietly listening.

After a short discussion, Jon said, "I'll notify you within an hour of our planned departure. Thanks for the information. *Semper Fi.*" To Ana he said, "The Embassy will provide helicopter transportation to Don Mueang airport. A waiting military transport will fly us from there to Udon Airport. We can take a taxi the last thirty or so miles to Nong Khai."

When he left, she leaned her forehead against the door frame and smiled. She felt safe and went to bed.

A light sleeper, she awakened when a chinchuck fell onto her bed from the ceiling, bounced, and scurried off. She tried to slow her sudden rapid heartbeat. Jon had told her *chinchucks* were harmless.

"Is my bed your trampoline?" She turned on the light. Not seeing the lizard, she hesitantly opened her mind for a search. Instantaneously there was a mental intrusion.

Hello. Who are you? It was telepathy from the same man as before.
You're the intruder, she responded. *Wouldn't it be proper for you to identify yourself first?*
My apologies. My name is Santad. Her mind picked up his slight amusement and sensed another mind slide silently into the conversation.
I'm Ana Masterson. Who's your friend?
!!!!!!!!!! His name is Boonrith.
She loved his mental exclamation, likening it to the feel of a bubbling chuckle. She asked, is there anything specific you want or need?
No one in Thailand used mental touch before. He used the Queen's English. They withdrew before she could respond.
She'd never conversed using telepathy because she had never encountered a telepath. Telepathy had always been in one direction, from her. Apprehensive and yet delighted to have this communication opportunity, she checked her watch. It was after midnight. She wondered if they would contact her again. Her hands shook as she grabbed a notepad and pen.

* * *

In another part of the city, Santad and Boonrith looked at one another in consternation.
The only other person Santad knew with psychic skills was Vaji, an elderly monk in Laos. When Santad was born in Thailand, Vaji was instantly aware of him from hundreds of kilometers away. Just as easily, Santad had picked up Ana's telepathic power across a city with over twelve million inhabitants. What concerned him were malignant thoughts he'd picked up about the American woman from a man near her location. Speaking in Thai, Santad spoke to his telepath apprentice, Boonrith.
"Did you feel the mind of that evil man near the American woman?" At Boonrith's slow nod, Santad asked, "Why would someone hate her so? From hearing her mind, I think she is a good person."
Boonrith suggested, "We need to learn more about both of them."

Santad contacted the American woman again. Entering her mind with a tone conveying bowing submissiveness, he began, *Please, Madam Ana, why are you are in Bangkok?* *To find a strong telepath,* she answered. *Were you born in South Africa?* He pulled out of her mind. Concerned, he asked his friend, "Is she looking for me?"

Boonrith answered, "You're the only telepath in Thailand."

"Why did she mention South Africa?"

"Ask her."

"I will talk with her later." He projected into Ana's mind, *Prung! Nee. Tomorrow. We'll talk tomorrow.* He stayed in the peripheral edge of her conscious mind.

* * *

Ana had enjoyed the friendly warmth of Santad's send. She felt a strange emptiness when he left her mind. As adrenalin surged through her, she shook with excess energy. She could barely finish writing notes for Jon and hoped Santad contacted her again. She needed to talk with him about VESPER.

She said Andy's name aloud several times. There was no response. Knowing all sounds were recorded, she related facts about interactions with her first telepathic contact. She ended her story with, "I'm uncomfortable being slammed in the mind without notice. I know that's what I'm supposed to expect, but it's unsettling to not control the conversation. A new experience for me."

CHAPTER 18

Wat Pho Temple
Bangkok, Thailand
31 August 12:07 AM ICT

Resting under a tree in their temple compound, the dark skinned Santad and his lighter skinned friend blended into the night. Their robes of the Theravada Buddhist sect of monks were in different saffron colors, a common sight. From a distance, mottled city night lights filtered through the trees. Saffron hues of their robes and the dim lights created a scene resembling an impressionist painting.

Boonrith was seated on the grass in a lotus position with his hands resting on his knees, palms up. Slender Santad squatted beside him seated on his heels, his robe tight around his legs. Boonrith brushed his hand lightly over the soft growth of emerging hair on his shaved head. Like other monks, they had their heads and eyebrows shaved twice a month at full and new moon phases. Evil spirits couldn't grab their hair to hang on to them if they were hairless.

With wisdom beyond his twenty-two years, Boonrith suggested gathering facts before trying to solve problems created by the American woman.

Santad made mental scans in her vicinity. He identified the killer, an Asian man whose directive was to kill anyone in his way when eliminating the American woman named Ana Masterson. Hesitant to become involved in an international terrorist dilemma, The two monks agreed to proceed slowly.

"It makes no sense," Santad said. "Her mind sounds, the tagline of her soul, is wholesome and uplifting. You can't fake that." Under trees in a grassy area within a large compound, the two were tired.

"Did you misread her?"

Santad presented the figure of a tall holy man as he stood, more slender compared to the shorter and large-boned Boonrith. He deliberated before replying. "Let me try to find him again."

When originally communicating with the American woman, Santad had been accidentally drawn to the nearby killer who had been thinking her name. The killer had a bizarre and unpredictable mental chaos of one whose brain had been damaged by drug use. Such a compromised condition translated into additional danger.

With concentration, he found the assassin and slipped into the murderer's mind. The opened thoughts exposed one of most evil sociopaths of Santad's experience. Discovering the man wanted to kill Ana because of her telepathic ability, he quickly withdrew and told Boonrith of his findings.

Boonrith whispered, "If the murderer learns we are telepaths, we may become targets."

Sitting on his heels, Santad's attitude was dismal. "What do we do? We can't let him know of us."

Boonrith agreed. After a long discussion, he suggested, "We should distance ourselves from this American woman." At Santad's nod, he continued, "We have many decisions and much to do. Let us proceed with caution."

Santad gazed at the wat, the main temple. "When I invaded her mind, I learned why she is here and about the man who travels with her."

"Her husband?"

"Bodyguard. She is on a dangerous quest. Helping her may prove difficult and make us vulnerable to the same threats." A jagged intake of breath exposing his emotion, he stood. "She needs to know about the murderer following her. What do you say? Should we tell her?"

Boonrith answered thoughtfully, "Yes. When?" He raised his eyes to Santad. "Are you still within her mind?"

Santad gave a small nod.

"Should you still be there?"

"My friend, there is no directive in the Buddhist Basket of Rules about telepathy. That written guide for holy men does not address the subject. Because of this omission, the two of us need to meditate, clear our minds and see the truth of this situation.

We have to honor life and Buddha and do what is morally and ethically correct. Staying in her mind, in my opinion, is the right thing to do." He paused. "The American is not aware of me." He sent a mental message to Boonrith which contained mirth. *After all, I have a light touch, yes?*

Boonrith laughed. *Yes. A very light touch.* Becoming serious, he asked, *What will happen when she learns you invaded her mind? Or that you remained there? She may not appreciate your invasion. As holy men, we have an obligation to be morally correct in every aspect of our lives.*

They continued discussing the American woman, her problems, and possible solutions. After analyzing options open to them, the two men decided to outwit the man bent on harming her while remaining in the background. Knowing the mission to help find terrorists was currently the most important goal in Ana Masterson's life, they vowed to help without getting personally involved. After all, she was a woman. Buddhist rules applied to prohibitions concerning females. Even though what she was doing was admirable, they had to keep their distance.

Santad held hope that his childhood mentor could help them purge her assassin. To apprise the senior Laotian monk of the situation, he began a mental send. Traveling at a speed equivalent to light, the telepath let the elder Laotian monk know what had transpired.

In flawless British English, the Laotian monk immediately replied. *Most gracious Santad, I see a woman wanting to rid the world of recent evil. She searches for a Johannesburg, South Africa, person. Yet, someone wishes to harm her.*

Santad sent. *Yes, honorable Vaji. What should we do?*

Vaji replied. *There must be a separation between the American woman and her would-be assassin. Have her travel to the northern part of Bangkok at dawn. Enter the mind of her assailant when we finish this conversation. Mentally persuade the man to travel south into Malaysia. Send the American woman to me when the assassin is heading toward Malaysia and she is safe from harm. I know one for whom she searches and will begin preparations for their meeting. Thank you for allowing me to assist you, Santad. I pray we will reach a satisfactory conclusion for everyone's benefit.*

Benevolent and calming love emanated from the elderly monk. There had never been hate, greed, or vanity. He was so advanced in mental techniques, Santad never knew whether Vaji was within his mind or not and didn't care. Since Vaji often stayed in mental contact with him during his youth, Santad had no qualms or moral ethics of lingering in another's mind. The younger monk deeply appreciated and honored his unseen and unmet mentor.

Santad sent respectfully with a smile, *Thank you honorable Vaji. I look forward to the day we shall meet.*

Vaji replied, *I also look forward to such an eventful occasion my young friend.*

With anticipation for what he knew was to become a true adventure, Santad hastily turned to his friend. "Boonrith, we need to persuade the American woman to go to Laos. You plan well. Tell me what we should do." They discussed how to handle the situation.

Santad sent Ana a telepathic message: *After breakfast, go north of Bangkok with your man friend.*

* * *

In the hotel, Ana awakened, alarmed at having no control over mental invasions from Santad. She reached too late for the bag of melted ice slipping off her shoulder. It fell and splashed to the floor. Blinking, she replied to Santad telepathically. *Excuse me. What did you say?*

Upset that Santad could enter her mind whenever he wanted, she admitted to herself she was guilty of the same thing. In a revelation about her past attitudes, she whispered, "How rude I've been." She abruptly sat up. "He entered my mind while I was asleep. Could he have changed it? Or tried to control me?" She shivered. "No, his mindsong is pure."

The realization of why others had been wary of her telepathy hit home. "I've been so selfish." She thought of all the people she must have hurt in the past with her flippant attitude about telepathy. "No wonder I was attacked as a kid." Self-revelations about her life and how she could have been more respectful to others continued. Then she thought about Jon Coulter and panicked. "I need to apologize to him. It's a wonder he's still here."

She was wide awake and thinking. Each idea was processed instantly as quadrillions of connections between glia and neurons transmitted her reasoning. There was plenty of space for such energy to flow as thirty-thousand neurons merely equaled the width of a human hair.

Santad had patiently waited for Ana to calm herself. Then he sent, *After breakfast, please hire a car and driver. With your gentleman friend, drive to north Bangkok for the day. I leave you now. Do not be frightened, my American friend.*

He slipped out of her mind as unobtrusively and quickly as he had entered.

Santad's departure from her mind created a vacuous sensation. She wondered why he thought she was frightened. Apprehensive, she felt something significant was going to happen.

I don't know Bangkok, she sent back. *Can you give me an address?* She waited. There was no response. *Are you still in my mind?* There was no response. She was unsure if he received her message or how to proceed.

* * *

Upon mentally locating the assassin, Santad made a clandestine telepathic incursion into the man's mind. He inserted information that Ana Masterson was currently driving south on the International Asian Highway to Singapore, Malaysia. The assassin was directed to immediately find and follow her. It was with satisfaction Santad knew the implanted directions would work. Within the hour, the assassin was driving south out of Bangkok.

CHAPTER 19

A Hotel
Sukhumvit Road
Bangkok, Thailand
31 August, 7:00 AM ICT

Before dawn, Jon grabbed a taxi and headed to the American embassy. He picked up his SIG and ammunition from a Marine guard. He'd missed the heft of his pistol. Now loaded, he slipped it into his waist holster and secured it under his right pocket. With a Marine guard watching, he adjusted the retention strap and positioned it to rest securely against his body. The open muzzle design of the holster allowed the barrel to be contained comfortably. To an observer, it would appear Jon had his right front pocket filled. The holster was comfortable enough for him to wear twenty-four hours a day. A loose shirt or jacket effectively concealed both holster and SIG. If he decided to go shirtless, it was designed to be hidden by his slacks. He could also tuck the weapon under his back waistband.

At breakfast in the hotel cafe, Ana explained what had happened the previous night and let him read her notes about conversations that had taken place. She apologized for her past attitude and promised he would find her easier to work with in the future. After explaining Santad's directive to drive north, she confessed at not understanding why they were requested to do so or knowing where they would end up.

He reminded her, "Andy ordered me to follow any telepaths' lead. He's assuming they all have high morals and know what's happening around us. Do you think your Santad is right?"

"I think he has high morals." She explained what she had learned about the man through his mindsong.

Jon said, "To find other mindreachers, you need to keep your awareness open all the time or periodically."

"Maybe once every fifteen minutes?"

"Why not? If Santad's one, let's hope he'll want to help VESPER."

"He may not be a mindreacher."

"He'd still be useful."

While Jon arranged for a driver and car, Ana went to the hotel jewelry shop. Shown samples of her birthstone on a black velvet tray, she selected two. Before the shop closed that evening, in a rush job, the larger black star sapphire would be mounted as a pendent and the smaller one in a ring. She had always loved mythology which called her birthstone a holy gem. Since they were mined in Thailand, she knew they would be meaningful souvenirs.

Once in the car with their driver, they left the hotel heading north. Traffic moved slowly and was deadlocked on most thoroughfares. When the traffic signal changed, their driver gracefully waved his outstretched arm up and down out the window to signal a left turn. Turning drivers behind them encroached and copied the action, overlapping their cars to the inside of the turn by several feet. Five cars trailed out in the turn as one long row of over-lapping vehicles. They effectively obstructed oncoming traffic as they completed the turn. In Bangkok's major traffic hang-ups, drivers had learned if they didn't fendergate other vehicles during turns, they may wait a long time for the next opportunity to make a turn. Bangkok had major traffic problems.

They were stuck in traffic when Ana received a telepathic message from Santad.

Where are you? Uhhh, a moment...

She waited while he visualized the vicinity using her optical senses. *Nii aria! Too far south!*

Leaning forward, she directed the driver, "We need to drive north."

"*Khao! Jai,*" the driver responded, motioning to the traffic. "I try. Too much traffic."

She sent to Santad, *Where are you?* She expected to see him soon.

I don't have to be close to hear your mind. I want to be sure of your intentions and ... sincerity.

Anyone who would drive in this traffic to meet you must be sincere, she sent with a grin. *Don't you agree?*

!!!!!! You are sincere. We meet later. In two days.

What? Can't I see you today? Apprehensive, she wanted to know who and where he was. All she knew was his first name. She wanted to meet and talk with him.

Jon asked, "What's up?" He had seen her stiffen and look anxiously around. He pulled out his SIG. It was obvious something was happening. When she didn't answer, he assumed she was using telepathy. Not knowing what to expect or from what direction danger might arrive, he went into high alert mode. "Telepaths," he muttered with impatience.

I will contact you later, Santad sent in a relaxed manner. E*njoy the city. Stay in north Bangkok until sunset.*

Wait! I want to talk with you.

I repeat, stay away from the city until evening. A man at your hotel wants to hurt you.

He already did.

Another man.

Frightened, she sat back heavily into the seat and saw Jon holding his SIG. "Why'd you take out your gun?"

"Damned if I know. You tell me." He holstered the weapon.

A tingle of fear shot through her. She relayed Santad's information. "We should believe him."

Jon warned, "Do you realize you're leaving me out of the communication loop? Remember what Andy said? We're a two man team. Team building depends upon how we communicate with each other. Did you hear the word 'communicate' just then? You are not communicating. Not before, during or after your mental modes. I get nothing! Hear me? Nothing! I don't even know when you're doing your mental gymnastics. What you tell me later, if at all, is only what you think might be essential. Without realizing it, you're probably leaving out important information. How do I know what you're talking about or what's being planned? Help me out here."

"I'm sorry," she began. "I told you what happened."

His voice rose in volume. "Your telepathic friend tells you we're safe if we stay away from the hotel. He gives us no facts or explanation. We don't know who he is or whether he's telling the truth. He could be leading us into more danger. What can I base decisions on if I have no data?" Jon paused to calm himself. "Listen. Missions are normally discussed and researched. Intelligence is gathered. Maps and photos studied. Reconnaissance completed. All this before a mission. Have you noticed that's missing here? I'm running blind and wondering what in the hell just happened."

"Santad is safe. I'd know if there was deceit in his send."

"You trust him absolutely?" She nodded. "You'd stake your life on him?" She dipped her head again. "Both our lives?"

"Yes."

"I'm not reassured. Could be a set up. If he's a powerful mindreacher he could make you believe whatever he wanted."

She tried to placate him. "It isn't a set up. I'm not trying to hide anything." She massaged her sore shoulder.

Agonizing over her lack of understanding, Jon fumed and glared at her. "Do you think I can plan tactical positioning without knowing what's happening?"

"I don't know what tactical positioning is."

"A Marine's prepared for anything and ready to react when in the field. Around you, its twenty-four-seven. Having a little information would help. Has your Santad been inside my mind? If I find out he was, he's dirt."

"He's not *my* Santad. I don't know when he's in my mind so how can I tell if he's in yours?"

Inhaling deeply, he looked around. "This is unlike any mission I've ever been on. At least I'm armed." He spoke louder for Andy to be tagged with his comment, "Andy, I'm not the man for this job!" Not easily aggravated, he scowled and muttered words too profane for Ana to hear. That's when he realized how much he missed sharing obscenities during operations. "Damn!"

She positioned her face in front of his and shouted, "Double damn." She crossed her arms and leaned away. After silent moments she mentioned, "Santad's postponing our meeting."

"Why?"

She relayed what she knew.

* * *

An atmospheric temperature inversion was taking place over Bangkok. Heat aloft kept haze of exhaust fumes and smells of petrol near the ground. Ana scrunched her face at the heavy stench. After an hour of being in the midst of slowed traffic, they were finally seeing progress toward Bangkok's northern environs.

She relaxed. "Traffic's horrible. How do these people get back and forth to work without being late?"

"I think local businesses keep nearby apartment buildings for key employees. Guess why there's a wind sock on so many roofs?"

"Helicopters for the owners?"

She pointed to a water buffalo standing in muddy water near a klong bank. A teen-aged girl stood on the animal's back holding a ten-foot long bamboo pole. A small white fishing net was attached to her pole like an upside-down parachute. The girl lifted the net in and out of the water catching flopping minnows. Throwing them back into the water, she dipped the net again and caught a larger fish. Reaching hand over hand on the pole, she pulled the net closer. Gathering the fish, she placed it in a rectangular, plastic, water bucket strapped to the buffalo's side. She then extended the net to continue fishing.

When they drove by an open air market, Ana requested the driver to stop. Jon agreed they could take a short break and they exited the car.

A sweet, caramel aroma of fried bananas filled the air. Chattering of roadside merchants and shoppers mingled with the laughter of playing children. Walking at her back left, Jon continually scanned the area looking for anyone giving Ana undue attention. Vendors wore such baggy clothing, any of them could conceal a weapon. He kept a hand softly pressed against her back in case he had to quickly move her out of harm's way. The driver walked behind the duo. The crowd eddied around them.

Sheet-sized, cotton canopies of vibrant, spectral colors billowed skyward. Tall bamboo poles anchored canopy corners to create individual vendor stalls. Fruit, vegetables, clothing, handmade crafts, electronics and miscellaneous items were displayed on fragile tables and the ground.

Ana didn't recognize most of the produce on the tables. Her hand hovered over one. Their driver surprised her by pronouncing the fruit name. She repeated the gesture over others and listened to him say mangosteen, jackfruit, pomelo, durian and custard apple. On the ground, spread newspapers were partially covered with slabs of meat. Vendors waved rolled up paper over the meat to disperse milling flies. Nude children, about four years old, wore gold chains around their waist and played tag with one another. One saw Ana, screamed, and ran to hide behind his mother's long skirt.

"Not to worry, please," their driver consoled. "Child has not seen *farang* before. Your round, blue eyes frighten him."

Jon reminded her, "You don't have a Mongoloid or Asian eye. You're a round eye. A monster to kids who haven't seen a blue-eyed blonde."

She looked to the child's mother and smiled before bargaining for a papaya with the woman.

Using a machete, the female vendor peeled half the papaya with a practiced motion and dribbled lime juice over it. Halving it, she handed half to Ana.

Taking the fruit nestled in a folded newspaper, Ana hesitantly took a small bite, expecting a sour lime taste. The lime, however, had made the papaya more delicious than any she'd ever eaten. While encouraging Jon to share in the delicacy, she watched him tense. The direction of his glance was an elderly, white haired local woman heading toward Ana with a determined walk. Jon began to intercept and then stepped aside. As the woman passed she touched Ana's arm, smiled, and sheepishly hurried on her way.

Their driver commented, "Is good luck to touch pale *farang*. Like touching starlight." Laugh lines crinkled the corners of his eyes. "Old people and children touch for luck." He touched her arm to demonstrate and hesitated. Touching again, he looked astonished. "You have hair on your arm." He bent over to take a closer look. He ran his hand across her arm marveling at the sensation.

She hadn't noticed before, but none of the locals around them had body hair. Once again she was different, only this time it was amusing.

Jon instinctively tensed as two barefoot children wearing simple cotton shirts and short pants ran toward them. He relaxed when he sensed no ensuing danger. Their clothing was too snug for bombs. The youngsters lightly touched Ana's arm and ran away giggling.

Ana listened to area mindsongs. Because of similarities, she could easily match children with parents. She skirted an elderly woman whose wrinkled face was smiling. Her gray hair was pulled under a wide brimmed and tattered straw hat. Three scars on the woman's face seemed to curve toward her sunken mouth. Barefoot, the woman rested in a squatting position with both feet flat on the ground, bent knees spread, and buttocks resting on her heels. A faded, black, ankle-length skirt tightly covered her legs to her ankles. The woman's right hand topped a mass of green bananas at her side. A preteen girl, squatting beside the woman, supported a baby against her back. The child was secured within a sling of black fabric.

The woman laughed with a passing customer. Ana gasped. The woman's remnant teeth, gums and tongue were blood red. Seeing Ana's shocked expression, the woman laughed harder. Her amusement quickly lessened into a cackle.

Ana whispered to Jon, "That poor woman. Is she contagious?"

"It's not a disease," he replied. "It's from chewing betel nuts." At her confused expression he added, "They're used to treat glaucoma and are a mild narcotic. Stains the mouth blood-red. People who don't care how they look. They chew it as a stimulant. The stain lasts years."

Ana tried to remember where she'd heard the word 'betel' before. Enjoying an 'aha' moment, she finally understood why the famous red star in the constellation of Orion may have been named Betelgeuse. Both the nut and star created a red color.

Green leaf-wrapped packages resembling decks of cards tied with string were stacked symmetrically on two grass-woven trays to one side of the old woman. Locals stopped to buy several. Ana examined one. Jon selected two of the sweet smelling packages, paid for them and handed one to Ana. The driver hovered beside her.

"Is *khao lam*, Madam," the driver told her.

"Sticky rice," Jon added. "Giant rice grains, sweetened and steamed with coconut milk in a bamboo joint."

"Safe to eat?"

"It's been steamed." They each sampled a packet.

She licked her fingers. "Good stuff." She pointed to red and green chilies for sale. "Hot peppers?"

"*Prik kee nooh*,"the driver answered."Too hot for *farang*." He plucked one off a display and plopped it into his mouth with a confident smile.

Telepathically checking his taste senses, she found his smile an act. Tears of pain pooled in his eyes. She gave him an innocent look. "May I buy you some?"

He raised his hand palm outward and mumbled, "No, madam." When she turned away, he spit out the burning mass with a vengeance. With each passing stranger, Jon's touch against her back strengthened. Sensing Jon's forced vigilance, Ana ended her sightseeing excursion, they continued their drive.

* * *

Santad and Boonrith were pleased that Ana's assassin was driving toward Malaysia.

"I hope he stays in Malay," Boonrith declared.

Santad laughed and said, "If he returns, we'll make him go to Cambodia."

In good humor, they attended to temple duties.

CHAPTER 20

A Hotel
Sukhumvit Road
1 September, 7:45 AM ICT

The next morning, Ana knew she would not meet with Santad for another day. That gave her time to visit Bangkok.

During breakfast in the hotel, she pleaded with Jon to visit one temple. Against his better judgement, he relented.

When they arrived at the Wat Pho Buddhist compound, laughter of touring children and teachers merged with tinkling temple bells. Children in each group were dressed in identical colors, their well-groomed attire consisting of white buttoned shirts with dark-colored skirts or short pants. She appreciated seeing a pack of boys dressed in clean, brown, loose-fitting uniforms of the International Boy Scouts. Bright-yellow bandanas were anchored at their necks with a copper ring. The left side of each brimmed, khaki hat was curled upward and secured with a yellow troop badge.

Jon looked around. "What do you think?"

"The temple is magnificent. Why do they have carved wooden hooks along the roof?"

"Same reason temple doors are narrower at the top. To catch evil spirits. Have you heard from your mindreacher?"

"Give me a minute." She opened her awareness and was immediately contacted.

Sawadee Krup!!!!!!!

She answered his mental greeting while giving Jon a thumb up. *Hello Santad!*

Excited at his strong send, she looked around. Chattering tourists of all nationalities milled about as she sought her elusive telepathic friend. Leaning toward Jon, she whispered, "He's close."

"Where?" He surveyed the crowd.

Looking around at everyone, she admitted, "I don't know. Does anyone look interested in us?"

"Not yet." He lit a cigarette while studying the compound. He attempted to be nonchalant as he drew in a long pull of smoke. He exhaled in burps of circular donut shaped puffs. His eyes missed nothing.

Thinking Santad might be a temple vendor, she nudged Jon toward a vendor cart displaying stacks of temple rubbings. The smiling cart vendor attracted Ana's attention and gestured toward his wares. Dressed in a short-sleeved white shirt and black slacks, his tire-tread sandals looked new. She approached the man.

"Is your name Santad?" Jon critically watched others in the compound as Ana and the vendor talked.

"I not know Mr. Santad." He smiled and gestured at his wares. "Would you like to buy temple rubbing? I use only best rice paper."

To give Jon time to scan the area, she asked, "How do you make them?"

"Let me show you." The vendor dampened a piece of rice paper and pressed it gently against a three-dimensional plaster cast. With a briquette-sized piece of charcoal, he blackened his finger tips and rubbed them gently over raised areas of the rice paper. He made some rubs darker than others. Ana was anxiously looking around the compound. "Casts are used to protect our temple. Now it dries." He spread out some of the smaller three dimensional rubbings. "Very nice. Yes? I give you a good price."

She bought one, had him roll it up and thanked him for the demonstration. She and Jon started walking toward the temple.

He asked, "Any luck?"

She shook her head. "No. I thought for a minute I heard his mindsong, but it's gone now."

"Could he be blocking you?"

"With his power, he could do anything." Her eyebrows were raised and forehead creased. Her gaze covered the open plaza as she swept fingers through her hair.

* * *

His expression grim, he reflected that she couldn't help not being aware when opening her mind to others. He thought, using telepathy is why she's here. Protecting her is why I'm here. I have to quit dogging her. That she doesn't follow directions is dangerous. She's new at this. No training. Never been in combat. Her life depends on me and the existence of the United States depends upon her. She's trying to do her best. I need to stop being so critical.

Noting everyone's position, movement and clothing, he remained alert. He knew suicide bombers were nervous first timers. If they followed the Middle Eastern patterns, their clothing would be oversized to hide a bomb. They would be staring straight ahead and walking with a stiff gait. He looked for males showing lack of facial tan from being freshly shaven or having skin recently exposed from headscarf removal. Seeing none of the telltale signs, he hoped Ana might be safe for a while. He wouldn't let his guard down.

Inside the entrance of the main temple, they saw most persons were barefoot. When Ana began to place her sandals beside those lined up on the floor, he urged, "Carry them."

"You're supposed to put them here," she corrected, pointing to footwear lined on the floor against the wall.

He gestured toward worn shoes and flip-flops.

"Look at 'em. None are worth wearing. Yours'd be stolen. If you don't want to walk barefoot the rest of the day, bag 'em or hold 'em!" He didn't remove his shoes.

She slipped hers into her ample Ameribag.

"Santad's mindsong just intensified." Stepping deeper into the temple and out of the tropical afternoon brilliance, she strained to see in the dark interior. As her eyes adjusted to the darkness, her mouth fell open at the sight of a reclining, gold Buddha statue over fifteen yards high and half a football field long.

"Look at the size …," she began. She noticed two monks perched precariously on the statue's raised shoulder. They were trying to spread a saffron-colored silk banner diagonally across the statue's chest from shoulder to waist. Intent on controlling the billowing, two-meter wide cloth, the monks kept glancing at her. She had almost walked to the foot end of the statue when a realization hit. Santad and Boonrith worked together. Two men were on the statue and Santad's mindsong was strong. Flushed with excitement, she looked back at the monks and whispered, "Santad and Boonrith are monks!" It was at this moment she received a send from Santad.

So blonde! He sent with a mental grin.

She looked at the monks, smiled and sent, *Can we meet now?* Awaiting his response, she looked at the intricate mother of pearl inlay designs in the bottom of the massive statue's feet. She peered around the feet to see the monks. They were gone.

She called to Jon, "Follow me!" She took off and ran toward the head of the statue.

He ran with her, scanning for danger. "Why are we running? What's happening?"

She stopped at the head of the statue, nervously ran a hand through her hair and looked around. "Did you see where they went?"

"Who?"

"The monks. The men on the statue."

"Probably outside." His head swiveled to eye everyone he had visually memorized inside the temple. He found no additional persons.

She quickly slipped on her sandals before heading toward the door. She called mentally to Santad, *Where are you?* There was no reply.

They rushed to an open patio. All four sides of the rectangular patio had a roof covering raised walkways to create colonnades. A gathering of nearly thirty monks were seated in three rows along the east walkway of the open portico. One third of the monks sat in a row cross-legged in a Lotus position along the concrete walkway. Their hands were palm up on their knees. Other monks sat on two rows of wood benches behind them, their hands also palm up on their knees. They were listening to an older monk walking back and forth behind them. The elder monk spoke, gave them time to contemplate, and repeated the process.

Ana had never seen so many holy men in one place. They appeared almost identical. Every head was shaved. Saffron-colored robes of different hues were wrapped and folded in the same manner. She tried in vain to identify Santad.

"I don't see him," she lamented and told Jon about the blonde comment. "He must have been one of the monks on the statue. They were moving around so much, I didn't get a good look. The taller one was slender. The other had an average build." She hesitated, thinking. "I wonder which was Santad?"

Retracing their steps, the duo walked past a statue of Buddha at the patio center to where holy men were seated. They slowly walked past the monks, examining their faces and looking for a sign of recognition. As a unit, the gaze of the monk's eyes followed Ana, their heads turning in unison as she walked.

"You're quite the novelty," Jon murmured, standing taller. He enjoyed being with a woman who drew attention.

"They're not looking at me … or into my eyes. They're looking at the blonde and blue colors." Ana told him. "Feels weird."

Santad sent to Ana, *What you think of our statue?*

Surprised, she looked at the statue at the patio center. *It's very nice.*

I refer to the reclining Buddha in the temple, he corrected, sending a mental image of the massive temple statue.

He was surprised at her reaction, recognizing it was the first telepathic image she had ever experienced. Without permission, he mentally illustrated the neural path she needed to follow in order to send such a detailed, visual projection.

Ahhhh…. She grasped the link as he led her into the depths of her mind. She let him repeat the process allowing her to remember the technique. *I hope I can remember this. Thank you. To answer your question, I didn't expect such a large statue.* She initiated a visual projection of herself dwarfed at the statue base and sent it telepathically to Santad. She still didn't know where he was.

There is much you have not experienced.

Ana knew he implied with innuendo there was more than a statue at stake.

He continued. *Your friend needs to learn telepathy.*

I thought it was something you were born with.

He sent, *Anyone can learn with the right teacher. It takes desire and mach mach time.*

Mach? What is mach?
Much much time. Your friend has courage. He is an
exemplary warrior. He does not hesitate to protect you. Has
knowledge of life. Is strong in mind and body. An asset. Be
mindful. These lands are not filled with all gentle people. You
are fortunate he is with you. He refuses to accept defeat.

Her shoes scraped pebbles as she made a full turn looking
for the monk. The smell of garlic and plum blew through the
compound.

Your passing rouses curiosity.

Ana's eyes took in the monks more closely. They filled only
one side of the colonnaded portico. The bold and multiple earth-
tone colors of their saffron robes created a striking contrast with
the white portico walls and azure blue sky above. Lining the wall
behind the seated monks were tiered, concrete pedestals four feet
high below a decorated red ceiling. The pedestals were inlaid
with semi-precious gems and carved stones. Upon each pedestal
rested a gilded statue of a seated Buddha. The hands of each
statue were in a prayerful attitude. A gossamer, five inch wide,
silk sash was draped diagonally across each Buddha chest. The
statues towered over the three rows of monks seated in front of
them. Such statues were placed along all four sides of the
portico. The serenity of the view with the vivid color palette
created a feeling Ana wanted to remember. She didn't know the
Wat Pho temple complex contained the country's largest
monastic order for the study of Buddhism and meditation.
Monks from many temples studied there.

Her eyes glanced over the solemn monks again. With a
double take, she saw one looking into her eyes, not at them. His
intensity made her blink.

You see me, the monk sent with amusement and flashed a
smile.

She recognized Santad's mental touch and smiled. *I do.*

You are not familiar with strong mental touch.

She had no words to describe the euphoria his full blown,
telepathic awareness caused. She compared it to mega-
endorphins released from her brain.

You have a good touch, Santad sent. *The symphony of your
mindsound is beautiful.*

She compared his mental presence to a soft touch resembling the tip of a small, soft feather traipsing through her mind so as not to overpower her. The other end of the diminutive feather was attached to a mighty eagle. It was a sensation she would never forget.

Conversations with him were instantaneous. As soon as one of them thought something, it was in the other's mind. Never before having contemplated telepathic velocity, she thought it to be at the speed of light. If telepathy energy travels at light speed, she thought, it may be electromagnetic in origin. As fast as our minds think, we communicate. When the Joburg babies communicated, she thought, it must have been the same way. They created an extended family of peers through mindreaching. Their parents were needed only for food, clothing and shelter. If I were one of their parents, she thought, I'd probably think my kid was an alien from outer space. She shuddered.

Continually scanning for danger, Jon was unaware telepathy had taken place.

CHAPTER 21

Wat Pho Temple
Bangkok, Thailand
1 September 9:27 AM ICT

Santad was aware of Ana's apprehension and awe of what he considered his minor telepathic ability. He worried how she would react to Vaji in Laos. Between the three of them, he figured they must encompass most of the world's telepaths.

Not to worry about my metal abilities, he sent. *Anyone with great power and still alive respects and nurtures life. They not harm it.*

She noticed his difficulty with English. *What do you mean, 'still alive'?*

Telepathy is rare. I am only one in Thailand. I teach Boonrith. Those who brushed their mind with telepathic power go crazymad. If Vaji had not shielded me as child, I would not be here.

She remembered close calls as an infant when she was trapped in another's mind. She sent him what she knew about remote viewers.

Ahhh, I know of such a man, he responded. *I helped one when I was young boy. A lay line connecting Earth's nearby magnetic field changed abruptly. Perhaps energy was dispersed into Earth. He was using a magnetic field line for something. When it moved, he was in trouble. Couldn't return to his body. He was very frightened. Why do they leave their body?*

For money, she sent.

?????

She laughed at his wordless question. *How far can you send your thoughts?* She watched the monks stand and begin to disperse, talking with one another. Santad remained seated.

Three young monks walked out the terrace exit to return within a few minutes with an elderly monk and four barefoot boys dressed in traditional saffron robes.

Santad sent, *How can I help you?*

The elderly monk and boys were placing large, brass bowls into across-the-shoulder slings of gold or saffron colored cloth. The bowls hung at hip level so the boys could steady them with an arm. She looked at the bowls with a questioning expression.

That holy man, Santad explained, *is preparing for alms with begging bowls. Every monk has an alms bowl. Some never use them. Monks of our wat are not allowed to touch money. We cannot buy food, soap, or paper. They must be received as a gift. Monks with no relatives to provide food could starve. Every morning, many volunteer monks walk the sois to obtain food from citizen donations or we don't eat. Food must be consumed before the sun passes overhead. Drinks may be consumed most of the day in this temple. We're allowed to drink cocoa, coffee and tea. These drinks are luxuries not seen at temples outside of Bangkok.*

She sent, *Does all of the donated food go into the same bowl?* She couldn't fathom such mingled flavors.

It is how we can feed our holy men and ill persons.

No wonder I've never seen a fat monk, she volunteered.

We try to end all desire. This is the best wat. We have a famous holy man. Santad sent the image of the elderly monk standing beyond them. *He is much loved. He gathers food for old ones not able to walk. We serve many people. When youth come to the city they want to get rich quick. No can do. This temple is, how you say ... a hostel. A community center. We try to guide them from crime. Encourage them to work hard. We help all. We are, how you say, inundated with many youth. We find them jobs, schools, hospitals. Give medicine from our dispensary. We are best temple in Thailand. Feed many. Other temples are understaffed. We remain to help others.* He sighed with satisfaction.

And the children? She motioned to the four barefoot boys in a line, from tallest to shortest. They stood patiently behind the elder monk. Their robe colors mimicked the elder monk. Chests puffed, they seemed proud to be with an honored holy man.

Boys are "dek wat" or temple boys. Novices. Attend monks, help prepare meals and wash up. On weekends, sweep temple grounds. From poor families. They are here to get a good education. No drugs in our school. In our classrooms they are taught Buddhist moral laws, mathematics, history, and the sacred language so they may speak and copy the book of Buddha, the 'Pali Canon.' The 'Pali Canon' contains Buddha's teachings. They read and learn in order to teach others.

The elderly, barefoot monk wore black, horn-rimmed glasses. As he walked off to gather food, the children strutted behind him according to height, the smallest last. Their darker skin contrasted with their white teeth making their proud smiles bright and beautiful. She etched the scene into her memory.

Santad walked toward Ana, stopping several feet from her. He put his palms together and bowed with reverence, the most beautiful sawadee she had yet seen. He sent to her, *Honorable monk is named Anu. All love him. People wait in sois with food for Anu to make his rounds. He is so beloved his bowl fills quickly. The children's bowls hold extra food. When people give food for temple monks, they gain honor toward nirvana. It takes many lifetimes to reach nirvana.*

Why do monks bow so low?

Bowing creates calm in our minds as we remember Buddha.

To Ana, Anu was the temple father figure and role model. *"Why is he so popular?"*

He has helped here long time. Many come here from all Thailand. Bangkok is different from their villages. They need friend. Anu is beloved friend to all for service and prayer. He nurtures all. We aspire to be as kind. All in Bangkok know his name. Our Lord Buddha blessed Bangkok and our wat with honorable Anu.

I understand your goal of reaching nirvana.

Heaven same same.

Not quite, she sent. *There are big differences. Can we meet or have tea or coffee together?* She hesitated, not knowing what was proper. *Or talk?*

No! Monk cannot be with woman. He brushed his saffron robe with loud thwacks. *Never. If the robe of holy man touches a woman, accident or not, he has to go through a three-day cleansing ceremony with help from other monks. They have much work and not like taking time for a cleansing ceremony. We must never meet in private. Communicate only in the open or with telepathy.* The sheen of sudden perspiration on his head glistened in the sun.

* * *

"Ana," Jon said with an expectant look. His head was tilted toward her, eyebrows arched in question. She had either ignored or didn't hear him.

In his military past, communication of conditions was primary. Situations were continually assessed with data from many intelligence sources. With Ana having no Counter Terrorism Center information, or any other intelligence source, he needed an effective way to stay in the communication loop. When she used telepathy, she put herself in danger. Not only did he have no idea when she was mentally communicating, she thrust his concerns aside. As wary as he was of telepathy, he realized having the gift was an advantage. He worried her mind could be controlled and desperately wanted to know when she was using telepathy. Ever scanning their surroundings for danger, he was becoming more frustrated by the minute.

* * *

She mentally asked Santad, *Do you know what Jon and I are about? Our objectives concerning terrorists?*

Boonrith and I are peaceful. We do not want be involved. We do not want to worry about dangerous people lurking at our temples to do harm. He looked into her eyes, for emphasis.

Who is Boonrith?

My friend. He is a telepathic novice. You need a telepathic guide. I cannot be. He looked away.

You help Boonrith.

We cannot help you. We do not wish to get involved in a terrorist affair. So sorry.

Jon's eyes flicked back and forth between Ana and Santad. He watched her expression change from casual to one of disappointment.

Santad was moving his head slowly back and forth while looking straight at her. Jon had no idea what was being exchanged.

She asked, *Are you from Johannesburg?* Santad shook his head. *Is there another telepath who can help me?* She glanced at Jon and changed her wording. *Help us?*

Yes. A man in Laos.

Was he born in Johannesburg?

No. However, he knows of the telepath you seek and agreed to introduce you. You will go to Laos, yes?

His mental touch was distracted. She wasn't sure she had his attention. *I have to discuss it with Jon.* Santad's' mind appeared to drift. In verbal communications with standing persons, she knew people began to shift their weight onto an outside leg while getting ready to walk away at the end of a discussion. This was a similar feeling. She wondered if such distancing behavior was correct etiquette when using telepathy or unconscious action on his part. She wondered if she did that.

The few still seated monks gathered their saffron-colored robes about them and stood, each placing a fold of the robe over their left forearm. They began to leave.

I must go. Santad smiled and backed away. Preparing to walk around the corner of the portico with others, he remained in her mind. It was a gentle, touch. *Shall I leave your mind?*

Please stay. In the past, if I heard more than one person, it was garbled. Why is it different with you?

I helped you. I moved into your mind and changed neural paths. Created correct patterns and connections. You are powerful, my American friend. It's a wonder you're not crazymad.

As powerful as you?

There was a long pause. *In time you will become more powerful than I. There is a monking ceremony tomorrow. You must come. There I will tell you of my Laotian friend who can help you.*

A monking ceremony?

He sent a benevolent smile. *Buddhist boy must become monk before considered a man. Before he can marry. It is a rite of passage to manhood.*

Ana's eyes opened wide. *Aren't you a monk all your life?*

No. Three days is the smallest time a boy can become a monk. Usually in the dry season when there's no work in the rice fields. Ver' difficult to find time in Thailand with three rice crops a year. You understand Buddhism. It was an affirmation.

He left her awareness to mentally attend to something, and was back in an instant. He told her the name and address of a small temple where they would have time to talk. He would expect them at nine o'clock in the morning.

She sent an affirmative to his invitation as he walked away and hoped to remember the name of the temple. Jon had remained beside her scanning for trouble. She linked her right hand over his arm and turned them both toward the entrance gate. Experiencing a comfortable feeling, she knew Santad remained in her mind.

Impatient, Jon interrupted her reverie. "Okay. Debrief. What should I know?"

As they walked past the vendors toward the gate, she related what had transpired. Determined to be at the monking ceremony the next morning, she went over the information about the Laotian man Santad mentioned. "We have to go to Laos."

"I wondered when we'd get a handle on that," Jon said. Nong Khai's a border crossing town into Laos."

"To meet a mindreacher. Santad told me telepathy can be taught. Oh, to see Andy's face when he reads this transcript." Her eyes twinkled in amusement. "He's also manipulating neural pathways in my brain to help me have more control."

"I didn't know such a thing was possible."

"He told me it was a miracle I didn't go crazy as a child." She caught her breath at the light scent of jasmine on the tropical breeze. It made her feel exotic. She was experiencing sights and sounds and smells she would never sense again. Temple bells tinkled in the background. She was beginning to love this beautiful country.

CHAPTER 22

A small Temple
Bangkok, Thailand
2 September. 9:01 A.M. ICT

Ana and Jon arrived at the small temple by nine o'clock in the morning. The temple was not ornate or in any guide book. There were no tourists.

Jon scanned for signs of danger while Ana searched for terrorist mindsongs. The temple grounds were clean and pleasant. Expansive areas of sparse grass, raked dirt and paths surrounded the buildings. Conversations around them were barely heard.

"A baht for your thoughts," Jon queried with a grin.

"Thinking about Santad."

"Is he Thai?"

No. My parents are from India, Santad sent to Ana with a humorous lilt. His essence had remained in her mind since entering it the day before.

"No, his parents are from India," she answered, her lips curving in a smile. She had accepted Santad's mental comment with ease. When previously told he would be with her, she hadn't thought about possible interactions or repartee.

Jon looked perplexed. "Did he tell you that yesterday?"

"No." She smoothed the skirt of her dress where it was wrinkled from sitting in the taxi. The bold, white-flower print on a navy background showed wrinkles readily. "He told me right after you asked."

Jon extended his visual scan. "I don't see him."

"He listened to you through me. I was a human transceiver." She grinned at Jon's incredulous expression.

His eyes narrowed. "I don't like this game."

"It's not a game." Her voice more harsh than intended, she looked away while shifting her weight back and forth from one sandaled foot to the other.

He grabbed her elbow and whipped her around to face him. His grip tightened. "What else do you two discuss?"

"Let go. You're hurting me." She jerked away and rubbed her arm.

"Put yourself in my position. How would I know who the enemy is? I'm supposed to protect you when you're using telepathy and are more vulnerable. Woman, you are the biggest paradox I've ever come across."

She lowered her eyes, "I didn't know he could hear you through my senses. I've done that in the past with others. I never thought of someone doing the same with me." She looked around the courtyard for Santad. "You have to admit, it's kind of funny." She chuckled.

Jon remained sober, his eyes squinting in anger, his forehead wrinkled. He moved with deliberation, scanning the compound.

This way. Santad sent her an image of the path she was to follow, creating a double image as it overlapped her visual cues.

"We're to walk around the temple on this concrete path." She led the way.

"Did he tell you where to go?"

"He sent me an image. Then gave instructions."

John grumbled, "I've spent most of my life fighting wars, but this assignment beats 'em all. I can't control anything. Out of the communication loop, I have to use extreme caution. If my team were here, they'd be waiting for commands that'd never come." Looking skyward, he shook his head in frustration and rolled his eyes. "This is asinine."

Santad sent to Ana, *If you crossed your fingers when using telepathy, it would help your friend.*

She asked Jon, "What if I cross my fingers when I use telepathy?" She crossed two fingers and held her hand high.

"Your suggestion?"

"His."

"Figures." Jon, blew air through clenched teeth. "It's about time one of you had a sensible idea." His glance erased her smile. "Keep your crossed fingers where I can see them. Which hand?"

"Left."

* * *

At the rear of the temple, a young man with a strong, smiling face was seated on a rusted stool. He wore only an ankle length, white cloth wrapped like a *pasin* skirt and knotted at his waist. When he saw them, he straightened. A saffron-robed monk with his back to them held a shallow, metal bowl of water. A folded hand towel rested over his arm. A middle-aged monk with piercing eyes stood holding a straight-edged razor. He was shaving the seated man's head as running children played tag nearby. The children laughed with squeals of joy. The monk holding the water turned, his gaze meeting hers. It was Santad.

She made a small sawadee and sent, *Why are his head and eyebrows being shaved?*

Santad tipped his head sideways and sent to her, *Don't forget to cross your fingers.*

She crossed them immediately and held them for Jon to see.

New monks have to have shaved heads. Evil spirits can grasp and hold on to hair. We remove temptation. He chuckled. It shows commitment to the holy life. A shaved head helps us remember our vows of poverty, obedience and chastity. *Heads are shaved every two weeks. Sometimes once a month.* He spoke aloud for Jon's benefit, "See the flowers his sister holds?" One of two young women held a circlet of fragrant jasmine flowers.

"Yes."

"After the head shaving, the wreath crowns him for protection from evil spirits."

Ana asked, "May I take pictures?"

The seated young man smiled and answered, "Yes. Thank you for asking. Are you touring the temple?"

"These are friends." Santad spoke. "Ana, Jon, this is Channarong who is going forth with the ordination."

"It is good to meet you, Ana and Jon." Channarong gave her a seated, social sawadee. Filled with excitement, he chatted in both Thai and English, creating laughter with his wit. Whenever Ana aimed her camera at the group, Santad turned away.

Why can't I take your picture? *You will not remember me? I think you never forget a face,* he teased. *Yes?*

Yes. She sighed and took pictures of everyone else. Invited guests emerged from different directions, each carrying a large-handled basket covered with clear cellophane. The baskets were filled with toilet tissue, soap, saffron-colored cloth, small towels and wrapped gifts. Realizing they were for Channarong, she glanced at her empty hands.

Santad noticed her consternation and explained. "Friends and relatives bring gifts to honor Channarong and other monks in our wat. They offer items monks need."

Ana's cheeks reddened. "You never said anything about gifts."

"It's for the *hawng! Suam!* ... the toilette. Not to worry. We know *farangs* not understand."

Ana was disappointed by her ignorance. She didn't know what was considered polite behavior for the occasion. "Still... I ... we... could have been prepared." When Santad sent a sympathy feeling she responded, "I'm okay. I wish you would have thought to let me know."

"So sorry for oversight. Be prepared to move. In a few moments, guests will march three times around the temple to frighten evil spirits and bring blessings."

The head shaving completed, water, shaving utensils and stool were removed. Channarong was given a pale blue, lightweight, silk robe to wear.

The two Americans joined the growing group of guests and spectators assembling for the march.

Channarong stepped up to a decorated, four-foot square platform and sat cross legged on a low chair. The platform had a pole at each corner anchoring a fringed, white canopy to cover the young man. Horizontal carrying poles were attached to the platform sides. Six men lifted the carrying poles, rested them on their shoulders and carried Channarong to become part of the parade of revelers marching around the temple.

Smiling Channarong watched his guests converse while strolling the pebbled path. Most held their baskets chest high. Some women warded off sunshine with bright, painted paper umbrellas while others used plain cloth umbrellas.

Young girls were dressed in white or pastel dresses and boys were dressed in short-sleeved, bright-colored shirts and dark shorts. Excited younger children skipped and danced among them. Thai women were clothed in western style dress or traditional garb of silk. Most men wore white, short sleeved shirts and dark slacks. The few Caucasian men who wore ties and suit jackets removed their jackets in the growing heat.

Children flocked around a marching old man who created a marching cadence by repeatedly hitting a small, brass gong with a wooden mallet. Everyone paraded three-times around the temple enjoying conversation and laughter. Jon and Ana joined in the parade. She had not known there was pageantry associated with Buddhism. That made her think about what Santad and other monks must have to go through to gain their holy status.

Everyone quieted upon entering the temple sanctuary. Attending monks accepted gift baskets and placed them on gilded tables at the entrance. Ana observed two elderly holy men sitting cross-legged on a carpeted platform to clearly indicate their higher status. The platform, one- sixth the size of the sanctuary, had been built in the southeast corner. A three-tiered bank of lit candles rested on gilded tables against the back wall of the platform. A large gilded Buddha statue was positioned at the highest point on wall shelving between the tables.

Guests sat on the floor along the wall opposite the sanctuary entrance. With a monk on either side of him, Channarong was the last to enter. Crowned with jasmine, he approached the platform. Two monks removed his blue silk coat to reveal a white novice robe. His father and mother acted as attendants. His father accepted the folded blue robe and handed it to his wife. She held it respectfully with two hands. Channarong stepped to the platform and kneeled before the altar on a brocaded cloth. A foot-high, triangular-shaped bolster of the same brocade provided a pointed surface upon which he rested folded hands.

Ana was awed by this new experience. A boy was becoming a man.

Except for Jon, all eyes were on Channarong. Jon continually checked the crowded sanctuary for suspicious activity. He periodically glanced at Ana's left hand. Her fingers remained uncrossed.

Channarong spoke with the older monks before leaving the platform. He'd repeated oaths and been given a new *Pali* name for the duration of his ordination. He'd promised to abstain from harming or taking life. He vowed to not partake in sexual contact, false speech, eating after midday, any type of entertainment, and not accept or hold money. Twelve younger monks in saffron robes crowded around Channarong to hide him from view. Ritual words were spoken during movement within the circle.

Ana whispered, "What they're doing? I can't see."

In a few moments her question was answered. Channarong's carefully folded white robe was handed out to a waiting novice monk, who placed them at the platform edge. When the circle of monks opened and stepped away, Channarong stood clothed in saffron-colored monk's garb. There was a hushed silence with murmurs of reverence. Large smiles graced faces. Children began clapping.

After a short benediction, guests moved to the lawn to form a line toward beaming Channarong. Each man congratulated him with respect and honor. Females stood back. They were not allowed to touch him or his clothing. He was forbidden to accept anything offered by a woman. His fiancée would keep her distance until his ordination ended in three days. She helped serve refreshments under the trees amidst jovial conversation. Giggling children threw cake to the ground for the birds and flapped their arms in delight. Tinkling temple bells brought an ambiance of reverence to the occasion.

Ana distanced herself from the monks. She didn't want Channarong to endure a three-day cleansing ceremony because of her inattention to protocol. Opening her awareness, she intercepted the reason for the rushed ritual. There was a barely perceptible second mindsong within Channarong's fiancé. Ahhhh, thought Ana with a smile. That's why he's a monk for only three days. She's pregnant. They want to be married soon.

Remembering to cross fingers of her left hand, she sent Santad a request. *Can we talk now?* Santad motioned to a set of folding chairs in the shade. Jon remained standing at Ana's side scanning the compound.

Santad said, "We will speak aloud for your friend." He proceeded to tell them how he tricked the potential assassin into driving toward Malaysia. "I know a powerful Laotian telepath who will guide you to a mindreacher. You have to travel to Vientiane to meet him."

Ana straightened. Her heart beat so fast, she could hear pulses in her ears.

* * *

Jon's eyebrow rose at the implication. When he'd encountered Ana, he'd been surprised by her abilities. Then along came a more talented Santad, who was now discussing a third person telepathically superior to him. If these psychics were not from Johannesburg, he questioned, how many more telepaths they would find and how powerful would they be?

"When I was a young boy," Santad related, "I gave my Laotian friend and mentor permission to enter my mind anytime. He helped me immensely over the years. Now I will pass the favor forward to help you."

"And Boonrith," she said.

"He wants to learn and needs much help." He chuckled, knowing Boonrith was listening telepathically to the discussion.

"Was he on the reclining statue with you?"

"He was."

Knowing anything she said would be transcribed to Andy, she said aloud, "Telepathy can be taught. Santad is teaching Boonrith telepathy."

"Yes," Santad affirmed.

Jon switched his glance from one to the other, as though watching a tennis match. He asked, "Santad, are you telling me I should learn how to do this mumbo-jumbo?" He remained repulsed by the idea and wanted no part of it.

Santad smoothed his robe over his knees. "Ana can teach you."

Ana exclaimed, "Me?" Eyes wide and mouth open in shock, she looked at Jon.

"I'll show you how." Santad studied Jon as though looking for qualifications and winked. Ana laughed when he said, "May take long time." To Jon he said, "You keep tight control of your mind." He stood and looked around. "I must leave now. Please go to the border crossing at Nong Khai, cross the Mekong River and go to Vientiane. My friend there knows your mindreacher."

A glance passed between Ana and Jon. Since leaving Johannesburg, Nong Khai had been their destination. They were on the right track, but moving too slowly. They needed to find a mindreacher as quickly as possible.

"My Laotian friend will arrange for someone to greet you in Nong Khai. He will know where you are. You will be escorted to his temple in Laos." *Goodbye for now*, he sent to Ana. Using a fast gait, he walked away.

Are you still with me? She crossed her fingers.

* * *

On the way back to the hotel, Jon took out his satellite phone. "I need to call Andy."

"Why the phone? Use the implant."

"Transcriptions may not reach him for a day or two. Anyway, he's a minor electronic god ... plugged in to his phone even while asleep."

"Minor god, indeed." She laughed.

Jon made the call and described the situation to Andy. He listened to the reply and cut the transmission.

"What did he say?"

"He has our visas for bordering countries on hold at the American Embassy."

"What are all the countries included in that?

"Myanmar, Cambodia, Laos, Malaysia"

Ana's eyebrows were raised. Her lips pressed together.

Jon reassured, "Worry won't solve anything. We'll do what we can and hope for the best. Are you packed?"

She nodded. "I have to pick up something from the hotel jewelry shop." With a sweep of her hand, she smoothed her hair.

When they arrived at the hotel, checking the time, Jon said, "I'll have the concierge get our luggage. Meet you there in a few." She nodded.

In the jewelry shop, she put on the ensemble of a matching black star sapphire pendent on a gold chain and matching ring. As Jon walked in, she asked, "How does it look?"

"You look good," he observed, looking her over.

"The necklace." She blushed.

"Beautiful," he said with the same inflection. Leaving the small shop, he called the American Embassy. Introducing himself to the answering Marine guard, he said, I need a flight to Nong Khai." He was told the helicopter was at his service and would follow his time table.

"Two passengers. Thirty minutes, depending upon traffic." The guard confirmed his request and said a helicopter would transport them to Don Mueang airport. They would transfer at Don Mueang to a waiting C-130A. He and Ana would be the only passengers to Udorn.

Ana asked, "Everything set?"

"It is. We'll fly to the same airport where we landed in Thailand and fly to Udorn in a C- 130A."

"A C-130A?"

"An older aircraft. Primarily used for medical evacuation."

"Why not take the helicopter all the way?"

"It flies low and makes a good target."

At the embassy, Jon hefted his gear pack and Ana's small rolling suitcase. She draped her Ameribag over her right shoulder with a wince at the sudden pain and moved it to her left shoulder.

At the embassy, a Marine guard told them, "Helicopter's out back, Major Coulter." Motioning with his arm, the guard continued, "This way please."

Ana asked, "Won't a helicopter call attention to us?"

"It's used regularly for expediency," the guard replied. "We've been informed you have a following. It's imperative you use the chopper. The Skytrain may be dangerous." Jon's eyes searched the compound perimeter for any unusual coloration, movement or attention being focused on them.

She asked, "A following?"

"Someone watching your movements."

"Who?"

"Unknown, Ms. Masterson."

They were airlifted to Don Mueang International Airport and landed beside a diverted C-130A military medical transport. They hustled aboard as the only passengers. Ana sat in the navigator's seat behind the copilot. She swiveled to face the cockpit and compared the instrument panel to airplanes she had flown.

Remaining near the aircraft entrance door, Jon flipped down a wall seat in the cargo area. In solitude, without ear protection, he listened to the engines. The rumbling vibration of his seat shook him as the aircraft moved down the runway. The shaking stopped when the wheels left the runway. From Don Mueang they flew to the former U.S. Air Force base of Udon Thani, south of Nong Khai.

During the flight, the pilots told Ana about Nong Khai. They included that it is a border crossing to Laos with an American retirement community population of about sixty-thousand. They recommended a guesthouse overlooking the rain-swollen Mekong River saying, "The owner's been friendly to Americans since the Vietnam War. It'll keep you off the map."

CHAPTER 23

VESPER Facility
2 September. 12:00 AM DST

Phillip Arnold wished he were sleeping instead of placing Masterson's location on his illegal website. One Bangkok assassin was dead. Another left word he was chasing Masterson to Singapore. From the Satellite Pit, Riggle reported she was traveling north. Arnold bet on Riggle to be right and contacted his previously contracted Laotian, Sri Lankan and Thai al-Qaeda teams.

The Sri Lanka contact, forty-three-year-old Virote Rehmanjee, was in northern Thailand with his son, Sadun. Virote was considered the top sniper in Southeast Asia. Until his son had joined him as a witness to confirm contracted kills, few had been verified. Virote had responded to Arnold stating he looked forward to killing his first blonde. A blonde in the land of dark skin and black hair, he relayed, would make an easy target.

Arnold had arranged for several teams to eliminate her in case Virote and his son failed. He included a southern Thai cell that sounded promising. He arranged for them to have access to the mainframe computer in the subterranean emergency preparedness facility. It was a boon they happily accepted.

His elimination teams would be kept aware of her lats and longs. He expected to hear of her death by noon. Once she was eliminated, VESPER would be safe for him until the next telepath arrived. No one else could identify him as a terrorist. Telepaths were so rare, he expected to be safe for a long time.

He dialed PhotinT, the government's Photographic Intelligence agency, to get visuals on her coordinates.

"Phil Arnold here with the VESPER Project. I need the most recent photos of a few work sites in Southeast Asia ASAP. I'll FAX lats and longs.

An hour later, his clasped hands rested on maps. Relaying geographic coordinates to execution teams, he ordered in bold caps, "SHOOT THROUGH THE EYE." With a few, deft key strokes, he closed links to servers he'd been using for illegal data drops and called it a night.

Rubbing his hands together in anticipation of Masterson's death, Arnold knew her removal would set back the government timetable of finding terrorists. Sporting a wry smile, he was pleased there was enough information for him to begin scouting for his own mindreachers. He'd find them and persuade them to join him. The power they'd have as a combined force would be formidable.

CHAPTER 24

A Wood Shack
Near Pattaya Beach, Thailand
2 September. 10:00 AM ICT

Natiphong, the local leader of the southern Thailand Barisan Revolusi National (BRN) terrorist organization, gazed out a square opening cut into the wall of his one room shack. He resented being stuck near the Gulf of Siam with little income. Having to steal food and goods to sell was difficult. Received baht was designated for building up the team arsenal.

Decaying risers kept the shack elevated a meter above the ground to discourage invasions of crawling insects and snakes. Walking caused the structure to tremble. The thatch roof leaked in multiple places. A wooden chest with firearms and ammunition had been placed in the room's only dry corner.

At dawn and dusk, when the sea or land breezes stopped, the air became infested with mosquitoes and "no see ums." Hungry bats by the thousands migrated to a nearby tree at dusk. Their appetites allowed Natiphong to sleep in peace. The bats left before dawn.

With a shrug, he smoothed the ample black cloth wrapped several times around his waist. Secured with a rope, it covered thin bowed legs. His bare chest was small for a man his size. Over dark eyes and sparse eyebrows, his short hair was thick. A wide nose emphasized hairless, wrinkled cheeks. One single dark hair, over four inches long, grew out of a mole on the right side of his chin. Natiphong eyed the small pile of clothing stacked in a corner. His weekly wash amah, hired to hand wash his clothing, was three days overdue. He couldn't pay her the last time. If she showed up today, he would be extra nice to her. He still had no extra baht.

At the shack of a friend the previous day, he'd used a computer to search al-Qaeda internet links for paying assignments. Through the Jemaah Islamliya terrorist network, he found a request to kill an American woman who was heading for northern Thailand. Realizing he'd just been given an opportunity to fill his pockets, he'd called a meeting. Sitting on a woven grass sleeping mat he waited until his two summoned lieutenants hunkered to rest their buttocks on their heels. Their elbows rested around outspread knees.

Speaking Thai, their leader began, "Our next assignment will bring *mach baht*. We're to kill an American woman who can read minds. Who wants the job?" His lieutenants looked at one another. Neither volunteered.

Mongkut was a recently recruited middle-aged fisherman. He was dressed in a greying white loin cloth that exposed moles covering his lower back. Years of ocean sun exposure had darkened and wrinkled his skin. The fingernails on his little fingers were each an inch long. He let them grow to make others think he was a man of leisure. He rested his arms on his knees. His fingers were misshapen from rheumatoid arthritis and stained from years of tobacco use. They dangled between his knees. Mongkut's splayed toes and thick stained calluses on the bottom of his feet were evidence of a shoeless life.

Mongkut suggested, "We should sell her. She's just a woman and will do what she's told." He rolled a cigarette and lit it.

The shorter man rubbed the back of his neck. "Are you sure?"

"Of course," Mongkut replied. "Men command. Women obey. Where is she?" Smoke swirled lazily about his head. The smell of cheap tobacco permeated the small room.

"Nong Khai area."

"What about Hamza? He's buying weapons in Korat. That's halfway there. Doesn't he have friends on the Mekong River?"

Natiphong said, "Yes. He and his friends can pick her up or kill her if she resists. Either way we get paid."

Mongkut agreed. "You can report we killed her. We collect for the kill and get more when we sell her."

The third man said, "Maybe we can have an auction. Women are sold all the time. If we do this right, we'll have enough baht for several years."

With trepidation, the leader looked forward to meeting this supernatural woman. "I'll put out feelers to see what might be offered for her skill. She'll make a unique toy others will want to play with. Mongkut, leave in the morning to meet with Hamza. I'll let him know you're coming. Dress as monks so no one will question you." Mongkut was handed adequate baht for the assignment. "Head for Nong Khai. Call me for the American's position. You can find her using the phone's GPS app. Think in Thai so she won't know your thoughts." After Mongkut gave a sawadee and left, the leader smiled. They were going to be rich.

CHAPTER 25

Udon Thani, Thailand
2 September 3 PM ICT

Upon arrival at the Udon Thani International Airport in northeast Thailand, Jon hired a taxi for the thirty minute ride to the recommended Nong Khai guest house.

After examining their rooms, they visited the spacious outdoor dining veranda. Sitting at the eastern side of the open air veranda above the high Mekong River bank, they gazed at the mile-wide river panorama. Small ferries transported cargo and passengers up and down the river and to the opposite Laotian town of Tha Dua. Locals preferred traveling in cheaper longboats rather than land taxies or bus. The long boats were so named because of the long propeller shafts sticking out behind them. Moving propellers in and out of the water to control speed, the drivers created cascading sprays with associated alternating engine noise. Clouds of heavy burned engine oil created grey trails of exhaust lying atop swiftly moving water. As wide as a rowboat and four times the length, centered burlap bags and cargo crowded passengers to the front and rear of the crafts. Longboat drivers, adept at maneuvering when overloaded, skillfully kept gunnels a few inches above water level.

Boats plied the river. Workers and students threaded their way up and down the banks with trade goods in bundles on their heads. Several women had babies strapped against their backs with black sashes. Two unencumbered women carried paper umbrellas to protect themselves from the sun. Most women wore red and orange woven bags with black straps diagonally across their torsos. Three had straps resting across their forehead with filled bags bouncing against their buttocks at each step. Persons arriving and departing the country via the footpaths had passports examined by Royal Thai Police at the top of the bank.

Like other guests, Jon wore his shirt loose. It covered the fact he was armed. He glanced at Ana, enjoying how the sun highlighted the teal in her eyes.

Massaging her sore shoulder, she whispered, "Are you armed?" At his slight nod she continued, "When we get back to the States, will you teach me how to shoot?"

"Why?" He rubbed his thumb against his cleft chin and gave a mischievous grin. "Think I need help?"

"I want a concealed carry permit."

"Learning how to use a firearm and using it in self-defense are two different things. You need training and acclimation to use firearms for self-defense. They can be easily removed from you."

"Not if you teach me how to keep it." She crossed her arms and put them on the table.

"You're not very strong."

"I heard you don't need to be strong. You just have to know what to do."

"Leave fighting to me."

"Because you're at the top of the food chain?"

He shrugged and rescanned the scene to orient himself if action became necessary. The scenic view from the veranda made it a popular rendezvous point. They sat along the railing with a good view of the river and Laos beyond. Four metal folding chairs surrounded the wooden table.

Her gaze followed his to the river. "Can you believe the height of these river banks? Must be a hundred feet." Pale blue sky reflected off river turbulence creating slashes of blue crisscrossing light brown water. She made memory images to recall later. Looking across the river to eastern Laos in this late afternoon, she was uncertain where land ended and sky began. They blended into obscurity. Inhaling, she had expected pungent cooking odors from evening preparations. Instead, melded scents on the breeze were mild. Boat engines could be heard along with occasional shouts below and conversations on the veranda.

Jon motioned to the waiter.

"*Sawadee Khrup!*" the young man bowed with deference.

"Do you have diet water?" The waiter looked at him with a perplexed expression before relaxing in laughter.

"Yes sir. Have diet water. Taste ver' good. Also have iced tea, cold beer, and wine." He smiled at Ana. A young man, he was dressed in a short-sleeved white shirt, long black pants and worn sandals. Slight in build, like most Thai men, he had no facial hair. A green jade Buddha pendent attached to a thick gold chain adorned his neck.

Ana craved calcium. "Do you have pasteurized milk?"

"Yes, madam."

"I'll have one large glass of milk and an unopened bottle of water, please. No ice."

"A local beer for me," Jon requested.

"Beerlao Lager is on tap."

"Make it a tall glass."

Ana gestured toward the river. "Is the water deep?"

"Mekong changes ever' day. Sand and rock drop to bottom when water slow in dry season." He smiled and gestured to the river. "Is monsoon season. Water fast. River bottom change over four-meters during wet season. Get ver' deep."

Jon said, "That's hard to believe."

"Is true," Pong said and pointed to the menu. "Would you like *mu yaw*? Is 'ver good today."

Ana asked, "What is *mu yaw*?"

"Mu yaw is appetizer. Numbah' one food with beer." He flashed a smile. "And milk."

She smiled. "What's your name?"

"I am Pong," he announced with a *sawadee*.

"He's talking about pork jerky," Jon volunteered. "Bring some *Mu yaw*, Pong."

Nodding, Pong kept a *sawadee* pose as he backed away, menu tucked under one arm. Ana noticed his splayed toes. "Thank you, sir," he directed to her. He turned and hurried into the guesthouse.

"Sir, am I?" Laughing, she examined food others had ordered at nearby tables. "It looks like they have pudding on the menu. From the color, it must be plum. I think I'll order one for dessert."

"Excellent choice." Jon grinned. "Curdled blood pudding is a local gourmet treat."

She grimaced. "Scratch that idea."

Ornate wooden bird cages hanging from the veranda wall housed colorful birds, one per cage. They sang occasional trills. At the northeast corner of the veranda, a two-foot high, miniature, Buddhist temple sat on a shoulder-high white pedestal.

She motioned with a nod of her head toward the structure. "Did you see that temple statue?"

Jon turned around to see it, lit a cigarette, blew smoke toward the banister.

"Ever hear our surgeon general's warning about smoking?"

He ignored her comment. "If anyone constructs a building in this part of the world, they believe a spirit moves into it." After inhaling, he blew smoke rings over the veranda's edge to drift past Ana. At the same time, he studied people milling about on the river bank.

"And …?" Ana swirled her hand through a smoke ring and watched it dissipate into haze. She took off her sunglasses and put them on the wide banister.

"Building owners provide a miniature temple for any interested spirit previously living on their land. Protection of the larger building is their rent. Like a spirit house for a guardian spirit." He watched river traffic and pedestrians.

She admired a small vase of zinnias and smoking incense sticks in front of the spirit house. A sandalwood fragrance was barely noticeable. A draped, silk vestment around the pedestal moved in the breeze. It was the same saffron color as those adorning the Buddhist statues at Wat Pho temple in Bangkok.

She asked, "Wouldn't spirits rather stay in the larger building?"

"Every day servants provide fresh flowers and incense to keep the spirit happy. Monks seasonally drape and bless the spirit house."

"Like the changing vestments in churches." She looked at Jon. "Do you believe in spirits?" She leaned forward to hear his response.

He gazed over the river toward the eastern horizon. "I'll tell you some day."

"They must be small to fit in such a tiny house," she speculated, amused by the gist of the conversation. A heavy breeze descended. The air now smelled of sandalwood, pungent garlic, onion, sweet cakes, and sewer. The wind direction had changed. She took a shallow memory breath. "You've been in Southeast Asia before."

He nodded. Knowing what to observe, his eyes scanned everyone and everything. On the open veranda high above the river, bullets could penetrate the thin bamboo banister. Thick teak decking planks, however, might provide protection from weapons discharged from below. He glanced along the bank for metallic reflections. He and Ana were the only round eyes on the veranda. Assassins could be any nationality.

Ana quickly drank her milk when Pong brought their drinks, and ordered another.

"I should have had the water first," she commented.

Jon asked, "Did I tell you Andy confirmed we're being tailed?" She leaned forward to hear his lowered voice. "Details of the Joburg Project are becoming known throughout the intelligence community. He knows of one death contract on you. We may end up facing the bad guys. I don't look forward to a wet job in civilian territory."

"I'm afraid to ask what a wet job is."

"A bloody one."

She grimaced.

"Andy suggested our implant communications may have been intercepted before the encryption was installed. He's not sure if they're still encrypted. He's going to query the *Citadel where the U.S. intelligence agency is involved with communications. He must be trying to backfill them by stopping the information flow. Agencies wanting VESPER info are now officially on a need to know basis."

"If the leak's at VESPER, how would they find it?"

"Andy has a dangle operation to fish out the operative. It began with ghost surveillance on VESPER technicians. They'll be observed to learn if they intercept our satellite signals and transmit them elsewhere. Something to remember … here in Southeast Asia, a human life can be snuffed out for thirty dollars or less." He silently vowed again, even without the support of flashbangs or grenades, he would complete the mission and bring her home safely.

"Shew," she exclaimed. "Lives are cheap here."

"Including ours." He lowered his eyes. Tapping the implant site, he whispered, "Don't forget, terrorists want you dead. We need to be very careful."

She tossed back her head and looked at the sky. Her shoulders lowering as she breathed out with a large sigh and an extended lower lip. "I know."

"You're going to change the world. With your help, mindreach teams will become international emblems of moral right."

"With your help, I'll stay alive long enough to do so." She twisted her hands. "I know I keep saying this, but I don't think I'm the right person for this job."

"You're VESPER's only hope to locate a mindreacher." He tipped his head and looked at her from the corner of his eyes. "I'm the one who's not right for this job." She raised an eyebrow. ""Because of VESPER training. My luck, I just happened to be in the right place at the right time." Annoyed when she crossed her fingers, he asked, "Listening to Santad?"

"Mindsongs. People at other tables." She uncrossed her fingers. "No terrorists here."

* * *

Jon studied her. As attractive as she was, he thought it best to remain professional with no personal entanglements.

She pointed out the magenta bougainvillea blooms draped over the banister at the west end of the veranda. The cooling breeze picked up.

He glanced at the river bank below them to see natives scattering from three men who had just stepped off a long boat. He readied himself for action.

Ana leaned down to catch her sunglasses blowing off the banister as Jon heard a shot.

"Down," he commanded.

Pong was delivering their appetizer when his face exploded. His face, blood and brains hit her. His knees buckled and he collapsed to the floor. A second report of a gun hit their ears at the same time Pong's metal tray hit the table edge, scattering contents in all directions. Had she not been reaching down for her glasses, her head would have been hit by the first bullet.

"AAEEEEEEEEE!" she screamed.

CHAPTER 26

A Riverside Guest House Veranda
Nong Khai, Thailand
2 September 5 PM ICT

Jon palmed his SIG, jumped over the table and pushed her to the floor before crouching to create a human shield between shooters and Ana. He shot at one assassin. Bullets flew at the veranda from the river landing. With a downward motion of his arm, Jon shouted to others, "GET DOWN!" His command broke them out of momentary shock. They dove for the floor. Bullets whizzed past. A report of each shot followed after a miniscule time lag. Ana was covered in blood above the waist.

"Where're you hit?"

"I'm not." She wiped a bloody hand across her cheek.

"Good. Stay down." He glanced through the railing. Locals near three men carrying rifles had distanced themselves from the shooters and hugged the terrain. That created a safe margin of space between them and the shooters. He could return fire without hitting a local. The distance was a stretch for his SIG, but was downhill. Gravity would help. Taking variables into account, he aimed and fired again. One gunner dropped with a hole in the center of his forehead.

Moving along the veranda perimeter, whenever Jon looked over the banister a bullet whizzed by and he took a shot. The bamboo blocked sight, not bullets. Eight bullets sprayed where they last sat.

"They're shooting blind. Stay out of sight," he commanded. One bullet hit the balustrade of the deck wall. It knocked off a chunk of wood supporting two-bamboo bird cages. Agitated birds, screeching alarm, flew off when their cages shattered on the floor. Guests on the veranda appeared dazed and frightened.

Frantic calls punctuated the noise of those rushing to escape between rifle volleys. Those not trying to escape remained flat on the floor protecting heads with their arms. Crying children were tucked into adults wrapped around them.

Jon fired twice, dropping another assassin. A third shooter ran to his longboat at the bank and jumped into it. Full throttle, the boatman turned to speed upstream and was swiftly gone from view behind trees. In one swift motion, Jon ejected his ammunition clip, pocketed it, and inserted another.

After a minute of silence, Ana wiped Pong's blood from her eyes with the back of her arm. She blurted loudly, "Andy, we've been attacked."

Santad immediately invaded her senses. *Are you okay?*

She answered him, *My waiter's head blew apart right in front of me.* She shivered. *It's horrible! I'm so stupid. I should continually scan for terrorists and mindreachers.*

Santad requested, *Tell Jon another assassin is seeking you from southern Thailand. He should arrive at your location tomorrow.*

She kept rubbing her bloody hands against her clothing. The smell of blood was everywhere.

Jon slipped the SIG into its hidden holster and shouted to the veranda crowd, "Stay down," Pandemonium erupted. Many on the veranda crawled inside the building. Shouts were heard from the river bank. He examined Pong. With a napkin, he covered what was left of the waiter's head. Tears streaming because of the grisly scene, Ana kept wiping her face as though to remove her painful and bloody memory. Tears mixed with blood streaked her face.

Jon rose to examine a now empty dock. Fearful of being targets, drivers of all but one longboat had fled downstream. The remaining driver had taken cover behind boxes stacked at the center of his craft. Travelers peering from behind shrubbery watched the veranda high above them. Amidst the horror of a bloody scene, nature continued the evening's advance with a darkening sky. Venus shone bright in the western sky. Soon under power, the last longboat filled with travelers and accelerated downstream. Waves fanning out from its wake reflected the deepening reds of sunset.

After eyeballing locals on the shadowed bank to gauge reactions, Jon knew the shooters were no longer a danger. Locals were emerging from hiding places and exposing themselves.

On the veranda, he gave first aid to victims. One attractive middle aged Asian woman with a chest wound was dead. When an emergency medical team arrived, he continued to help.

Ana asked, "How do you know who to treat first?"

"Critically wounded are quiet. You help them first. Screamers have energy, so they're usually less critical." Soaked with blood and perspiration, he wiped an arm across his forehead. The few left on the veranda cautiously crouched or duck-walked to safety. When Jon finished applying first aid to one prostrate man, he moved Ana inside the guesthouse. Conversations among staff discussed the plagues of local hoodlums.

Machine-gun toting military troopers and Royal Thai Police questioned stragglers before permitting anyone to leave. Jon kept knowledge of the intended target from the authorities.

They moved to Ana's room. A large ceiling fan hung from her high ceiling. The tops of the white walls had painted borders of blue and green. There was one queen-sized bed, a futon sofa and two wicker chairs. A round end table beside the bed contained a small brass lamp with a low wattage bulb. The solid door had two deadbolt locks. Jon closed and locked the single veranda window above the air conditioner. Satisfied the room was secure, he called room service and ordered two dinners.

"You'll be safer if I sleep here," he announced.

"Should we go to one of the big international hotels?"

"We're better off sequestered here. The owner's placing a flock of geese on the veranda."

"Geese?"

"They're territorial. If anyone approaches, they'll make an ungodly racket and attack. They're vicious and can kill." He lifted his head and looked into her watery eyes. "How're you doing?"

Fighting tears, she replied, "I'm okay. But Pong's death is my fault. That poor boy. Think of his family."

"You didn't cause his death. An assassin did. Remember what Andy said. Any mindreacher you find will nail terrorists. They want you dead before you find them."

"If mindreachers are so almighty powerful, why didn't they help find terrorists before?"

"Why didn't you?"

She crossed her arms. "I never thought about it. VESPER's expecting mindreachers to jump on the antiterrorist bandwagon. There's no guarantee they will."

She looked at her bloody self and grabbed clean clothing. "I need to shower."

"I'll lock you in and be right back."

He returned within a few minutes with his gear pack. After ordering room service dinners, he sat at the round table, took out a small triangular kit and began to clean his SIG.

Her hair damp, Ana stepped back into the room clothed in a black T-shirt and shorts. Steam and an aroma of lavender followed her. She sat on the bed, resting her back against the wall. She pulled out her digital reader and selected a good adventure novel. Not having her glasses, she enlarged the print before escaping into the story.

After Jon showered and dressed, he pulled the dinner cart into the room and spread the fare on a coffee table. They sat on the futon to prepare their plates.

Ana took a bite of meat with rice. The pepper afterburn brought tears to her eyes. She downed a small bottle of water and said, "That sauce is so hot, it probably cooked itself!" She wiped tears from her eyes. "You should've warned me."

"Sorry. I didn't know." He handed her the milk glass.

"Thanks." Her throat became less painful. Between bites of fruit salad, she admitted in a whisper, "I was so frightened. I keep seeing Pong's face explode over and over."

Jon propped his right ankle on the opposite knee and shot her a sympathetic look.

She asked, "What?"

"You've been through some hard times this past week and survived. You're finding out what you're made of. I want to know who the mastermind is." In frustration, he muttered, "Hotel Sierra," amidst other profanities. She pretended to not hear.

Admiring her pleasant demeanor as she finished her orange, he asked, "Is Santad with you?"

Goodbye. Santad winked out of her mind.

"No."

After dinner, Jon finished lubricating his SIG while they discussed what tomorrow might bring. He asked, "Want me on the bed or futon?"

She glanced toward him, tilted her head toward the futon and thumbed in the same direction.

He placed his SIG on the end table nearest his head. He next lifted one of two pillows off the bed, plumped and draped it over the other sofa arm. Resting his legs over the pillow, the back of his head flat against the seat cushion, he folded muscular arms across his chest and relaxed. He closed his eyes to enter an alert-sleep mode. He would awaken at the slightest noise not originating from Ana. If he knew how he did it, he would learn that he slept with only one *hemisphere of his brain resting at a time. Only at his Montana ranch did he feel safe enough that both hemispheres slept at night.

She asked, "Do you mind if I turn on the air conditioner?"

"Sleep powder can be put in it to be blown into the room. We don't want that, do we?" Unspoken was the fact it would mask what he needed to hear. "Use the overhead fan. It's quieter."

"There's no such thing as sleep powder."

"It's common in this part of the world." He opened one eye and looked at her. "Sleep's on my agenda."

Ana scrutinized him. He had intelligence and internal strength. He protected her. She wished he were telepathic. Oppressed by the enclosed space and the heat, she felt the need to open a window. Knowing fresh air would make her feel better, she tiptoed to the window. Since the large, brown geese were milling about the far end of the expansive veranda, she began to open the window. Honking raucously with flapping wings, feathered guards rushed to investigate the movement. Deciding fresh air wasn't necessary, she closed and locked the window.

Jon frowned at forgetting her claustrophobia.

She interpreted his expression as anger toward her for interrupting his rest. Considering whether to apologize, she settled into bed. Thoughts of recent attacks on her life ricocheted through her mind to the point of overload.

"Jon?"

"Mmm?"

Embarrassed by her frailty and feeling of loneliness, she confessed, "I don't feel so great."

His expression softened. "And …?"

"Would you massage my shoulders? They are so sore."

He did.

CHAPTER 27

A River Guesthouse
Nong Khai, Thailand
3 September. 6:00 AM ICT

At dawn, the sound of honking geese broke through to Ana's
*consciousness. She reached for Jon's comforting mindsong
only to find he was gone. She was just beginning to extend her
mental reach when someone scratched on the door. She heard
Jon's voice and opened the door.

The smell of tobacco mingling with aftershave impacted her
senses. He held a tray containing two mugs of coffee, a small
pitcher of cream, two pastries, bananas, oranges, eating utensils,
two small plates and newspapers. She closed the door as he
placed the tray on the coffee table. As he moved, she saw a
Marine who was tough, mean and lean, yet gentle and
considerate when needed.

She inhaled. "The coffee smells delicious".

"These tea drinkers don't know how coffee's supposed to
taste. It's instant and triple strong.

"Tell me again, what's the currency rate in Laos?"

"Several thousand *kip* per dollar. Changes daily."

She tasted her coffee and grimaced. "Whoa, that is strong!"
She removed a pastry from the tray and placed it on a plate.
"What do I need to know?"

"Our visas are for two weeks. That should be all the time
we'll need. By the way, your foot's pointing at me."

"So?" She wiggled her toes toward him.

"It's poor manners in this part of the world to point your
feet at anyone. When seated, notice where your toes are pointing
from now on."

"You're joking, right?"

"I'm not."

Giving him a disbelieving look, she changed the position of her feet and offered him pastry.

"No thanks. I brought sweets for the sweet," he replied with a wink. He peeled an orange as she sampled the pastry. "In this part of the world, I rarely eat anything I can't peel or boil."

"Any other advice?"

"Buddhists make sacrifices to pleasure others. Decline any first refreshment invitation. Accept the second. By declining the first politely, you acknowledge their offer to give you pleasure. The second time it's respectful to accept their kindness." He chewed the orange segments one by one.

Savoring the citrus aroma, she peeled the remaining orange. "What else?"

"A *sawadee* in Laos is called a *nop*. The source of all that is you, your head, is lowered in respect for another as you bring your palms together like a Thai *sawadee*."

"And...?"

"Don't touch anyone on the head. It's sacred. A temple for the soul and closest to heaven. No mortal should come between a man and his God. I once trained a Thai who was a practicing Presbyterian. Fooling around one day, I bopped him on the head with a rolled map. Everyone froze. According to them, I committed an unpardonable sin and had to apologize."

"What happened?"

"He lost face in front of his co-workers and avoided me after that. I didn't think he believed in Buddhist traditions. Big mistake."

She grinned. "You admit to a mistake?"

He grunted. "Another thing, use cash. Credit cards are cloned when pulled through card readers. Use it once and Andy'll be getting bills by the thousands when the number is sold."

She excused herself to prepare for the day. From inside the bathroom she called, "How do we get to Laos?"

"A bridge south of us. The first major bridge to span the Mekong. Australia paid for it." He lowered his voice. "Mind if I smoke?" His grin broadened when she didn't hear him. He lit a cigarette and said louder, "After we get our passports stamped, we'll ride the shuttle bus across. Fill your gear pack for two days. The customs office on the other side of the river will sell us visas if they don't accept the ones we have. To buy a visa, we need the exact amount in greenbacks, no kip or baht. They don't give change. Then we'll grab a cab to Vientiane, about twenty klicks."

"Do you think the Laotian customs will be hard to get through?"

"I doubt it."

"Santad said someone would meet us here. They're supposed to know where we are." She was dressed in a black T-shirt, spidersilk safari style jacket and cargo pants. Waving a hand at cigarette smoke, she complained, "I don't like breathing second-hand smoke."

"Glad to see you wearing spidersilk," he said. "It won't rot in the tropical sun."

"It's rough. It desperately needs fabric softener."

"The bulletproof fibers in the material make it rough. Here in the tropics, cotton and natural fabrics disintegrate after a few months of being washed and dried in the sun. Spider silk should last years.

"This'll last a century." She grinned. At least I can wear it as a jacket or a shirt.

"You've got eight pockets in your shirt and more in your pants. Put anything important in your pockets. That includes water filters, fire starter, mirror and your fist sized thermal blanket. Don't use a purse."

"Sounds good to me.

"Got any condoms?"

"No."

He tossed her two packs. "Use them to hold and carry water." He looked around the room and added, "Wear hiking shoes. We don't know where we're going. Are they broken in?"

She nodded. "What else?"

"Wool socks. It's wet season. The monsoon rains daily. T-shirt and pants. The shirt jac should last several weeks without cleaning. I packed an extra, long-sleeved shirt to keep mosquitoes at bay. I have cigarettes, water and this." He patted a metal vodka flask before slipping it into his back pack.

"I don't have wool socks."

He tossed her two pairs. After calling the front desk to arrange a pickup and storage of their suitcases, he finished stuffing his gear pack.

At a light knock, he opened the door to greet two hesitant middle-aged and bowing Buddhist monks. They were so slight in stature, their combined weight would not have equaled his. Their shaved heads and different-hued, saffron-colored robes looked out of place in the hallway of the guesthouse. Jon ushered them into the room.

"*Sabaai-dii.* Hello," the shorter monk said. "My name is Kasemsan." Gesturing to the man beside him, he said, "This is Sawat." In broken English, Kasemsan explained they were sent to escort Ms. Masterson and Mr. Coulter through the border formalities and to the senior monk at a Laotian temple. After a short discussion, the four left the guest house and walked to the bridge. Locals bowed to the holy men. Border guards treated them like royal emissaries.

Ana whispered to Jon, "This man we're going to meet must be special if his reputation spilled into a bordering country. His monks are highly honored."

Jon told Kasemsan and Sawat he would pay for any transportation. Buddhist monks were forbidden to hold money, drive or own vehicles.

They were soon on a shuttle bus in slow moving traffic over the Mekong River on the Friendship Bridge connecting Thailand and Laos.

Ana saw two monks on the pedestrian crosswalk furtively keep their backs to the bus. They appeared to be snacking on what resembled dried beef. She recalled Santad telling her monks ate once a day and rarely snacked. Another oddity was the absence of wrinkles in their garb.

"Jon, don't monks wear natural fibers?" At his nod, she pointed at the two monks they just passed. "Look, no wrinkles. They must be wearing polyester. And one's overweight. Did you ever see a fat monk?"

With traffic at a standstill, Jon studied the two men. The suspicious monks turned their backs to his pointed observation.

She asked, "What do you think?"

"I'll keep an eye out for them."

CHAPTER 28

A Buddhist temple compound
Near Vientiane, Laos
3 September 12:42 PM ICT

The two Americans were escorted into a partially walled, historic compound outside Vientiane, Laos. Vivid pink bougainvillea blooms adorning the concrete walls gave a stately appearance to the ancient compound. Since they were on the Mekong River floodplain, buildings within the compound were elevated several feet above ground to protect them from seasonal flooding.

A little person, her white hair cut to less than an inch, swept the ground with a handmade grass broom. Each sweep created a cloud of pale, suspended silt which the breeze carried to the rear of the compound. Barefoot, she wore a clean, white, threadbare, sleeveless and hand-woven cotton shirt. Her ankle length black skirt was secured with a rope around her waist. The woman watched Ana, a smile wrinkling her dark, weather-beaten face. Ana smiled in return. They walked past a weathered dormitory. If they could see into the screenless windows of the cell-like rooms, they would learn each contained a rolled, woven, grass sleeping mat and little else. In the absence of electricity, there were no lamps or electrical appliances.

Escorted by Kasemsan and Sawat to the open sanctuary of the temple, Ana's stomach churned with excitement. Her gaze wandered. The sanctuary was about forty by thirty feet in size. She admired the rich patina of the teak floor, ceiling, and walls. Ornate painted designs decorated vertical posts and ceiling beams. Openings on the east and west walls provided light and views of clear sky. Her eyes took in contrasts between bright blue sky, dark-brown teak of the temple interior and the monks in bright saffron-robes walking over pale brown earth.

She luxuriated in the inner calm created by the ambiance. After removing their shoes, they were escorted to the sanctuary center, their damp stockings leaving footprints on the pristine floor. In the hushed atmosphere smelling of jasmine and sandalwood, her eyes were wide open with reverence. An elderly monk sat on a raised platform at one end of the sanctuary. Two young monks kneeled beside him. She tried to memorize the moment. Goosebumps lined her arms.

Beaming with goodwill and gesturing with an open palm toward the older, meditating monk, Kasemsan whispered with a deep, bowing *nop,* "Honorable one."

Kaseman and Sawat bowed as they shuffled backward to squat and sit on their heels near the room's eastern wall by the entrance. Their saffron robes, tight across spread knees, ended at their ankles.

The elder monk turned his attention to the Americans. His peaceful demeanor created a rush of tenderness in Ana. Seated in a lotus position, his leathery and wrinkled skin suggested decades of sun exposure. He stood to greet them, his right hand forming half a *nop.* Their eyes met. The monk introduced himself in a gentle voice. His British enunciation and presence commanded attention. "My Laotian family name of multiple generations has been Vajiralongkorn and comes from the ancient Sanskrit epic, the Ramayana. It is difficult to pronounce. Please call me Vaji."

With deep bows, Jon and Vaji showed respect to one another. The monk looked into Jon's eyes as his arthritic fingers came together in the prayer attitude of the Laotian *nop.* Jon and Vaji simultaneously gave the formal, silent signaling salute of the martial art form, Shorinji Kempos. To anyone not familiar with the form, their actions would resemble only a bow common to Laos. Both now knew the other was Kempo trained and would need no assistance in combat.

Jon knew he shouldn't be surprised at the monk's Shaolin Martial Arts signal. The Shaolin Temple in China's Henan Province was a Chan Buddhist Monastery. Because Vaji was older, Jon assumed the monk was a Shaolin Master. Jon had trained at the Chinese Shaolin temple only four-years. The experience changed his attitude on life. Like himself, the monk made no unnecessary motions.

The Shorinji Kempo discipline and martial art form was based on Buddha's teaching of building self and spirit. It was created by blending Chinese and Japanese martial art forms. Citizens around the world from diverse religions, ethnicities and cultures strove to achieve excellence during their training. Since life is respected, the discipline evolved into a protecting martial art form. Fighting and force were to be used only when there is no alternative. Through learning Shorinji Kempo techniques, Jon gained a strong mind and body. Students of Shorinji Kempo help protect their community and work however they can for world peace. Peace was the reason Jon had joined the United States Marine Corps.

Looking into Jon's curious eyes, the monk acknowledged and honored Jon's admission of knowing Shorinji Kempo by dipping his head farther. When the top of his shaved head became visible, Jon's mouth opened in astonishment. Skin at the top of the monk's shaved head held two lines of four small, circular burn marks, as though from the ends of cigarettes. Each mark designated a milestone of outstanding achievement by a monk. For a Buddhist holy man to have one burn mark was rare. Two were unheard of in this day and age. This monk had eight. Jon had been unaware a man this honorable and distinguished existed. The holy man named Vajiralongkorn had to be legendary.

Jon was being given knowledge others wouldn't recognize. He smiled and bowed lower than Vaji. In a quiet voice he remarked, "Thank you, honorable one."

The lighter of Vaji's two saffron-colored robes covered his left shoulder. A darker saffron wrap created the rest of his attire. Stubble of white hair circled his head. The man exuded an impression of understanding. Round, wire rimmed glasses sat toward the end of his wide nose and moved when he smiled. Although some of his darkened teeth were worn, his captivating smile radiated peace and love. Ana and Jon smiled in return.

Welcome to Lane Xang, Vaji sent telepathically to Ana while saying aloud to Jon, "Welcome to Laos."

CHAPTER 29

3 September 1:10 PM ICT

A mercenary from Sri Lanka and a noted sniper, Virote Rehmanjee, had been contracted by Phillip Arnold to kill an American woman. Virote zeroed in on her GPS coordinates supplied by Arnold while in the back seat of a dilapidated taxi. His son, Sadun, occupied the front passenger seat. Both wondered what the vegetation would be like at their site. They wanted to infiltrate the location and remain hidden until the perfect shot was arranged. Virote planned to be situated higher than his blonde target if at all possible.

Looking at himself in the cracked rear view mirror, Virote saw no outstanding facial features. He looked like most Ceylon males. Once he killed the Masterson woman, his umber-colored skin, small brown eyes, black hair, and small stature would allow him and his son to blend into the local scene as they escaped.

Sadun looked like a young Virote. Both were slender, healthy and well trained. Prepared mentally and physically for encounters with an enemy, they could run many kilometers. Both wore brown shirts and pants for camouflage. Jewelry had been removed to eliminate potential reflections.

Studying his GPS unit, Virote used a satellite phone to talk with his American contact. Phillip Arnold relayed the target's current latitude and longitudinal coordinates. After describing an aerial view of the Buddhist compound from satellite imagery, Arnold verified both Americans were in the temple compound, most likely inside the main temple. Severing the connection, Virote stored the waypoint on his GPS. Using waypoints, he could document locations of past kills. He appreciated having technology's ability to locate targets. In the past he would spend hours or days finding his victim.

A yawn showed a flash of gold-covered incisors as he watched longitude seconds change on his GPS. When the instrument pinpointed the taxi had nearly reached the set waypoint, Virote ordered the driver to stop. After paying the fee, he carefully removed his metal case from the taxi. Sadun removed two smaller, similar packages from the front of the vehicle. The two men stood quietly on the side of the dirt road until the taxi made a U-turn and disappeared into a dust cloud.

Virote surveyed the area before moving off the road. He gently shuffled his sandaled foot back and forth atop the ground. A light-brown cloud of disturbed silt wafted skyward, hovered, and gently moved with the breeze. "Move carefully," he told his son. "Any motion will raise dust and announce our position. Don't make yourself a target. We don't know how many guards are posted." Small drops of moisture formed on his upper lip.

Not knowing how far the American telepath could read minds, Sadun suggested, "We should think or speak only *Sinhala or Tamil from our homeland so the American woman can't read our minds."

"Or think music," Virote replied. Drops of sweat from his nose splattered to his shirt. They entered an elevated site filled with bamboo. The temple entrance in the distance was beyond its compound wall. "The elevation will provide a good shot."

"Hummm," Sudan murmured, "this is good. We're hidden from the road and temple compound."

Virote agreed with a nod. By placing himself in the copse of vegetation, he could see through the thicket to the entrance of the temple with no impediments while remaining hidden from view. He determined the distance to the temple was about four-hundred-fifty meters, or five-hundred yards. It was a good distance for either rifle.

In the shade, Sadun used binoculars to search the compound. He saw no guards.

Virote readied himself for his kill shot. He unwrapped and opened the long metal case containing a *Robar RC50 bolt-action, fifty-caliber sniper rifle, appreciating that it had a five-round magazine of ammunition. To him, the weapon looked as beautiful as it was lethal. He loved to feel its heft. The balanced, long-shafted barrel warmed to ambient air temperature within a few minutes. Attaching the telescopic lens, he lifted the rifle to feel the smooth grained stock against his cheek. Tucking the butt of the rifle against his shoulder, he sighted through the scope at different objects, ending with the temple entrance. There was a small sweet spot within the lens through which to focus targets perfectly. He knew from experience where the sweet spot was located. Gently massaging the bolt handle, he quietly and smoothly moved it through its motions. To have the weapon work so perfectly, Virote knew it was created with care. One day he would tour the factory where it was constructed.

The rifle was finally his after years of payments. At over seven-thousand American dollars, the Robar was the most expensive piece of equipment he'd ever owned. Handling it with respect, he placed the rifle onto an oiled cloth on the ground. Having cleaned the rifle repeatedly and lovingly for the last three days, this weapon of their livelihood was ready. On this contract they would evacuate quickly and leave the weapons behind. Virote wasn't worried. The kill fee would cover expenses.

He stacked the two metal gun cases for a base. Opening the bipod legs of the Robar, he rested the rifle on the top case and lowered himself into position behind it. After making minor adjustments to the telescopic sight, he located the sweet spot of perfect magnification. Seeing an edge of a blonde hair just inside the temple, he smiled. His American contact was correct. Blondes do make easy targets. He made his angle more perfect using the elevation adjustment knob. With patience he waited for the perfect opportunity.

Meanwhile, Sadun dug a trench the length of the rifle cases and twice as deep. He lined the trench with plastic and oil cloth wide enough to be later overlapped. Once buried in their cases, the rifles could be retrieved later.

Virote loved the feel and odor of the oiled wood stock. When he fired, the stock would be tight against him. He had to be careful when handling it. The trigger was adjusted for a light touch. When the bullet passed through the woman's head, he and his son would bury the weapons and immediately leave the site. If he didn't kill her, he'd destroy the whole complex using *incendiary ammunition to start the conflagration.

Lying on the ground behind the weapon, Virote checked ammunition, debating which to use for the fire, if needed. He decided on blue-tipped incendiary ammo and placed it to his right. The resulting inferno would destroy the main temple and the woman in it. Surrounding buildings would also burn. He mumbled, "I love a good fire."

Sadun agreed with a grin, his eyes sparkling in anticipation.

Virote relished planning a kill. Anticipation filled him with excitement. He didn't try for fancy shots with the Robar. He usually aimed for body mass center. At forty-six inches long, the Robar was a "one shot kill" weapon. He never missed and enjoyed watching bodies blow apart. He was curious to see if the blonde's light skin would make a different color explosion.

Sadun handed his father a headset to protect his ears. Before Sadun worked with him, Virote had to listen for sounds of others approaching and used no ear protection. Consequently, his hearing had been damaged. With his son guarding the perimeter and calling out range, Virote didn't mind losing awareness to ear protectors. The protection he used blocked all noise once a weapon was fired. Otherwise, he could hear his son.

Sadun placed the loaded Finnish Sako sniper rifle next to his father. Virote insisted it be loaded, ready to fire and placed next to him in case the Robar misfired. Its telescopic sight was easier to use than the one on the Robar as it provided a wider field of view. The smaller Sako used Remington .223 caliber ammunition. At over eleven kilograms, it was as solid as the Robar.

He grasped the Robar with his left hand. It was secure and steady on the bipod legs. His body acted as an extension of the rifle due to the many hours of dry firing. He adjusted for distance as the light breeze continually changed. Any breeze would alter the trajectory of the fired bullet. He told Sadun to move from the hillock. He wanted no distraction. He had to remain concealed until the blonde moved directly into view. The sight adjustment perfect, he readied the Robar and waited for a lull in the breeze and a clear view of her head.

Virote hoped for a bonus with a clean kill. He glanced at his son who was spotting for irregularities. Sadun would tell him of any wind change. Virote lifted his face to feel the breeze and looked around the temple compound. Silt movement from people walking allowed him to calculate variables of wind speed and direction. Smells of burning wood and food from the nearby village made him hungry.

Readjusting his head, he again made a mental picture of how he and the temple were situated. Creating a mental trajectory for the bullet, he decided to aim for the nose or lower to get the requested kill shot. He hoped to see her rip apart. Killing and watching death masks appear were his hobby. He preferred a close kill with a hand gun so a little blood would "accidently" get on him. He loved the unique aroma of blood mixed with gun powder.

Knowing the ground slope gave an illusion of a shorter distance to the target, Virote adjusted the telescopic sight again using the top dial. Practicing tactical breathing calmed his nerves. Breathe in, breathe out, breathe in, breathe out one hundredth of a second and hold. Having used the Robar often, he relaxed and brought forth muscle memory to recall how it was going to feel. He waited vigilantly for a blonde head to show and didn't look away. He was afraid to blink.

Sadun reminded him, "We'll leave right after the kill shot." They would immediately wrap the weapons in oil cloth, put them into their cases and bury them before disappearing into the brush. They needed to rush.

* * *

In the temple courtyard, Mongkut and Hamza from the southern Thai al-Qaeda cell conferred quietly while studying an electronic device. Being dressed as monks enabled them to hide their weapons. The two men marveled at the ease with which the GPS had narrowed their search for the American woman. They decided when she left the temple they would approach. Her husband was always looking around at scenery and would be easily distracted. They'd kill him if they couldn't handle him.

Their leader, Natiphong, had previously suggested offering the telepath money. Women loved cash and baubles. If she could not be persuaded to accompany them willingly to the Gulf of Siam, they would sedate and abduct her. Punching on a cell phone with a dry mouth and a tremor in his voice, Hamza, who spoke poor English, requested Natiphong stay on the line in case a translator was needed. Squinting in bright sunlight, both men waited for the telepathic woman to emerge from the temple.

CHAPTER 30

A Buddhist Temple Sanctuary
Near Vientiane, Laos
3 September 1:10 PM ICT

Upon hearing silent and verbal greetings from Vaji simultaneously, Ana raised her eyebrows with a winning smile, remembering to cross fingers on her left hand.

With an impish look, Vaji crossed two fingers and lifted his left hand. Jon's face showed surprise Vaji knew Ana's signal for telepathy taking place. The monk said, "For now, we will talk." The two men sat cross-legged facing one another, Ana at Jon's left. She had gracefully folded her legs to one side making sure her toes pointed away from the two men.

They accepted Vaji's second offer of refreshments. An elderly, white robed, holy woman provided hot tea to the Americans.

Seeing the woman's inch-long hair, Ana asked, "Is she a nun?"

Vaji supplied, "The *Pali* word is '*bhikkhuni.*' A fully ordained, female, Buddhist *bhikkhuni* may perform like a monk, but is not respected as much. No temple woman of Laos is ordained. White robed women prefer to be called a 'monistic.' Two monistics cook and clean for us. They learn *Dharma, a Pali* language, meditate often and rest when work is finished. They receive food and some financial aid. You will recognize them by their short hair and white robes."

Watching the Americans silently drink tea, the elderly monk occasionally nodded his head as though communicating with someone. He requested two attending monks to leave after tea was consumed and the implements removed. Smiling, he leaned back. Putting his arms out toward them, palms up, he said, "Shall we discuss what brings you to Laos?"

Ana shifted to a kneeling position, gratified to be in his presence. His mindsong broadcast resonance and complexity. She timidly began, "Because of Santad, what I say may be redundant. Have you read my mind yet?"

"Somewhat. You are more complicated than I thought." He crossed his fingers for Jon to see. Using telepathy, he encouraged, *Think of all that has transpired. I will learn from your thoughts.* Within seconds, he pulled forth information, learning the history of the Johannesburg babies and VESPER. Jon looked back and forth between them waiting for an explanation.

"My dear Ms. Masterson and Major Coulter," interposed the elderly monk, "I judge others by knowing myself. Ms. Masterson, your thoughts and dreams are similar to mine. I have planned for your arrival and am at your disposal."

"Please call me Ana. This is Jon."

"It has taken a long time," Vaji continued. "What I have anticipated has finally arrived. Please know, Buddhists accomplish meritorious deeds and gain nothing in return. We do them to show gratitude to our ancestors and to this beautiful home we call Earth. In the celestial record of all we do, hopefully my name will be associated with evidence of more kind than unkind acts."

Rarely impressed by anyone not associated with the military, Jon listened carefully to the holy man seated in front of him. Few would ever rank one-tenth as high on a lifetime achievement scale. He scanned the sanctuary, admiring the gilded, wood carvings and paintings as he listened. Highly polished surfaces of the temple's dark teak interior reflected a patina of age. Walls above the openings were decorated with intricate and colorful inlays of different hued woods to create multiple patterns from ancient designs. Between walls and ceiling around the sanctuary were ornate, painted carvings in reds, blues, and greens. They were embellished with a rich, twenty-four karat gold leaf. The seated, smiling Buddha statue on the staging area was covered with gold, much of it in loose flakes.

The gold reflected hues and shades of saffron and amber. Floating dust motes danced in shafts of brilliant beams of sunlight. Sunlight flickered through the red-orange blooms of surrounding flame trees outside the temple.

An occasional light breeze wafting through the blooms caused them to shuffle. The tenuous breeze also caused small brass bells at the temple rooftop overhangs to tinkle softly. The bells seemed to be a continuous reminder of the temple reverence.

Constantly assessing his surroundings, Jon extended his view beyond the compound walls noticing there were multiple higher elevation sites that could hide snipers. He wondered if Vaji had appointed anyone to secure the compound. He maneuvered himself to a position between Ana and the entrance.

Vaji cleared his throat to refocus Jon's attention. "There is little I can do to help you except in a mental capacity or to delegate others. Unfortunately, we must take terrorists into account when planning your meeting with the mindreacher. The terrorist mind is an evil and strange thing."

A thrill of excitement moved through Ana at the mention of a mindreacher. The elderly monk swayed back and forth as he spoke. "I've learned most terrorists cannot be guided to see the light of mankind. They don't realize a single good deed is worth much in our lives. Instead, they believe killing others will be rewarded in heaven." Smiling, he requested, "I want you to hear what transpires today, Major Jon Coulter," and held out his left hand, fingers spread apart to imply no telepathy. "Consider this question, Ana. How do you feel I may best help you?"

Thinking about the implants, Jon remained silent. He glanced outside to the conversing pseudo monks he had seen on the bridge. They were standing where they could observe Ana.

Alerted by Jon's inattention, Vaji glanced to where he was looking. One of the monks studied a small instrument in his hands. True monks did not touch such instruments.

Ana was unaware of any distraction. "Do you know a family by the name of Jayachettha?"

Jon interrupted. "Excuse me." He inclined his head in the direction of the courtyard. "Vaji, are those two monks from this temple?" Ana leaned toward the door to better see the monks outside.

* * *

When Ana leaned forward, Virote finally had her head perfectly in sight through the telescopic lens. He instantly tightened the butt of the rifle into his shoulder pocket and moved his finger to the trigger. His left wrist remained straight and locked. The cross hairs were unmoving. With a blonde head lined up, Virote steadily pulled the trigger. He anticipated catching an instantaneous expression of horror before it was blown off her face. "Ah yes," he whispered, "the best part."

* * *

Vaji's expression changed with extended awareness. He shouted, "Ana, move!" Using mental powers with which he was born, but rarely used, he slowed the projectile heading toward her. He lamented not being aware of the bullet soon enough to stop it. He could only impede movement.

The bullet hit Ana's left shoulder. Had she not moved, it would have hit her head. The momentum of the bullet's impact spun her around and to the floor. Immediate pain and burning began as energy of the speeding bullet reverberated through her body. The shoulder of the multi-layered, bulletproof shirt had absorbed much of the impact. Her skin burned. Her eyelids flickered before her expression showed agony.

Yelling profanities, Jon reached for her.

The elderly monk had a sad expression, his eyes weary. Although he had mentally slowed the bullet, he had not thought quickly enough to deflect it.

* * *

Virote was usually in charge. He determined who lived and died, when and how. He was confused by the delayed impact and saw no body explosion. He'd never had a cold bore shot move so slowly. He inspected his firearm to find what variable interfered with his shot. He pulled the bolt back and canted the rifle to the right. The spent casing dropped to the ground. He reloaded. He realigned the Robar to take into account a trajectory change with a warm rifle bore. The instant he saw her head he fired again. Unfortunately, she moved. The bullet time interval was normal.

He muttered, "Damn! The woman's a witch. She changes my shots."

Sadun looked at the temple through binoculars. "A miss?"

* * *

Quiet, Ana was pale. She said, "No blood."

Jon checked the wound site. Relieved at seeing no entry wound, he sniffed for the smell of cordite to determine if the shooter was upwind. He moved her further into the temple.

"Must be two snipers. There were different time lapses between shots and bullets." He knew where Ana had been and where the bullet hit. He visually searched the terrain where he thought the bullet may have originated.

She moaned. Her mouth dry.

"Vaji, take care of her." He pulled out his SIG and took off running in a zigzagged motion toward a bamboo copse in the distance.

"It hurts so much." She hunched her shoulders and looked down, pulling her shirt away from the injury to see it.

Vaji sent to her, *I slowed the bullet. Had I paid more attention and extended my awareness earlier, I could have stopped it. I didn't think fast enough to deflect it. My deepest apologies. You must release healing from your mind.*

She squinted her eyes at him in confusion before releasing endorphins. She marveled at his comments.

Not that way, he sent. *You cannot keep healing energy in your mind. You must release it. Your mind was created to do this. It is similar to faith healing and most effective when life is in danger, for then it is stronger. I will show you how to begin. It will also cleanse your mind. Remove anger or shame.*

He entered her mind and taught her how to begin healing by visualizing herself healed and healthy. *Believe yourself being healed.* Energy rippled through her nerves. Pain began to recede. *Do not speak to anyone of your healing.*

Why not?

You do not want healing energy to escape and weaken your healing. After a healing, even your Christ said, "Tell no one." Vaji continued telepathic instruction. *When you have experienced intense situations with someone, that person becomes important to you. That is why Jon and his military brothers are so close to one another. They reciprocate intense feelings experienced during life-threatening situations in combat. In the process, they are molded as brothers for life. Please transfer your attention to him in this situation, not me. Intense connections that healing creates cannot be made with me. It is forbidden.*

Saddened, she sent, *I know. You're a holy man. Is anyone else hurt?*

No.

She thumbed toward the pseudo monks standing outside the temple and said aloud, "They act like they're frozen. What did they shoot me with?"

Vaji replied, "It wasn't them." He lifted a corner of his mouth and tried to tease a smile from her. "At least you're not leaking." Encouraged by seeing a grin, he continued. "Your padded shirt stopped penetration, not impact force. You've got soft tissue injury and swelling."

She massaged the impact point through the spidersilk and felt something hard. Through the hole it made in the multi-layers of her shirt, she twisted the object out. It was a partially smashed, bullet. She held it for Vaji to see. "It's huge!"

In a subdued voice, he replied, "It could have killed you."

"I wouldn't be alive if not for you." Tears welled in her eyes. She put the remnant in a small zippered pocket. "I'm going to save it. Otherwise, my friends will never believe me." She tried to move and gasped in pain. "I'm saving the shirt too. For proof I was shot." She wiped moisture from her face with a sleeve and winced at pain the small movement caused. Both shoulders now felt useless.

Vaji spoke a sharp command to someone unseen in the wings of the temple. With a shuffle of bare feet, three monks rushed to guard the pair of pseudo monks in the courtyard.

CHAPTER 31

A Bamboo Copse
Near the Temple Compound
3 September 1:40 PM ICT

Virote was puzzled. His aim had been perfect. The time factor between his pulling the trigger and the arrival of the bullet had been off. How could that be? After waiting to watch the effect of his kill, there had been no repercussion. Nothing. He wondered if he was going crazy and stared through the scope. There was no explosion of blood after a perfect shot. The smell of discharge cordite usually lifted his spirits. Today it brought disappointment.

Seated Sadun had been scanning the area for intruders during the set up and action. He turned to see his father's confounded expression. "What's wrong?" Sadun's question, diverting their attention, caused them to miss seeing a man running toward them from the temple compound.

Virote answered, "Nothing." He didn't want to lose face in front of his son and waved him away.

Forehead lined in worry, Sadun watched his father.

Virote, lips pressed together and eyebrows flexing in anger, ran a shaking palm over the warm rifle barrel before grabbing incendiary ammunition. He visualized an explosive inferno incinerating the Americans before he destroyed the compound.

* * *

On the temple steps, Vaji gathered helpers to him. He waved his arms and projected mental warnings simultaneously in English and Lao.

Naipadchuban! Naipadchuban! Kandoanoenngan kab koaaephnghin kabkhunpaibon! Now! Quickly! Run to the back of the compound!"

Diminutive monks ran out of the buildings shouting questions in confusion. Vaji called to Ana, "Come."

Two male temple workers half carried her while Vaji held a section of his robe out to block her view from the sniper. Vaji continued warning calls and encouragement as he loped behind Ana.

Reaching the concrete wall, she collapsed and curled her body against it. Two temple monistics arrived to stand over her. An excessive amount of endorphins, healing enzymes and hormones flowed through her body, numbing her fingers

"Is okay," one woman said to her, and patted her back.

* * *

The instant incendiary ammunition was shot, Jon spotted two men through the bamboo at about two-hundred yards. One held a rifle. He fired at their heads, killing both, and ran to them, continuously scanning for additional assassins. There was no evidence of a third man. He swore at not spotting them earlier while rushing back to find Ana.

It was too late to save the ancient temple, now engulfed in fire. Wood, tiles, and debris flew into the air within a rising fireball. Flakes of gold leaf glittering with reflected sunlight rose in the maelstrom. A flaming, saffron sash floated aloft with a slow, languid and graceful twisting motion in the blackened air currents as though being pulled up by a puppeteer. Burning chunks of temple rained to Earth. Sparks arced from billowing white and yellow-orange flames rising from other buildings.

* * *

"Fai! Fai!" Shouts of fire throughout the compound alerted nearby villagers. They were mingled with calls for help. *"Suay dae! Suay dae!"* Those who reached the safer walls to the rear of the compound inhaled acrid smoke. Exposed skin and clothing grew hot from nearby flames.

Vaji took a few minutes to check on Ana.

"Chao hu suk aenv dai? How do you feel? Do you know how to relieve your pain?"

"I do."

"Then do so. I repaired one cracked rib. Another is bruised. You have flesh damage."

As pain retreated she became more coherent. "I don't know how to mend bones. Will you show me how?

"I will be pleased to do so. You will soon be healed." In a squat, he sat back on his heels to rest a moment and sighed in relief.

Grateful for the monk's attention, she spoke with wonder in her voice. "Thank you for saving me."

"I am fulfilled by helping others."

She looked at the devastation. "I caused all this. How many more people will die or get hurt because of me?"

Jon arrived, furious with himself for not being able to have stopped the sniper earlier. He said, "We need to get out of here."

She nodded with guilt-ridden eyes.

"You escaped death again. It's the 'again' part I don't like." He scanned the area for threats before checking her shoulder.

The three of them surveyed the damage. Flattened structures were flames and smoldering rubble. Monks lining the concrete wall were covered with black ash. Like a firebreak, the compound's dirt perimeter had stopped burning grass from advancing toward those huddled for protection.

Through the conflagration, shouts could be heard as faithful villagers came running from all directions to see what had happened. Gathering his robes, Vaji stood and ran barefooted toward the main gate to the village, dodging his way through pockets of hot destruction. Two younger monks followed him.

With effort, Ana tried to stand. Jon moved in front of her. "What do you think you're doing?"

"I've got to help Vaji. He's too old to be running around."

"You can't help. You don't know their language and you're hurt. I don't even know if you can travel anymore."

Frustrated, she leaned against the wall and collapsed to the ground. Using a soft touch, Jon massaged the back of her neck. With tears in her eyes, she said, " Everything's gone. His people are hurt and burned. It's my fault. If I weren't here none of this would have happened." Tears coursed down her blackened face. "Now both shoulders hurt." She told Jon about Vaji slowing the bullet.

Astounded, he asked, "Can you do that?"

"No way!"

He speculated such a skill would be invaluable in combat. If such control over bullets could be taught, he would become an avid pupil.

One of the suspicious monks and a novice monk had been killed during the attack. Once the bodies were removed from the ruins, a monk delivered cool water in a large wooden bowl and a small cloth. Jon dipped the cloth into the water. Wringing the compress, he slipped it against Ana's wound. In the absence of ice she relied on evaporation for a cooling effect. She sighed in relief.

"You're hot," Jon observed. "How do you feel?" He questioned his ability to protect her. Her safety had been compromised yet again.

"Overwhelmed." She shuddered, looking around. There were no buildings left in the compound. "It was such a beautiful holy place. How could anyone destroy it? We're lucky Vaji's awareness is far-reaching."

"It's unacceptable that you're injured again." Jon's eyes were intense with frustration. "At least we know reinforced spidersilk works."

"If Vaji hadn't slowed the bullet, I'd be dead."

Jon assessed the situation. "The attacks have to be directed by someone knowing our location. It's our implants." With a light touch he wiped tears off her cheek with the back of his hand. "We need to get you out from under satellite coverage and get rid of these implants. Find a hole to hide in." He wasn't familiar with the area and didn't know where to go.

Hurrying to them, Vaji arranged his hands for a *nop* and bowed his head. "I ask you to please forgive this attempt on your lives." His British accent became more pronounced. "We have never had such a deed take place at our temple. Meditation, prayer, and sanctification of this holy site must take place to cleanse it before repair begins. Do not worry. It shall be rebuilt more beautiful than before. It is you I am concerned about."

She murmured, "I'm okay." She looked from one to the other of her two protectors.

Vaji gestured toward the horizon. "Here in Laos, we must repay the kindnesses bestowed upon us by the United States government. I am mindful of gifts given our nation by your country in times of war and peace. Thus spoken, please know I am determined to aid you in your quest." He took a deep breath. "My dear American friends, have courage to face this horror unleashed on Earth. VESPER will obtain what it needs, at least that which is in my power."

"Thank you," Ana told him while surveying the burning rubble. "What'll happen to that fake monk who survived?"

"His home is near the Gulf of Siam where terrorists proliferate. He will be detained. Two marksmen from another country injured you and destroyed the compound. Jon took care of them."

A young novice approached and whispered to Vaji. The elder monk said to Ana. "The surviving man dressed as a monk was instructed to plan your abduction, not your death. He will be handed over to the police from the local substation."

Ana queried, "And then what?"

"We are a poor country. Not all villages have jails like the United States. Our places of confinement are well-constructed enclosures made of bamboo or rattan. Normally stacked three high, they're large enough for an adult Laotian prisoner to sit or squat. Once given a sentence, the accused are not removed from their confinement until the term of their sentence has been carried out. This Thai man will most likely spend considerable time being retained and questioned by the police." Vaji smiled and added, "Most of the policemen live nearby and completed their monkhood inside this wat. They take care of us."

Jon straightened. "Jails here aren't pretty." He thought of American prisoners of war during the Vietnam conflict who were kept in such cages. "Bodily functions take place with little or no water and no paper such as you use. Prisoners in the lower cages have to be aware of those above. Without a family member to bring food and water, it's a lonely, hungry and exhausting experience. Can be fatal. They're given enough food to sustain life, but the water may not agree with them. Many don't survive such incarceration. They can't stand or stretch. Large Anglo-Saxons like us have a difficult time."

Ana said, "I'd go crazy. Even being able to see out wouldn't stop my claustrophobia. I can't imagine such confinement."

"To the locals it's SOP. To citizens of developed countries, it's considered torture. However, it'll keep this fellow out of our hair."

Vaji rubbed his bald head and grinned, his eyes twinkling. "Kanchana is the name of your mindreacher contact. Kanchana is moving north from Cambodia. We will meet in a village on the Mekong River southeast of here. The auspicious name of Kanchana means "golden one." Ana continued to lightly massage her shoulder. Vaji warned, "Dangerous men converge on this site with intent to harm you, Ana."

Jon scanned the area. He was disturbed at his lack of information. Vaji had not shared any details. He asked the monk, "Do you know how much time we have before the assassins arrive?"

"I am not sure. They travel at different speeds. The first should arrive tomorrow evening."

"There's more than one?"

"Two so far. I have ways to help in this strange situation. As you protect Ana, you'll be guided to a safe place near the remote village of one of our monks." He looked at the sky as though observing drones or satellites. "Our monk cannot stay with you. It is forbidden for a Buddhist holy man to sleep with un-ordained males more than three nights. Nor can he lie in the same sleeping area with a woman."

Ana asked, "Where are we going?"

"Think of it as an 'Outward Bound' experience," Jon proposed.

"Outward Bound?"

"An American organization that takes groups of people into the wilderness. In the process of learning how to survive, they form cohesive, corporate teams and leaders." Jon knew a former SEAL had headed the organization at one time. That bumped its standing up a notch in his mind.

Vaji stood and brushed his robe. Black ash flew from its bottom with each smack, exposing blackened feet. He crossed two fingers of his left hand for Jon to see.

To Ana, he sent, *Those converging on this wat must not find you. As far as they are concerned, I am just a simple monk with whom you spoke. I will have no information for them. They will not learn of your destination.* He sent to her in a flat tone, *I will manipulate their minds with suggestions. You will be elsewhere. You should be safe. I will now show you how to heal bones.*

He moved through Ana's mind with skill. He illustrated the process she would use to heal bones using residual electricity stored in her body.

"I didn't realize electricity was the healing agent."

"Yes. It is surprising. When cats purr they give off a vibration which also heals bones. If you break a bone, place a happy cat beside it to let it heal more quickly. Did you ever see a cat with a broken bone?"

She burst into laughter. "Dogs, yes. Cats, no. Does purring keep their bones strong?"

"What do you think?"

She thanked him, but doubted she would remember the complex healing technique. "When do we leave here?" Wary of traveling on foot in the tropical wilderness, she added, "I didn't bring survival gear. I have a high tolerance for pain, but don't know if I can manage my gear pack."

All will be fine, Vaji sent. *I will remain here a while to settle my people. You will meet the one you seek.* His mindsong softened in volume. *You have a beautiful mindsong, Ana. I am honored to know you with the harmony and order it brings.*

She blushed. *Are all mindreachers alike?*

Are all humans alike? He bowed to her as a gesture of respect, placing his hands with palms touching, arthritic fingers pointing to the heavens. *Dear child, you and your VESPER organization have finally brought expectations of world peace. Please know that a monk is forbidden to be alone in the presence of a woman, travel alone with a woman, or even sit in a room alone with one without a male companion. Monks are usually forbidden to carry on conversations with women or become emotionally involved. I have vowed a lifetime of celibate living. Even though we are compatriots, it is inappropriate for me to continue to follow you with my mind. However, it may be necessary at times. At this time I require a mind-strong companion to be with me and have called Santad to join me.*

He'll be thrilled to finally meet you, she sent. *What about his friend Boonrith?*

The fledging is learning and will accompany Santad, Vaji replied with an emerging smile. *Please find time to meditate when you are in your safe place. Contemplate on how to best work with a mindreacher. You are destined for greatness as your power grows. In the future you will become more valuable to your government.*

Surprised at his prophecy, she was comforted.

Vaji turned to a monk seated nearby at the compound wall and asked in their native tongue, "Kittichai, please lead our gracious guests to one of the hidden caves near your tribal village in the morning."

The younger monk stood, performed a bowing *nop* and replied in stilted English, "Of course." Compared to Vaji, Kittichai was large-boned and healthy. The fringe of growing hair on his shaved head was dark. Like the other monks, there was no hair on his face, arms, or visible lower legs. His robe was a deep amber hue, his bare toes splayed. He stood and bowed as Vaji introduced him to the Americans.

To Ana, Vaji directed a send in his precise British accent, *With the unexpected confluence of assassins coming to this wat, we will take precautions to assure your safety. Staying in a cave within a honeycomb of nearby caverns should remove any threat of detection by satellite.* He repeated the information aloud for Jon.

Ana stood, hands on her hips. Although intelligent, in a battle zone she was out of her element. She watched curling smoke and steam rise from smoldering temple remains while villagers and police searched rubble for injured persons who might have been overlooked. Ana didn't tell Jon what was said during telepathy.

"As much as I want to get Ana out of here," Jon looked pointedly at Vaji, "what's the possibility of your making an error in judgment? My commanding officer ordered me to follow leads of Ana and those with telepathic power. I'm ignorant about psychic realms and am going into this blind." Wary about relying on a cave for safety from satellite detection, Jon recalled Colonel Walton saying the capability of the NAVsop satellite energy transmissions would go through underground buildings. A first priority had to be to safely remove the implants.

* * *

Vaji addressed his concerns. "As for my judgment, let us hope I am correct. You may trust Kittichai with your life."

Jon gestured around the compound and beyond. "Not having information or intelligence about our surroundings has been a major liability." "Being telepathic, you're aware of much more than I, but ---"

Waving a hand in dismissal, Vaji cut him off. "It is best this way," and reassuringly bobbed his head. He explained, "Kittichai knows the land and has consented to guide you to a safe place." He tapped a finger behind his ear implying knowledge of the implants. He spoke a few words to Kittichai who immediately left, bare heels flying under his robe. He sent to Ana, *I told Kittichai to have the washama help him.* Speaking aloud for Jon, he reassured, "Kittichai will find what is necessary. One of the monistic women will help him."

Ana fretted. "What about you? Time is ..."

Vaji cut her off. All will be fine.

She murmured, "I sure hope so."

He sent, *I make preparations for your meeting with a mindreacher, Kanchana.* He had sent the message with an encouraging feel. "All will be well. Do not be concerned."

Ana enjoyed listening to Vaji who never used contractions. She thought he spoke and acted like a royal. One day she would learn he was.

* * *

Frustrated, Jon continued scanning the compound perimeter for enemy activity. His posture beside Ana illustrated concern for her safety. If threatened, he had been trained to act with speed, surprise, and deadly action. He had a difficult time being proactive around telepaths and was anxious to get moving with Kittichai. A cave would be better than nothing. If Andy hadn't directed him to follow the telepath's instructions, they'd already be gone. He longed for execution of the familiar mantra, "get in, do the job, get out."

"Food for you," informed a young monk handing Jon several wrapped cloth packages, four water-filled canteens, and a well-used, wooden-handled parang knife with a hand-made plastic sheath. He guessed the parang weighed about one pound. The total length of the parang was less than twenty-inches with the blade a foot long. Jon slipped his belt through the sheath loop to let the parang hang from his left hip. Pulling it out several times with each hand, he hefted the well-balanced parang. Remaining items went into his gear pack.

* * *

Feeling exuberant, Ana thought "Kanchana" over and over, thrilled to have the man's name. She sent to Vaji, *You've no idea how much I want to succeed.*

But I do, he assured with significant confidence and glanced in the direction Kittichai had run. *You will succeed. When the danger is gone, Kittichai will lead you to a rendezvous site. You will meet with Kanchana and myself.* He bowed and stepped away.

She felt relieved. *You'll be there?* He nodded. *What'll I do if the mindreacher refuses to help?*

We will see. He shrugged and said aloud, "Do you wish sleeping mats?"

Jon said, "I'll take one for Ana."

Vaji strode with them to a nearby village home raised on stilts four feet above the ground. "You will stay here this evening. In the morning you will be escorted to safety." He introduced them to the homeowners, who were gracious and happy to help their priest. The male head of the household spoke enough English to make them comfortable.

Three smiling, curious children of the home were under the age of five. Asked to give the guests privacy, the cautious children peeked around their mother's skirt in awe of a blue-eyed blonde *farang.* They stepped back in fright whenever Ana moved. The young parents gave Ana and Jon food before leaving. The Americans had the elevated, one room home to themselves for the night.

Later, sitting on the floor, Jon rubbed his implant site. Swearing, he remarked to Ana, "I don't know how to remove 'em or turn 'em off. Andy considers these our safety net."

With a grim expression, she said, "There's a growing rip in our net." She felt sore, dusty, thirsty and discouraged. Never liking to sleep on a hard surface, she knew her woven, grass sleep mat would be as hard as the floor under it.

Jon placed a hand in his pocket and told her, "Vaji's a superior telepath. I'll follow his lead. I hope he knows what he's doing. Just in case we need to move fast, stay alert. Follow my directions." He looked into her eyes. "You've been functioning at a demanding level with daily death threats. Most civilians couldn't operate with such stress. You're an extraordinary woman, Ana. You'll find our mindreacher."

Jon knew he had to continue with cool competence in what was the weirdest situation any military officer had yet encountered. He questioned how to motivate a telepath such as Ana and hoped she stayed compliant.

Her lips pressed together, with a sigh, she said, "You're the expert."

CHAPTER 32

A Small Village
Near Vientiane, Laos
4 September, 6:30 AM ICT

The next morning, Jon rearranged items in their gear packs to distribute weight. He would carry the most weight. Ana would use her gear pack.

Barefoot Kittichai approached in civilian clothing. Acknowledging them with a deep nop, he asked, "*Jao paak phaasaa lao dai baw*? Do you speak Lao?"

Jon answered, "No."

Kittichai requested, "Follow please."

"Lead the way." To Ana he whispered, "I don't feel good about this."

Ana replied, "Vaji knows what he's doing." She and Vaji exchanged telepathic goodbyes.

Kittichai took them to a waiting taxi.

* * *

When the trio reached the Ngum River, Kittichai hailed a passing longboat to transport them southeast. With the treacherous flooded Mekong River and speeding long boat, it was a fast trip. Near the town of Ban Na Sen, they disembarked and began a trek into uneven and higher terrain. They followed an ancient, overgrown path.

Kittichai was a lean man with no Western fat on him. He maintained a fast, rhythmic pace.

Since they had to remain inconspicuous, they circled settlements. Not having the "Himalayan slope," a trademark feature of Asian eyes, Caucasians stood out. Blonde with pale skin, blue-eyed Ana was an anomaly in the region. She'd be remembered if seen. A canvas hat hid her hair. Sunglasses hid her eye color. The men took turns slashing foliage which slowed forward movement, switching hands often.

Jon repeatedly checked to find the parang sheaf was securely attached to his belt, his SIG tucked into his waist holster, and small wooden clave in his pocket. He attacked brush hindering their progress by slashing with the parang knife. The force of his actions created agony in his wounded shoulder. Cursing pain, he vowed, "If others can heal from combat injuries and return to active duty, so can I." Leading with renewed vigor he powerfully cut into the foliage. There had been a trail, but they had to blaze a new one through the overgrowth. Between him and Kittichai, the tunnel-like trail lengthened.

Ana had time to think about mindreachers and her surroundings as she walked between the two men. It kept her mind off the pain.

The trek also gave Jon time to think about their situation. He became more disgusted with the implants every day. Treading through heavy foliage, he called, "Andy!" He repeated the name two more times in hopes Andy was listening to his transceiver.

Within a short time, Andy facilitated the uplink by responding through the transceiver imbedded under the skin behind Jon's right ear. His deep voice boomed, "What's happening?"

Aware a VESPER technician should have transcribed every spoken word for Andy, he began to provide more details about the latest attempt on Ana's life when Andy explosively interrupted.

"WHAT?" Andy yelled. "No attacks have been reported in my transcriptions." With deep conviction and profanity, he said, "I'll find who did this. No excuses. Damn, I should've been more vigilant."

Jon was shocked to discover Andy didn't know about any of the attacks on Ana. Their communications had been compromised and data altered. He said, "We have implant headaches."

"Get rid of them," Andy commanded.

Removing the transceiver implants would protect Ana from exposure. No one could locate her without the NAVSOP data.

"Thanks, buddy."

"How's she doing?"

"Sore. Anxious. Can't believe she's still upright. Sure has stamina."

"Are your friends with you?"

"Affirmative." Jon felt again for the reassuring presence of the loaded SIG in his waist holster. "Friendly cuss, warmed right up to me." On the narrow encrypted frequency band, the two men discussed the presence of ongoing intelligence operations in Southeast Asia and the location of safe sites. Jon added, "I have no idea what's going on with her voo-doo telepathy."

"Trust issue?"

"Affirmative."

"You'll work it out. Some good news. The Intelligence Oversight Board has been alerted to what is now officially being called the Joburg Project. They want to fund VESPER through continuous tax dollars. We're fielding calls from the National Reconnaissance Office, the Office of the Coordinator for Counterterrorism, the National Security Advisor, and the intelligence divisions of the Department of State. Several new national security systems plan to use the Joburg mindreachers once they're located."

Jon commented, "Maybe they're no longer telepathic."

"Then we're up that proverbial creek! The President wants a seed pod of three to identify terrorists ASAP."

"If these mindreachers are as powerful as you anticipate, he'll only need one."

"The DCI is trying to gather Ana's DNA and background information. They want to see if her telepathy is genetic."

"The Director of Central Intelligence! We're not secret anymore, are we?"

"No. Stay alert. Charlie Mike."

Jon didn't know Andy's first order of business after his call was to conference with CEO Herman Wald and try to uncover the in-house traitor. If he had his way, security for the emergency government hive under the airport would soon require optical fibers. That would hamper wiretaps. Since new generations of computers can crack normal encryption systems in minutes, rather than years, he would recommend quantum-key servers which no current system could hack. In his opinion, a matching, quantum-enabled satellite for secure transmission of data should have been installed. That would have stopped infiltration of data and interception of communication from the satellites.

*   *   *

Used to walking with longer athletic strides, Ana felt inhibited as she picked her way behind shorter Kittichai. Watching his feet, she attempted to match his pace by stepping in his footprints. Ever mindful of not touching the monk, she had to be careful to not tread on his shoeless heels. Where they trekked with little natural canopy, jungle plants grew so dense they couldn't see what they were stepping on. Where the trees blocked sunlight, the forest floor was fairly void of plant life and easy to navigate, but seemed more ominous.

Footfalls bounced the gear pack against her back. She tried to arrange weight more evenly over aching shoulders. Having earlier removed her brassiere in the way women do without removing clothing, she inconspicuously threw it away. She next adjusted her back pack to alleviate strap pressure against her wounds. Spidersilk caused chafing no matter what she did. As much as her pack hurt, she wasn't going to ask Jon to carry it. She was part of a two-man team and would hold up her end.

Loud caws and soft trills of bird alarms preceded them. Overgrown vegetation and mist blocked views of distant landscapes. She wasn't perspiring as much as she expected, but wasn't worried. Sweat stopped evaporating with high humidity. Feeling poached, she folded her sleeves higher and pulled a navy blue bandana from an inside pocket. Folding it diagonally, she moistened it from a canteen and wrapped it around her neck for a cooling effect.

Lulled by a steady pace on their serpentine path, she watched Kittichai. His large pack of supplies looked heavy. The rough calluses on the bottoms of his feet appeared thicker than the soles of her shoes. Thinking of her blisters, she began to appreciate his life style. Never having been confined by footwear, his toes splayed outwards to leave an unusual print on the soft loam. Paying attention to his footprints, it took a few minutes before her brain registered there were animal prints in the soft soil.

"Kittichai," she called, stopping his forward progress. "What made these?" She pointed to the large prints paralleling their path.

Before answering, the monk glanced at Jon, who dipped his head in an abbreviated nod. "Is cat," Kittichai spit out.

"Good heavens! What kind? These prints are huge!"

Jon pointed to nearby spoor. "We have cougar in Montana, but nothing this big."

Kittichai said, "Tiger."

Jon had spotted the prints earlier and had been examining the terrain. Noises they made trekking through the area would either scare the cat or attract it. Readying his body for a big cat encounter, he took the lead.

Ana stepped into a large paw print and grimaced. It was comparable to the length of her size nine shoe.

She hiked between the two men.

Jon hacked a path in front while Kittichai brought up the rear. She was relieved when the cat tracks moved off the trail and out of sight. Remains of snakes appeared beside the path whenever Jon led. With Kittichai there were none.

She asked Jon, "With all the noise you make cutting a path, why don't snakes skitter away?"

"They're predators. We could be their next meal. Let me know if you see one that looks good. We'll save it for dinner."

The presence of snakes intimidated her desire to take a break.

Jon cautioned, "If one bites you and I'm not around, kill it, lie down, and call me."

"Kill it? Why?"

"So I'll know why you're dead when I find you later. Kill it so I know what snake bit you so I can treat you for snakebite. The first priority is to learn whether the snake bite was venomous or not." He explained he could often tell the difference between poisonous and non-poisonous snakes by the shape of their head.

She shivered. "I hate snakes."

"Laos has 'one step' snakes. After they bite, you can take one step before you die. I don't want you bitten. It's you or them. I choose you."

When she adjusted her posture again to stop the gear pack from hurting her back, her legs cramped. She didn't know if cramping was from over exercise, lack of water, lack of potassium, or all three. She was unable to decide which shoulder hurt more, the one wrenched in Bangkok or the one hit by a bullet.

* * *

After an hour of clearing trail, Jon dropped back to let Kittichai lead into a region of lighter plant growth. He removed his wrist cloth and twisted it, wringing out the accumulated sweat. Ana walked between them. Thinking aloud, Jon commented, "I can't decide if it's a single mastermind or an international organization gunning for you."

"I've been asking myself how they found out about me so fast." As the heavy foliage increased, Kittichai slipped to the rear and let Jon lead.

"I feel responsible. Your arrival on the scene put a killing machine into motion. Someone's using resources from around the world to target you. Their only constant is impatience."

"We both know it's the implants," she declared. "They always know where we are. Whoever it is doesn't value life. They'll kill anyone in their way."

"I should have gotten the switch-off procedure from Andy."

Exasperated, she said, "Aren't they like cell phones? They give off signals whether they're on or off."

Jon fingered his healing implant scar as he hiked. "If they're super glued to bone, removal will be impossible. Maybe ...," he paused.

After several moments passed, she felt her implant wound. "Maybe what?"

Hacking at foliage, he suggested, "I could pulverize them with a squeeze."

"Would they release a toxin?"

"Your guess is as good as mine. By the way, I'm impressed you're able to keep pace with us."

She blushed. "This trail's so overgrown it must be ancient."

"Or used by pygmies," he mused. "No one taller could get through"

"At least trees'll help block us from satellites." They dodged vines and branches impeding them from all directions. Slashing against plant bases, Jon backhanded his blade. Using his good left arm, he hit plants so they would fall away from him. Lacerations covered his hands. After clearing each obstacle, whoever led made sure the other two could pass through. Jon slipped back to let Kittichai lead.

Ribbons of sunlight streamed through tall tree canopies into dark shadows. Within them Ana saw sparkling reflections. Looking closer, she saw light reflecting off dew drops hanging from gigantic spider webs quivering in the breeze. The spider webs were ten or fifteen feet across. Climbing on them were monster spiders with legs over a foot long. Attached to the highest web, a giant spider lowering itself was caught in a gust and blew toward them on its tether.

She stepped back, hands outstretched to break a fall. "Holy moley! Look at the size!"

Jon remarked, "Like tarantulas on steroids. It's a good thing those webs are high." He chuckled. "Think of the spider silk those monsters could produce." He took photographs of the gigantic webs and spiders. Once the pictures were delivered to the spider silk manufacturers, he expected research teams would make a beeline for this location. "Imagine breeding this species." He made an audible note for Andy to verify the waypoint and sent off photographs with his satellite phone.

She was amazed at the suspended colony. "If their webs were at ground level, I bet they'd stop a tiger in its tracks." Swatting at insects buzzing her eyes, she had more appreciation of her spider silk clothing.

"Webs low near Mekong," Kittichai swept his arm toward the glittering webs. "Not go near ... can kill."

"Not us," Jon joked. "Wearing spidersilk clothing, they'll think we're family." Ana laughed. His attention kept returning to her. Her humidity-frizzed hair looked like a halo when she moved through sunny areas.

She was hot. The tropical heat was relentless and their shirts didn't allow air flow. During the debriefing back in the states she planned to recommend designers put ventilating mesh in the underarm areas and under a flexible back yoke on the shirts. She remoistened her bandana and tied it around her forehead. Cooling was immediate. Watching Kittichai swing his parang blade back and forth against the shrubs and tall grass, she understood why he didn't kill animals. He warned them away.

* * *

"Ana," Jon called. "Got a headache or muscle cramps?"

"No to the headache. Yes to cramps. Why?"

"Dehydration symptoms. Haven't seen you drink much water."

"I'm okay, just hot." In the presence of a monk, she couldn't open her shirt to cool off. She rolled sleeves to her shoulders. "Why do insects keep buzzing my eyes?"

"They're after salt in your perspiration. Lower your sleeves to keep them from your armpits."

Mumbling about the heat, she followed his advice with her head lowered and back slumped.

"If we're going to a cave," he said loud enough for her to hear, "we have to face the possibility it may become a little theatre of war. We need to use the site to our advantage no matter what it looks like. Need to picture all directions an enemy could infiltrate. Have to conceal you. Act fast. Surprise intruders commando style. Any satellite could see our trail."

Out of habit, he studied bird flight paths. Straight and low flight meant they were heading for fresh water, a survival necessity. From flight paths, he knew there was surface water nearby. Clues provided by animal and insect life were indispensable for existence. Nostalgic jungle smells brought forth memories of special ops training he'd led in Southeast Asia.

* * *

Ana tripped over a root and fell against Kittichai. The monk helped her regain her footing, removing his touch as though being burned.

"I'll be more careful. I'm so sorry." She felt deep regret that touch had occurred.

"Watch your step," Jon admonished. "You're in the boonies now."

Straightening, she replied, "This place is the ultimate boony of all boonies." With each grueling step, pain radiated through her back and arms. Discoloration and swelling from the bullet impact had spread across her chest. Figuring there was internal bleeding; she refolded her neck bandana, dampened it and put it under the gear pack strap at her left shoulder to ease pressure. She grabbed another from the pack side pocket and used it to tie the straps closer together. That reduced the pain in her side and took the load off her shoulders.

"Jon," she called.

"Yes?"

"Legs cramping. Feet in agony. Blisters, I think. What do you suggest?"

He called for a halt and had Ana remove her shoes. He used vodka from his flask to clean his fingers and the blisters. He sterilized the tip of the smallest blade in her Swiss army knife with his lighter, broke the blisters and worked out blister fluids. After spreading antibiotic ointment on her wounds, he covered them with a bandage and duct tape.

"That'll do it," he said.

As she pulled on clean socks and her shoes, she experienced leg spasms. Jon gave her more water to drink before he massaged her calves and thighs. Then he helped her stand.

"When we reach our destination," she asked, "would you teach me martial arts? That might help me get in shape for things like this."

"I think your shape is fine," he said with a sexual innuendo.

"You know what I mean."

"A Marine will always be of service to a lady in distress," he answered with a salute. "Want me to carry your gear pack?"

"I'll be all right." In reality, she was exhausted.

"Drink. Your muscles need water. Let's have some grub." He pulled out food a monistic woman had packed.

"You never get tired. You look like you could run all day."

He laughed. "Marines do that, you know."

"You never talk about it. What is it with you guys? You're so secretive."

He dipped his head at an angle. "My assignments were classified."

With a forced smile, she asked, "How can I protect myself without knowing martial arts?"

"There're no rules when fighting for your life. Catch 'em off guard. Act crazy. Spin. Spit. Snarl. Snap. Scream profanities and gibberish. Bite. Hit. Kick. Claw. Hurt. You know where to kick a man. Look for a weapon. Use the flashlight's sharp edge. Cut and slash as deep as you can. Aim for the face, eyes, neck, anything! Rip off their nostrils. Get your thumbs or fingers in their eyes. Then run. If they catch you, repeat the process. Otherwise, you're dead."

She grimaced.

"Or, leave fighting to me."

CHAPTER 33

They finally arrived at a south-facing, sandstone cave with no evidence of habitation. The cave was about fifteen feet deep. The opening, strewn with boulders, was about ten feet wide. Climbing around boulders made access difficult. Their surroundings became eerily quiet. Kittichai looked around.

Ana's legs shook with fatigue. Clenching her teeth in pain, she let her gear pack drop and slumped against a cave wall with a moan. Insect noises beyond the cave began, increasing in loudness over time. The wilderness was filled with tireless creature buzz. Her dehydrated thigh muscles cramped again with excruciating pain. She couldn't sit, stand or walk. To move was agony. She grabbed her canteen and drained what was left in it. Jon handed her another, which she emptied.

"Thanks." She tried to stand, but could not. She knew the water would eventually release the muscle cramping if she relaxed.

Squatting on his heels, arms around outspread knees, Kittichai ordered, "Rest here. I go to my village. Return tomorrow." He rolled his gear pack to the ground. "*Sohk dii der.* Goodbye." He walked around a bamboo grove and was soon out of sight.

"At least we don't have to stay here long," she remarked.

"Hate to burst your bubble. In this part of the world," Jon predicted with a smirk, "the word 'tomorrow' means some indefinable time in the future. He could be gone a day, a week, or more." Her eyes flashed surprise. He turned his face into the breeze. It held no human odors.

"I didn't know his pack was for us. Do you have more water? My muscles are crying for liquid. My body is one big cramp."

"Take this." He handed over his last canteen before rummaging through Kittichai's pack. It was half full of water containers. Jon had not realized Kittichai had carried such excess weight and admired the monks' stamina. "He left us rice, water-filled plastic jugs, dried food, mangosteens, guava and papaya, two tin cups, a battered cooking pan, two bowls and spoons."

She emptied the canteen. "What kind of dried food?"

"River weed." At her confused look, he added, "Grows along river banks. They're simmered in sauce, dried and spiced up."

"With what?"

"I don't know. In this part of the world, probably ginger, tomato or garlic. The dried sheets are cut into edible portions."

"Would you eat it?"

He shrugged. "It's been boiled."

"Which is mangosteen?" He picked out an orange-sized, purple object, pressed firmly on the outside and twisted. The inch-thick rind came off to expose a soft white fruit resembling a large garlic head. He removed one section and gave it to her to taste.

"Mumm. Sweet." He handed her the remaining mangosteen. "Does this grow on the ground?"

"Like an apple." Rummaging in the pack, he found jerky. He was surprised, since Buddhists refuse to hurt animals. He hoped it wasn't dog. He pulled a packet of reusable Graphair water purification filters from his shirt pocket. After checking to ensure the pack was in good condition, he returned it to the pocket and buttoned the flap.

"I'll smooth out a sleep spot," Ana said. "Gotta' move. Muscle cramps." Resisting the urge to sleep, she folded the bandana into a large triangle and tied it over her nose and mouth. Then she rolled over until she was on all fours. With excruciating pain, she forced herself to stand. On quivering legs, using a leafy shrub for a broom, she attacked debris at the back of the sun-warmed cave. Powdered silt and sand billowed into the air.

* * *

Rubbing his chin, Jon decided to forego shaving until they headed toward civilization. He moved around the campsite perimeter evaluating defensive positions. Glancing at Ana, he watched her examine a side opening in the cave. It looked like she could fit through it. He thought she was changing daily. According to Vaji, she's growing more powerful. He reflected with a crooked grin, "Better keep on her good side." He called, "Hungry? I hear frogs." She shook her head. "Birds?" She looked away. "They're like chickens," he persuaded. "Asians put a whole cooked sparrow in their mouth at one time."

"No, thank you."

Examining the site to find escape paths in case of attack, he pondered the surrounding plant growth impeding their view. There were mountain laurel, pine trees, and trees he didn't recognize. Having passed cypress on their hike to this site, he was disappointed to not find it here. Trees would help conceal them and yet restrict escape. He pulled up a small, leafy shrub and handed it to Ana for a fresh broom.

She asked, "Is the open cave entrance safe?"

"Safer than the trail we hacked," he replied. At her questioning glance, he pointed with his thumb, "Look at our footprints. Locals go barefoot. We left large Anglo Saxon size depressions from shoes. Each step we took left our signature. He tapped his implant site. "As long as these work, we're in danger."

Finished with sweeping and tamping sand into depressions to level and smooth a sleeping area, she clapped to rid her hands of silica dust and stepped beyond the cave for fresh air. Dust had turned into a silt layer on her damp bandana. She took it off. With a flick of her wrist, she snapped it to remove dust. Infrequent light beams sprinkling through the jungle canopy highlighted suspended dust. They created dappled shadows dancing on the ground. Inhaling decomposing jungle plant musk made her sneeze.

She'd dreamed of traveling to new and exciting places. No matter how dangerous, she felt lucky to be in this wild and magnificent environment. The problem was, they were running out of time. Muscles aching, she sat on a large boulder wishing for milk and ice.

Jon said, "Enjoy the scenery. It'll help you relax."

She beamed. "Believe me, Jon, sore or not, I am enjoying this." She refolded her bandana and tied it over dusty hair.

"We should stay in the cave. No one's coming to rescue us. We might as well do what we can to stop the bad guys from finding us."

"What about Kittichai and the men in his village?"

Jon rolled his eyes with a resigned sigh. "They're farmers. They may not have fighting skills or education."

"No schooling?"

"Missionary schools are too far away. They can't read a map because they've never seen one. They have no idea what the rest of the world is like. The more immediate problem is the village chief. Villagers will believe what they're told. If the village chief tells them you and I are good people, we're in like gold. If he says we're bad, run for your life."

If Ana were closer, she would have heard profanity muttered under his breath. Having finished his tirade, he turned his back to her and sat on a boulder at the cave's edge tossing rocks into the jungle while muttering expletives. The more he thought about their situation, the more anger consumed him. He thought Ana teetered on a psychic fulcrum. She was in the air one minute and down to Earth the next.

She interrupted his contemplation. "How do such remote people earn money?"

"Except for weaving homegrown cotton or cultivating opium, they don't. They barter."

"How much can they earn from an opium crop?"

"Maybe a thousand dollars a year, if they're lucky. Usually a dollar a day.

"You've seen a lot of the world, haven't you?"

"Ye shall know the truth and the truth shall make you free." He turned his face to the breeze and inhaled, alert to any change in the air.

"Bible quote?"

"Book of John. It's cut into a marble wall of a building I used to frequent." He pictured the CIA headquarters in Langley, Virginia, and speculated about how many people had read that quote over the years. He scraped an insect nest off the cave wall that Ana missed and rolled out her woven, grass sleeping mat. Twilight was approaching.

"What's your specialty in the Marines?"

"I put out fires."

She looked at him with admiration. "I'd never enter a burning building."

"Our fires are international hotspots needing attention. We go in, do our job and get out." Wary, he said, "You, my dear, have become a roving hotspot which our enemies want to extinguish."

She paled. "How can I help you?"

"Follow my orders."

She squirmed at his comment.

Birds nearby ignored them. Trills, whistles, peeps, and song patterns from near and far were nonstop. The eastern sky had become blue-grey. A mass of layered purple and pink clouds highlighted the western sky. Venus appeared. Animal calls and tempos softened with the deepening twilight. Insect noises increased.

"I don't know how I'll sleep with all this noise," she lamented.

"Did you ever fall asleep watching TV?"

"Don't we all?"

"If you can sleep with a TV going, you can sleep here. I'll gather rocks for a fire pit and some wood," he offered, "You know how to cook rice?"

She stifled a smart retort. "Actually, I'm a good cook."

"Your specialty?"

She gave him a wide smile. "Brownies. If you're wanting rice, let's find some herbs." They reconnoitered the area and found wild onion. At the cave she watched him adjust rocks to hold the cook pan above a small fire.

"We can cook with these." She pulled a Velcro flap from a pocket on her cargo slacks and removed a small white box. "A cook's gift from Andy. These pills have capillary pumps with fuel to burn several hours. Power to go. May I use your lighter?" She placed a pill-sized fuel pellet on a flat rock at the fire pit center. "Andy told me these have several fired clay layers. The bottom layer is saturated with fuel. The lighter's heat goes down the center hole and ignites the fuel. Capillary action pulls the fuel into a flammable vapor." She took his lighter and aimed the blue flame at the miniscule hole in the pill top. A smoke veil blew past as the blue flame was pulled into the miniature disk's cavity. A flaming vapor streamed out of the pellet like a gasoline torch.

With a soft whooshing sound, the flames reached over a foot high.

"Impressive," he commented. "May I?" Extending his hand, he examined the remaining pellets in the dimming light. "Should be standard in field packs. "

They used water Kittichai left to cook rice. The aroma from the dented pan soon whetted their appetites. As they ate, Jon pulled a protein drink from his gear pack and offered it to her. She drank half and handed it back. He chugged what was left and passed over some jerky.

"Thanks." Holding a hand over her chest she said, "I'd love a tall glass of iced mocha and a good book right now." Seated on the ground, she wrapped her arms around raised knees and relaxed her back.

"A reader, huh?"

"Not without my glasses. Must have misplaced them. I can increase the font size on my reader." She didn't remind him her glasses fell and broke during the Bangkok murder attempt. "Andy told me to bring a second pair. I didn't. Big mistake."

* * *

After eating, in the early twilight Jon raised his head and sniffed. "I smell water." Walking southwest they found a stagnate pond. Scooting floating algae out of the way, he used rough grass to clean the cook pan and filled it with water.

At the cave site, Ana filtered water into canteens through a Graphair purification filter and made tea.

Jon said. "Mask your nose and mouth with your bandana when you sleep. This area has screwworm flies. They deposit eggs in nostrils."

"You're kidding?"

"Do I lie?"

In the cave, Ana quickly collapsed into a deep sleep. Jon arranged his sig for easy access before entering his sleep alert mode.

CHAPTER 34

VESPER Facility
3 September. 12:00 PM DST

Phillip Arnold remained apprehensive. Masterson was still alive. In addition, a satellite had been having periodic glitches. Although cowboy Derek assured him it wouldn't last long, an hour ago one tracking satellite stopped processing. VESPER was now limited to two satellites. Three were needed for triangulation and good coverage. He passed Masterson's lats and longs to several al-Qaeda teams. The team that lost men in the Nong Khai attempt still needed funding.

"They better be successful this time," he agonized. "At least one team should be close to killing that psychic bitch. Why so many attempts? Her bodyguard must be more talented than I thought. Since shooting at her doesn't work, this next effort will," he snorted in disgust, "or no one gets paid a cent." He had hired an Asian martial arts assassin reputed to be one of the best trained in the world. Finding him had been a boon. He and his men would be well rewarded after the kill.

Visiting the communication Pit, Arnold found the Masterson position in a remote Laotian area. Using a desktop computer, he examined a topography map of the region. Seeing the contour lines close together on the chart, he knew their terrain was steep and rugged. He questioned the topo map accuracy. He also questioned how Masterson had lived through several attempts on her life. He wished he had a video feed of each attack. He desperately wanted to know how she managed to survive.

CHAPTER 35

Wilderness area
Laos
5 September. 5:30 AM ICT

Mist began to dissipate in dawning twilight. Ana awoke to see a shirtless Jon slamming his forearms as fast as lightning against small tree trunks, a Shaolin exercise routine. He danced over the ground with soft steps. Scars across his chest, right arm, and back provided evidence of a warrior life style.

She called out, "Good morning! How are you today?"

"Invigorated. Fired up. Motivated."

"You're supposed to feel that way. You're a Marine!" He made a quick head dip and continued his routine. She called, "I'm going to wash," and headed for the small pond.

"Make noises to alert animals. Stay where I can see you." As an after thought he added, "Don't go wading. Hear?"

She gave him a thumbs up.

Muck surrounded the brackish pond. Dense green algae floated on the surface. Pockets of reflected sky were visible between algae groups. Rolling her cargo pants above her knees, she slipped off her shoes. Glancing to ensure she wasn't visible to Jon, she stepped into the water and began to wash. Cool liquid against her skin took her mind off their predicament. The duct tape over her blisters was waterproof. Seeing no danger, she relaxed.

"Jon's over protective. Why would he not want me to go wading? It's so refreshing." She took another step. Thinking of snapping turtles, she smacked the water. Cool, creamy, wet silt squished between her toes at each step. Her feet sank to ankle depth in the silt. She moaned. "This feels so good."

She questioned when Kittichai would return. If anything happened to him, she might not meet Kanchana. Instant fear flowed through her. She rolled her pants higher, appreciating they were baggy. When the algae mat began to settle back toward her, she splashed it away and stepped into a liquid balm. "You think you can fool me," she addressed the algae with a grin. "I know you're hiding energy. You'll be harvested one day when coal and oil are gone." Insects skimmed the water. Swarms of flying gnats were highlighted by a sunbeam filtering through the overhead forest canopy. Birds pecked along the swampy bank foraging for creatures displaced by her arrival and lapping water.

Inhaling jungle musk with all the unique aromas, she marveled at her situation. "Here I am," she whispered. "Who would have known a few weeks ago I'd be halfway around the world fleeing terrorists? Been put through the pits. Have to admit, I relished every second. And I thought pilot training gave a rush."

Ignoring the water's rank smell, she splashed her face. Feeling what she thought were minnow nips, she sculled the water to frighten fish. Sliding hands across her legs she felt a small bump and then another. They were smooth, slippery and larger than her thumb. She couldn't lift her leg to see what they were. Her feet were stuck in the muck. Twisting her feet to break the suction, she stepped out of the pond to see what caused the bumps.

She was horrified to see swollen, worm-like objects attached to her legs. About three inches long, they were black and shiny. Engorging on her blood, they seemed to enlarge as she watched. She didn't know they had stomachs three-fourths their size, or could hold eight times their weight in blood. She was going to learn fast. A breeze created a damp chill. She was frustrated her thumb and forefinger kept slipping off the slimy parasites.

"Slippery little suckers." She watched in astonishment as one released babies. A few attached themselves to her. Mommy had brought them to dinner. Parting cattails, she stepped into tall grass. Algae flowed off her legs. Some remained stuck in clumps around the black animals. Leaves in surrounding trees fluttered in the breeze as though asking, "Now what?" Her lips narrowed into a hard line. She shook her legs and stomped to dislodge the creatures. Grabbing her bandana, she stretched and twirled the material between her hands. With a whip-type smack, she tried unsuccessfully to dislodge the blood-suckers. Growing desperate, she cried out, "Jon, I need help." At her call, animal and insect noises stopped.

He ran to her expecting danger. He had to bite the inside of his cheek to stop a chuckle when he saw her predicament. Reaching toward one of the parasites he stifled a smile.

She jerked in reflex as he touched one of the black objects. "What are they?"

"Leeches. Stand still." Without looking at her face, he said, "You ignored my advice." She said nothing. He nudged the small end of the largest creature attached to a soft spot behind her knee. Goose bumps appeared.

She cringed. "How do I get them off?" She heard him chuckle and tapped her foot. "You laughing at me?"

"Nooooo," he answered, looking away to hide a grin.

Screeches and caws of the jungle animals began again. Birds called tentatively. She inhaled Jon's aroma and admired his muscular, glistening chest. She flinched with revulsion when touching a leech. "They're black worms."

He remarked, "But with panache." He spoke calmly with tenderness in his eyes, "You need to be still so I can remove them. Some species slice skin to stick their heads inside and suck blood. They can leave microscopic parasites."

As hard as it was for her stop shaking, it was harder for Jon to hide his amusement at her discomfort. On past missions when his men had moved through water, they stripped afterwards to pick off leeches. The higher the water, the more leeches they accumulated.

"I hope," he began, "you didn't pick up an amoeba. They live in warm freshwater. Can infect the brain. They enter through the nose if you splash water on your face. That's why you don't dunk your head in warm lakes, ponds or rivers without holding your nose shut. All we need to make us more miserable is for you to get sick."

"I never saw a leech before."

"Microscopic parasites, amoeba and leeches are in ponds, lakes, and rivers throughout the world." He placed his fingernail next to a leech and nudged it sideways with a shove to break the seal it had made with her skin. With his other hand he pushed and bothered the sucker at the other end of the leech. Once the main oral sucker detached from her skin, it tried to attach itself to his finger. He flicked it off. "We need to be careful. An accidental squeeze could make it regurgitate into your body. Bad stuff."

Lacking salt to kill the leeches, he took a cigarette from his pocket. Leeches jiggled as she shivered again. Jon crumbled the tip of a cigarette with spit and dropped it onto a leech. The animal released its hold. He knocked it off. "Tobacco kills 'em."

"I always knew tobacco was harmful," she said with a smile in her eyes.

He laughed and removed leeches from the back side of her legs. "It's easy to do. Try it," he suggested.

She took a cigarette and methodically removed the remaining leeches. Their injected anticoagulant at bite sites caused blood to dribble. Insects attracted to the smell of blood milled around her. She reached to unroll her trousers.

"Not yet." He rushed her back into the cave, dug into his gear pack and pulled out the flask. "Your legs look absolutely ravished …ah, excuse me, ravishing." He grinned. Using a small cloth, he swabbed the wounds with vodka. "Sterilizes. I know you think you got them all, but one leech species slices skin and slips inside to begin their families. Check your legs for lumps."

Her eyes widened and face paled. "Really?"

With a nod, he asked, "Want me to run my hands over your legs and feet to check for the telltale bumps of imbedded leeches or will you do the honors?"

"I will." In a grim mood she began the dreaded task, horrified that leeches could be inside her.

"Check from the top of your legs to your feet. Especially between your toes. Baby leeches love gourmet hidey holes." He watched intently. She slid her hands over her legs and feet, prodding for bumps. If she hesitated, Jon checked for telltale signs of leech intrusion.

"Double check the soft tissue below your ankles." He examined the duct tape for leaks.

Completing the task, she rubbed off remaining algae and unrolled her slacks. She slipped into the cooler cave recess and watched nearby plants deepen in hue as the sky grayed with thickening clouds. Jon walked to the innermost wall and sat. He took his cigarettes out, lit one and deeply inhaled. He enjoyed watching smoke rings deform against the rock. Soon they were listening to pelting rain.

Drops cascaded off the cliff face to pool in some areas and sluiced downhill in others. They formed multiple rivulets similar to a miniature braided river. Rain was so heavy she couldn't see over ten feet. There was a flash of light and a crack of thunder. Rain pouring off tree leaves splatted to the ground.

Jon advised, "Make a slurry of mud. Rub it over exposed skin to keep off insects." After muddying her skin, she dozed off within minutes.

* * *

When the deluge stopped, the sun shining through the rising mist created a luminescence around them. Jon decided to forego fire pellets. He started a small wood fire at the edge of the cave. Crackling flames soon flickered and brought Montana memories. He ran the tip of his tongue across dry lips.

"I'm going to find some water. Don't go anywhere."

"I won't." She dozed.

He surveyed the terrain for edibles and located three banana plants growing in a sunny spot. Surprised to find them at this elevation, with his parang he removed the largest smooth and variegated green leaves of one plant for padding under Ana's sleeping mat. The leaves were as large as she. He sliced a ripe banana bunch off one plant and a green banana hand off another before cutting the trunk to a foot high.

He carved a well in the stump center with the blade's curved edge and used both hands to scoop out the cavity. Water rose in the bowl-shaped hollow from the underground stem and root system. When it filled the depression, he swiped it out. After it filled again, he drank the water and covered his new water reservoir with two trimmed banana leaves to keep out insects. He peeled one of the ripe bananas. It had little flesh and many black seeds, each seed about one-fourth of an inch thick. He ate the tasty banana with relish, spitting seeds out. Being competitive, he tried to best himself with each spit.

* * *

When Ana awakened, her first thoughts were of Jon. She pitied him for being saddled with her. "That poor guy," she said. "He probably never had to put up with someone like me. I've done nothing but cause problems."

Jon returned and took her to the new water hole. He scooped water from the banana tree trunk depression with the cooking pan and passed it over for her to taste. When her lips touched the cool water, she smiled.

"It tastes so clean." She emptied the pan. Jon made water holes in another plant and explained why she should place green bananas in a dark gear pack to ripen swiftly.

"You know a lot about living in the wilderness."

He raised an eyebrow. "Ever hear of counterinsurgency training?" When Ana shook her head, he related, "I trained military once near here. Taught 'em to live off the land."

"Do you think we're safe here?"

He ignored the question. "I've been scoping the area. Did Vaji tell you how long we'd be here?" She shook her head. Trained to assess and meet needs, on past missions he'd had backup and support with his team. He remembered pledging to not fail his comrades and to shoulder one hundred percent or more of the tasks. With Ana there was an absence of any mutual plan. He hoped for wisdom to do what was right when action was needed. To take her mind off their situation, he asked, "Want to learn a few tricks of the wilderness?"

"Such as?"

"Finding water or food? It'll help pass the time."

"Lead the way." Not wanting to contaminate the canteens with impure water, she carried the cook pan to hold any water they found. "With this humidity, we should be able to scoop water out of the air." She waved the pan in a figure eight and laughed.

Jon grasped her empty hand. "For safety." His thumb massaged her palm. "How're your shoulders?"

"Swollen. Sore from my pack." He gently massaged her shoulders a few minutes. "Ummmm, don't stop." She missed being touched and felt reassured. Her thoughts wandered to home.

"You have stronger neck muscles than most women."

She grinned. "Sports."

"Really?"

"I was a girl athlete. Trampoline and tennis teams, National Ski Patrol, Water Safety Instructor, gymnastics and such.

"You'd be easy to train in martial arts."

"You can teach me." She looked away smiling. She had always wanted to learn martial arts for self-protection.

Walking amidst wet foliage, he called her attention to plants with cup-shaped blooms for rain reservoirs.

"Because of microscopic parasites in the topics, if you run out of your Graphair filters, boil drinking water. Too bad we don't have a *microbiocide. By the way, anyone who has spent time in the tropics should never donate blood."

"Parasites?"

He nodded.

With the return of blazing sun, translucent leaves surrounding them greened the area in hundreds of hues. Sweet aromas wafted by. The never-ceasing animal alarms changed frequently in volume as they trekked.

With his parang, Jon cut off a young stalk of bamboo below a stem ring and shook it. Hearing water splash inside, he chopped a hole in one end and drained liquid into the cook pan and handed the pan to Ana.

"If you cut notches in a bigger standing plant, you'll get more water, but the wood is thicker and will be harder to cut. If you need water, let me know and I'll cut notches for you. You should be able to drink it right away, but let's not take chances."

He grabbed the top of a young green bamboo, bent it over and tied it down with paracord. He made a hole in it. The bamboo began to drip water from the cut. Using short sturdy branches anchored into the ground, he positioned an open condom under the drips to gather moisture.

They returned to the cave and strained the *bamboo water with a Graphair filter.

"Not bad," she said after tasting it. "Clean taste. Kind of like well water."

"You'll never run out of water around here "if you have a way to cut the stalks."

He tied a second trash bag around leafy foliage. "Plants give off moisture. The theory is they give off more liquid than you need. They don't, but we'll get a trickle you can try later. Every little bit helps."

"Handy thing, that transpiration," she quipped. "I can't believe how much I've learned on this trip. You must think I'm a dumb blonde."

"You were never a dumb blonde." Jon had been witnessing her metamorphosis into a more aware telepath and wondered how much more she'd progress. Off and on during the rest of the day he taught her a few basic marital art moves for self-protection and to loosen her muscles. She was an avid learner. They cooked and ate light with food the monistics provided.

In preparation for sleep, Jon had her tuck her pants into the tops of her socks. She reapplied a thin mud slurry to her face and neck. While occasional black flies visited with fierce bites, no-see-ums bit non-stop.

She announced," I'm sleeping here," and unrolled her sleep mat under the trees.

"Better not. You'll attract animals."

"I'll hear them if they get too close."

"See those black spots in the trees above you?"

She looked at ponderous, overhanging limbs in the canopy. "That fungus?"

"They're tree leeches. Put yourself beneath 'em, and they'll drop onto your nice, warm, delicious, blood-filled, body." He moved her sleeping mat to the back of the cave. "Some have three jaws and a hundred small teeth. They'd love your soft skin."

"What an imagination."

"It's the truth."

She shuddered. "How would they know I'm here?"

"Each one has ten pairs of eyes." She rolled her eyes. "I'm not exaggerating. Plus, your body heat would attract them. Getting ready to sleep out there you'd be advertising, 'Here I am, eat me, eat me.' " He coughed to camouflage a laugh.

She scratched a few bites which began bleeding. "Should I worry?"

"Not much blood loss from a leech cut. Let's hope you don't get infected or develop an allergy. We're in the middle of nowhere without medical supplies. I'm here because of your faith in Vaji. Just because someone has telepathic ability doesn't ensure they know what needs to be done to protect you. Grab a bandana."

She pulled one out of her gear pack. "Now what?"

"Mask your nose and mouth when you sleep. Screwworms. Remember?"

"You're worrying me." She smeared mud on her face.

"Good. Be proactive. Prepare for the worst." He analyzed the situation, observing what he heard and smelled. He spoke aloud for Ana's benefit. "If I were an enemy, how would I raid this site? Wouldn't carry anything large. Trees are too tight for an air assault. It'll be from the ground. Trees, bamboo and shrubs limit the line of sight but will conceal us from intruders." Feeling uneasy, he planned to sleep with one eye open. With no support team, equipment or supplies, he had to rely on cunning.

"Ana," he began, "your telepathy got me to thinking. If you weren't trying to find a mindreacher, do you think you'd be interested in traveling with a military team on assignment?"

She asked, "Have you thought about combat teams being trained in telepathy? If you did, no one would have to talk during operations. Think how that would change team effectiveness and combat readiness. They'd know enemy thoughts and positions at all times."

"You don't sound civilian anymore."

She grinned. "I've been around you too much."

"One of the hallmarks of a good military is constant improvement. But training troops in telepathy?"

"The President would love the idea."

He twisted his mouth in thought. "The problem is time. There's nowhere to add telepathy in overcrowded training schedules."

"Maybe one telepath could go into combat with each squad."

He looked toward the ceiling in thought. "Good idea for command to think about."

* * *

Later, fully dressed to keep the insects at bay and ensconced in the farthest reaches of the cave, Ana's legs itched. Fully dressed to protect them, she rubbed her pants legs over the itchy sites. Shivering as the air cooled, she murmured, "Jon?" He made a gravelly noise in his throat. "I'm so cold, would you mind if we shared some body heat?"

He arched an eyebrow. "Sure."

Ana moved next to him. When he pulled her closer, she snuggled into a spooning position to get some body warmth.

"Mmmm, you smell good," he murmured. He moved the pistol and clave behind him and nudged a *tactical pen in a front pocket to the side.

"Leech bites itch."

"Scratching makes 'em worse," he admonished. "What's clinking?"

"My flashlight. In case I need to leave for a minute. Makes me feel safer since you showed me how to use it as a weapon."

Before he could protest, she released the flashlight. Due to its shape, it rolled in an arc with a bump before bouncing off a rock and skittering toward the cave opening. After a quiet interlude she whispered, "Thanks for being my bodyguard."

He had a crooked grin. "I enjoy guarding your body. I just thought it would be easier."

Not entering the privacy of his deep reflections, she let her mind skim his surface thoughts. She recognized one half of his mind was going into sleep mode. She knew warriors never let both sides of their mind sleep at once. Wanting him to totally rest with both sides of his mind, she invaded the pituitary gland of his endocrine system and released chemicals allowing him to relax and sleep. She waited until his breathing became heavy and regular. Then she moved his pistol to a position against the cave wall behind him. She didn't want him to roll on top of it and awaken.

With the thought they were we're hidden from satellites and miles from civilization, she asked herself, who could find us? She joined Jon's oblivion.

CHAPTER 36

Laos Wilderness
5 September 11:27 PM ICT

The cadence of chirping cricket harmonies stopped first. Other animal and insect noises stopped next. One animal screeched an alarm before there was quiet.

Ana opened her eyes at the eerie silence. No animals stirring meant a nocturnal predator. Remembering the tiger prints, she questioned if the predator was human. Raising her head, she spotted movement of upright, shadowy upright figures beyond the cave entrance. Focusing for mindsongs, she flinched at hearing the demonic noises of assassin minds. Only within the youngest mindsong could she sense a trace of humanity. The feel of night changed from nice to nasty. Condemning her lax behavior, she was angry at not being alert to mindsongs. She thought, I'm such a fool.

Nudging Jon's arm, her pressing hand cautioned him to freeze as he tensed into wakefulness. He'd know what to do and take care of her. At that thought, she remembered drugging him. A flash of fear passed through her. She reached into his mind and released adrenaline into his body. Lurking doubts about his hampered ability crowded her thoughts.

* * *

Startled, Jon's eyes opened. Ana's warning touch didn't immediately put him into alert mode. Instead, he felt groggy.

"What the...?" He felt energized as adrenaline flowed through his body. His mind ratcheted into warrior mode.

Seconds had been wasted. Fully awake, he saw stealthy movement beyond the cave. Whoever they were, they moved with trained precision to remain unnoticed. He pictured the steps he would take when they tried to enter the cave.

"When I create a diversion," he whispered into Ana's ear, "take off through the side opening." He felt her nod. Suspecting it would be a fight for life, he knew she was the most formidable hope the United States had in the fight against terrorism. His distraction had to be good. Ana had to escape the killing zone. He felt her prepare to move at his order. He reached for his firearm to find empty space. Careful not to touch sand and make a noise, he groped where he had placed it, sweeping his hand above the sand. He seethed. Ana moved his SIG. He found the gear pack. It could be hefted across the cave as a diversion. He stealthily rose, gaining enough leverage to sling the pack with a lateral motion toward the far wall.

At the appropriate time the cave shape would funnel intruders along the other wall. He smelled their curry breath before counting four, barely perceptible moving shadows. The haloed first quarter Moon created a dim light and a moonbow beyond wispy, cirrostratus clouds. The bow meant precipitation, but this was monsoon season. It would rain every day. The Moon would set at midnight. Needing a weapon, he grasped the pen in his pocket.

Knowledge in practiced fighting with a shobo, or ninja tool, had let him understand the full defensive and attacking potential of any held object. Feeling the tactical pen in his pocket against his hip, he instantly decided to use it as his shinobi-shobo. Any object consisting of a short shank of rounded wood or metal, such as his tactical pen, could be utilized as a deadly weapon

His mind automatically brought up muscle memory of practice when he was a teen. He'd held pens while striking objects and as a shuriken-type weapon which he threw at his handmade targets. The pen would reinforce his fist like an interior brass knuckle if he hit anyone. His fist would be injured, but it would hurt his attacker more. With the pointed end of his pen, he could rip flesh or, using it as a dagger, imbed it into a vital area of his attacker's body, especially areas on the face and neck. He could also use it to extend his reach when holding off an attack. He had practiced throwing writing pens as a youth so many hours that he intimately knew their aerodynamic characteristics.

Jon calmed. A Shaolin warrior must have calm readiness in mind, body and spirit and be ready to die in achieving their objective. In an instant these thoughts passed through his mind. His iron arm was ready, tongue at the top of his palate, breathing deep and steady.

Knowing any safety net was full of holes, he placed the gear pack at his left. Leaning on an elbow, he placed the pen lengthwise in his other hand, the pointed end near the tip of his middle finger. Creating a lengthwise groove for the pen between his index and ring fingers, he folded his thumb over the pen to secure it. The make-shift weapon was ready to sling with leverage, bo-shuriken style.

He was reminded of his teens when he'd practiced day after summer day throwing his mother's ballpoint pens, bo-shuriken style, at trees and home-made bulls-eye targets. One side of his mouth curved upward, remembering her anger at finding smashed pens in her desk. He'd long since graduated to more complex methods of warfare. Yet the feel of this pen in his hand was comfortable.

Several minutes passed before they heard motion. It would have been indistinguishable from blowing leaves, if not expected. A tight, green helium laser beam swept across the cave at shoulder height. The handler listened for a reaction. Jon pressed Ana down and flattened.

A thrown piece of flat, twirling metal hit the cave wall behind them. A spark flew off rock as it was deflected toward the ceiling. It proved the invaders were not only lethal, they were not sure of Jon and Ana's positions. Using the strength of a side toss, Jon slung his pen at the intruder who had thrown the metal. Had the man not moved, it would have entered his shoulder. Instead, it penetrated the man's left eye.

"*Mai chai! Mai Chai!* No!" In shock, the man jerked at the pen. Parts of a gelatinous mass emerged from his eye socket. Seeing what he held, with shaking hands the man recoiled, tossing the vitreous orb and pen. Glistening in the soft reflected moonlight of its moving arc, the orb disappeared into the darkness. The wounded intruder dropped to his knees, covered his bloody eye socket with his hands, spewing vomit in all directions.

Recoiling, Ana scuttled to the side of the cave and tried to squeeze through the opening. It was too narrow. She couldn't escape that way. She panicked.

* * *

Jon heaved his gear pack. Three men rushed into the cave. Knowing these were well-trained, hardened killers, he hoped Ana was quick enough to escape. The pack hit the opposite wall and slid to the ground.

One man slipped on her flashlight. It lit and twirled in the air. The beam circled the cave's entrance twice while falling. It landed close enough for her to grab and douse the beam. In that short interval of time she saw a man flip backwards into the opening and land deftly on his feet, body arched forward and arms outstretched ready for action. His grotesque face showed beady eyes, a broad nose, and no chin. Another intruder groped empty space. A third rushed around the cave perimeter seeking targets, one hand trailing the wall as a guide.

Using stealth and rapid action of a Shaolin trained martial artist, Jon closed in on the runner. He ran up a wall and jumped upon one dark figure. A reverberation of a gunshot within the small cave was followed by a sharp pain in his sternum. He grabbed his chest. Instead of blood, his palm hit a dart needle.

Smashing a hand across his chest to thrust it aside, he hoped there had been no time for liquid to be injected. His brain was in unity with his heart, his heart with his mind, his mind with his breath. His mind was tranquil. His breath permeated his extremities. He placed the tip of his tongue to his upper palate. His spirit felt strong.

"If I live through this," he vowed, "I'll never be out of condition again. Ever!" Knowing time may be short before the drug took effect, he screamed with feral fury, "OOO-RRRAAAHHH!"

His left side faced one opponent. Arms out, he quickly swirled and brought his right leg around and up in a swift kick to the man's head. The man fell to the side as Jon brought his leg down and back. As quick as lightning, his rock-hard, right hand struck forward to punch another intruder in the chest. It caused the black-garbed attacker vascular spasms and internal damage.

The man fell at Jon's feet. Jon's healing shoulder reacted with pain.

Attackers surrounded him. Striking with every part of his body as though hitting sand bags, with each effort Jon shouted, advancing harshly. He stopped extraneous thoughts. His body positions gave him strength. He dropped intruders or they rolled out in different directions. With the force of eagle claws, using three fingers he crushed hand and wrist bones. He grew dizzy.

Surprised by Jon's assault precision, his opponents coordinated their attacks and ricocheted off walls with metal batons in their hands. They targeted, bludgeoned, and kicked his head and damaged shoulder. He questioned how they knew of his combat wound. They appeared to be dumbfounded he was still moving.

In motion, Jon was a deadly weapon. If not for the chemical dart, the intruders would be dead. Pain sluicing through him lessened. His right arm became useless. He became lethargic. He had the will to fight but could not easily control his body.

* * *

Ana hid behind a boulder. The man she ironically called 'Nochin' found her. He gripped the front of her shirt and whipped her body side to side. Remembering Jon's earlier suggestions, she acted crazy by screaming, twirling, and flailing arms and legs. With a firm grip, she held the cutting end of her flashlight outward. Each time he tried to swing her, she created a dead weight in the opposite direction. She slashed, cutting at hands, arms, and neck. Frustrated she couldn't grab an earlobe, she was pleased his ear hung in pieces. When Nochin released her, she flew into the back of Jon's legs.

"GET OUT! MOVE! MOVE!" Jon yelled, barely holding on to consciousness.

"I'm trying," she called. When she stood, her muscled attacker grabbed and twisted her arm trying to heave her out of the cave. She brought her arm to her chest, pushed against his and rolled her body around him while screaming. He released her with that hand and grabbed her with the other. She slammed the sharp edge of the flashlight into his wrist, lacerating flesh and tendons. He released his hold and knocked the flashlight out of her hand. She turned to run. He grabbed the back of her shirt.

Whirling with full body weight, she pulled away hoping the spidersilk shirt would rip and free her. Unfortunately, it held.

* * *

The chemical dart slowed Jon's thinking. Seeing Ana struggling with an attacker, he shouted, "USE TELEPATHY." Pounded with kicks, fists, and batons, his arms felt heavy. His vision grew impaired. Fearless, he fought using every ounce of decreasing strength.

* * *

The assassin backhanded Ana's face. She felt her nose crack. Blood sprayed. She slammed her bare foot against his instep in an attempt to pulverize his arch. It didn't bother him, but almost crippled her foot. By holding a bent arm at the wrist and quickly turning, she used that elbow as a battering ram against his neck while mentally entering his visual senses to hide her presence.

At his confused hesitation, she smashed her knee as hard as she could toward his crotch, hitting his inner thigh instead. Face-to-face with him, she slashed his arms, neck, and face with her fingernails and kept hitting as hard as she could. He kept trying to grab her. Slick with sweat, she kept slipping from his grasp. She mentally dulled his visual sense again.

Surprised, he shook his head. Still blinded, he rubbed his eyes and tried to see.

Dropping, she rolled from him, protecting her face with her hands. Emboldened by freedom, adrenalin pumping, she skirted boulders and ran. Hearing grunts and blows of fighting, she didn't look back. Terrified of the dark unknown jungle and the life-threatening melee' behind, she ran zigzagging to become a difficult target. She tongued teeth on the injured side of her face. They were loose.

Feeling an adrenaline rush after her narrow escape, she slammed into another man. His hands grabbed her throat and squeezed. She tried to mentally anesthetize him. She straightened index fingers of both hands together into a point and jabbed them upward as hard as she could into the hollow at the base of his neck. He released her. Before he recovered, she kneed his groin. This time she was on target.

With a harsh grunt, her assailant bent over and fell sideways. She ran until she slammed into a tree and recoiled to the jungle floor. Whimpering at the impact, she rose wearily to all fours and crawled into heavy brush. Spider webs wrapped her face. Thorns and knife sharp leaves grabbed her clothing.

The assailant beat bushes to find her, his noise masking her escape. His screaming rage pursued her into the night. She figured someone at VESPER had to hear what was going on through the implants and send help.

The racket behind her diminished with distance. Thorns lacerated her face and hands. Had she not been wearing protective spidersilk, her body would have been ripped to shreds. She ignored the pain. Her toenails were torn to the quick as debris of the jungle floor ripped her bare feet. She sucked ripped fingernails to alleviate pain and spit blood. Feeling alone and vulnerable, she tried to breath calmly while silently walking and wiping insects off her skin. To lull chattering animals alarmed at her passing, she sent them a mental sense for calm and quiet.

Tears of relief coursed down her cheeks. She'd escaped. Jon saved her life. Fear parched her mouth. As the adrenaline overload faded, she craved water. Her hands shook.

"*Kill 'em, Jon*, she sent. When her toes cracked against another rock, she collapsed to the ground, listening and smelling for danger. Running fingertips over her feet, she felt rips. She continued moving. The farther she ventured from the fighting clamor, the more slowly she progressed. Grim and weary, she continued a haphazard flight with no comprehension of direction except to keep the fighting noise diminishing behind her. Groping her way, she slipped on damp undergrowth. The absolute dark created by the setting moon made progress difficult. However, if she couldn't see, neither could her attackers. She collapsed, shaking with the adrenalin high.

Grabbing handfuls of dirt, she spit into it, kneading it into mud. With diagonal smears, she wiped it on her clothing, face, neck, and wrists for camouflage. She smelled her wrist. "Good," she announced in a whisper to the trees, "I smell like dirt!" She next muddied her blonde hair. Trembling, she found concealment, a depression in an overhanging cliff deep enough to give protection from the elements. She rolled into a ball and took quiet breaths, listening.

Ana felt lucky to have stumbled across a shallow cave. Periodically checking her skin, she wiped off chiggers and occasional larger insects. Knowing some insects injected an anesthetic so she couldn't feel them, she swiped often at her clothing to remove imagined, attached animals. Apprehensive about leeches from trees slipping under her flesh, she ran a hand through her hair. Tangles kept her busy until she fell into a worried sleep.

CHAPTER 37

Laotian Wilderness
6 September 6 AM ICT

By dawn, Ana calmed and visually checked her skin for parasites. During the night, insects had climbed inside her cargo pants and attacked her left knee. It had swollen to about the size of her thigh but didn't hurt. She figured the insects anesthetized her with each bite. It was the same knee she'd injured in a skiing accident the year before.

Dehydrated and exhausted, she stood and fell against a tree. She released a double whammy of endorphins from her mind. Within seconds there was no pain. Sitting in dawning light, listening to jungle noises, she could smell decay in the tree against which she rested. As the sun rose, tropical heat began to warm her drowsy body. She shook herself awake. "Have to hurry. The airport bombers won't wait. Neither will my thirst." A cry escaped her lips. With a shiver of fear and sagging body, she thought, I don't think I can do this.

A parasite plant's vase-shaped blooms on a nearby tree held liquid. She fit a Graphair filter between pursed lips and teeth before pouring the small amount of water into her mouth. She wiped residue off the filter off before placing it in her chest pocket. Her thirst somewhat sated, she sat to rest. Opening awareness, she found Jon's mindsong.

"He's alive!" She stood and began moving toward his weak mindsong.

* * *

About forty-five minutes later, her nostrils flared as she neared Kittichai's cave. She shortened her stride to maintain stealth. She got the feel of the terrain by walking with bare toes touching the ground first, the ball of the foot next, and then the heel. Putting her body weight forward on one foot, she slowly repeated the process to get closer. Her lips pressed together in concentration, she heard no terrorist mindsongs. Crouching behind a tree, she magnified her senses. Moving tree to tree, she wished for shoes. Her feet were in agony.

Sighting the cave, she saw strewn debris and Jon. He wasn't moving. If not for his faint mindsong, she would have thought him dead. She was outraged at what he had endured for her. A body lay near his feet. Another with a bloody eye socket and grotesquely twisted head lay outside the entrance. "There's two," she said, looking around. "Where's the others?"

She put her fingertips at Jon's neck artery to check his heart strength. She urged, "Talk to me, Jon. Come on. Open your eyes. It's Ana." That's when she saw his implant hanging by a skin flap, his skull visible below it. Biting one side of her lower lip, not wanting to touch the bloody flap, she squeamishly removed the slippery transceiver from his head and threw it to the ground. She grabbed a fist-sized rock. Expending rage, she slammed the rock against the miniature transceiver as hard as she could again and again.

Listening to Jon's shallow breathing, she ran her fingers over his arms and legs to brush off accumulated sand and dirt. Telepathy gave her the location of his broken collar bone and punctured sternum. His right side was lacerated and discolored from beatings, his pulse slow and weak. He had no conscious thoughts or feelings. Examining the torn skin flap on his scalp, she whispered, "If your hair were an inch longer, I could weave knots to hold your wound closed." She found her emergency stash and retrieved three safety pins. She used them to close his implant wound.

"Not perfect, but effective." Keeping his head and neck aligned with his body, she managed to roll him onto his back.

Rubbing her own implant scar, she mumbled, "Have to remove this. They can't find me again. They just can't!" Reaching into her deep, right front pants pocket, she unzipped the hidden inner pocket to grasp her Swiss army knife. Clasping it to her bosom, her thoughts centered on when and how she would cut the implant from her head. She shuddered.

"It'll be slippery. What if I make a mistake? I'll do it later when Jon's safe." Pocketing the knife, she sat to address her exhaustion and pain.

From her brain's apothecary, she released more endorphins, her body's natural opioid. She worried about overdosing on her own enzymes. When her pain began to diminish, she located her shoes. It was difficult to put them on over sore and bloody feet.

At the banana tree stump Jon had cut earlier, she found enough pooled water to satisfy her thirst. Trash bags left to collect dew had a few swallows of water. She drank that before stuffing their belongings into gear bags. She found and pocketed Jon's cigarette lighter.

She was determined to make a travois with which to pull Jon to the safety of her new cave. She scavenged to find suitable rattan or bamboo for side supports. His parang was used like an axe to cut the stalks.

To make the travois, she opened and placed his small tarp next to him. It was not much wider than his body was long. She rolled sturdy rattan along two sides of the tarp, anchoring them in place with para cord. The clothing strewn about was used to strengthen travois ends. While working, she made comforting comments to unconscious Jon and hummed.

Pulling a rolled bandana out of her pocket, she tied it around her forehead to keep perspiration from burning her eyes. Removing her slacks, she wove the legs into the travois frame end for additional support and stepped back to examine the result. Exhaling air from puffed cheeks, she exclaimed, "If spidersilk'll stop a bullet, it'll support a Marine."

How she was going to pull the travois became a challenge. Blistered, bruised, and bleeding, her hands presented a dilemma. She flexed her fingers. "I don't know if I can lift you, let alone pull you. You're soooo heavy." Tears fell from her eyes as she leaned over to pat his chest. "Don't worry big fella', we'll be okay."

She wiped her hands on grassy weeds, felt something hard and grabbed.

"What ...?" A small, smashed GPS rested in her hand. "They may return with a new one." Spotting Jon's flask, she hefted it. It felt half full. She dribbled vodka over the safety pins to sterilize his implant wound. She next removed the bandana from her head and put it around his to keep insects from the wound. Massive swelling around his right shoulder helped keep the broken collar bone immobilized. After securing the flask, she walked around to find anything of importance and came across another body. "NoChin! Jon killed three of them. Where's the rest?" She listened, but heard no terrorist mindsong.

With effort, she pulled Jon onto the travois and buttoned his shirt at the neck. She next unrolled his right sleeve, buttoned it at the cuff and a second time to his neck button. The secured sleeve created a temporary sling to immobilize his arm.

Getting in position between the travois poles, she tried lifting it. Sharp pains spiked across her back and legs. The poles slipped out of her hands. Jon crashed to the ground. She whispered, "Oh Jon, I'm so sorry." She removed her shirt and used what was left of the Paracord to knot the shirt tails securely to the pole ends. Squatting in front of the travois, she tied the shirt sleeves around her waist, thereby anchoring the poles to her body. "I can do this." She braced the handles on her hips and tried to stand. After struggling, exhausted and angry, she managed to stand.

"Andy, get us OUT OF HERE," she screamed." Sobbing, she flexed her hands and fingers and grabbed the poles again. "Okay. An object at rest remains at rest until an outside force acts upon it. Pull!" Except for straining her back, nothing happened. Again she put all her weight into the exertion and shouted, "PULL!" The travois moved less than a foot. "I have to rethink this." She glanced at Jon. "If you were awake, you'd tell me I'm doing this all wrong. What should I change?" She leaned forward. When she straightened her legs against Jon's weight, the travois moved slowly. Her whole body quivering, she complained between pulls and grunts, "You weigh a ton. Man, I have mega pay backs coming!"

Staggering during the tortured journey, she kept releasing pain relieving chemicals from her brain. She wrenched her back. Insects attacked exposed skin. She felt tortured. If the travois had not been strapped against her, it would have dropped many times. To keep it from tipping sideways, she held the poles tight against her hips. The pressure abraded her skin. Had the path not been downhill, she would have failed.

"When we get there and my legs work again, I'll go back to Kittichai's cave to cut out my transceiver. First, I have to hide our trail." Between breaths she muttered, "Better not use endorphins again. Need to keep alert." Fear flowed through her. She called telepathically, Vaji? Santad? Then she screamed, "ANDY? DO SOMETHING. SAY SOMETHING." There was no response. "How can you guys ignore us? This is a death game. I want to change the rules!"

Arriving at the second cave in agony, she held the travois against her hips and untied the shirt sleeves. Her leg muscles seized in a locked position. She could barely lower Jon to the ground. When she did, her hands wouldn't open. Once freed from the travois, massage finally loosened her fingers. She put on her spidersilk cargo pants and shirt before dribbling water into Jon's mouth from the canteen lid. He took a few sips. His eyes remained closed.

"I'm glad you're unconscious. You've suffered too much because of me." Reaching into her mind to once again release more than the normal quantity of pain easing endorphins, she felt her back pain lessen. She frowned. "I wonder if I can overdose on my own chemicals? If I sit, I'll never get up."

Feeling alone, she broke off a small tree branch and swept cobwebs from along the cave edge, gathering them for use later. She dragged the travois into the cave and collapsed beside it. Her muscles expended, she slept several hours until thirst awakened her.

She hated to leave him, but needed to retrieve supplies. She grabbed the flask and retraced her path to the first cave. While walking, she rubbed fingers through her hair to remove dried mud. She felt guilty being alive while Jon was hurt and unconscious. She wanted Kittichai to return. They had a mindreacher to meet.

Fear haunted her as she neared the cave opening. When a bright light hit her peripheral vision, she whipped around, expecting to find a killer. She was relieved to see a buckle from Jon's gear pack reflecting sunlight. She rifled through the pack, keeping canteens, food, clave, ammunition, extra lighter and cigarettes. She located Jon's SIG where she had placed it and continued to gather what could be salvaged.

She sat on a large boulder and flipped out the narrowest blade of her Swiss pocket knife. With Jon's lighter, she heated the metal. When it became too hot to hold, she anchored it between two rocks and continued to sterilize the metal. She let it cool and visualized the squeamish task of removing her implant. When ready, with a calm mind set, she grasped the blade between thumb and finger to expose a millimeter of blade point. With a sure movement, she sliced the skin in a circle halfway around the implant. Pain shot from the still tender site, a reminder of her frailty.

"Hope I don't hit an artery. It hurts ... oooowwww."

With a grimace, she pulled one side of the slippery skin away from her skull. Using a jagged fingernail, she tried to pry the miniature transceiver from the bone. Both raised arms began to cramp. She didn't dare stop. Blood ran from hands to elbows to armpits and down her body. Wiggling the implant to make it move more freely, she felt something stringy attaching it to her body.

"Vein? Nerve? Surgical thread? Euugh! I hate this."

Nauseous, she shuddered and lost hold of the implant. Her arms fell. When cramping subsided, she took a deep inhale and breathed out through her nose. She grabbed the implant and sliced, freeing it. It looked repulsive with tissue and blood attached. She shook her fist at the sky and screamed, "I swear, Andy, you'll never attach another bionic bastard to me." She reached back to gain momentum. Underhanded she tossed the implant as far as she could. "I knew I should have played softball!"

She opened the flask. Using fingers over the opening to control the liquid flow, she held open the skin flap and gritted her teeth against the coming onslaught of pain. When a few dribbles of vodka fell into the open wound, she arched her back in searing pain before lowering her head in relief.

"Thanks for the vodka, Jon. I'll keep some in my emergency stash after this." She took a swig, coughed, and capped the container. Aching with the effort, she made narrow braids in her hair over the implant site to seal the wound. When the blood dried, it would anchor the braids in place. She used a bandana to keep insects from the blood.

On her journey back to Jon, she used branches and leaves to brush the ground in an attempt to eradicate travois ruts and signs of their passage. Each swath of the branches dispersed fungal spores from the ground. A spore fog enveloped her sweaty body before she reached the cave.

A monsoon cloudburst removed any signs of their passing. The rain impacting soft, loamy earth mellowed the noise of its frontal attack on the cliff. Steam rose from heated rocks. When the rain stopped, she cut nearby rattan shoots and filled a canteen with water. Her strength giving out, she collapsed into a deep sleep.

CHAPTER 38

New Cave
Laotian Wilderness
7 September 7:42 AM ICT

The next morning, Jon awakened disoriented. He didn't recognize his surroundings. His eyelids hurt. His right shoulder was numb. His whole body ached.

Struggling to rise, he flexed muscles to find where he hurt the most. A soft croak emerged when he tried calling Ana. When he couldn't straighten his right arm, he figured out the jerry-rigged sling. Wind blew through the trees pushing the loamy smell of earth into his nostrils. Nuts dislodged by wind thudded occasionally to the ground. Sunlight made overhead translucent leaves a thousand shades of green. Wilderness sounds seemed normal.

Through one partially opened eye he saw Ana, bloodied and lying on the ground with a disfigured face. He couldn't see motion of breathing. Before passing out, he took a shuddering, acknowledging breath. He'd failed. She was dead.

Ana awoke at the thud of Jon's fall to the ground. Crawling to him on hands and knees, she saw the bruises now extended past his rib cage. She kept watch over him.

When he next awoke, he kept his eyes closed to keep from seeing her body. Upon feeling a soft hand on his forehead, he opened his eyes to see her alive. He relaxed when he heard her ask if he was okay. He was lying in a shallow recess against a cliff. Wondering how he'd arrived at their current location, he thought a cold beer or three would hit the spot. "Where are we?"

"Someplace Kittichai may not find. On the other hand, the terrorists won't either, I hope." She described her ordeal. "If you weren't so fit, you'd be dead."

"Did I just hear a compliment?" She smiled at his question. He groped inside his gear pack beside him to grasp the hard cigarette box and relaxed. It wasn't lost.

"You know what I think about smoking."

Noting dried blood at her implant area, he felt behind his ear. "What the…?"

Shrugging, she said, "Safety pins. Sorry. Didn't have anything else."

"Where's my implant?"

"I hit it a few times with a rock."

"Please tell me that was after you removed it."

She laughed. "It was hanging out. I clipped it off. Left mine as a decoy. I hope some animal attracted by the blood will swallow it to make a false trail." She pushed hair from her face.

"Good thinking. How did you get yours out?"

"Thanks to the Swiss army." She lifted the damaged knife.

"I bet it was hard to cut yourself like that."

Tears walled up in her eyes at his acknowledgement. They drank water, snacked and slept.

*   *   *

The next morning during a light refreshment of water and fruit she had found, Ana held out her hand. "Here's your satphone." The glass was cracked and sides dented.

Jon frowned and grumbled. Multiple cuts and bruises made his face grotesque. "Probably won't work." He slumped to the floor. "Being directed all over Southeast Asia by telepathic monks is crazy. I have no working technology. I'm isolated in the wild with a telepath. I have no idea what's happening most of the time."

She suggested, "Maybe you should go back to your special ops team."

Annoyed, he muttered, "Don't I wish. You reading my mind?"

"You told me to stay out." Her lungs began to vibrate. As she inhaled, the vibration increased. She suddenly couldn't breathe in or out. Desperate, she visually searched the area, but saw nothing out of the ordinary. Stronger vibrations caused a paralyzing resonance within her chest cavity. She collapsed to the ground.

Jon saw her struggling for breath. "Something caught in your throat? She shook her head, her eyes closed. "What's happening? What am I looking for?"

She sent telepathically, *I don't know. Can't talk. Can't breathe. Lungs vibrating. Help me.* She opened her mouth to suck in air. Her lungs wouldn't work. She squeezed her eyes shut and grimaced. *What's causing it?*

He kneeled on the ground beside her and began mouth to mouth resuscitation. He could feel her lungs vibrating. Each time he blew air through her mouth and then pressed on her vibrating diaphragm, a light wavering air flowed out.

Birds began screeching alarms. She zeroed in on one bird's audio sense and recognized a roaring sound below her hearing range. Mentally exploring the audio source, she felt a feline touch.

It's a big cat. Sent out low-frequency sound waves to paralyze some animal. *Infrasound. Got me too.

Between breaths he said, "I don't see a cat."

She pointed toward the sound source. Bushes hindered his sight. He felt the vibration in her lungs diminished as the cat's roar became audible.

"I hear it now," he whispered.

She pushed Jon away and gasped for air. *It's a tiger. Big one.* She frantically tried to breathe while gagging and dry heaving. Shaking, she asked, *Why weren't you affected?*

"No idea. I don't even know what happened. You were fine. Next thing I knew, you were suffocating on the ground. I thought a mindreacher was trying to kill you. How could I counter that?" He rubbed her arm. "Sorry you had to experience that."

"Me too." She gave him a penetrating look. "Want to hear the sound that caused it?"

"Try me."

She sent her memory of the upper range of inaudible roar to his auditory senses. She let him feel the energy of the infrasound at the upper frequency range to enable his mind to barely hear the bass sound. When the low frequency energy impaled his mind, his head vibrated.

"Didn't know I had an internal woofer. Man! That's incredible."

"That's a demonstration of infrasound used as a weapon."

"Can that damage your ears?"

"Yeah. Big time." She tried to sit up, but felt dizzy.

"Lie still 'til you're okay Is that cat still around?"

She nodded and asked, "Can it smell us?"

"When was the last time we bathed?" He chuckled. "Bears in Montana can smell food thirty-five miles away. I imagine it's farther for a big cat with a longer nose."

"Partially. When air hits the inside of your nose, neurons take notice. If you sniff harder, neurons work harder detecting odors. Dogs and cats have bigger noses. More smell neurons. I'm glad I can't smell that well. This world stinks." She shifted. "Our man eater's sniffing us, but he just ate. Keep your gun handy in case he gets interested." She rubbed her forehead and had Jon's brain release pain killing hormones. "Think it's safe to build a fire?"

He checked his SIG and slipped it between his back and cargo pants. "Build a bonfire if you want. Smoke'll get lost in these trees." From the cave, he eyed their surroundings. "Wonder where there's water around here?"

"I have some. If you feel like moving around, keep an eye out for that cat."

"Don't worry about me." He watched her create a rock ring and use a fire pellet to provide heat for cooking rice.

In a gear bag she found Kittichai's dried fruit and jerky and handed it over to Jon. He used his teeth to rip a bite of jerky from a larger piece and chewed with relish.

She lowered her gaze. "I want to apologize to you."

"For what?"

"I caused your mind to release a something to make you sleep. Then I moved your gun so you wouldn't roll over on it. I worried it might go off."

"I'm responsible." He kicked at the wall. "I thought this assignment would help me get reactivated for combat."

"Don't knock yourself."

A lopsided smile grew on his swollen face. His bruises were turning yellow at the edges. He sat with the parang blade in one hand and a chunk of fine-grained rock in the other. He wet the rock and used it as a whet stone to sharpen the blade.

"You know," she pondered, "I've been thinking. If I practiced enough, maybe I could mentally control people."

"If someone's trying to kill you, I guarantee you won't try to mentally control them. Your first instinct will be to run for your life!"

"I need to train."

"If you're serious, focus and plan. Figure out on paper what needs to be done and do it. Don't react in panic. You'll become competent and confident with practice." He looked at her. "Is Santad with you?"

She shook her head. "Do you think terrorists got to them?" She lowered herself to the ground. "Santad told me it was possible to teach you telepathy."

"Oooo...kay," he replied skeptically, and leaned against the cave wall. Small rock fragments fell as he moved.

"If Boonrith can learn telepathy, so can you. Plus, it would be a diversion from pain," she urged.

"Hummm, that's good motivation." He stretched and seated himself more comfortably.

They embraced minor telepathy experiments. After each success, she advanced another step. She brought his awareness to a baby bird. Through the link with Ana's mind, he listened to the bird and felt it taste raw food fed by its parent.

"It can't sing," he said.

Birds use a template in their brain to imitate their parent's song.

He listened patiently to the bird. After minutes of silence, he confessed, "I've been thinking. For the good of the Corps, I should learn this stuff."

"What did you just say? The man who hates psychics is interested in becoming one?"

"A soldier trained in telepathy might create safer combat conditions for himself and others. It'd be a win-win situation. A win for the psychic population and a win for the military to have correct and positive directions in the field. Commanders and troops wouldn't have to outguess the enemy. They'd know enemy positions and enemy battle strategy ahead of time."

While he talked, Ana kept a poker face. She visualized the importance of telepathy in combat conditions.

"Tell me more about your telepathy."

She told him about her parents warning her to never use it. She recounted about not being allowed to have friends visit and feeling alone as a child. "Animals never told me to go away. Through their minds I learned about the world." She gave him a curious glance. "Tell me about your family."

He stared into the jungle and snickered. "Poor mom. She had four rowdy boys. We owned a ranch. We learned to shoot rifles from horses before we were old enough to go to school. My brothers and I designed shooting competitions for the last Saturday of each month."

"A family Top Gun competition?"

"Full of shooting, laughs, food and memories. Yet, I wanted something different. After high school I spent several years learning martial arts." He told her about his travel to China and training four years in martial arts at the Shaolin Buddhist temple complex.

Two brown *gibbons played in nearby trees. The male gibbon kept hooting and venturing back and forth, skittering within twenty feet of them. Curious, it sat on his haunches watching them while grooming himself. His right hand located parasites. With his left hand, he picked them off his skin and ate them. He also mimicked Jon's posture. Growing bolder, he somersaulted and moved closer to Jon. His mate jumped limb to limb nearby, far enough away to be safe. She watched her mate.

She sent a mental nudge to him. *Be still. Open your eyes.* His face mirrored pain. *Want pain relief?*

"What do we have?"

Telepathic help. Trust me?

Reluctantly, he nodded.

Moving through his mind, this time with permission, she had his brain release a small amount of endorphins. A week ago she knew only to self-release pain killers. To do so with Jon gave her a sense of satisfaction.

He closed his eyes, cleared his throat, and relaxed as pain receded.

When you learn telepathic skills, you'll be able to help wounded without morphine. They remained quiet with the frolicking gibbons creating humorous breaks. She sent, *Ready to enter a new psychic realm? You'll experience animals in a way others would never consider or fathom.*

CHAPTER 39

Laotian Wilderness
9 September 2:23 PM ICT

Ana thought about how to approach the task of opening Jon's mind to larger animal senses. Sitting in the shallow cave studying him, she figured he'd either love it or hate it.

She sent to him, *I'm going to introduce you to gibbon senses. You'll find it amusing.* What she didn't tell him was that his consciousness would expand in the new situation.

When he blinked in acknowledgement, she entered his mind to move through tenuous senses. At the same time she used similar neural paths in her own mind. Deftly, and with caution, she moved their consciousness to the male gibbon's senses.

* * *

Jon and the gibbon flinched simultaneously. He felt the creature's alarm. It ran away on all fours. Mesmerized by the senses perceived by the animal, Jon wondered if gibbons had thoughts. Astonished by the clarity of the gibbon's primeval senses, he listened to jungle grunts, screeches and calls intensified through the animal's primitive mind and stronger sensory input. Smelling himself through the gibbon's senses, he wrinkled his nose and vowed to bathe as soon as possible.

Human olfactory receptors, Ana sent, holding up her thumb, *are the size of your thumbnail. You can identify billions of smells. A gibbon sense of smell is ten times stronger.*

Both gibbons returned. Cautious, they looked from human to human. The male inched closer. Ana slowly vacillated Jon's awareness between the two animals. Within minutes he could tell which gibbon mind he inhabited by smelling pheromones of the other gibbon.

When the male gibbon hit his shoulder twice, his mate joined him on the ground. She closed in to sit beside him. Parting her mate's fur in a grooming search, she picked out and ate parasitic insects one by one. Jon experienced a pungent tang when the insect was crunched by gibbon teeth before being swallowed. Ana continued facilitating his explorations into gibbon senses.

After an hour, exhausted from working with four minds, she concluded the session. Both gibbons fled when she moved to stretch and stand. Jon remained seated.

She smiled and twisted to stretch oblique muscles at her sides. They were still sore from dragging the travois. "Well," she asked. "What do you think?"

He said, "Using telepathy, you truly experience the world, don't you? You've learned aspects of this world others would never imagine. Do you pity the rest of us?"

"No. You may be in awe of telepaths while I admire musicians and mathematicians. Astronomers and oceanographers. Biologists and artists. I could never duplicate their thoughts even though all minds are pretty much alike."

He raised his eyebrows and leaned toward her. "I sensed a hundred things at once. I could even tell when you jumped me gibbon to gibbon. I've been a physical 'give me a tough job and I'll do it' kind of guy. I'm not used to mental manipulations." He cleared his throat. "No wonder telepathy cuts you off from the rest of the world. It involves all your senses at once. I didn't think about anything else." He looked at her. She seemed different. He didn't know if she had changed during this trip or if he had. He watched the breeze play with her hair. "Woman, you challenged my beliefs. I'm forever changed."

"In what way?"

"You validated what telepathy is about."

"Experiencing animals is my hobby. Makes me who I am."

"It boggles my mind. Gave a peek into your universe." He grinned. "Also took my mind off food. One question, can telepathy damage your mind? "

"I don't think so."

He stood, leaning against the cave wall. "I'm so stiff from sitting, I can barely function."

"Me too. My butt's numb." She rubbed her buttocks.

"They may return. I'll take first watch if you want to sleep."

Her mind heard a feminine and echoing baby's mindsong similar to that of Kittichai. She whispered, "We have a friendly visitor."

Jon assumed a non-threatening posture.

A young Laotian woman appeared through the foliage and regarded them. Pointing west she greeted them with a slight bowing nop and pronounced, *"Sabaai-dii."*

Ana answered with a bow. "Hello."

The woman gushed, "Hello. Hello." Continuing her pointing westward she declared, Kittichai." Pointing to herself she said, "Nit."

Barefoot, Nit wore a thin cotton blouse over a faded, tubular pasin skirt wrapped sarong style and secured with a thick and folded reddish-brown, cloth sash. A black sash wrapped diagonally around her chest supported a dark-haired baby peeking over her shoulder. A homespun black muslin turban gave the woman an older appearance. Ana estimated the young woman was still in her teens. From mindsong similarities, she knew Nit was the child's mother.

The young woman squatted on thick callused heels while unknotting the ends of the reddish-brown sash. With the baby resting against her back, she leaned forward to balance herself, smiling and nodding. Talking in the Laotian singsong dialect, she seemed oblivious to their incomprehension of her language. She would not look into their eyes. Each time she was caught staring, she lowered her face in subservience.

While hunkered, Nit placed her sash on the ground, unrolled it and removed several small packets wrapped in green leaves. Opening the first, she mimed eating and handed them to the Americans.

Ana made a *nop* motion of thanks and took the packet. It contained sweet rice enriched with cinnamon, nutmeg, and mace. As they savored the taste, the child put his cheek against the girl's shoulder and sucked a thumb.

Nit held up a palm to motion stop and then pointed to herself. She made a walking motion with her fingers while saying, "Kittichai. *Hak mai"*

Jon said, "I think she wants us to stay here. Must be from Kittichai's village. She'll let him know where we are." He pointed to his chest and the cave to let her know they would remain where they were. He then made a *nop* with his hands and bowed his head slightly to thank her.

Nit responded with a wide smile and nodded enthusiastically. After placing additional rice packets on the ground, she folded and refastened her now empty sash. Standing, she backed away. Bowing with prayerful hands in front of her chest, she disappeared into the jungle.

* * *

Before nightfall, Kittichai arrived laden with food and water. Ana had tears of relief as she greeted the monk.

In his broken English, he related information Vaji sent him. The day after the three of them left the temple compound, two Thai holy men arrived. For over an hour they sat silently beside the burned temple with Vaji.

"Using telepathy," Ana suggested. "Guess who the two monks were?"

"Santad and Boonrith," he answered." They chuckled.

Kittichai related, "Twice, new men came to temple area seeking Madam Ana. Venerable Vaji and his friends stayed quiet. Each time, the visitors became confused and went away.

Jon asked, "Mental manipulation?"

She dipped her head. "I think so."

Kittichai showed Jon a paste concoction made of plant blossoms, leaves and roots. "Is *Hak mai*. Good medicine. Jon applied the paste to his open wounds using the monk's instructions.

Jon brought the monk up to date with information of the surprise attack at the first cave.

Kittichai responded. "Angry man came to village to find you." Relating how the village elders rebuffed the intruder, He described in detail how villagers, in a go-down-in-tribal-history-skirmish, ended up having to kill the man. No one had recognized the language he spoke.

"Must be the one who got away," Jon suggested.

"Vaji sent a message," Kittichai continued, tapping his head. "At the Mekong, we take longboat to Mueang Hinboun."

Ana asked, "Is that a village?"

Kittichai nodded and pointed south.

Jon warned, "The river's swollen and dangerous. Without life jackets, we'll have to be careful."

"We leave *phrung nii.* Tomorrow." Kittichai announced. "Will be *yaak,* uh … difficult." He looked frustrated at having to use English. "Travel to Mekong and rest one night. On river next day half day. Okay?"

Jon nodded.

"I return with dawn." Before they could respond, he disappeared into the jungle.

"At least he didn't say "tomorrow," she commented.

CHAPTER 40

Back in New York, Phillip Arnold was worried. Colonel Anderson had alerted VESPER security and the Secretary of Homeland Security about the altered transcriptions. Arnold told Anderson that Homeland Security wasn't needed. As Communications Director, he'd find out what happened. He'd later blame the problem on computer transcription malfunctions. He planned to immediately send the cowboy on vacation. Al-Qaeda contacts were told the new order of the day was mental warfare using telepathy. He got their full attention and was asked for additional information. Planning to contract al-Qaeda teams to do his bidding, he knew his dreams were coming true.

Assessing the potential of assembling his own cadre of mindreaching terrorists, he was determined to find a Joburg mindreacher before Masterson did. The transcriptions would tell him what he needed to know. Thinking aloud, he reflected, "After the last attack, signals from her bodyguard stopped. She hasn't moved." After a pause, he boasted with glee, "She's dead. She's gotta' be dead." Pumping a fist, he said, "Both of them."

An online contact from Northern Thailand reported an old monk with an entourage moving downstream on a flooded and dangerous Mekong River. Arnold was told that particular old monk never ventured out. His travel must therefore be significant.

He asked himself, "I wonder if it's the same monk Masterson met in Vientiane? Why go downstream on a flooded river? Must be important. To meet her? No. She's dead. Maybe he's going to warn a mindreacher. Better find out." He ordered an assassin to follow the Monk if it wasn't too late to do so. Villagers may have seen him pass by.

CHAPTER 41

Mueang Hinboun Village (Muanghinboun)
Laos
10 September. 7:32 PM ICT

It was dusk. After trekking out of the mountain and experiencing treacherous episodes on the swollen Mekong River, Jon smelled cooking food. He and Kittichai made eye contact. Kittichai nodded toward buildings on the Thai river bank. The Laotian bank varied. Where it was flat, water buffalo lingered within a bamboo fence. At steeper bank areas, vegetation grew to the water. Dirt paths were infrequent. In an open area they saw bamboo huts with thatched roof at the river's edge. Tall, permanent poles near the huts each held an open, three-sided, white fishing net suspended about ten feet in the air by ropes.

They neared their destination, Mueang Hinboun village in the Khammoun region of Laos. Forested mountains filled the Laotian landscape beyond the flood plain. Cultivated plots of land bordered the Mekong. Unpainted, wood flat boats were anchored along steep river banks.

Kittichai had the boatman turn in along the bank bordering the village. Two rows of homes, above the bank and about a hundred meters from the Mekong, were concentrated along a road paralleling the river. Jon estimated the village contained less than two-thousand souls. There was no temple. The larger village on the opposite Thai bank had several temples.

Ana opened her awareness to find Vaji. She heard Santad's mental send announcing her arrival.

She's here! Ana's here!

His joyous message cheered her. She had no idea where he was.

He sent to her, *I met Vaji! He's wonderful!*

Boonrith echoed the accolade. *He is indeed!*

I think so too, she sent to her unseen friends. The two monks came into view at the top of the river bank. The three exchanged glowing smiles.

After climbing the bank, Santad led the group to a nearby home. It was the last building on the downstream end of the dirt road. The road extended beyond the home over a quarter mile to a tributary emptying into the Mekong. The road ended at a dirt ramp for launching boats.

A vibrant mindsong invaded Ana's mind, cascading through her multiple senses. As soon as one level of consciousness within her mind was revealed, another was pried open. Surprised someone would invade her mind unasked and so easily, she looked for the gentleman named Kanchana. Instead, she saw a middle-aged Asian woman with large, almond-shaped and intense brown eyes staring at her. She hadn't expected Kanchana to be female. She recognized a similarity to Vaji's face and eyes. About five feet tall, the woman wore a long-sleeved, flowing, grey Mandarin collared shirt over black silk palazzo slacks. Her sturdy sandals appeared bulky on her petite and manicured feet. A gold bracelet surrounded each wrist. Gold adorned her neck and earlobes.

In Southeast Asia one never knew when you might be forced to flee your home and bank account. Many adults wore their accumulated wealth in the form of gold or precious gems as earrings, necklaces, bracelets, or in hidden pockets sewn within their clothing. If threatened, they could leave at a moment's notice, taking their wealth with them. Precious metals and gems could be traded around the world for cash.

Hello, Ana, began the woman's telepathic send. A glow of happiness permeated her British-accented mind speech. *I'm Kanchana Jayachettha. Uncle Vaji speaks well of you.* The woman raised her hands together and gracefully bowed the Laotian *nop* greeting. A smile transformed her face to a welcoming expression of warmth and beauty. Kanchana glanced at Jon. He was carefully observing every characteristic she exhibited.

Ana crossed her fingers and replied, *Vaji's your uncle?* Kanchana smiled. Euphoric to find a mindreacher, Ana examined Kanchana's mindsong. She recognized a familial similarity to Vaji's mindsong. The feminine mindsong was enchanting until Ana noted with unease that it contained a barely perceptible undertone of deceit. Unable to block it, the ensuing resonance of a mental greeting within her mind showed evidence of immense, controlled power. Radiating high levels of energy within Ana's mind, Kanchana's mindsong created a resonance as magnificent as several orchestras. Ana remarked, "Kanchana is an unusual name."

Kanchana grinned. To Jon she said, "You've been hurt. May I help you?"

"Yes, thank you," Within a second he relaxed as pain began to recede.

Ana said, "I relieved some, but it kept returning. You'll have to show me how to make relief last longer." She paused before asking a question burning in her thoughts, "Were you born in Johannesburg?"

"Conceived, not born there."

"Did your mother work for Dr. Reginald Beckman?"

"Yes."

Tears of relief at finding a mindreacher began to well in Ana's eyes. "You're the reason we're here. Do you know if you're telepathic because of Dr. Beckman's machine? Or through genetics?"

"Both. I'm more powerful than Uncle Vaji. He suggested the doctor's machine may have increased my inherited psychic potential. I inherited telepathic ability from my mother."

Jon said, "If you're not one of the original Joburg children, there's a change in the probable count of existing mindreachers. I need to let Andy know."

"Andy would be …?"

"Colonel Andrew Anderson of the United States Marine Corps, a psychiatrist and VESPER's Medical Director. He traveled to Johannesburg when information about the genius babies hit the news wires over forty years ago. The papers said nothing about telepathy. Andy couldn't locate Dr. Beckman. He recently brought mindreacher abilities to the attention of VESPER."

Kanchana squinted her eyes and tilted her head. "Explain what VESPER is."

After Ana and Jon supplied details about the recently formed organization, Kanchana said, "I believe you're on the right track to locate terrorists through telepathy. If I decide to work with VESPER, I could find terrorists and alert authorities who could remove them from society. There should be enough mindreachers to rid the world of terrorists. Through the years I've had inklings there were others. Sometimes when a commercial airplane flew over I'd sense a strong telepath on board. I wondered if they sensed me. To save time, Ana, may I use thought-transfer with you to learn what I need to know?"

"Is it safe?"

"Yes. Leave it to me."

To Ana, the transfer of information felt as though tendrils of static electricity stretched neurons and glia within her mind. It was a good physical feeling like stretching your legs before running. Taking only a few minutes, the information exchange included all information of their existence since the first cell division of their creation. The mental block Ana had earlier created disappeared as though it had never existed.

"It'll take me a few hours to digest this," Kanchana said. "I'll enjoy getting to know you through your memories."

Ana excitedly ran her fingers through her hair. Then, waving her hands as she talked, she said, "It'll take me years to digest this information. Is there a shortcut?" She loved learning new ideas and techniques. With Kanchana's help, she was learning so rapidly she could feel her world expanding.

"I transfer mind data when gathering information. With you, I'll learn about life in the United States. Having transferred so much information in the past, I'd venture to guess I have the educational equivalent of advanced degrees in many fields. It comes in handy at times. You've lots of memory space, Ana. May I show you how to work it?" When Ana nodded consent, Kanchana taught her how to store data in alternate memories. "What you'll find interesting is, we'll know each other so well it'll be easy to predict reactions and behavior."

"When you skim my memories," Ana commented, "you'll learn about American teenagers."

"Lots of fun stories?" At Ana's nod, Kanchana chuckled in anticipation.

Ana said, "I thought Santad was a powerful telepath until I met your uncle. Now I see you're more powerful than both of them put together. I'm thankful to know our first mindreacher is peaceful. I love your laughter. It's so deep and rich."

I know you've been worried, Kanchana sent.

"I can't wait to take you to VESPER."

Vaji approached. "I see you've met my niece, Kanchana Jayachettha." After a brief greeting, Vaji described how Kanchana's parents were blackballed for employment and forced out of South Africa. They traveled to Vaji for help. When born, Kanchana was given her mother's historically honored and royal Laotian name. "The family returned to her father's village of Siem Reap near the ancient ruins of Angkor Wat by Tonle Sap Lake in Cambodia. When my sister and her husband were killed during a political skirmish. Their friends unofficially adopted Kanchana. Since my sister and I were both psychic, we assumed Kanchana inherited the telepathic gift from her mother. Until I entered Ana's mind, I had no idea Kanchana was part of a select group of mindreachers with advanced skills. With her psychic inheritance and Dr. Beckman's intervention, she may be the most exceptional mindreacher on the planet." Santad and Boonrith joined the group.

Ana asked, "Kanchana, how do you keep in touch with Vaji?"

"Uncle Vaji kept a mental link open between us. He listened to my thoughts and chatter. Some children have an imaginary friend. Mine was real. Unless I asked him for privacy, he was with me every second."

Santad boasted, "He helped me too."

Ana commented, "I'm soooo envious."

"Holding dual citizenship, I knew I could live in Laos. I'm not sure I want to make a change of residence." She hesitated and raised her hands, waving them about as though casting a spell, "In Cambodia, I was recognized as a fortune teller."

Jon said, "Logical job for a telepath." He glanced at Ana. "Ever think about that?"

"Never." She and Kanchana exchanged smiles knowing Ana had just lied. "well, maybe once or twice." That Kanchana knew every thought Ana experienced was going to provide amusement.

Rubbing her forehead, Kanchana's eyes squeezed shut in pain. "My headache is excruciating."

Ana felt Kanchana's forehead. "No temperature."

"Stress migraine," Kanchana said. "Jon's the one who should have a headache. Really, Ana, safety pins?"

"I didn't have anything else."

With a wounded expression meant to garner a smile, Jon gingerly tapped the safety pins behind his ear. He asked, "What do you think about VESPER?"

Kanchana replied, "When Uncle Vaji sent an invitation to meet you, I wished to honor him. Since I was a child, whenever I thought his name, he listened and helped me. Until now, he'd never requested my help. His wanting to help you get rid of terrorists is important to me."

"True," Vaji admitted. "Kanchana must make a decision which will affect the rest of her life. If knowledge about her extraordinary abilities is made public, living in the United States could bring her fame and fortune. It could also bring ridicule, fear and death. To date she has shied from notice."

Kanchana bowed her head toward her uncle. "I've been brooding about what to do. Looking from Vaji to Ana to Jon, she shrugged. "Word will soon spread that I'm a strong telepath. Since terrorists don't want to be identified, I'll be targeted whether I join VESPER or not."

Jon said, "VESPER may not be the safest alternative for anyone right now." He studied her. "Are you concerned about repercussions of joining VESPER?"

She nodded, watching him. He resembled a gladiator preparing for battle.

He said, "I want medics to mentally begin healing the wounded in combat by using their minds. You can teach them how to do that. VESPER will give you that opportunity."

Kanchana glanced at everyone. "To heal others, I begin activating stem cells in damaged organs." At Ana's perplexed look, she added, "Every body organ has stem cells. When an organ is injured, stem cells are triggered to work replacing damaged cells. I just give a little electrical stimulation through the nervous system to speed stem cell production. I knew these healing agents existed, but never knew what to call them until the last several years. The stem cell name fits." She paused, her expression serious. "I'm going to tell you something you may think strange. Remember this because it is fact and special. Why it happens no one knows. Daily meditation or prayer as short as twenty minutes increases the number of positive stem cells throughout your body. Stem cells heal the body. Whether you feel ill or not, pray or meditate. You'll be healthy if you do. Teach that to military troops and you'll see a higher mortality rate."

Jon said, "Good to know."

"Something else. If you crave something, your body must need it. I always crave milk and dairy products which is difficult in Cambodia."

Ana asked, "Are you familiar with the term, glia?"

Kanchana shook her head.

"They used to be called grey matter in the brain. Scientists are now beginning to learn their importance. They outnumber neurons three-to-one and exist basically on calcium. They're more important than neurons because they enable chemical communication within brain neurons. Without glia and their calcium nets, we'd lose the use of a major part of our thinking brain. Your glia needing calcium is why you crave milk."

Kanchana said, "I always wondered about that. Uncle Vaji doesn't eat any dairy foods." She rubbed her forehead with the fingers of both hands. "It's ironic. I can heal others but not myself. Man, this headache!"

At her obvious distress, Vaji told her to rest. After she left, he said, "Pretending to be a fortune teller, she uses telepathy to learn about others. Then she advises them how to help solve their problems."

Ana guessed the deceit feelings she felt were caused by Kanchana lying to patrons about her fortune telling.

Vaji sent to her, *I am sending this only to you, Ana. I want you to know that Kanchana has a serious weakness.*

She looked at him with apprehension, eyes open wide.

Vaji sent, *She is an addict.*

Of what? Heroin? Opium?

Neither. She self-medicates with chemicals from her mind's apothecary.

Endorphins?

Yes, he replied. *And *dopamines, the body's opioids for killing pain and stopping thirst and hunger. She is constantly trying to lose weight. She releases endocannabinoids for the same thing and to give her pleasure. She continues to require more and floods her brain with chemicals. She will not admit such use has changed her synaptic connections. It is not reversible.*

Ana sent, *I am so sorry.* Her eyebrows raised and eyes filled with worry.

Vaji continued, *I recently learned she can also release hormones and chemicals totally unknown to me. They're an anesthesia to stop pain and relax her body. The effects on her mind can last months. Chemicals accumulate in her brain and body. I worry that her effectiveness may at times be impaired. True, she is brilliant. Such an attribute may help overcome any of her self-medicated anesthetic effects.*

Worried, Ana sent, *Do you think her critical thinking and analytical ability have been affected?* Worried about the quantity of mindmeds she had personally used in the past two weeks, Ana questioned if she was an addict like Kanchana.

Vaji thoughtfully stroked his chin before sending, *I will find out. My niece tries to block me. I let her have her way. At least until now.* He winked.

She sent, *Will I be able to tell when she's using mindmeds?*

There are physical signs. I will show you. He sent imagery for her to identify physical signs of Kanchana's chemical use.

Ana was pleased the techniques he passed to her were ones she'd used in the past to identify opioid drug addicts. She had yet to determine when and if such verifications were measurable on a mindreacher of such superior ability and how they would affect Kanchana. However, if Vaji mentioned it, he must think it significant. Lowering her head, she glanced at Vaji and sent, *I've used mindmeds too. Endorphins.*

Not to worry. Non-telepathic persons do so without thinking about it. They unconsciously release endorphins when in a happy state of mind or laughing. I have used them. Look in a mirror to see if you are overdosed, my dear. Kanchana uses mega doses. Yesterday she swore she was clean, but it is her weakness. Tell no one unless a situation arises and you feel it is necessary.

Will it affect her decision making?
Usually not.

Ana was concerned with the word 'usually.'

Vaji picked up her thought. *As with most drugs, most obvious will be affected pupils. She's good at hiding her condition. Memorize her mindsong in this healthy state and you'll know in the future if and when it changes.*

Thank you for the information, she sent, and contemplated whether to tell Jon. *Vaji, being a doctor, will Colonel Anderson be able to tell she is on drugs when he meets her?*

Vaji shrugged. *If he is a doctor, he should be able to.* He turned and walked away to meet with villagers.

Ana shook her head knowing she had some serious thinking to do before returning to VESPER. "It can't be kept a secret," she whispered, thinking aloud. "Andy needs to know."

After dinner, Santad and Boonrith led a discussion concerning differences between the thinking mind and the physical brain. Sitting off to the side, Vaji removed safety pins from Jon's head and began healing damaged tissue before everyone retired for the night.

CHAPTER 42

Mueang Hinborn
Laos

The next day Kanchana told Ana, "My telepathic power is stable. The powers you have are different. They're a taste of what you'll become. In the manipulations of your thought processes, you're stimulating your mind and awakening areas that have lain dormant. Be forewarned, advanced telepathy might be thrust upon you unexpectedly. The metamorphosis of your mind becoming similar to a mindreacher may create mental turmoil. Plan for periods of confusion. Sit back and relax when necessary."

Are you sure? Ana crossed her fingers for Jon.

Kanchana sent with a twinkle in her eye, *Have you noticed how much you've changed since arriving in Southeast Asia? Your mind should feel more open since you've created additional neural pathways. You're like a sapphire just mined from the earth. When polished, you'll become a star sapphire with rays of hope spreading across the world. You may become one of the best identifiers of terrorists. The transformation will take less time than you can imagine. Remember, you are what you think. Your worst enemy can't hurt you as much as your own thoughts.* She smiled at Ana's rapt attention and said aloud, "To be as well-spoken as you, highly educated and disciplined in your telepathic endeavors is a blessing. It's amazing you had no help. You were a brave child."

Ana believed her talents had grown under the influence of Santad, Vaji, and now Kanchana. She questioned where these emerging talents would lead.

Inclining her head with a knowing smile, Kanchana said, "Be careful. Don't demonstrate all your talents. Nontelepaths, the NT's, will become envious, jealous and angry with you. Not understanding will bring fear. You and mindreachers will be considered dangerous freaks."

With a resigned expression, Ana asked, "What's new?

"Don't worry. You'll know when to use your powers. Keep most of your talents hidden until perfected and needed. Experiment if you must to strengthen them, but never on humans."

Ana asked, "Anything important to look out for?"

Kanchana spent some time explaining the relationship of telepathy to the warp of ripples in the earth's magnetic fields. *The Earth's magnetic field grows weaker in some places and stronger in others. You can latch on to the magnetic energy flow to boost the distance of your send. When there's a strong mindreach taking place, a slight flux or waiver occurs in the magnetic field. When you grow stronger in your telepathy, you'll feel that flux.*

What will it feel like?

Kanchana sent, *Let me show you.* Remembering how it felt, she telepathically sent the feeling to Ana's mind.

Oh, Ana sent, *what a soft fluttery feeling.*

Vaji approached the women. "You've had time to think, Kanchana. Will you join VESPER?"

"I don't know. Ridiculous as it seems, I can solve problems of others but not my own. What do you think is best for me?"

"Not all mindreachers will wish to help VESPER," he answered. "You must become the first. Be their role model. They will need someone morally correct, ethical, and extremely intelligent. You fit all categories. Because of your psychic heredity and that vacuum machine in Johannesburg, you will be the most intelligent and powerful of them all." He turned his head as though straining to hear something. Straightening, he turned and sent to all of them, *Two terrorists are coming. You must leave. NOW!* To Kanchana he sent, *Go with Ana to New York. To them, I am an insignificant monk and will not be targeted. But you are new to the area and a confident mindreacher. Anyone with half a mind will sense your power.*

You are in danger. With my love and prayers, you must leave. I will help you escape.

Never having heard her uncle express fear in a send, Kanchana scrambled to gather a small pack of belongings. Santad loudly warned the others. Palpable tension infected them all. Hearts beat faster. Adrenalin rushed.

Ana's hands trembled as she lifted her gear pack. She feared Kanchana wouldn't travel to New York.

* * *

Jon was increasingly frustrated at not knowing what's going on and having to rely on psychics. He asked Vaji how many terrorists there were, weaponry, and their present location.

In a rush, Vaji didn't answer. He herded them to the house. He wouldn't tell anyone where they were going or how they would travel until two motorized somlars arrived. Vaji, Santad, Boonrith and Kittichai boarded one. Ana, Kanchana and Jon boarded the second one. They traveled south on the small, rutted dirt road. The treeless vegetation was primarily low grass until they reached a small river flowing into the Mekong. They stopped behind an old airplane parked above the river bank. A newer Cessna aircraft rested nearby.

"A *Cherokee!" Ana sighed with pleasure. It was the same color blue as the Cherokee she had used during her flight training. She brushed her hand over the ailerons. Grabbing the rudder, she moved it back and forth. The low-wing four-seater looked its age, but flyable.

"What a junker," Jon complained. He peered through the Plexiglas side window. "Vaji, I'm no pilot."

"Ana can fly it."

"Ana?" Pointing to her with his thumb, he barked, "Just because she's telepathic doesn't mean she can fly an airplane!"

Vaji chuckled, clasped his hands together in front of his chest and looked innocently at Jon over the top of his glasses. "We must hurry."

In a derogatory tone Jon demanded, "Ana, tell Vaji you can't fly this scrap metal." He smacked his hand against a wing. The airplane shuddered.

She stepped back to examine the aircraft. "Looks fine to me."

He bellowed, "You're a pilot? Why didn't you tell me?"

Ticked off with his attitude, she reproached him. "Vaji's provided a way out of here. You should be ecstatic, not dogging on me."

Jon's second language being profane, he turned away to stop blasphemous words forming in his mouth. With teeth grinding and tendons stretched taut in his neck, he balled his fists and walked to the other side of the Cherokee. Ana's ability to fly was their escape route out of Laos. Pacing, he looked at her with reluctant admiration. "A pilot," he muttered with a crooked smile. "Better be a good one."

Terrorists are close, Vaji sent to everyone.

Ana studied the oil stained wheels and fuselage. There was no time for a preflight inspection. She had to trust Vaji.

Jon asked, "Using the grass or road for a runway?"

"Road."

"What about the ruts?"

"I'll try to avoid them."

The Cherokee was parked near the road which ran parallel to the Mekong River. The treeless south end of the road ended at the banks of a small river emptying into the Mekong. A dirt boat ramp led up from the river. Ana surveyed the area, deciding she would taxi north, turn around and take off toward the south. She had to be aloft before reaching the boat ramp.

HURRY, Vaji screamed in her mind.

She released a charge of endorphins throughout her body to relieve pain. To help Kanchana board the airplane, she showed her the handgrip on the side of the airplane. The mindreacher stepped on to the worn, black strip at the edge of the wing and into the Cherokee. She was relegated to sit on the hot metal floor in the back of the airplane. The back seats had been removed.

Ana tossed her gear pack in and told Kanchana, "Sit close to the seats to center the weight."

Having been sitting under the tropical Sun, everything inside the airplane was hot to touch. The heated air inside felt like it burned their lungs.

Taking the left front seat, Ana opened the small window vent. They felt the airplane lean to the right when Jon climbed on board and sat in the right seat. The second yoke in front of him pressed against his legs. Perspiring, he moved the seat back.

"Those mountain pygmies must have been here too," he joked, remembering remarks from their earlier trek. Ignoring the safety harnesses, seatbelts were reconfigured to fit. Kanchana had none. She would hold onto Jon's seat.

Jon reached out to close the door.

"Leave it open," Ana ordered. "That's our air-conditioning." In the absence of a preflight checklist, she mentally ran through take off procedures hoping she didn't forget any.

Outside, Santad was waving his arms, shouting and running toward five *dingo-type, feral dogs resting on the road near the boat ramp. Snarling and snapping, the dogs moved into the taller grass and disappeared.

Riddled with minute cracks and striations from age and tropical sunlight, the Cherokee's Plexiglas side windows had lost most of their transparency. The windscreen above the instrument panel was discolored to a pale yellow. The sweltering aircraft smelled of mold and sweat.

Checking the fuel gauge, she switched the fuel lever between tanks to feel the notches, deciding to use the fuller right tank. Jon would be sitting to the right and she would empty that tank first to balance the craft.

Holding the brake, out of habit she put her mouth to the small window vent and yelled, "Clear" to let people know the propellers were going to move. She turned on the fuel pump, primed the engine, turned on the master switch and magnetos, pushed the starter and prayed. She had not pre-flighted the plane and was rushing through startup procedures.

The propeller made a half turn. The engine coughed. On the second attempt, the engine started and died. Ana's breathing stopped and started with the engine. The motor finally caught. Props spun. Oil pressure began to rise. She grabbed the flaps control. Due to the heat outside and subsequent lack of lift, she put in two notches of flaps.

Vaji screamed in her mind, *GO! GO! GO NOW!*

She taxied the Cherokee north on the smoother side of the rutted road before reaching the trees. She turned the airplane to face the open area to the south and braked. Feet hard on the brake, she locked the throttle full open. She needed maximum power for a quick take off. The engine accelerated. The plane vibrated. She snugged her seat belt with a tug. Without headsets, the engine noise was deafening.

"I was told sex was dangerous and flying was safe," Jon called out. "Now I wonder if that's true."

She gave him a questioning look.

He reassuringly patted a hard pack of cigarettes in his shirt pocket and yelled over the engine noise, "Do you know what you're doing?"

She ignored him, waiting for oil pressure to rise. It was not where it should be, but they had to leave. Wind was blowing the grass to the north. That meant heading south would give a strong head wind to provide good lift.

She demanded, "Close and lock the door" while sending to Kanchana, *Hang on.*

Jon slammed and locked the door as the brake was released.

Kanchana anchored her arms around Jon's metal seat supports. Using telepathy, she listened to Ana's technical analysis of steps to follow in flying this airplane. She was fascinated with Ana, a budding mindreacher.

The airplane jumped forward. Hot air began to move through the small window and vents under the instrument panel.

Behind them, a three-wheeled, motorized samlor holding two men waving pistols raced after the Cherokee. Not seeing them, Ana didn't react. She felt the nose lift off the road at fifty knots. Bullets pelted the fuselage. Jon grabbed his SIG. Without an open door, he couldn't return fire.

At sixty knots, the airplane felt smoother. Wheels skimmed ruts. Bullets pinged off the aircraft. At eighty-five knots, they were airborne. Ana waved the wings to the monks and veered north so she could eyeball the river on her left.

She received a message from Vaji. *Fly to Nakhon Phanom airport. It has commercial flights to Bangkok.* He included a visual map of the Mekong River bordering Laos and Thailand. She laughed. He had highlighted the name of Nakhon Phanom airport in her mental image with as if using a yellow highlighter pen. The river image faded and changed to Vaji's view of the terrorists who were hot wiring the Cessna airplane. She figured one of them must be a pilot. Since they had guns and the Cessna had a more powerful engine, she was in trouble. Her back began perspiring. She couldn't read the instrument panel because her view was overlaid with Vaji's mental images. Then his sending stopped.

* * *

Kanchana was mindreaching her uncle's optical senses when she saw the terrorists through a veil of red. Frightened, she asked him, *Are you okay?* There was no answer. She accessed Santad's optical senses. All she could see was a bloody carnage. Her uncle and a *samlor* driver were on the ground. The other driver was bloodied and running away. Boonrith was rushing toward her uncle. In the midst of sending Santad encouragement to help her uncle, her body lifted off the floor and slammed back down. She barely managed to hang on to the back of Jon's seat.

Oblivious to the fighting on the ground, Ana sent to Kanchana and Jon, *Those air bumps are caused by thermals. Heat off the land makes air rise unevenly. Think of them as potholes in the air.*

* * *

Jon's experience with airplanes was primarily diving out of them at high altitudes for night infiltration missions. He felt undressed without goggles, multiple gear packs, and no team to lead in a free-fall mission. He saw only trees and rough country below.

"We'll be jostled 'til I get some altitude," Ana told them over the engine noise.

Remembering Vaji's Nakhon Phanom image, she checked the positions of the sun and river. The sun would orient her to the cardinal points. Plus, the river was to her west. Knowing in her mind approximately where Nakhon Phanom should be, she scanned the horizon. With a look of pleasure she said, "I don't know where we are or where we're headed, but we're making good time!" Having left danger behind, she relaxed against her seat. With a big smile she murmured, "I always wanted to say that."

With no English-speaking air traffic controller to contact for assistance, she kept the transponder off. There would be no identification of their airplane on any airport radar.

Look for any hand held instruments, she sent to Kanchana.

Startled when his head hit the cockpit ceiling at an air pocket, Jon tightened his seat belt and joked. "Can we please stay in the middle of the sky?"

"I'll try, but we have a storm coming." She motioned to the west.

"This plane has only one propeller. What'll you do if it stops?"

"I aim for two trees."

He looked down to the trees. "Won't one do the job of killing us?"

"We go between them. Let the trees take the wings off. The fuselage should remain whole and protect us." She fiddled with the radio. "Not working."

What's this? Kanchana handed a small grey object to Ana. It was wedged in the pocket behind your seat.

Ana felt Kanchana's worry. What's wrong?

Uncle Vaji's hurt. She sent details to Ana who paled and turned to Kanchana.

Jon asked, his forehead creased, "What is it? The engine?" He listened to hear an irregularity.

"The plane's okay," she answered. "It's Vaji. The murderers want no witnesses on the ground."

Jon pulled out his SIG. It was armed and ready to use.

"It's not your fault," Kanchana told her.

So many have been hurt because of me.

Ana fingered the device Kanchana had passed to her. *It's got power.* She found their latitude and longitude. "Now I know where I am. I just don't know where I'm going." Using the rudders to steer, she stayed in Laotian airspace trying to match the river out her window with the shape and curves of Vaji's image. She examined the Garmin, thinking someone might have stored airport waypoints.

Kanchana handed Jon a limp and folded road map. He unfolded it, blocking most of the windscreen.

"Hold the yoke steady," Ana requested and took the map. John held the second yoke in front of him while she matched Mekong River meanders on the ground to those on the map. After a few minutes she announced with relief, "Found Nakhon Phanom. We're heading north, should be heading south."

Jon said, "That's a former United States Air Force base. I've never been there, but it should have two runways."

All eyes were on churning, black-bellied storm clouds approaching from the west.

"When we land," he suggested, "let's remain inconspicuous. I'll contact Andy on the way to Bangkok."

"Good." *Kanchana, how are you doing?*

I'm looking at the scenery. Vaji is healing himself. Feeling better, Kanchana enjoyed the view. *Flying is beautiful,* she sent with a feeling of pleasure. *There are so many colors of green. I can see where farmers planted crops. I wish I had a camera. You know, I'm going to enjoy this spook stuff.*

You're joining VESPER?

Uncle Vaji wants me to.

Ecstatic, Ana replied, *I'm so glad we found you.* She received the mental image of an airplane at eight o'clock from Kanchana. Twisting around, she saw the Cessna and pulled on the yoke to gain altitude.

"I'm going lose the Cessna in those storm clouds."

Jon queried, "Is that safe?"

"There'll be updrafts," she hedged. She didn't tell him it wasn't safe because she only had VFR certification, Visual Flight Rules. In the states, she wasn't allowed to fly within five-hundred feet of any cloud." Her hands were slick from perspiration. "There might be wind shear. The upside is, that storm should hide us and let us escape."

Jon tightened his seat belt. Alarmed, his wide eyes flicked back and forth at the growing cumulonimbus cloud.

"I know. I'm a female pilot and you don't feel safe." His expression confirmed her guess. She scanned the heading. The Cessna veered off as cloud mist enveloped them. They were jammed into their seats as the Cherokee hit the turbulence of an updraft. Kanchana held on to the passenger seat's metal supports attaching it to the floor of the fuselage.

Jon leaned over to see the altimeter climbing. "Rising too fast?"

"It won't bother a Cherokee. This is the easiest airplane to fly. Practically flies itself."

The jungle beneath them disappeared from view as darkening clouds thickened. The cockpit grew dark. Blind to their surroundings and unable to see instruments, Ana flipped the switch for the red overhead light used at night to illuminate the instrument panel. Nothing happened. Rain pelted the windscreen. Tossed about, the airplane surfed on the wind. "I didn't think it would be this bad," They were jerked around with violent turns and abrupt drops.

Kanchana had a hard time holding on.

Jon asked, "How can I help?"

"By staying calm." Small hail bombarded them. At one big bounce, Kanchana was thrown to the back of the fuselage. Jon extended his hand to provide an anchor. She was too far back to grab it.

Afraid of wind shear pushing them to the ground, Ana decided to leave the storm. "It's getting so dark I can hardly see." With no visuals, she couldn't orient herself. "Something doesn't feel right." She desperately searched for the horizon. "I should have known better than to take this old plane. The instruments aren't working right."

Jon stiffened. "All of them?"

"How's the engine sound to you?"

"Different."

With their descent, the clouds grew thinner and the instrument panel became more visible. Internal signals from her senses made her doubt the instrument panel. She tried to guide the craft from the storm. Their surroundings grew lighter. Taking in the situation, Ana uttered in astonishment, "Why didn't I feel this?"

The airplane was in a deadly spin and out of control. Fear and panic rushed through her. A glow of sweat covered her body. She swallowed to hold in vomit. She thought she could stop the spin by increasing airspeed in a dive, but her altitude was too low.

Trying to see through the swirling, thinning cloud mass, Jon leaned back in resignation. "We're dead."

CHAPTER 43

Western Laos
3,200-feet in elevation
11 September 12:20 PM ICT

Squeezing her yoke with both hands, Ana looked back. Kanchana had been pulled against the back of the cabin. Her weight helped start the spin. The centrifugal force of the spinning kept her there. She was flattened against the flat vertical back wall of the fuselage with no handholds.

Ana sent, *Kanchana, move up here. Your weight at one end of the plane with the engine at the other is making us spin like a barbell.*

Kanchana inched her way as though a giant hand pulled her back. Her knees were cut from raised rivets and metal seams in the fuselage floor. Struggling, she reached toward Jon's seat, slipped back and started over. By the time she grasped his seat again, they could hear her sobs.

The Cherokee dropped into a lighter area of clouds. Their world was spinning. The turn indicator needle confirmed they were spinning to the right.

During flight training Ana had never practiced a spin. Having heard horror stories of flying in storms, she had only flown in fair conditions. She pounded her thigh. "I'm so stupid. Why did I fly into that cloud?"

Kanchana yelled in a breaking voice, "Will we be okay?"

As though by instinct, Ana rolled the airplane upside down to release the wing stall.

Thrown about, Kanchana screamed. Her left elbow slammed into metal under her body weight. She grasped her arm. Glaring at Ana, she sent, *You could have warned me!* The spinning stopped. With relief, Ana regained control of the airplane.

Reflex action. Happened too fast. Are you okay? She wondered if Kanchana was under the influence of self-induced mind drugs.

Kanchana did a double take, looking at Ana. *You know about my addiction?*

Ana blew air between clenched teeth. *Are you monitoring my thoughts?*

With my life in danger? Yes.

Vaji told me.

Rubbing her elbow, Kanchana sent, *Don't let anyone worry about my addiction. I'm good. Are we flying sideways? Will we make it?*

Of course we'll make it, Ana sent.

We're upside down.

We'll make it.

You forget I know your thoughts. You have no idea what to do.

Ana sent back, *I've never flown upside down. One wrong move and we've had it.*

Jon reacted by grabbing and pulling on the yoke in front of him. He'd been told that was how you made an aircraft go higher. He had no flying experience and didn't immediately realize that in an inverted position, he had accelerated them toward Earth.

Ana screamed, "LET GO!"

"YOU'RE GOING TO KILL US," he yelled, tightening his grip.

Not able to rip control from him, she reacted by hitting his mind with high frequency sound waves at the loudest decibel level she had ever sent. He grimaced and slammed his hands over his ears, releasing the yoke.

KEEP YOUR HANDS OFF, she sent to his mind, pushing the yoke in to release back pressure. She needed the ailerons to work.

The engine sputtered.

"Fuel," she cried out. "It's not getting fuel."

Working the throttle, she snapped the fuel pump switch off and on several times.

"Aim for blue, Ana. Aim for the sky. Get the rubber on the green side. Wheels to the green!" The yoke controls were backwards in their upside down world.

It was difficult to work the rudders. She looked through the windscreen. Fast approaching jungle above her and blue sky at her feet. "Don't stall," she pleaded. The airplane began to level. The rudder became more effective as the nose rose. She worked the ailerons. The airplane was leveling, but was still upside down. Her mind racing, she relinquished her paralyzing mental hold on Jon.

His eyes burning into her were full of anger. Squinting, he took deep breaths through his nose. His lips were pressed together in a fierce grimace of revulsion. Hanging upside down from seat straps, he slammed his fists into the metal above his head and pushed to remove seat belt pressure on his legs.

Ana knew she let Jon know about a power she'd not exposed previously. She figured he was in shock at her mental outburst and wondering what else she could do to an opponent. He appeared watchful, as though expecting another mental onslaught.

She glanced at him and said to lighten the situation, a curl on her lips. "Some people freeze at the strangest times." He continued to glare at her.

To have successfully maneuvered the airplane out of a spin gave her a glow of satisfaction. A few minutes more and the airplane would have augured into the ground.

Barely audible, he said, "I could've lost my hearing."

"I had to stop you."

He glanced outside. "Speaking of flying, aren't you supposed to fly this thing right side up?"

She called out, "Hold on Kanchana!" With a quick turn of the yoke, Ana righted the now controllable airplane amid creaks and groans of tortured metal and the thudding of Kanchana being slammed around. Out of the corner of her eye, Ana thought she'd seen the right wing flex during the maneuver.

Kanchana sent, *I don't appreciate being thrown about without a warning.*

Are you okay? She turned to see Kanchana grasping Jon's seat struts.

I'm okay since we're right side up! You didn't warn me you were flipping the plane again. You just said to hold on. Kanchana rubbed her neck with one hand while tightening her grip on Jon's seat with the other.

"Jon, check your wing." She increased altitude.

"Looks okay, but what do I know?" He slammed his elbow against the door.

"They're at seven o'clock," Kanchana told her. "Higher than us. Dropping closer to our tail." She craned her neck. "Their passenger door is missing."

"They waited for us to pop out of the clouds," Ana admitted, squeezing the yoke to keep her hands from shaking.

Jon suggested, "They expected us to crash."

After a questioning glance toward him, Ana checked the instruments to verify straight and level flight before looking out the window. The Cessna was out of her visual range.

Jon patted the cigarette box in his pocket. Temperature was critical for the cigarette bombs to work. The minibombs wouldn't work if it was too hot.

He asked, "Any idea how hot it is outside?" He reached into his shirt pocket and began to open the cigarette box.

"The higher you go, the cooler it gets," Ana remarked. Seeing him reach for cigarettes, asked, "You can smoke at a time like this?"

"Cover your ah ... never mind," he said. "Just fly the plane!"

A pinging diverted Ana's attention to the left wing. Another ping. Bullets sheared paint off the wing near the fuel cap. "They're shooting at the fuel tanks!"

Holding the cigarette pack in his teeth, Jon unbuckled his seat belt and opened the door.

Ana screamed, "Close the door!"

"You told me to do something. Women! Always changing their minds." He began to stand, bent over in the low overhead space, and leaned out the doorway.

"It's suicide to go out there."

"Nice view," he replied, bracing his body against the door to stop it from blowing shut.

Her left hand on the yoke, Ana grabbed Jon's pant leg as he leaned toward the wing. His motion pulled her toward the door. The lean made her left hand pull the yoke to the right. That wing dipped and Jon was heaved farther out the door as the airplane banked in that direction. He grabbed the doorframe. He had one foot anchored against the seat base supports. Bullets whizzed past his head.

"We're doing a hundred-forty knots," Ana screamed against the raw noise of the engine and wind. "Get in and close the door!"

Kanchana reached toward him. *I'm afraid he'll pull me out if I grab him. What do I do?*

Protect yourself, Ana responded. *He's out of his mind!* Furious, she glared at him. Air turbulence with the open door required both hands on the yoke to keep the airplane steady.

With a foot still anchored inside the airplane, he leaned out to find the chase plane. The wind buffeting him was cool. Emptying his SIG at the Cessna, he pulled out the empty magazine and threw it into his seat. He grabbed a full magazine from his left pants pocket, slammed it into the SIG and continued firing. Bullets from the assassins continued to career off the Cherokee's fuselage in all directions.

Afraid he'd fall out, Ana kept the airplane steady. She was perplexed at seeing him release cigarettes a few at a time into the prop wind. She couldn't see each of them being pushed by the Cherokee slipstream toward the Cessna. Explosions shook the Cherokee. Fire lit the air. Shrapnel flew in all directions.

Jon pulled himself inside, closed the door, and strapped back in. "Proceed on course," With a broad smile, arms crossed over his chest, he announced, "Problem solved."

Hands shaking on the yoke, she marveled at his calm. "What did you do?"

Amazed, Kanchana answered her. *The cigarettes had some kind of bomb in them. He blew that plane out of the sky.*

* * *

Deep in thought, Jon knew he didn't have experience in a cockpit to make a correct judgment and could have caused their death. He always heard that to go up, pilots pulled the yoke toward themselves. Then Ana had attacked in a fury. He couldn't fight her mental assault. To be hit with an incapacitating mental barrage he couldn't repel had been a shock.

He didn't know she could do that or that such a thing was even possible. She'd lulled him into thinking psychics and telepathy were good things. They were not, especially if you were on the receiving end. His former repulsion toward all things psychic had been justified. It was no wonder Ana was afraid of mindreachers. She had illustrated one power. How many did she have? She never told him she could attack and incapacitate someone with her mind. Yet, she considered herself a minor telepath. If she could put someone out of action by just thinking about it, what could someone with more mental power do? Like a mindreacher?

He glanced at Kanchana. He'd considered her a benefit to the United States government. Having been exposed to Ana's mental attack, he wondered what mindreachers would be like when angry. Kanchana's female, he thought. How stable is she? I've always been told women were irrational at times, especially during their menstrual cycle. I never believed it. I do now. I need to talk with Andy.

He looked out the window to reflect. Vaji had told them telepathic powers could be taught. Santad was teaching Boonrith. Ana had given him a little instruction. He wondered if he could be taught to overpower someone mentally during combat. If so, how many men could he repel at one time? He looked at Ana. He had no idea what talents she had. He'd thought she was just an innocent school teacher who could tell what someone was thinking. His strength, training and martial art techniques amounted to nothing compared to her mind control. He wondered if Andy had any idea what VESPER was getting into or what changes mindreachers would make in the world? In war? During peace talks? How many damned mindreachers are there? He glanced again at Kanchana. Sweat covered his body.

* * *

Ana spotted Nakhon Phanom's runway to her west. With no transponder, there was no reflected radar identity signal for the flight tower.

"You guys see any airplanes in the air?"

"No."

"No."

"Me either." Finding a wind sock to give her ground wind direction, she knew which end of the runway to use for a touchdown. She approached runway thirty-three with a heading of three-twenty-five from the east. She estimated the runway was about eight-thousand feet long. Originally rebuilt for USAF Phantoms on bombing raids during the Vietnam War, it was more than perfect. She put wheels down on the runway numbers. Her instrument panel showed an elevation of five-hundred-fifty-five feet. She greased the landing and turned toward the terminal at the first taxi lane. The cabin heated quickly at ground level.

"Turn on the air-conditioning," she requested. Jon opened the door, holding it against the prop wind with a knee. The cabin cooled.

"Not much ground activity," Kanchana remarked.

Ana said, "It is kind of quiet." She taxied to a tie down area holding small, private airplanes. "About that airplane spin…."

Jon interrupted, "What about it?"

"People may not know they're going into a spin. Forces on the body and inner ears can belay sensations of motion." She could tell Jon didn't know whether to believe her.

Parking near similar aircraft, she began the engine shut-down procedure. When the prop stopped rotating, Jon stepped to the tarmac. He placed the airport's provided wooden chocks at the front and back of the wheels to hold them in place and secured the wings with rope attached to ground tie downs. Kanchana grabbed a rope anchored into another ground hook and tied down the airplane tail. Ana completed shut down procedures, locked the Cherokee door and walked around the airplane to make sure it was secure. Although it was riddled with bullet holes, no fuel leaked.

The sign above the terminal entrance announced they were at the Nakhon Phanom Royal Thai Navy Base. The three walked toward the main entrance to find a customs officer.

Flanked by Ana and Kanchana, their arms around his waist, Jon draped his arms over their shoulders and admitted, "I thought we were goners."

Ana said, "Me too. I never learned how to get out of a spin."

"We noticed," Kanchana remarked. Jon laughed.

"The FAA required parachutes for spin practice, " she said. "We never had any. Guess I was flying by the seat of my pants."

"Nope. Other end," Kanchana replied, tapping her head. She sent to Ana, It takes intelligence to fly an airplane safely. "Good news. Vaji just sent a message he's better. I told him where the owner can find his airplane."

Jon remarked. "Good landing, Ana."

"Thanks".

"You know," he mumbled, "if I'd been the pilot, you'd be carrying me off this field in a wheelbarrow!"

Ana glanced at him. "Why? Legs too rubbery?"

"Nope. Boys too big," Ana blushed as he and Kanchana roared with laughter.

CHAPTER 44

Embassy of the United States of America
Bangkok, Thailand
12 September 4:23 AM ICT

After resting at the American Embassy in Bangkok while awaiting transportation, Ana, Jon and Kanchana were ready to head stateside. Orders from Washington expedited their departure. Embassy staff rushed around them.

A diverted *Gulfstream G650ER was waiting for them at Don Mueang International Airport. With a range close to 7,000 miles at Mach 0.9, it had sleeping facilities for ten persons, the luxury airplane would make a comfortable and fast trip to JFK in less than seventeen hours.

Double encrypted calls and radio transmissions flew between the embassy and VESPER headquarters. Commercial tickets were purchased and embassy personnel similar in appearance and using the names of Ana, Kanchana and Jon, were assigned to take the public flights as a diversionary tactic. The diversion team would spend an overnight in Tel Aviv to take more time. True flight knowledge of Kanchana's freedom flight the New York City would be on a need to know basis.

Employees at the Embassy rushed at their tasks to ensure nothing involving Kanchana was left to chance. Her immediate stateside arrival was imperative. She could identify terrorists threatening the United States.

The trio awaited final clearance before leaving the Embassy. Rotating blades of the helicopter outside created a sense of urgency. It would transport them to Don Mueang to land beside their assigned aircraft for their freedom flight to New York.

Kanchana took in the scene. "Why is there such a rush?"

Ana reminded Kanchana about the looming nuclear bomb threats.

Jon added, "We have an additional passenger on the helicopter."

Kanchana looked around with raised eyebrows.

"A DSS employee assigned to you. She'll be your escort and remain with you until relieved. That's a pretty special honor."

"DSS is …?"

"Diplomatic Security Service. They're special agents and federal law enforcement personnel assigned to protect the Secretary of State and important foreign dignitaries. They work with American ambassadors. For a civilian to be authorized their exclusive protection is unheard of. The Ambassador assigned additional security to you in the form of six armed Marine Guards. That'll leave him short staffed, but replacements will arrive soon."

Kanchana asked, "Marines to guard me? I thought they just guarded the ambassador."

"Marine guards," Jon informed her, "aren't here to protect diplomats. Marine guards are stationed at embassies to help process and protect classified information vital to national security. You are the classified item they have to protect. They also shore up security after attacks. They protect embassy buildings and host CIA personnel. The President wants you isolated and safe. The Marines here in Bangkok are the best trained to do just that. They are to be proactive in securing you. Stateside, you'll be assigned your own impromptu FAST team."

"Assembled in a hurry?"

"Fleet Anti-terrorism Security Team. Also called American Special Ops. The Marine Corps Security Force Regiment is a security and counter-terrorist unit of the United States Marine Corps. It's an elite security force on standby to respond to threats to the United States Navy, the Marine Corps or other American government interests throughout the world, anytime and anyplace. You are the prime government interest right now."

She asked, "Why are Marines at embassies? Why not the Army or Air Force or Navy or Coast Guard?"

Jon answered, "The U.S. Marine Corps was the only military organization that would sign an agreement with the State Department to provide twenty-four hour armed security at diplomatic posts worldwide. None of the other military branches would take the job. The Marines exceeded all expectations."

"Aren't you a Marine?"

He replied with a strong voice, "Absolutely."

"Have you been Special Ops?" He gave one short nod. Kanchana watched activity near the helio pad. "Don't you think that helicopter's too small for all of us?"

Jon told her, "Your Marine guards are at the airport waiting to escort you between the helicopter and a private aircraft donated for our mission. They'll board last to provide protection until replaced stateside. You'll have twenty-four hour protection indefinitely."

"So, I have a DDS agent and six armed guards?"

He laughed. "Guarding a telepath is no easy job. When permanent guards are assigned, you need to train them in telepathy. Otherwise, they'll be out of the information loop. They need information to plan advantages and procedures. For military personnel to not know what's happening in their surroundings leaves 'em wide open for infiltration and attack. Such telepathic training will have to take place throughout the military. I don't know who'll create such a plan, but its coming. It has to. We can't recognize terrorists. They could be losers from al-Qaeda, ISIS, the Taliban, Shiite, Sunni, or home-grown rebels. They join because of propaganda or to be part of a gang. A brotherhood. Being a nobody to begin with, they expect their actions'll get 'em noticed with a little acclaim. They hate everyone, are unpredictable and require vigilance. We can't be complacent."

Kanchana replied, "You're right. Sounds like there will be much work to tackle in law libraries."

"You're our only mindreacher so far. We'll protect you with our lives. The laws keep changing. It used to be that if terrorists charged you, according to laws created by Washington politicians, we were not allowed to fire at them. We were required to give them the benefit of the doubt. We had to wait they fired on us and were positively identified as terrorists. Then their intentions had to be proven. Meanwhile, they're raising weapons with fingers on triggers. I would guess no politician who voted for those rules of engagement was ever in a combat situation or had military training." Inhaling deeply, he scanned their surroundings.

Kanchana bit the inside of her cheek and mumbled, "Because of your rules of engagement, my lifespan may be shortened. Plus, I may never be alone again. Could you stand never having solitude? I hate the idea of long-term invasion of my privacy. A year would be stretching it."

Ana tilted her head and asked, "Could anything change your mind?"

"I'll see what incentives I'm offered. I can be swayed."

Ana teased, "I wouldn't mind six handsome Marine guards as my escorts."

"True," Kanchana said with a chuckle. "That should prove interesting."

CHAPTER 45

JFK International Airport
13 September 12:23 PM DST

Refreshed after sleeping most of the trip, Kanchana had been prepped and prepared to begin her first aerial search for terrorists over New York City. No time would be wasted. As soon as they landed at JFK, she was to take off to search for terrorists.

VESPER's Herman Wald wanted no incidents to stop her surveillance. Using an encrypted satellite link as she traveled, Kanchana assured Wald she would be able to hear terrorist mindsongs at low altitude and low speed. She wasn't familiar enough with aircraft to know what the altitude and speed should be.

At the President's orders, Wald had two Sikorski HH-60Whisky Pave Hawk helicopters on standby with United States Air Force pilots awaiting Kanchana at JFK airport. The Pave Hawk was chosen because it is used in civil search and rescue and counter-drug activities. Each Pave Hawk uses a secure radio anti-jam communication system, an infra-red jamming unit, an infra-red imaging system and encrypted SATCOM satellite communications in addition to other standard issue safety equipment.

The FAA had been notified of government incursions over the city. Two designated Flight Controllers were assigned to work exclusively with the USAF pilots using encryption-enabled radio frequencies. Normal pilot chatter would not be heard.

In case of attack on Kanchana, the Pave Hawk could cruise at speeds over two-hundred miles per hour. When Kanchana boarded the aircraft, gun ports on the sides of the fuselage were to be manned with 0.50 caliber machine guns. The President didn't want to take any chances with her life. As the only known mindreacher, she could not be easily replaced.

As soon as Kanchana's airplane landed at JFK, she was escorted to and boarded the lead Pave Hawk with her DDS agent and two armed Marine guards.

At Kanchana's entrance, the pilots introduced themselves, told her where to sit, how to strap in, helped adjust the headset to her head size and positioned the mic in front of her lips.

"Move the mic aside if it's in your way," the pilot said. "Whenever you talk, I'll hear you. If you want the world to hear, press this switch." He showed her the com switch for her mic.

She couldn't stop exclaiming how beautiful the city had been from the air as she arrived, even the purple smog line. She asked the pilot, "How fast does this go?"

"Cruise speed's over two-twenty."

"We need to go slower."

"You're the boss."

"When I find the perfect speed, I'll need quiet."

Her communications headset doubled as a noise suppressor. Once aloft, she opened her mind to hear terrorist mindsongs. She was worried she wouldn't be able to locate terrorists. The pilot in command had been instructed to fly a grid pattern over New York City until Kanchana determined optimal elevation and speed for her mindreaching capabilities After about fifteen minutes, the optimal speed and safe altitude for her telepathic ground searches was determined.

. All other aircraft were forbidden to fly within forty miles of the city. That would allow her full airspace access during their overflight with no impediments or delays. Since the survival of the United States was dependent upon her success, no interruptions or distractions could be permitted. Coulter and the remaining USMC guards would fly as escort in the second Hawk.

After forty-seven minutes, she located seventeen terrorist mindsongs at one New York City site. She suspected she found them because there were so many in one place. Hovering above the building, she gave specifics of their meeting.

A local judge, unaware the gathered information was from a telepath, immediately issued a search warrant for the site.

While continuing their search pattern, Kanchana learned the FBI coordinated with three local law enforcement SWAT teams on standby awaiting her information. Upon entering the terrorist apartment, one man firing at them was killed. Fifteen men and one woman were arrested. According to documents found, all had infiltrated the United States illegally.

Four city Islamic terrorist cells sponsored the arrested terrorists. Authorities expected the headquarters of Jamaal E-Islami, Hezbollah, Al Muhajiroum, and Hamas cells would soon be located by Kanchana. They expected to find answers to stop the November airport nuclear bomb threats.

Landing back at JFK, Kanchana was escorted into a secured building and placed in a room with a two-way mirror. The arrested terrorists were placed in the room one at a time. She could see the occupants of the adjacent room without them seeing her. Without their knowledge, Kanchana read their minds. Speaking softly into a microphone as each was scanned, she was able to give authorities exact locations of twenty-two dirty plutonium bombs scattered around the city. When teams went to the bomb sites noted by Kanchana, they found bombs but no bomb construction materials.

Because twenty-two bombs were found, compared to the number of terrorists identified, it was believed at least five other terrorists remained at large. Public and business video camera records near the terrorist meeting site were requisitioned as discreet inquiries began throughout the neighborhood. The NSA was contacted to supply cell phone, email and Internet surveillance data of suspects. Electronic voice queries were captured and analyzed to pinpoint who did what in planning attacks.

Mile-high drone images were requested along with satellite images and data. Homeland Security coordinated facial searches around the globe. If any terrorist arrested had appeared in public during the past three months, it would be known where they were seen, with whom, what businesses they frequented, flights they took, and so on. Terrorists would be traced back in time and new leads revealed. If luck held, there would be international repercussions from this raid.

Arrangements were made for future flyovers of nearby areas.

Tendrils of the NSA began to flow outward.

* * *

By ten o'clock the next morning, Kanchana and her protective entourage met Ana and Jon at VESPER in Herman Wald's office. Four Marines stayed outside the office door.

Kanchana felt Ana's claustrophobic fear barely being kept under control. She sent to her, *Would you like to have some help with your claustrophobia?*

Is that possible?

Certainly. She entered Ana's mind for less than a minute. When she pulled out, Ana was no longer claustrophobic.

Oh my gosh! Thank you Kanchana! Ana took a deep breath and relaxed for the first time in the subterranean VESPER facility. She had no idea how Kanchana solved her claustrophobia problem and was amazed it was nullified so quickly after a lifetime of suffering. No one in the room knew the healing had taken place.

Kanchana was introduced to VESPER's Medical Director, Colonel Andy Anderson. As a goodwill gesture, she offered to perform a mindreach scan of the VESPER facility for terrorists, if allowed.

Wald accepted her offer saying, "Right now, I think we're pretty secure." Andy shot him a questioning look.

"It'll take a few seconds," she whispered, and closed her eyes.

* * *

On another level in the facility, Phillip Arnold was enjoying a mug of black, decaffeinated coffee in his office. Seated against a wall and confident of the future, he was saying last goodbyes to staff members as they wished him well at his new vocation. He didn't worry about the mindreacher or Masterson. He'd be long gone by the time the commercial flight out of Bangkok arrived stateside.

* * *

In Herman Wald's office, Kanchana looked at Wald and began, "I didn't think I'd find anyone ---"

"Great," Wald cut in with a big smile. He slapped his desk top in relief.

"But, I did," Kanchana exclaimed. Not knowing names of corridors, she drew a quick sketch of the terrorist's location on a white board.

After she named Phillip Arnold, Jon gave Andy a slow nod. Andy closed his eyes and inhaled deeply. He said, "I can't believe how stupid I was about him."

Wald leaned back in his chair. "Are you sure, Kanchana? He's our Communications Director."

"I'm so sorry. I never dreamed you'd have a terrorist employed here." Dismayed VESPER wasn't perfect, she provided Arnold's thoughts to prove her accusation.

"That murdering bastard," Wald lamented and relayed Kanchana's information to Security Director Shelly White. He told the Marine guards to accompany them to Arnold's office, but to stand down upon arrival. He wanted VESPER's armed security team to take care of the traitor. Everyone was to meet outside Arnold's office.

Eyes narrowing and fists clenched, Andy said, "Our Communications Director! He's the one who tapped our phones and compromised our satellite transmissions." He growled, "Wait 'til I get my hands on that traitor!" He started out the door at a fast pace.

"Stop," Wald commanded. "We have to go by the book."

Andy whipped around, gripping the door frame. "What book, Herm? No legal procedures for mindreaching accusations are in place. How would anyone prove Kanchana's mental evidence in a court of law?"

Ana suggested, "The President may provide help in clarifying that."

"Your civilian courts," Kanchana said, "put terrorists away more effectively than federal or military courts."

Ana tilted her head and scrunched her eyebrows. "Why do you say that?"

"Your President Bush used civilian courts for the Shoe Bomber and al-Qaeda agents named the Lackawanna Six. Your current president may be just as obliging."

"It's true," Wald acknowledged, loosening his tie. "President Bush set a precedent so terrorists can be tried in civilian courts." As they hurried toward Arnold's office he added, "We need to make sure Kanchana is given access to him. She can learn what he knows about the airport bombers."

"Don't waste time talking. Let's hurry," Andy interrupted. "I want to watch security apprehend the bastard. Taking Kanchana's arm, he walked faster. Wald, Kanchana's DDS bodyguard and Marine guards followed.

Jon grabbed Ana's arm when she went to follow. "No. He'll know you."

She pulled her arm away. "He'll know Kanchana anyway."

"He may be the one who contracted your assassins. He wants you dead."

"So? I'll be protected. I want to see who he is." Surprised by her answer, he acquiesced. Catching up with Kanchana, Ana slowed. "Kanchana, can you tell if Arnold hired someone to kill me?"

"I signed a loyalty oath at the Embassy in Bangkok to not use mindreaching within any government facility. I've already broken it here at VESPER."

Wald replied, "It's waived." Kanchana gave him a questioning look. "I've the authority."

Hands fidgeting, Andy complained, "This elevator's too slow. Where is he now?"

"Same place," Kanchana answered.

"Doing what?"

"Small talk. Saying goodbyes. He's heading for Houston." When the elevator stopped at the next level, they rushed into Arnold's hallway.

Wald asked, "Is he wearing an earsphere?"

"No," she replied.

"Can you read his thoughts?"

"Aloud?"

"Yes."

She reported Arnold's polite verbal response and derogatory thoughts about each person while saying goodbye.

"Those are superficial thoughts," Wald commented as they walked. "Can you go deeper?"

She did. Kanchana exposed Arnold's terrorist connections and his desire to reach Joburg mindreachers before VESPER.

"He's deranged," Andy said. They approached the communications office. Four armed and stern-faced security guards with Shelly White approached from the opposite direction.

Wald walked into Arnold's office followed by his entourage. Their irate expressions focused on Arnold. When Andy moved to approach Arnold, Wald grabbed his shoulder and stopped him.

Seeing Marine guards in the hall, Arnold stood abruptly and accidently sent his full coffee mug to the floor. He gave Kanchana a murderous look as White's security guards entered the room. Two guards approached him.

Wald repeated his order for the Marine guards to stand down by the entrance. He wanted VESPER guards to take down the traitor.

Jon kept himself between Arnold and Ana. White's team moved closer. The few employees in the room flattened against the walls.

Arnold defensively stretched out his arms palms out to stop them and moved a step forward. "What do you want?"

"You murdered someone here at VESPER," Kanchana accused. She nodded pointedly to White. White acknowledged agreement with a slight inclination of her head. Security guards had placed themselves equidistant from one another surrounding Arnold.

Arnold's accusatory glance included everyone. Eyes widening, he tore his half glasses off and slammed them to the desk. With a raised voice he said, "I didn't kill anyone."

Wald shouted, "You deranged murderer." He motioned to the security team to close in.

Arnold raised his arms as though surrendering. "Don't shoot. I'm unarmed.

Andy said, "Man, you are one hell of a good actor. I never suspected you."

"I'm no murderer." Arnold's glance kept darting between Kanchana and the guards, resting longer on the mindreacher each time. Employees began gathering in the hall. Word was spreading through earspheres. The VESPER murderer had been identified.

Arnold sneered at Kanchana. "I know who you are." He spat at the floor in her direction. "You mind freak!"

Before anyone could react, he grabbed a concealed pistol from his waist band and fired at her twice. As she collapsed to the floor, Ana screamed and rushed to her.

Two VESPER guards grabbed Arnold. He twisted and fought. Two Marines stepped in. Arnold's weapon was removed as he was lifted off his feet and slammed face down to the floor. One Marine held him down with a knee while the other cuffed him. The action happened so fast, most observers in the room didn't realize anyone was shot.

The right side of Kanchana's blouse grew red. Blood streamed onto the floor. Andy knelt and applied pressure to the wound.

White ordered the security man nearest her, "Call for topside medics. Meet them at the terminal entrance as escort so they can find us."

Ana pleaded, "Fight this, Kanchana. You have to survive." She lowered her head. "What'll I tell Vaji?"

Kanchana kept her eyes closed and sent to Ana, *He knows.*

The bullet had hit Kanchana's underarm and entered her chest. Now beside her, Andy ripped clothing from the wound. White pulled a large, thick syringe from a gear bag and ripped off the sterile plastic covering. The syringe had a black plastic cap over the end which White flipped off. Slipping the syringe into Kanchana's wound as far as it would go, she depressed the bulb. Unseen, sterilized, pill-sized sponges were forced into the wound cavity. White's sponges absorbed blood, expanded with moisture, and applied pressure inside the wound. They were effective in stopping non-arterial blood flow. Each sponge had been marked to show up on x-rays to ensure they didn't get left in a wound.

Wald pulled a first aid kit off the wall and laid it on the floor beside Andy. Sterile dressings from the kit were pressed against the wound. Blood flow slowed.

Wald asked, "How is she?" He knew Andy was a medical doctor, as well as a psychiatrist, and that Kanchana was in good hands.

Andy answered, "I don't know where the bullets are."

While applying first aid to Kanchana, Andy asked Wald, "Why'd you hold me back? You know I could have taken care of Arnold."

Wald answered, "By keeping my hand on your shoulder, I stopped myself from attacking him. I should've let us both go at him. He'll be taken care of. This country doesn't take kindly to turncoats." He leaned over Kanchana. "Thank you for locating our traitor. You are fantastic. I knew the Joburg bunch would be good. I just never dreamed how good. Arnold's right about one thing. Telepathic evidence isn't valid in any court of law."

"Yet," Andy replied. To Kanchana he whispered, "Stay with us, Kanchana. You're going to be okay."

Kanchana blinked and tried to smile. Unknown to anyone, she had already begun several healing techniques while releasing endorphins from her brain to relieve pain. She knew she'd survive.

Wald lamented, "I should never have asked the Marines to stand down." He thought their only hope to find terrorists may be dying right in front of him. He held onto a desk to steady himself.

A wide-eyed man and woman from the airport emergency medical team were soon escorted through the door pushing a wheeled stretcher. Two uniformed medics followed them.

Handing them the empty syringe, White told them, "These sponges have to be removed within four hours. Let's get her ready for the ambulance topside." The medics helped stabilize Kanchana for transport to the nearest trauma unit. As she was wheeled out of the room, her security team followed the fast-moving gurney.

When pulled to his feet, a red-faced Arnold threatened, "Your charges won't hold in any court of law, Wald! I'll sue you for all you've got!"

"Go ahead," Wald replied.

"VESPER's compromised. You're not secret anymore!"

Wald gave the traitor a disgusted look. "We'll learn a lot from you." To White he demanded, "The medics are not to discuss what they saw or anything about this facility. Once Kanchana's safe, debrief them about what they've witnessed." She acknowledged his concern with a brief nod and left the room.

With a maniacal grin, Arnold screamed, "Don't press your luck. She's dead. She got what she deserved." The growing crowd parted as security personnel removed a screaming and resisting Phillip Arnold from the room. As he passed through the door, he turned his head and smirked. He knew everyone thought it was because he shot Kanchana. In reality, it was because he had successfully infiltrated the massive, emergency preparedness computer installation shared with VESPER to create a memory drop for international terrorists. A memory drop he'd placed so deep within the bowels of the massive computer installation, no one would ever suspect or find it. He would use it again one day. Future hackers finding the memory drop would also find access to every bit of information contained within the computer system and links to every government organization.

Whispering began and grew louder when Wald called out, "Get back to work, people." No one moved. He shouted, "Everyone out. NOW!" The crowd dispersed.

To those listening, Wald announced, "I'll request lawyers to help draft legislation concerning telepathic evidence used in court. It'll have to be good to be passed by our current politicians."

With a break in the action, Jon touched Ana's shoulder. "You okay?" He watched her feeble nod. "You need to get you away for a few days. Ever ridden a horse?"

"Why?"

"I've a little pinto in Montana you might enjoy. If we're lucky, maybe you'll have time to cook some brownies." He was thinking he wanted to learn more about combat use of telepathic power.

She replied with smiling eyes, "Thanks. As enticing as that sounds, I have to decline. I need to stay close to Kanchana. Excuse me while I talk to Andy. There's something he needs to know."

CHAPTER 46

Office of Medical Director
VESPER Facility
14 September 4:46 PM DST

Andy sat at his desk, his expression was glum. "I understand we need to talk."

Ana took a deep breath, sat straighter and said, "We expected mindreachers to be perfect. They're not." She clasped her hands in her lap so they wouldn't shake.

"Tell me about it."

She related what Vaji told her about Kanchana's addiction. He dropped his head and sighed. "We're learning more about chemicals such as the more common endogenous opioids or endorphins. Some are neurotransmitters in the brain. They can affect the brain for a long time. Large amounts may be life threatening. Yes, it's a pleasure chemical, but serves other purposes. It helps the mind determine how to behave to obtain rewards. From what I understand, it must be present to feel pleasure from anything, from a great cup of coffee to a roller coaster ride. It stops the tremors you often see with Parkinsons. Does Kanchana have tremors?"

"I haven't seen any. Vaji told me she excretes other chemicals from her mind."

"If she follows normal progression, she'll become confused. She'll crave and release chemicals such as dopamine to get satisfaction. She'll experience withdrawal with depletion. That'll cause more craving for the chemical. She'll relapse back to releasing more. Damnation. She's addicted to her own hormones."

Eyes intense on him, she said, "I am so sorry."

"You're not at fault."

He called the hospital and requested a doctor by name who had a high security clearance. That particular doctor was always put in charge of anyone who might be a security risk under sedation. Once connected, Andy informed the doctor of Kanchana's self-medication. That knowledge would enable the doctor to test her for chemicals prior to ordering hospital dispensed medications. They need perfect medication during emergency treatment and recovery."

"Will her addiction affect how she helps VESPER?"

Andy rubbed a hand over his chin. "It'll affect her frontal cortex which affects attention and executive functions. She'll find it hard to concentrate. She could become impatient and careless. Maybe the newness of VESPER will keep her excited enough to overcome negatives. I'll alert Mr. Lopez. With his help, we'll keep an eye out to judge her self-administered chemical levels and help get her through this addiction."

She gave him a questionable look, eyebrows raised and eyes wide.

"Let's be positive. We'll have guards and staff with her all the time videoing her life. That will document changes in her condition."

Relaxing his elbows on his desk, he tapped tented fingers together. "Ana, you may be surprised to know over sixty percent of the general population in our country uses drugs, legally or illegally, equivalent in strength to heroin. Back in 2018, in major cities that number made a dramatic jump to almost eighty percent. Startling, huh?"

"I knew it was bad, but not that bad."

"Many of those addicts are in positions where they fear letting anyone know about their drug use. Don't want to hurt their families or jobs. There are too few rehabilitative facilities throughout the United States. Of those existing few, not many will take users into treatment as outpatients. We have only one in the United States for classified personnel. It's a national crisis. We're just beginning to learn how to cope and provide help to those who want it."

"I had no idea."

He responded, "Talk to any crisis center involved in rehabilitation. It's bad. The crisis may get worse. The only thing that will help will be the proliferation of drug rehabilitation centers. Every town needs several."

"Her uncle's a mindreacher. He could monitor her. Use mental floss or something when needed."

"She needs to be informed of decisions concerning her well-being." Andy looked around the room. "What we're doing is so new, working through this drug abuse with Kanchana will help us prepare for other mindreachers who may come aboard with similar problems."

He looked at her discolored facial bruises and swollen nose. "Has your nose been X-rayed?"

"I had it X-rayed at the embassy in Bangkok. It's okay. I just look horrible."

"I'll check with Herm to see what his priorities are for you two."

"I don't think Jon wants to be saddled with a telepath. Don't blame him. You wouldn't believe the mental anguish I put him through."

"He has no say in the matter. I don't know how soon Herm is planning to send you two after another mindreacher. I expect you need a break. Everyone is relieved most of the November bombers have been found.

"Me too."

"Herm wants to speak with you two in his office. He's waiting for us."

When they reached Wald's office, Jon was waiting in the reception room. Ana was asked to remain there with Jon.

Wald met privately with Andy before they were called into Wald's office. As they were being seated, Wald and Andy exchanged knowing glances. Wald cleared his throat, placed clasped hands on his desk and said in a somber voice, "I don't know what this concerns, but the White House called. The President personally requested both of you for an immediate classified assignment."

THE END

A NOTE FROM THE AUTHOR

Thank you for reading my book. Please let me know what you think about it by writing a book review on Amazon.com, with Barnes & Noble, Good Reads, etc. I will enjoy reading your comments and appreciate your support. Book reviews for Amazon may be posted at my authors' page :

https://www.amazon.com/author/irenebaron

I invite you to explore my websites to sign up for contests, newsletters, blogs, RSS feeds, and make comments. You will learn about other mindreacher adventures, see what was left out, sign up for the latest free books, printable handouts, and information. Look for the sign-up list at the bottom of each web page.

www.mindreacher.net
http://www.irenebaron.com/
www.maryknew

If you enjoyed this story, you won't want to miss the next MINDREACHER adventure to be published soon. Watch for it:

MINDREACHER-The Galapagos Affair.

GLOSSARY

AL-QAEDA: Also known as al-Qaida, al-Qadr, Group for the Preservation of the Holy Sites, International Islamic Front for Jihad Against Jews and Crusaders, Islamic Army for the Liberation of Holy Places, Islamic Army for the Liberation of Holy Shrines, and Islamic Salvation Foundation. Al-Qaeda is an Islamic extremist organization cofounded by Osama bin Laden, Mohammed Atef, and Abu Ubaidah al Banhirir to make the Jihad international. According to Yonah Alexander and Michael Swetnam in their book Usama bin Laden's al-Qaida: Profile of a Terrorist Network, al-Qaeda began in 1989. It consists of numerous terrorist organizations which continually evolve. The al-Qaeda goal is to unite all Muslims and establish a global government based on sharia law.

Alexander, Y., Swetnam, Michael S. *Usama bin Laden's al-Qaida: Profile of a Terrorist Network.* (Ardsley, NY: Transnational Publishers, Inc.) 2001.

AMERIBAG: An Ameribag is a "healthy back bag" worn over either shoulder, or cross-body. It is contoured to the natural shape of the human back. The more places the bag touches when worn, the lighter it feels. Numerous interior pockets offer security, organization, accessibility and comfort. Angled exterior pockets fasten differently to enable the wearer to remember where they put supplies. Heroine Ana, in the MINDREACHER novel uses an Ameribag as her daily purse, as does author Baron.

http://www.ameribag.com   Accessed December 14, 2017

BAMBOO WATER: Bamboo grass (Bambusa Schreb) has over 1,000 species with giant bamboos being the largest member of the grass family. Called tree grass, it is one of the fastest growing plants in the world and grows up to a meter per day. Water may be found in the vascular bamboo stem cavity between the rings. To access the water, a notch is cut at the base of each cavity between the rings.

BIOFUSION: An Automatic Chemical Agent Detection Alarm system is an alarm system based on technology to detect different airborne agents with a response time of less than two minutes. Thousands of types of chemicals that can be detected in vapor clouds within a 5-mile radius include blister and nerve agents. The DOD recommended point detectors which are man-portable for placement but must be stationary to function correctly. The Biofusion detectors can be used with a gas chromatography system. Such a system can weigh over 100-pounds and require a 120 or 220V AC power supply. They can operate continually after they are started and can be utilized in battlefield situations. Such systems can also be linked to other automated warning systems. They can be created to produce an alarm which can be heard from a distance. In this novel, the detector is an advanced, stationary unit placed in a VESPER entry area to detect chemical agents in the vicinity of the unit. National Research Council (US) Commission on Engineering and Technical Systems

National Research Council. 1998. Review of Mass Spectrometry and Bioremediation Programs of the Edgewood Research, Development and Engineering Center. Washington, DC: The National Academies Press. https://doi.org/10.17226/6316

BO-SHERIKEN: The Japanese Bo-Shuriken consists of a thin single blade about four-inches long. It was often called a throwing needle. The modern weapon is often in the shape of a star. The weapon dates back to a professional swordsman of the 1500's. It is held between two fingers. A flicking motion of the wrist propels the lethal instrument straight to the intended target.

http://www.citadel.edu/root/c4-research

CARBON NANOTUBE: Discovered in 1991, carbon molecules of carbon nanotubes (CNTs) efficiently conduct heat, have unique electrical properties and are exceptionally strong. Science Daily of 29 July 2016 reports one end of the cylinder is often capped with a hemisphere of buckyball structure. The diameter of the tube is approximately 50,000 times the width of a human hair and up to several millimeters in length. Single and multi-walled CNTs exist.
.https://www.sciencedaily.com/terms/carbon_nanotube .htm Accessed December 26, 2017.

CARBON NANOTUBE SUPER-FABRIC: Due to their tubular structure, CNTs are 50-times stronger than carbon steel. Scientists speculate they will create applications to make a diverse range of materials stronger, from fabrics to steels. Techniques have been developed to extract CNT fiber from a soup of carbon nanotubes. Since they conduct and hold electrical charges, electrical devices could be incorporated into CNT fabrics. To date, a flexible sheet of correctly aligned CNTs will support 50,000-times its own weight. Ray H. Baughman of the University of Texas spun CNTs with polyvinyl alcohol. The human-hair- size-threads were 17-times stronger than Kevlar and 4-times stronger than spider silk. Baughman stated, "You could cover an acre with a sheet that weighs only four ounces." It is anticipated CNT *spinoffs will be used in artificial body parts, vehicles, heating elements, batteries, etc.
Winters, Jeffrey. Associate Editor. "Wonder Cloth," Mechanical Engineering, 146, no.4 (April 2006) Accessed 12 March 2011, https://www.asme.org/engineering-topics/articles/nanotechnology/carbon-nanotube-super-fabric

CITADEL: Citadel Cyber Communications Command maintains ongoing research by students and faculty mentors at the Citadel in South Carolina which crosses the range of communications. One such study is an Intrusion Detection system which identifies invasion activity from outside the primary network. The Citadel has much current research in communications which the United States government may adopt/use in security measures. Students under the direction of

faculty members have worked on building a "Prototype of Agents and deploying them in the Network to Detect Intrusions. Such agents would have prevented intrusions of satellite communication systems found in this novel
http://www.citadel.edu/root/c4-research

CONSCIOUSNESS: Tom Siegfried wrote, "Consciousness ... represented evolution's pinnacle, the outcome of eons of ever growing complexity in biochemical information processing." When our brain receives information from the outside world and organs within itself, it integrates that data to create reality. "At its core, consciousness is self-referential awareness, the self's sense of its own existence. It is consciousness itself that is trying to explain consciousness." Laura Sanders wrote in the Recipe for consciousness: "Somehow a sense of self emerges from the many interactions of nerve cells and neurotransmitters in the brain – but a single source behind the phenomenon remains elusive."

Sanders, Laura. Emblems of Awareness – Brain signatures lead scientists to the seat of consciousness. Science News. (11 February 2012) 23-27.

Siegfried, Tom. "Self as Symbol – The loopy nature of consciousness trips up scientists studying themselves." Science News (11 February 2012) 28-30.

DEFENSE ADVANCED RESEARCH PROJECTS AGENCY (DARPA): "For sixty years, DARPA has held to a singular and enduring mission: to make pivotal investments in breakthrough technologies for national security. The genesis of that mission and of DARPA itself dates to the launch of Sputnik in 1957, and a commitment by the United States that, from that time forward, it would be the initiator and not the victim of strategic technological surprises. Working with innovators inside and outside of government, DARPA has repeatedly delivered on that mission, transforming revolutionary concepts and even seeming impossibilities into practical capabilities. The ultimate results have included not only game-changing military capabilities such as precision weapons and stealth technology, but also such icons of modern civilian society such as the Internet, automated voice recognition and language translation, and Global Positioning System receivers small enough to embed in myriad consumer devices."

The MINDREACHER author accomplished research, directed aerial photography and authored two sections of the classified counterinsurgency book, MEKONG RIVER while working with DARPA in Thailand. She was under contract with Battelle Memorial Institute for the Office of the Secretary of Defense, ARPA, Research & Development Center, Supreme Command, Thailand. DARPA completes research in cooperation with academic, corporate and government partners.

https://www.darpa.mil/about-us/about-darpa

DHARMA: There is no one word translation of Dharma in Western languages. It refers to law and order. What the word means varies with the religious context in which it is used. In the writings of Buddha, it is in the Pali language and includes descriptions of ways individuals should live to be moral and follow the path of righteousness. The Dharma concept has been in use by many religions for centuries.

https://en.wikipedia.org/wiki/Dharma

DINGO: Dingo is a term for feral dogs in Southeast Asia. They are considered the first native dog in the Americas. The original term relates to a dog native to Australia, the Canis lupis dingo. As an adult, they may reach a mass of 44-pounds with a height of 2-feet at the shoulder. The dingo is able to turn its head about 180-degrees in each direction.

https://www.smithsonianmag.com/smart-news/dingoes-arent-just-wild-dogs-180950384/

DOPAMINE: A neurotransmitter, dopamine can flood the brain to create a euphoric state that suppresses the amygdale and brings pleasure. Dopamine gives an overall sense of well-being and meaningfulness, which is felt mostly in an area of the pre-frontal cortex. It brings a sense of cohesiveness. The amygdala, in comparison, is ready to generate anxiety and gloom. Too much of the dopamine neurotransmitter causes hallucinations, paranoia, over-excitement, euphoria and exaggerated feelings of meaningfulness. Too little brings feelings of meaninglessness, lethargy, misery, depression, lack of attention and withdrawl. MINDREACHER heroine, Ana Masterson, can release dopamine from her mind.

Godwin, Malcom. *Who Are You? 101 Ways of Seeing Yourself.* (New York: Penguin Books. New York, 2000. 39.

EMBEDDED TECHNOLOGY: Using micro and Nano engineering, embeddable devices have been created for energy harvesting and storage. They were designed to be self-sustaining systems. Most are used in the medical field to store, process and transport data. They can generate codes for ultra-secure encryption for improved security and accuracy. A few were developed to be used as Nano sized transceivers using atoms and molecules to function. The A. James Clark School of Engineering at the University of Maryland continues research in that field of study. (A nanometer equals one billionth of a meter.)

www.ece.umd.edu

FULLERENES: A fullerene is a form of spheroidal carbon molecule consisting of a hollow cage of atoms. Sometimes called "buckyballs," they were named after Buckminster Fuller, they were discovered during research at Rice University in 1985. Much research has taken place with the fullerenes, including layering them between graphene sheets. They were combined with other products in this novel to create the bulletproof spidersilk fabric.

GIBBON: The tropical forests of Southeast Asia has over twenty species of gibbons. They resemble a monkey with no tail. They have longer arms and a sound sac in their throat to amplify their "hoot" which is often vocalized as a duet with another gibbon of the opposite sex.

https://www.britannica.com/animal/gibbon-primate

GLIA: Glia cells in the brain account for over forty percent of brain weight. They "…influence the way chemical and electrical signals travel from neuron to neuron and may shape the way information is stored." (ScienceNews 8/22/15. 19) They may also help protect the brain. Glial cells in the brain

outnumber neurons. Neuroscientists Robin Franklin and
Timothy Bussey of the University of Cambridge stated there is
compelling evidence that the humans' superior learning and
memory skills are partially due to glia which support neurons
and help form the blood-brain barrier.

There are three types of glia (R.D. Fields/Nature 2013): **A)**
Microglia enlarge before attacking invaders that enter the brain.
They consume dead or dying cells and clear out unnecessary
nerve cell connections. (ScienceNews:11/30/13,22).
    They travel and respond to nervous system injury and
infection and monitor electrical activity in neurons. Their
dysfunction is involved in most nervous system diseases.
    Yeager, Ashley. "Maestros of Learning and Memory –
Glia prove to be more than the brain's maintenance crew.
Science News, (August 22, 2015) 19-21.

Glial stem cells stabilize blood vessels feeding the brain with
ten times more oxygen and nutrients than other body organs.
Since Alzheimer's disease is characterized in part by brain-
wide vascular/blood vessel problems, the glial cells may be
insufficient. (Irene Baron suggests since glial cells require
calcium, a diet low in that element may be partially responsible
for initiating Alzheimer's disease.
    Moyer, Melinda W. "Without Glia, the Brain Would
Starve - Blood vessels break down if certain glial cells are not
present." Scientific American MIND (May/June 2013) 17.

Eric Newman and Kathleen Zahs, physiologists at the
University of Minnesota, have shown glia release calcium
which has "a direct impact on the firing of the neurons." Since
fictional Anna Masterson in this novel has more glia than
normal, she requires more calcium and craves milk as her
beverage of choice.
    Morrison, Chris. "New Knowledge of Neural
Neighbors!" Only On Science Friday Online. (22 December
2004) Accessed 23 December 2006,

http://www.sciencefriday.com/pages/features/0698/glial/glial.ht
ml

GORE-TEX: Gore-Tex fabric is waterproof and breathable by repelling liquid while allowing air to pass through. It was created using Teflon. The trademark is registered with W. L. Gore and Associates.

GRAPHAIR: © Copyright CSIRO Australia
Scientists with the Commonwealth Scientific & Industrial Research Organization (CSIRO) "have created a type of material to create a water filter that can make highly polluted seawater drinkable after just one pass." It uses a one-atom-thick carbon material, Graphene, as a filter. That material has microscopic nano-channels allowing water through, but stops most other particles, including sea salt. By adding a layer of a new carbon material, called Graphair (made from soy bean oil) 99% of the contaminants were stopped from passing through the filter. Eventually, filters will be made small enough to carry for personal water purification and large enough for industrial use. Permission was granted by CSIRO to use their information.

Starr, Michelle. *"New Graphene Invention Makes Filthy Seawater Drinkable in One Simple Step."* Science Alert. (February 16, 2018): Accessed February 18, 2018, www.ScienceAlert.com/graphene-film-water-filtration-drinkable-seawater

Readers may also wish to access this author's GraphAir blog articles at:

Http://www.irenebaron.com/irene_baron_blog1/water_filter_perfection_with_csiro1/
http://www.irenebaron.com/irene_baron_blog1/clean_water_worldwide/
http://www.irenebaron.com/irene_baron_blog1/plastic_found_in_bottled_water/

GRAPHENE: Graphene is used in bulletproof clothing. New uses for the material are being invented continually. Andrew Grant wrote, "It's strong yet flexible, it's an impenetrable wall for molecules trying to pass through, and it's a fantastic conductor." By adding calcium it can move current resistance-free.

Grant, Andrew. "Graphene turned into superconductor." Science News. (3 October 2015)

GS RATING: The General Schedule (GS) is the pay scale for federal employees. It consists of 15 grades, GS-1 to GS-15 with 10-steps within each grade. This author held a GS-13 rating when assigned to government contract work in southeast Asia. At the time that rating was equivalent to a U.S. Army major.

GULFSTREAM G650ER: According to their website, the G650ER was designed to be the most technically sophisticated and comfortable private airplane. Flight deck capabilities allow pilot controlled onboard computers to be changed to full automatic to monitor the flight. When on automatic, computer adjustments create smoother flights. Using the PlaneView II flight deck, information from the Flight Management System and the primary flight display are shown on multiple large format screens.

Pilot controlled two side-mounted Gulfstream-designed Cursor Control Devices (CCDs) integrate with PlaneView II. Pilots select and scroll where and how they want to see airways, airports, radar weather and other data to increase situational awareness and their response. The Enhanced Vision System (EVS) II, or the nose-mounted infrared camera, images can be seen on an instrument panel screen. The aircraft cruises at 51,000 feet which is above commercial traffic and weather.

For passenger comfort, the cabin is replenished with 100 percent fresh air every two minutes. Such oxygenation "reduces fatigue and ensures a more alert and refreshed arrival many time zones later. At a cruise altitude of 45,000/13,716 meters, a G650ER cabin is pressurized to an altitude of 4,060 feet/1,237 meters. That cabin altitude is almost two times lower than commercial airlines."

http://www.gulfstream.com/aircraft/gulfstream-g650er

Being a pilot, author Irene Baron chose this aircraft as the one in which she would enjoy sitting right seat as an observer.

HEMISPHERIC SLEEP: Christof Koch of the Allen Institute for Brain Science in Seattle wrote, "… the capacity to awaken from slumber distinguishes sleep from coma." Studies have been made using electric signals from the brain. They show some animals keep one hemisphere of their brain awake when sleeping. When not fully relaxed, humans also sleep with one of the mind's hemispheres in alert mode. When fully relaxed, both hemispheres will enter the restful sleep mode.. Long term effects of sleeping with only one hemisphere at rest are unknown.

   Koch. Christof. "To Sleep with Half a Brain – Sleep and Wakefulness Are Not All-or-none States Of Mind. When we sleep, one side of our brain can be awake." Scientific American MIND. 7. No 5. (September/October 2016) 22-25.

INCENDIARY AMMUNITION: Much of this ammunition has been banned by NATO. Highly explosive, this ammunition is used to punch holes and catch objects on fire. If it has a Tetryl explosive compound at the tip, it will have an internal firing mechanism. At impact the firing pin will strike the explosive Tetryl compound which scatters the incendiary material and flames. The tip color of the bullet defines use. Red or orange is a tracer. Black is armor piercing. Red atop a black band is an armor piercing tracer. Light blue or silver is basic incendiary. The initial flame is 3,000-degrees Fahrenheit. This type of ammunition is dangerous and restricted in many states within the United States. Always be responsible, respectable and safe with firearms.

IFRASOUND: Sound is a vibration the human ear can detect. Infrasound lies at the extreme low end of our hearing range with vibrations occurring fewer than 20-times per second. This frequency can travel over a thousand miles. When not audible, infrasound has been described as a rough or popping effect, or a chugging, whooshing sensation which can be felt.

http://www.infrasonicmusic.co.uk/background.htm

Author Irene Baron has felt the "popping effect" from passing earthquake waves.

The female lead of this novel experienced infrasound from a tiger which incapacitated her. Elizabeth von Muggenthaler, a bioacoustician from the Fauna Communications research Institute in North Carolina, presented her research at the Acoustical Society of America meeting in Newport Beach, CA. She discussed her work concerning the paralyzing affect that a tiger's roar has on animals, including humans.

American Institute of Physics -- Inside Science News Service. "The Secret Of A Tiger's Roar." ScienceDaily. Accessed 18 March, 2018: www.sciencedaily.com/releases/2000/12/001201152406.htm

To enable a more accurate description of Ana's lethal effects from the tiger's infrasound, during research, this author discovered the report by Alex Davies, "Bioeffects of Sound." He wrote that infrasound can kill animals by setting up vibrations within their body. He reported lung collapse (pneumothorax) has been triggered by infrasound vibrations. Air may enter the cavity between the lungs and chest wall causing lung stress or collapse. The victim experiences breathlessness and chest pain. During the vibrations, lungs may vibrate at the same frequency and cause loss of breath.

Davies, Alex. "Acoustic Trauma: Bioeffects of Sound." SCRIBD. (November 5, 2012): Accessed December 2012, https://www.scribd.com/document/127555222/Acoustic-Trauma-Bioeffects-of-Sound-pdf

The Max-Planck Institut fur Bildungsforschung has announced humans can hear sounds lower than had previously been assumed, down to 8 Hertz. This was discovered when 8 Hertz activated the primary auditory cortex of the brain. The brain picked up the vibrations while the human heard nothing. There is controversy as to whether infrasound causes hearing damage. Research is ongoing.

Bergomin, Fabio. "Lattice Structure Absorbs Vibrations.".ETH Zurich. (July 29, 2016): Accessed November 2016, https://www.ethz.ch/en/news-and-events/eth-news/news/2016/07/lattice-structure-absorbs-vibrations.html

Not affected by ground cover, tiger infrasound can incapacitate animals up to five miles away.
Staff. "Conference Report – Acoustics." New Scientist. (03 May 201) 21.

Although not used in this novel, a most intriguing comment by Sarah Angliss was, "Infrasound can cause seemingly paranormal experiences." Perhaps readers will visit the zoo more often to check that out.
Angliss, Sarah. "Organ Pipes & Haunted Sites." National Physical Laboratory. Brighton, UK. (April 2003). Accessed July 2016,
http://www.sarahangliss.com/portfolio/infrasonic

MICROBIOCIDE: A water treatment, microbiocide is an alternative water treatment used to destroy bacteria, algae and fungi. The product was developed using regulatory approvals for environmental fate, toxicology and performance data. It is used primarily in industrial cooling water systems, mist air-washers, and paper mill manufacturing. In the near future it is hoped an American chemical company will have smaller amounts applicable for use in purifying drinking water for third world countries, primitive areas, and during national disasters when clean water is unavailable.
Hack, T.K., Lashen, E.S. and Greenley, D.E "The Evaluation of Biocide Efficacy Against Sessile Microorganisms" Developments in Industrial Microbiology 29 Suppl.3. (1988) 247-253.

NAVIGATION VIA SIGNALS OF OPPORTUNITY (NAVSOP): The British NAVSOP (Navigation via Signals of Opportunity) system is used for determining locations within 3-meters. Using a diverse range of existing transmissions including mobile phone, radio and Wi-Fi signals, NAVSOP provides security in urban, isolated or underground regions lacking GPS/satellite access. It also eliminates hostile jamming opportunities created by singular transmission signals.

PIPER CHEROKEE PA-28 : Built by Piper Aircraft, the Cherokee was designed for flight training, transport and personal use. The metal aircraft is not pressurized and has a single engine with low-mounted wings. It can have two or four seats. The landing gear is a tricycle configuration. First built in 1960, the Cherokee is the fourth most produced aircraft in the world.

Author Irene Baron used a Cherokee to obtain her VFR certification. She said it is one of the easiest airplanes to fly and a favorite of owners.

REMOTE VIEWING (RV): According to Paul H. Smith of the International Remote Viewing Association (www.irva.org), "Remote viewing is a mental faculty that allows a perceiver (a "viewer") to describe or give details about a target that is inaccessible to normal senses due to distance, time, or shielding." They relate it to "so-called psi," such as clairvoyance or telepathy.

During research, viewing targets have included international sites, astronomical objects and enclosed areas. The RV act is a learned discipline. The viewer accesses the subconscious in their mind to view the world. The process is also called "Out of Body" (OUB). The Farsight Institute (www.farsight.org) wrote, "Remote viewing is a controlled and trainable mental process involving psi (or psychic ability). It is used to transfer perceptual information across time and space. It is clear that remote viewing works in complete violation of the accepted "laws" of quantum and relativistic physics.

Smith, Paul H. "What is Remote Viewing," International Remote Viewing Association. (March 18, 2018): Accessed March 2018. https://www.irva.org/

Over two decades of research on parapsychological or psi phenomena took place at Stanford Research Institute (SRI). H.E. Puthoff was the first director of that research. The project began with "…increasing concern in the intelligence community about the level of effort in Soviet parapsychology being funded by the soviet security services." By 1976, remote viewers in the United States were hired by SRI as consultants. The CIA, and Defense Intelligence Agency (DIA), during the life of the program used remote viewing for the military organizations. Between 1986 and 1995, military organizations requested assistance over 200 times for information not available elsewhere.

Puthoff, H.E. "CIA – Initiated Remote Viewing At Stanford Research Institute." The Intelligencer, Journal of U.S. Intelligence Studies. 12, No. 1. (Summer 2001) 50-67.

ROBAR RC-50: The Robar is a bolt-action sniper rifle. There are many manufacturers. One is the custom gunsmiths at the United States Robar Companies, Inc. Phoenix, Arizona. The Robar which author Irene Baron used for practice was 46-inches long with a telescopic scope. She repeatedly hit the bullseye of a 1" thick steel target at 500 yards. Using the bipod legs, she said the Robar was smooth and had no recoil. It is used as a sniper rifle in MINDREACHER novels. Always be responsible, respectable and safe with firearms.

https://robarguns.com/about/

SANDIA NATIONAL LABORATORIES: The Sandia National Laboratories are operated by the National Technology and Engineering Solutions of Sandia. The main labs in Albuquerque, New Mexico make up one of three National Nuclear Security Administration research and development laboratories and has a budget of over 3 billion dollars. It is a contractor for the U.S. Department of Energy's National Nuclear Security Administration and supports other federal, state and local government agencies and companies.

www.sandia.gov

SECURITY LEVELS: Working with classified data, individuals must have a clearance at that level or higher. Single Scope Background Investigation (SSBI) is required for TS, Q & SCI access. Standard checks include employment, education, organization affiliations, local agencies, different residences, foreign travel, assets, character references, and interviews with persons who know the individual, including family members.

Security levels vary in different countries. International security levels usually are:

Public Open Sources	May be read/known by anyone
Declassified	Previously classified and POS
Unclassified	Refers to information which may be illegal to distribute
Confidential	First and lowest classification level
Secret	Also known as Collateral or Ordinary Secret
Top Secret	Data that affects national security, counterterrorism, counterintelligence or other highly sensitive data
TS-SCI:	Top Secret - Sensitive Compartmented Information. Individuals within one compartment may not have access to information in other compartments.
SAP:	Special Access programs. Used when information is exceptional. L and Q clearances are Dept. of Energy. "Yankee White" is working with the President or Vice President.
USAP:	Unacknowledged SAP
Waived USAP	Temporary privilege to read/know USAP
ACCM:	Alternative or Compensatory Control Measures

Private Contractors	Exclusive CIA &/or Cliques
Them	Members encompassing high national office holders

SHAOLIN TEMPLE: Located in Denfeng County, Henan Province, China, the Buddhist Shaolin Temple was founded in the 5th century. The martial arts method practiced and taught at the Shaolin Temple, Shaolin Kung Fu, is considered one of the best in the world. MINDREACHER hero, Major Coulter, studied at the Shaolin Temple for four years after graduating from high school and before enlisting with the U.S. Marine Corps.

SHOBO WEAPON: A small piece of sharp edged, pointed wood with an attached ring at its center. The ring fits over the middle finger allowing the shobo to be hidden within the fist. With one in each hand, they are used by Ninja warriors to strike pressure points, paralyze or kill enemies without leaving a trace.

SHORINJI KEMP0: The martial art form of the World Shorinji Kempo organization originated in Japan in 1947. Founder, So Doshin, realized law and government required character and the "…way of thinking of the person" in authority." He stated "…everything depends on the quality of the person." After WWII he dedicated his life to "…educating youth with the spirit and backbone the country needed." He desired to train these future leaders to give them "…indomitable spirits and sturdy bodies," courage and confidence. He reformulated Chinese and Japanese martial arts to create a unique, technical martial art form, Shorinji Kempo. The nonprofit World Shorinji Kempo Organization is the global framework.

Editor. "History of Shorinji Kempo." Shorinji Kempo, East Portland Branch. (2013): Accessed 1 November 2017, http://www.portlandsk.org/history.

Editor. "What's Shorinji Kempo Organization?" World Shorinji Kempo Organization. (2018) Accessed 17 March 2018, http://www.shorinjikempo.or.jp/wsko/history/index.html

SIG SAUER: Begun in 1853, two men in Switzerland began a company which would become one of the most renowned manufacturers of small arms. Now headquartered in Newington, New Hampshire, SIG SAUER is the largest member of a worldwide business group of firearms manufacturers. They offer unparalleled design expertise and extensive manufacturing capacity.

Author Baron used the classic SIG SAUER P226 Legion SAO RX as the weapon of choice for hero Major Coulter because it is used by elite United States forces and been proven in combat. His 9mm SIG has a 4.4" barrel and non-reflective grey finish. Always be responsible, respectable and safe with firearms.

SINHALA LANGUAGE: Sinhala is the native language spoken by the largest ethnic group of people in Sri Lanka.

SITAR: The sitar is a string instrument originating in India and used in Hindu classical music. In the lute family, it is most like the banjo in proportion with a four-foot long neck. It usually has five metal strings and twenty frets. The "box" is often a made from a gourd.

SMART PILL: The cognitive enhancer, modafinil, has been known to improve memory or focus. Drugs which contain modafinil (brand name Provigil, normally prescribed for sleep disorders) include Ritalin (given to people with ADHD) and Adderall (a mixture of amphetamine salts). The British Broadcasting Company (BBC) announced the Academy of Medical Sciences in 2008 reported "...even a small 10% improvement in a memory score could lead to a higher A-level grade or degree class, and that is a big improvement." There have been no long term studies to determine side effects and risks of use.

Watts, Susan. "Do cognitive-enhancing drugs work?" BBC News. (November 9, 2011): Accessed November 14, 2011, https://www.bbc.com/news/health-15600900

SNIPER: "A marksman or qualified specialist who operates alone, in a pair, or with a sniper team to maintain close visual contact with the enemy and shoot enemies from concealed positions or distances exceeding the detection capabilities of enemy personnel. The U.S. Marine training manual, listed below, was the first source author Irene Baron studied before practice firing 50-caliber sniper firearms like the ROBAR.

U.S. Marine Corps Scout Sniper Training Manual. Scout/Sniper Instructor School. Marksmanship Training Unit. Weapons training Battalion. Marine Corps Development and Education Command. Quantico, VA. Lancer Militaria. 1989.

SPIDERSILK: Spidersilk can be compared to a biosteel. The spider gene, specific to milk producing animals, has been placed in goats. The milk produced will allow production of silk. Fibers made from spinning of goat milk create a biosteel with three and one-half times the strength of aramid fibers currently used in bullet proof armor. Areas of the government involved in the study and outcome include the NASA Langley Research Center, U.S. Air Force, DARPA, CIA, FBI, Southern Command, Atlantic Command, the Australian DOD, plus more. The two main characters of MINDREACHER wear bulletproof clothing with a composition including spidersilk.

Buchnell, Dennis, "The future is now." Future Strategic Issues/Future Warfare [CIRCA 2025]. Future Strategies Issues. (July 21, 2001) 34

SPINOFFS: Spinoffs occur when original products or techniques discovered during research are repurposed for other uses. Beginning in 1976, NASA documented annual spinoffs to private and commercial enterprises to benefit mankind. Other types of spinoffs may include: books, climate or ecological research, corporate mergers, education, electronic programs, entertainment, healthcare, movies, stocks, television programs and websites.

STAR GATE: Project Star Gate (1978-1995) was a Defense Intelligence Agency (DIA) codename for a US government project which studied psychic and supernatural phenomenon for spying and military uses.

The project goal was to establish a program using psychoenergetics for intelligence applications.
Psychoenergetics is when a person "can perceive, communicate or change characteristics of something or someone that it separate from that person in space or time. It also describes things such as remote viewing, where people can see things in another place, and telekinesis, where someone can move an object that they're not actually touching." Questions exist as to whether the program was actually shut down or just moved to a secret "Special Access Program" classification.

Griffin, Andrew, "Project Stargate: CIA Makes Details of Its Psychic Control Plans Public." The Independent Tech. (January 18, 2017)
https://www.independent.co.uk/life-style/gadgets-and-tech/news/project-star-gate-cia-central-intelligence-agency-a7534191.html

STUBBY HUBBLES: The National Reconnaissance Office (NRO) transferred two KH-11- type "digital imaging reconnaissance spacecraft" to NASA. They are often called SpySats.

One was refitted to look down instead of up for science applications. The telescopes are reported to have "high tech lightweight mirrors far more advanced than Hubble's." The mirrors were manufactured between the late 1990s and early 2000s. NASA and university astronomers found the mirrors superior to those in the Hubble Space Telescope, especially for detecting and imaging extrasolar planets and gathering evidence to define dark energy. They can be easily moved by ground control or onboard instrumentation.

Deployed telescopes, with an aperture of 2.4-meters. are reported to have the capability to zero in on terrorists and areas of interest such as Iran, North Korea, China, and the Soviet Union. Since the instrument bay is only 5-feet high, the newly acquired NRO telescopes have been dubbed the 'Stubby Hubbles.' Astronomers are calling them "Super Hubbles." They were designed for observing Earth objects up to 3.9-inch resolution from an altitude greater than 200 miles. NASA looks forward to funding in the early 2020's for research missions using the hardware. Although images taken with the telescopes are not being released, the instruments are currently unclassified.

Covault. Craig. "Top Secret KH-11 Spysat Design Revealed By NRO's Twin
Telescope Gift to NASA." AmericaSpace-For a nation that explores.(June 6, 2012): Accessed June 6, 2012, https://www.americaspace.com/2012/06/06/top-secret-kh-11-spysat-design-revealed-by-nros-twin-telescope-gift-to-nasa/
.

TACTICAL PEN: A tactical writing pen/defender that could save your life is an overlooked weapon that can be carried in a pocket. Often made with titanium or lightweight aircraft aluminum, the durable carbide tip breaks vehicle glass. They resemble and can be used as a normal ballpoint pen. They have a sturdy, non-slip metal grip. Either end of the pen can cause deadly lacerations. Their uses as a weapon include:
1. Flat end: blunt weapon to break bones, especially a skull
2. Pointed end: as a dagger in a thrust/stab/gouge, to rip nostrils or jaw, break heavy glass, ice pick, etc.
3. Hold inside a fisted hand to increase momentum and strike force
4. Throw as a bo-shuriken style weapon
5. In a spear grip extend reach for raking action
Author Irene Baron always has one with her.

X-CHROMOSOME/INTELLIGENCE: "The Y has a mere 100 or so genes, and there is no evidence that any of them are linked to cognition. This contrasts sharply with the 1,200-odd genes on the X chromosome. There is mounting evidence that at least 150 of these genes are linked to intelligence, and there is definite evidence that verbal IQ is linked. It suggests that a mother's contribution to intelligence may be more significant than a father's – especially if the child is male, because a male's one and only X chromosome comes from his mother. And in females, the X chromosome derived from the father is in fact bequeathed directly from the father's mother, simply setting the maternal X-effect back one generation, so to speak."

Badcock, C. Ph.D. "The Incredible Expanding Adventures of the X Chromosome." Psychology Today. (September 6, 2011) Accessed September 2011,

Https://www.psychologytoday.com/articles/201109/the-
incredible-expanding-adventures-the-x-chromosome

XHOSA/CLICK LANGUAGE: The mouth shape may be the
reason some persons in Africa can speak with click sounds. "In
recent research, Scott Moisik of Nanyang Technological
University in Singapore and Dan Dediu of the Max Planck
Institute for Psycholinguistics in Nijmegan, the Netherlands,
build biomechanical models that simulated clicks in vocal
tracks with alveolar ridges of varying sizes." The alveolar ridge
between the upper teeth and roof of the mouth is missing or
small in click speaking persons. Everyone can learn click
languages in varying degrees, but not without errors in
pronunciation and click consonants. Susanne Fuchs, senior
researcher at the Leibniz Center of General Linguistics in
Berlin stated, "The palate shape of an individual matures from
early childhood to puberty and … may be affected by frequent
productions of clicks." The question: is the absent alveolar
ridge an inherited palate configuration or the change of palate
caused by speaking the click language?

Pycha, Anne. "Linguistics. Speaking in Clicks."
Scientific American. (December 2017). 15.

REFERENCES

Akerman, D. 1990.*A natural History of the Senses*.New York:Vantage Books/Random House, Inc.

Alexander, Y., Swetnam, M.S.2001. *Usama bin Laden's al-Qaida: Profile of a Terrorist Network*. Ardsley, NY:Transnational Publishers.

Badcock, C. Ph.D. *"The Incredible Expanding Adventures of the X Chromosome."* Psychology Today. September 6, 2011; Https://www.psychologytoday.com/articles/201109/the-incredible-expanding-adventures-the-x-chromosome

Bergamin, Fabio. 2016. *Lattice Structure Absorbs Vibrations.* ETH Zurich. (Ju;y 29, 2016) Accessed July 29, 2016. https://www.ethz.ch/en/news-and-events/eth-news/news/2016/07/lattice-structure-absorbs-vibrations.html

Bodansky, Y. 2001. *Bin Laden – The Man Who Declared War on America.* Roseville, Ca. Forum/Prima Publishing/Crown Publishing/Random House, Inc.

Bruce, Cr II, Shafer, N. Editors. 1998. 1998 *Standard Catalog of World Paper Money – Modern Issues 1961-1998 III.* Iola, WI. Krause Publications.
Buchnell, Dennis, 2001. *The future is now. Future Strategic Issues/Future Warfare [CIRCA 2025].* NASA Future Strategies Issues. (July 21, 2001) 34

Campbell, R.J., M.D. 1996. *Psychiatric Dictionary.* New York. Oxford University Press.

Cohen. Tayar. 2017. *The Morality Factor - Overlooked in previous models of personality, moral character turns out to be key in predicting job performance and leadership potential.* Scientific American MIND 28. (January/February): 32-38.

Constable, G. Editor. 1987. *Mysteries of the Unknown – Psychic Powers.* Alexandria, VA. Time-Life Books.

Covault. Craig. 2016. *Top Secret KH-11,Spysat Design Revealed By NRO's Twin Telescope Gift to NASA.* AmericaSpace - For a Nation That Explores. www.americaspace.com/?p=2082.

Dang, Tri Thong. 1993.*Beyond the Known – The Ultimate Goal of the Martial Arts.* Rutland, Vermont. Charles E. Tuttle Co.

Dermietzel, R. 2006. *The Electrical Brain.* Scientific American Mind. October/November. 57-61.

Donald, D. ed. 1986. *The Pocket Guide to Military Aircraft and The ;World's Air Forces.* New York, NY. Gallery Books/ W.H. Smith Publishers, Inc.

Editor. 1990. *The Military Frontier – Understanding Computers.* Alexandria, VA. Time-Life Medical.

Editor. 1989. *U.S. Marine Corps Scout Sniper Training Manual. Scout/Sniper Instructor School. Marksmanship Training Unit.* Weapons training Battalion. Marine Corps Development and Education Command. Quantico, VA: Lancer Militaria.

Evans, M.D. 1996. *Beyond Iraq – The Next Move.* Lakeland, FL. White Stone Books.

Godwin, M. 2000. *Who Are You? 101 Ways of Seeing Yourself.* New York, NY. Penguin Books. 39.

Goldman, A.I. 2006. *Simulating Minds – The Philosphy, Psychology and Neuroscience of Mindreading*. Oxford, NY. University Press.

Grant, Andrew. 2015. *Graphene turned into superconductor*. Science News. (October 3)

Guinness, A. E. ed. 1991. *ABC's of the Human Mind - A Family "Answer Book*. Pleasantville, NY. Readers Digest.

Hester, T., Harfouche, Christian. 2005. *Bodyguard Mixing Styles*. Bodyguard Magazine. Issue 9.50.

Kaufman, S. F., Dan, Hanshi 10th. 2000. *The Martial Artist's Book Of Five Rings – The Definitive Interpretation of Miyamoto Musashi's ClassicBook of Strategy*.

Koch. Christof. *To Sleep with Half a Brain – Sleep and Wakefulness Are Not All-or-none States Of Mind*. When we sleep, one side of our brain can be awake. Scientific American MIND. 7. No 5. (September/October 2016) 22-25.

Kugler, L. 2012. *Survive Anything*. Outdoor Life. March 2012. 33-42.

MacYoung, Marc. 1993. *Floor Fighting – Stompings, Maimings, and Other Things to Avoid When a Fight Goes to the Ground*. Boulder, CO. Paladin Press.

Milius, S. 2012. *How Elephants Call Long-Distance – Air rushing through larynx produces infrasonic tones*. Science News. Society for Science & The Public. (September). 11.

Morrison, Chris. 2004. *New Knowledge of Neural Neighbors!* Only On Science Fri Online. December 22.): http://www.sciencefriday.com/pages/features/0698/glial/glial.html

Moyer, Melinda W. 2013. *Without Glia, the Brain Would Starve – Blood Vessels Break Down if Certain Glial Cells are Not Present.* Scientific American MIND.(May/June) 17.

Netanyahu, Benjamin. 2001. *Fighting Terrorism – How Democracies Can Defeat the International Terrorist Network.* New York, NY: Farrar. Straus and Giroux – Macmillan Publishers.

Papanek John. ed. 1994. *Secrets of the Inner Mind - Journey Through the Mind and Body.* Alexandria, VA. Time-Life Education.

Piven, Joshua., Borgenicht, David. 1999. *The Worst-Case Scenario Survival Handbook* San Francisco, CA.:.Chronicle Books.

Puthoff, H.E. 2001. *CIA – Initiated Remote Viewing At Stanford Research Institute.* The Intelligencer, Journal of U.S. Intelligence Studies. Volume 12. Number 1. (Summer) 50-67.

Pycha, Anne. 2017. *Linguistics. "Speaking in Clicks.* Scientific American. December 2017. P. 15.

Runchock, R.M. ed. *Countries of the World and Their Leaders Yearbook 2002.* Cleveland, Ohio: Eastward Publication Development, Inc.

Saferstein, R. 2004. *Criminalistics – An Introduction to Forensic Science.* Upper Saddle River, NJ: Pearson/Prentice Hall.

Sanders, Laura. 2012. *Emblems of Awareness – Brain Signatures Lead Scientists to the Seat of Consciousness.* Science News. (11 February): 23-27.

Schubert, S. 2006. *The Body Speaks - A Look Tells All.* Scientific American MIND. (October/November):26-37.

Siegfried, Tom. 2012. *Self as Symbol – The Loopy Nature of Consciousness Trips Up Scientists Studying Themselves*. Science News. (February 11): 28-30.

Silva, Jose' and Miele, Philip. 1977. *The Silva Mind Control Method*. New York, NY: Simon & Shuster Inc.

Sundt. W.A. 1992. *Naval Science 1*. Annapolis, MD. Naval Institute Press.

Sundt. W.A. 1991. *Naval Science 2*. Annapolis, MD: Naval Institute Press.

Tegner, B. 1967.*Complete Book of KARATE*. New York: Bantam Books.

Turner, B. ed. 2005. *The Statesman's Yearbook – The Politics, Cultures and Economies of the World*. London: Palgrave Macmillan.

Winters, Jeffrey. ed. 2006. *Wonder Cloth. "*Mechanical Engineering. (April).

Wiseman, John. 2004. *SAS Survival Handbook – How to Survive in the Wild, in Any Climate, on Land or at Sea*. United Kingdom: Harper Resource/Harper Collins Publishers.

Weissman, T.A. 2004. *Calcium Waves Propagate Through Radial Glial Cells and Modulate Proliferation in the Developing Neocortex*. Neuron, Vo. 43, No. 5. (September 2):647-661.

Yeager, Ashley. 2015. *Maestros of Learning and Memory – Glia prove to be more than the brain's maintenance crew*. Science News. (August): 19-21.

ACKNOWLEDGEMENTS

I give my appreciation and thanks to those who provided information, advice, encouragement and support. That includes medical advisor and good friend, Dr. Vicki Whitacre M.D. For practice shooting the ROBAR sniper rifle and other firearms on private ranges, thanks go to many U.S. Marine veterans who offered assistance. Numerous military personnel have advised me concerning military affairs including Sargent H.J. Lewis USMC 1950-1955 and Cpl. H.M Hzyan, USMC, Veteran.

Special thanks to Columbian artist, Leon Alegria, who provided cover art, "Mindgarden." Through color and movement, his interpretation of flowing telepathic energy exhibits his thoughtfulness and extraordinary talent.

My excellent editors include Catherine Frompovitch, Justine Wittich & Sandra Wickersham-McWhorter. Analysis by Cynthia Olcott has been pivotal. I wish to acknowledge first readers Kathy Brantley, Joel Worthington, Herb Worthington and Alex Manz for their suggestions. Many thanks to others who provided technical information across the military and science spectrum, including Jeff Deischer.

Thanks to Battelle Memorial Institute and the Office of Secretary of Defense, Advanced Research Projects Agency, Research & Development Center, Supreme Command-Thailand. Working with them over 4 years in Southeast Asia, I gained much knowledge concerning counter insurgency and experienced a multitude of cultures.

Photo by Brodie McLean

About the Author

Irene Baron began her writing career as an Information Specialist with Battelle Memorial Institute under contract to the Office of the Secretary of Defense, Advanced Research Projects Agency, Research & Development Center-Thailand. She sat left seat in Sikorski Helio 19 helicopters operated by Air America along the Mekong River bordering Laos, Cambodia and Thailand while directing aerial photography during the Vietnam War. Baron wrote sections of the Top Secret *Mekong River* book for use during counter insurgency if needed by American forces if Thailand had been invaded during the SEATO Agreement. A private pilot, artist and retired science teacher, she currently lives in the United States. Contact the author at: P.O. Box 1203, Zanesville, OH 43702, USA and through email on her websites:

www.irenebaron.com
www.mindreacher.net.
www.maryknew.com.

Made in the USA
Middletown, DE
10 June 2019